Praise for

THIS COLD COUNTRY

"No one I know of who is writing today gets what the Anglo-Irish are all about better than does Annabel Davis-Goff. [*This Cold Country*] is a tour de force of narrative detachment and involvement, a deft, subtle, caring and honest novel."

—*The Baltimore Sun*

"Crisply and gracefully, and with her habitual wry empathy, [Davis-Goff] shows us how Daisy comes to a singular discovery: that while loneliness can contort or destroy her ties to other people, it can have the opposite effect on her feelings about her surroundings."

—*The New York Times Book Review*

"Davis-Goff's prose is unadorned...but the emotional undertow of the book keeps churning even after the last page is turned."

—*The Seattle Times*

"Yet another marvelous Anglo-Irish novel of manners by Davis-Goff...Daisy is a charming character, and the lush but languishing Irish landscape of the 1940s is the perfect setting for this wartime love story. A rich and satisfying read."—*Library Journal*

"A satisfying story told without sentimentality or melodrama but with a fine eye for detail."   *klist*

"Davis-Goff is a talented writer...a   e
here in the way of elegant pr

                                                                    ekly

THIS
COLD
COUNTRY

ALSO BY ANNABEL DAVIS-GOFF

The Dower House

Walled Gardens

The Literary Companion to Gambling (editor)

THIS
COLD
COUNTRY

Annabel Davis-Goff

A HARVEST BOOK • HARCOURT, INC.

Orlando   Austin   New York   San Diego   Toronto   London

Copyright © 2002 by Annabel Davis-Goff

All rights reserved. No part of this publication may be reproduced or
transmitted in any form or by any means, electronic or mechanical, including
photocopy, recording, or any information storage and retrieval system,
without permission in writing from the publisher.

Requests for permission to make copies of any part of the work should be
mailed to the following address: Permissions Department, Harcourt, Inc.,
6277 Sea Harbor Drive, Orlando, Florida 32887-6777.

www.HarcourtBooks.com

Library of Congress Cataloging-in-Publication Data
Davis Goff, Annabel.
This cold country/Annabel Davis-Goff.
p.   cm.
ISBN 0-15-100847-7
ISBN 0-15-602738-0 (pbk.)
1. British—Ireland—Fiction.   2. Young women—Fiction.
3. Ireland—Fiction.   I. Title.
PS3554.A9385 T48 2002
813'.54—dc21   2001003817

Text set in Granjon
Display set in Water Titling
Designed by Cathy Riggs

First Harvest edition 2003
A C E G I K J H F D B

Printed in the United States of America

For my sister
Julia

>   . . . . for the world, which seems
> To lie before us like a land of dreams,
> So various, so beautiful, so new,
> Hath really neither joy, nor love, nor light,
> Nor certitude, nor peace, nor help for pain
>
> — MATTHEW ARNOLD, *Dover Beach*

Dunmaine, Shannig, Dysart Hall, and other Irish houses are loosely placed somewhere in West Waterford. The names of the nearby towns are fictional and are not based on any town with a similar name elsewhere. Petrol rationing in the south of Ireland has been anticipated by a few months and some other small liberties have been taken with the timing of rationing, both in England and Ireland.

BRITISH
ISLES

N
W   E
S

*Shetland
Islands*

*Orkney
Islands*

Loch Ness

SCOTLAND

*North
Sea*

ATLANTIC
OCEAN

Glasgow
Edinburgh

NORTHERN
IRELAND

Belfast

Bannock House

Isle of Man

IRELAND

Irish Sea

Liverpool
Manchester

Dublin

WALES

Dunmaine

Rosslare
Fishguard

Abernath
Farm

Birmingham

ENGLAND

Cardiff
Bristol

London

Isle of Wight

English Channel

PART ONE

Autumn 1939

CHAPTER 1

No one liked the rats, and only Daisy felt any affection for the ferrets. She liked the thickness of their coats, their efficient sharp teeth, and their stubborn refusal to establish a relationship with their owners, or—as Daisy, and maybe the ferrets themselves, thought of the humans who caged them—their captors.

The ferrets worked for their keep. No bargain had been struck. They did what they would have done in nature and in return were fed with food they would not have needed had they not lived in captivity. They seemed aware of this, Daisy thought, and their constant vigilance and ready teeth seemed to her less an instinctive reaction than a conscious wish to sink their teeth gum deep into the wrists of the humans who exploited them.

Although she was not unsympathetic to their plight, the rough treatment, the small, dirty, and foul-smelling cages in which they lived, Daisy was determined not to become an object of their revenge. She quickly learned how to grasp a ferret by the neck, lift the temporarily powerless creature, and drop it into the sack used to transport them.

It was a skill she had learned less reluctantly than when she had been taught to snap the neck of her first rabbit, the rabbit itself a victim of the unnatural alliance between ferret and man. It had struggled in her hands; she could feel its warmth, its weight, its terror. She had been appalled by what she was doing and had been clumsy, failing to snap the rabbit's neck at her first attempt; Frank, the shepherd who was instructing her, had had to finish killing it. She had vomited afterward—a little way off, behind a bush—and Frank had pretended not to notice either that or the tears that she wiped away with the sleeve of her jacket. Although Daisy had enlisted in a branch of His Majesty's Services the day after war was declared, it was the Women's Land Army and she had been sent to a farm in Wales—so far the only blood she had seen spilled had been that of rabbits, and the greatest danger she had faced had been a sharp nip from a ferret.

"Can I come, too?" A child, Sarah, stood on the badly lit landing outside the nursery bathroom. An only child, she was holding a tatty doll dressed in expensive baby clothes.

Daisy shook her head.

"Take Dolly back to the nursery and make sure Marmalade is there. Then close the door. I'll come and tell you afterward."

Sarah trotted obediently along the landing, proud of the responsibility. Daisy watched her go; Sarah's gait had a little bounce that made her seem to float for an instant between steps. It always gave Daisy pleasure. Although Sarah left her doll in the nursery when she took a bath, Marmalade—the old black Labrador—accompanied her every time she ventured into the chilly bathroom.

When Daisy wanted a long soak after a cold day's hard work—plenty of hot water was one of the luxuries at Aberneth Farm—she usually rousted the old dog from wherever she was sleeping and had her flop on the bath mat. Marmalade was more a talisman against the rats than a practical deterrent. The rats, far from desperate, were not likely to invade the bathroom while humans were there. But, if she entered the room quietly, there was sometimes a sinister scrabbling sound and occasionally even the glimpse of a naked, obscene, gray tail disappearing into the floor.

The rats came up under the bath. Where the pipes came through the floor they had gnawed the edge of the wood and were able, it seemed, temporarily to flatten their bodies and squeeze through before returning to their usual surprisingly large size. Under the bath and in one corner of the skirting board, pieces of tin cans had been hammered out and nailed over holes. Similar metal barriers, less skillfully worked, covered corners of the barn floor and the small room where the feeding grain was stored.

With her right hand—the ferret dangling helplessly from her left—Daisy locked the bathroom door. Losing a ferret was an eventuality as eagerly to be avoided as being bitten by one. The overhead light did little to alleviate the gloom under the large iron tub that lay close to the linoleum-covered floor. The narrowness of the dusty space between its heavy iron base and the hole the rats shared with the plumbing pipes made it impossible effectively to seal the gap.

The ferret averted his nose as Daisy pointed him at the small dark hole; then, when she persisted, pushing his unmuzzled snout down beside the drainpipe, with a wiggle, as she released him, he was gone.

Daisy stood at the window and waited. She did not expect the return of the ferret, which she had privately named Sebastian. Although the ferrets had not been given names, Daisy had once overheard the gardener—in whose shed they lived, and who fed them—call one of them Fred. His tone, if not of affection, then of familiarity.

Nevertheless, she had to stay. If Sebastian-Fred returned and she were not there, he represented a danger to the next person entering the bathroom. Or, she considered (for she spent quite a lot of her time exploring the logistics of "what if") what a problem she would have set herself if she were on the other side of the closed bathroom door attempting to enter in order to recapture a not so small, fierce creature while preventing it from fleeing, with or without a passing nip, between her ankles and disappearing into the recesses of the large old house—forever. Seen only when it came on food raids or waged intermittent guerrilla warfare against the legitimate inhabitants, a scapegoat and a reproach to Daisy for years to come. "Daisy's ferret" they would call it, she thought dreamily, pleasantly aware of the smell of baking drifting up from the kitchen below. The window overlooked fields and a copse of gnarled trees, behind which, unseen, lay the Wye. It was from here that Daisy had first seen the sky light up when the oil storage tanks nearly fifty miles away had been bombed.

A scream from the kitchen below suggested the return of Sebastian was now unlikely, and Daisy left the bathroom, closing the door carefully behind her; like many of the doors at Aberneth Farm, it required a tug after it seemed closed to ensure the click that prevented it slowly reopening when the house settled on its timbers, or when the persistent drafts in the upstairs corridors, supplemented by the wind outside, reached the proportions of a small indoor gale.

Hurrying down the back stairs, the thick wool of her stockinged feet (her muddy gumboots stood side by side outside the back door) catching unpleasantly on the dry splintered wood of the steps, Daisy reached the kitchen. By the range, Mrs. Thomas, the cook, remained on duty beside a large and fragrant pot, permitting herself only an expression of extreme disapproval while Elsie, the housemaid, stood to one side of the door leading to the scullery, intermittently screaming. Tabitha, the kitchen cat, an animal that Daisy had never before seen awake, now stood, arch-backed, bristling, on the table, a primitive, dangerous glare in her eyes. Daisy was not sure whether the stance was aggressive or defensive, but she knew it would not be wise to touch her.

"Where is he?" Daisy asked.

Mrs. Thomas's lips remained pursed, but Elsie pointed to the larder, a small dark room off the scullery. Daisy, following Elsie's pointed finger, stepped into the room, closed the door, and turned on the light. Behind her, the screaming stopped. She could hear the sound of the wireless from a shelf behind the range.

Moments later, she recrossed the kitchen, the ferret held out from her body, dangling helplessly from her hand. Elsie looked at her with an expression that contained both respect and disdain; Mrs. Thomas merely shook her head, indicating that were there not a war on, she would not, for a moment, put up with that kind of carry-on in her kitchen.

Hearing the newscaster's words, Daisy paused by the kitchen door. The two women looked at her pointedly; she had not been invited to remain in their territory, particularly not with that creature hanging, although apparently patiently, from her arm. After a moment, they followed her gaze to the wireless and they, too, heard and began to comprehend the words. Daisy silently indicated the set with a gesture of her head and Mrs. Thomas reached up and increased the volume, at the same time adjusting the tuning so that the voice, although still overlaid with static, was easier to understand.

The three women and the inert ferret stood still while a Welsh voice—the BBC broadcasting from Cardiff—announced the sinking of the *Royal Oak* in Scapa Flow.

THE LIBRARY WAS the warmest room in the house. Daisy closed the door behind her, aware that her entrance was heralded by a blast of cold air from the hall. As she came around the strategically placed screen, the change in temperature reinforced the impression of a small enchanted pre-war room, one in which now sat three young, attractive, and laughing people. Rosemary, Daisy's employer—for although Daisy had enlisted in the Land Army and had been issued a uniform, it was on Rosemary's farm that she worked, and Rosemary who paid her at the end of each week—sat in a low armchair beside the fire, a tea tray on a low table in front of her. Even the two men—one a little older than Daisy, the other perhaps in his late twenties—in uniform, smiling and healthy, suggested nothing more ominous than a stint in a smart regiment. At Rosemary's feet, Margo, the older black Labrador, snoozed; Rosemary looked up with a welcoming smile as Daisy entered.

"Daisy, you're just in time for a cup of tea," she said.

Daisy hesitated. She was aware of the figure she cut: stocking-footed, an inert ferret held a little away from her body. Rosemary, in contrast, was wearing a tweed skirt and a light brown twinset; her low-heeled shoes were elegant and well polished. Only her hands, her wedding and engagement rings emphasizing her short nails and reddened skin, suggested that she was not presiding over tea at a peacetime house party.

"Daisy, this is my cousin James Nugent. And Patrick Nugent, he's by way of being a kind of cousin too. Daisy Creed."

"I just came—" Daisy said awkwardly. "There's something on the wireless—I was in the kitchen. A battleship called the *Royal Oak* has been sunk. In the Orkney Islands—somewhere called Scapa Flow."

The two men exchanged glances—Daisy had the impression that the mention of Scapa Flow had caused a greater reaction even than had the sinking of the battleship—and the younger, James, turned on the wireless that sat on the table beside him. It was tuned to the BBC, and after a moment Daisy heard the same bulletin that had been broadcast in the kitchen. All four looked at the wireless and listened to the account of the *Royal Oak,* sunk at anchor by a German submarine. Seven hundred and eighty-six officers and men dead.

"Dear God," Rosemary said softly.

For an instant no one spoke or moved. Daisy felt as though she were part of a painting or photograph commemorating a moment in history. Then Rosemary poured a cup of tea and handed it to her.

"They aren't supposed to be able to get into Scapa Flow," James said.

"They tried during the Great War. In 1918, a submarine, manned entirely by officers, was destroyed in the attempt," Patrick said to Rosemary. "The tides and currents and the difficulty of navigating the channels were enough to keep the fleet safe from submarines . . . then. The Admiralty thought they still were."

"So what'll they do now?" she asked.

"Find a way of keeping the subs out, or move somewhere else. Rosyth, probably. It was the main base at the end of the last war. But now you'd have to worry about air raids."

After a moment the newscaster repeated information he had already read and the tableau unfroze. Daisy was aware of how awkwardly she was placed. She was unable to drink her tea since it was all she could do to balance the saucer and spoon while Sebastian twitched slightly in her other hand.

"There are drop scones. Delicious, although I don't know how you are going to eat them with that thing in your hand. Maybe one of you chaps would like to hold Daisy's pet."

Patrick reduced the volume of the wireless a little and turned toward Daisy.

"Isn't there somewhere we can park that brute?" he asked.

"Turn a wastepaper basket upside down and pop it under," James suggested.

"She will if you sit on top of the basket," Rosemary said.

"I will if you get him out afterward," Daisy said, the grasping of the ferret by the scruff of his neck being the only part of the operation that entailed either skill or risk.

"Put your cup and saucer on the table," Patrick said, indicating the round table that stood a couple of feet away. "That way you can drink your tea."

As Daisy sipped her tea, all four listened again to the sparse account offered by the BBC. Then Patrick switched off the wireless.

"We'll turn on again at six o'clock," he said.

Daisy put her cup down and went out to take Sebastian back to his cage in the gardener's shed. As she stepped into her gumboots outside the kitchen door she wondered what would happen if England lost the war. It was not a question she had ever heard asked.

RABBIT STEW FOR dinner. The two men had left, and dinner was, as usual, a female affair. Daisy looked forward to meals; she was young and hardworking and often she ate because she was tired. The food at Aberneth Farm was good. Maintaining a prewar standard of cooking was Mrs. Thomas's war effort. Mrs. Thomas complained about wartime shortages, but having accepted a sympathetic hearing as her due, she turned around and adapted her recipes.

Before she came to Aberneth Farm, Daisy had never eaten rabbit. The stew had a rich, thick brown sauce, made with herbs, and over the top were sprinkled toasted breadcrumbs. There was finely chopped parsley on the mashed potatoes; the potatoes, parsley, and the carrots in the stew came from the garden. Daisy ate heartily, but Valerie, the other Land Girl, picked at the meat. There was a small heap on the side of her plate, rejected as not immediately identifiable.

It had been agreed Valerie was conservative about her food. What Rosemary, and for that matter Daisy, really meant was Valerie was suburban, but they didn't say it, even when they were alone together. Although Daisy and Rosemary had become friends, Rosemary knew that if she were to preside over an efficiently and harmoniously run house and farm, there could be no suggestion of factions, favoritism, or, worse still, acknowledgment of—or alliances formed along—class lines.

Daisy thought that even if there had not been rabbit for dinner, Valerie would have been off her feed because she had missed the teatime visit of the two young officers. War, for Valerie, who had been born and bred in Tunbridge Wells, was a catalytic event that had divided the male sex into officers and others. The outbreak of war had, seemingly miraculously, provided her with an opportunity to meet, ensnare, and marry an officer who originated from somewhere more promising than Kent. The news that two young men from regiments not usually accessible had passed through the house unmet by her seemed unnecessarily unfair. Especially since she was ready for them.

Valerie prided herself on not having let herself go although she worked on a farm. She and Daisy were paid one pound a week and were entitled to a day off. Daisy saved a day each month and had accrued a few more when Valerie asked her to fill in for her in order to be able to attend some distant officer-heavy social engagement. Valerie was made of sterner stuff; every second day off was entirely spent in beauty preparations. Her hair was shampooed with Stablonde, a mask superimposed over her face, her hands encased in gloves filled with almond oil. Eyebrows were plucked and feet were pedicured. She would appear, those evenings for dinner, looking radiant; by the end of the evening when she went upstairs to bed her expression would have turned to one of vaguely confused disappointment.

Daisy had once accompanied Valerie to the small market town nearby and the two girls had shopped together at Boots. Daisy watched as Valerie shopped for beauty products that she, Daisy, had never considered buying and, in some cases, had not known existed. Once a month Daisy stocked up on sanitary towels and such minor necessities as shampoo, toothpaste, stamps, and writing paper. Otherwise she saved her wages. She felt rich and pleasantly aware that at some stage a treat would present itself—for she, too, knew that the war devastating Europe would offer her freedoms and opportunities she had not been brought up to expect—and then she would have the saved days off, and money to be able to indulge herself fully.

Queen-of-puddings followed the rabbit stew; Daisy helped herself enthusiastically. She was always hungry and ate three meals a day with appetite and enjoyment. Like the deep hot baths, well cooked food was a luxury she had not been used to before coming to Aberneth Farm; she associated it with the long days and hard physical work of the farm. She was happy, satisfied, pleasantly full of good food and aware that within an hour, before she had finished digesting her meal, she would be asleep.

"I thought Patrick was rather taken with you," Rosemary said, further depressing Valerie.

Daisy looked puzzled. There was nothing coy about her confusion; it was merely that she had thought James, the younger and more attractive of the two officers, to have shown more interest.

CHAPTER 2

DAISY WAS RIPPED untimely—half past five—from the comfortable warm dark of her bed by the alarm clock. The room was bitterly cold. The peacetime house was centrally heated—George, Rosemary's husband, was, if not rich, at least well enough off to live comfortably—but during the war all heat in the house emanated from either the Aga cooker in the kitchen or from individual wood-burning fireplaces. There was a small grate fireplace in Daisy's room and she had even once on her Sunday off, lit a fire and spent the afternoon reading in bed and napping. A morning fire was not justified since she needed to be at the milking shed fifteen minutes after she had forced herself out of bed. Dressing quickly, putting on her knickers and socks before she took off her flannel nightdress, and averting her eyes from the bed for whose comfortable warmth she would that moment have given a year of her life, Daisy struggled into her clothes: two pairs of socks, a woolen vest under a sweater, a cardigan, and her uniform britches. When she was dressed, she left her room, walked quietly through the dark and silent house—she was the first one up—down the stairs, across the hall to the small room in which fishing rods, guns, riding boots, game bags, and the other accoutrements and protective clothing of sport were kept. Not all designed for the seasonal killing of small, usually edible, animals;

there were also, for the summer months, a collection of tennis racquets in wooden presses and a croquet set. Dust and the occasional fine cobweb covered most of this equipment, since it pertained largely to peacetime pleasures. Though Rosemary, who was an accomplished fisherwoman, had occasionally spent a warm evening beside the small river that flowed along one side of the farm.

Daisy pulled on her gumboots, stuffed her wool-covered arms into her overcoat, put on her hat and gloves, and opened the front door. She bicycled through the icy darkness down the avenue, the cold of the frozen metal handlebars penetrating the worn rubber grips and thick gloves to her aching fingers. There was enough light from the moon to silhouette the trees on either side. Nothing moved; it was as though they were frozen in place. Had she not been so cold, Daisy would have found the landscape mysterious and beautiful.

The winter—the first winter of the war—was bitter, the coldest in many years. Flocks of birds had swept down on the berry-bearing trees and bushes and stripped them of every edible particle. Birds that now were to be seen dead, frozen in place on branches of the leafless trees.

Daisy was used to the crunch of her bicycle wheels on the frozen mud, and puddles that looked as though thin, opaque glass had been shattered to show the dark brown water beneath. The leafless trees had become sculpture, the evergreens self-contained or, in the case of the rhododendron, drooping and defeated, playing dead and waiting for the spring thaw. Frost, ice, and freezing cold were common at Aberneth Farm; snow was unusual and its consequences visual rather than practical. All that winter it could be seen covering the top of the distant hills.

Five minutes later she arrived at the milking shed. The cows were moving slowly, but with purpose, toward the shed. All but one—Duchess, the only mixed breed in the herd of black-and-white Friesians, and Daisy's favorite—would amble to their places, stick their heads through the bails, and begin to munch the hay provided to keep them from becoming restless while they were milked.

Daisy worked in the milking shed washing the milking machines and, if the milkers were shorthanded, stripping down the cows—hand-milking the last drops that the machine had not squeezed from their teats. Stripping down was the part of her work that Daisy enjoyed most. She liked cows; she found their unhurried gait calming. She liked their dreamy gaze and the way, in summer, they would stand immobile, chewing the cud, occasionally flicking away a fly with a swish of the tail, while staring at the horizon. She liked the sound milk made as it hit the metal pail and the simple rhythm set by the alternating jets bouncing off the bucket. She liked the smell of cows, and most of all, on those winter mornings, she liked their warmth. Sixty cows in a milking shed generated a certain amount of heat; an individual cow provided a warm flank for Daisy to rest her forehead on as she stripped down the teats so much warmer than her painfully cold and stiff fingers.

Unfortunately, though this morning was a stripping down morning—some of the milkers having claimed accumulated time off to sleep in before chapel—the greater part of Daisy's work took place in a cement-floored room adjacent to the shed. It was where she washed the milking equipment. The milking machines and churns were washed in cold water. They had to be kept spotlessly clean; every surface needed to be scoured and every angle and crevice thoroughly scrubbed. Daisy had a hose with good water pressure and scrubbing brushes of different shapes and sizes, but she suffered dreadfully from the pitiless cold. Cold water on the cold damp concrete made her feet ache, and her hands were raw, red, and, this winter, covered with chilblains.

The chilblains, three on her right hand, one on her left, had developed when the weather had first become relentlessly cold. In every other way, Daisy was healthier than she had been when she joined up. She took more exercise, she slept better, and she ate more and probably healthier food. The jacket of the coat and skirt she had worn on the last prewar Sunday no longer fitted her, although the skirt did; her shoulders were broader and she was sometimes surprised by the hardness of the muscles in her upper arms.

Daisy was hungry; she was tired; she was very cold. She felt lonely, neglected, hard done by, although she didn't connect all these feelings or add to them that it had been a very long time since she had felt an affectionate or prolonged touch from another human being. Instead, she felt a tear trickle down her cheek, and she thought, *I want my mother.*

Her mother, she thought, not without humor although a matching tear rolled down from her other eye, would not be much use to her this morning. Daisy's father had three services to conduct—Holy Communion twice and a sermon—and although the unemotional atmosphere of the rectory precluded panic, there would be the usual anxiety about surplices and misplaced glasses and gloves.

The rector had three surplices, none of them new; the household economy of the rectory did not lend itself to reserves of linen of any kind, either for divine worship or for bedding. Mrs. Creed tried to make the surplices last. She darned, snipped frayed edges, and tried not to launder them too often. During the summer it was easier; she left the drying laundry out to bleach in the sun. Bewildered bees would be thwarted on their journeys to the purple and blue flowers on the rosemary bushes by the voluminous stretches of white cloth, with embroidered and lace cuffs, that now covered them. The surplices, her father used to say, had a pleasant herbal scent that sometimes inspired—or distracted—him while conducting services.

Daisy leaned her forehead against Duchess's flank, feeling a little comfort from the sensation of life beside her; her hands were too cold to draw any feeling of warmth from Duchess's teats. Her fingers seemed as thick as the teats and she saw that one of her chilblains had split open; it was raw and oozing. She started to cry, without pausing in the rhythm that drew the last drops of milk from the independent cow's teats. Two or three of her tears dropped into the milk.

Rosemary greeted Daisy on her return to the hall.

"Happy Christmas, Daisy dear," she said, and then noticing the misery behind Daisy's smile, although the tears had long since been conquered, "What's the matter?"

"My chilblain burst," Daisy said, sounding to herself like a child. "And, like most of the population, I'm cold."

"Take off your gloves and boots, and I'll paint them for you." Rosemary had already given Daisy the medicine that ameliorated the symptoms of, but didn't cure, chilblains. But she knew that being taken care of would to some extent make up for Daisy not being allowed to warm her hands or feet by the fire or to immerse them in hot water, either temporary relief being the worst thing one could do for chilblains. The liquid that Rosemary dabbed on Daisy's toes and fingers was blue and seemed both old-fashioned and magical. When her toes were dry she slipped them into her bedroom slippers and went in to breakfast.

"Coffee," Rosemary announced proudly. "The last pound from before the war. And marmalade. Coffee and Seville oranges are going to be one of the great pleasures of peace."

Valerie was on leave, so there were only Daisy, Rosemary, and an overexcited Sarah at the breakfast table. Sarah was bouncier than usual.

"The smell of marmalade, the smell of freshly ground coffee—after the war I'll keep the door to the kitchen open."

"Look at Sarah," Daisy said. "She's the only one who doesn't think about 'after the war.' "

"She was awake all night—weren't you, darling?—I have to keep myself from apologizing to her for this modified Christmas."

"It doesn't seem modified to me," Daisy said politely, sincerely. "A fire at breakfast, holly on the mantelpiece, and real coffee and marmalade."

"I know, but I feel guilty and responsible and at the same time rather like a character out of *Little Women*."

"*Little Women*. It was the first chapter book I read for myself. My mother gave up in disgust just after the Christmas scene you're thinking of—I can see, now, it embarrassed her. I finished it on my own and wept over it."

"I'm afraid I might weep over it now with George away at the war and the small sad presents I'm giving this year."

"Presents," Sarah said. She gestured with her spoon, smiling and overexcited.

"After breakfast," her mother said, with unconvincing firmness. "When you've eaten all your porridge."

Sarah patted her food happily with her spoon, but did not use it to carry any to her mouth.

"Presents," she said again, this time almost in a whisper.

Daisy was reminded of the comparative privilege of Rosemary's life when she saw the presents for which Rosemary had, not only from good-mannered modesty, apologized. And again she thought how gracefully Rosemary carried that privilege. Sarah tore off the paper that wrapped her presents; the garish reds and crude greens of the botanically incorrect holly pattern, on any other day, would not have been found in the library. Sarah was the only one to tear into the paper and, even so, her mother managed to salvage most of it and sat, absentmindedly refolding it, as she watched her daughter's delight.

The Christmas tree was in the library. A wartime Christmas tree, a little smaller than the ones that had stood in the hall in the years before Daisy had come to Aberneth Farm. There was no practical reason for a smaller tree—regardless of the size, it would be cut from the woods at Aberneth Farm and the morning after Twelfth Night chopped up for firewood—but Rosemary had made Christmas a smaller, cozier celebration than it had been in the past. A more intimate, feminine affair.

When Sarah stopped tearing open packages to play with a dolls' tea set—tiny china plates, cups, and saucers that, without being antique or valuable, clearly had not come from a toy shop— Daisy and Rosemary opened their own packages. It had been suggested by Rosemary, and gratefully agreed to by Daisy, that not only all presents but also Christmas letters and cards should be saved for Christmas morning. Not for the first time, Daisy marveled that Rosemary—a grown-up married woman and a mother, but not so many years older than herself—should have such finely developed instincts and tact.

As though reading Daisy's grateful thoughts, Rosemary smiled at her.

"I'm glad you're here," she said. "For your sake, I'm sorry you're not with your family but, selfishly, for Sarah and me, I'm happy you're here. I'm not quite sure I could have pulled it off without you."

Sometime around the beginning of November, Daisy had started to worry about Christmas. She knew Rosemary would get it right, but she was less confident in her own part in the festivities. She gave a good deal of thought to presents, to what she should give Sarah and Rosemary. In the end, the problem had solved itself almost effortlessly. On leave, at home with her family, her grandmother—her mother's mother, who lived at the rectory, ignoring her son-in-law and quarreling with her daughter, more often the cause of problems than the solution to others not of her own making—had asked Daisy what she planned to give Rosemary and Sarah for Christmas. Without waiting for a reply, her grandmother told her that she would make Sarah one of her patchwork pigs. She added that she was already embroidering six small linen handkerchiefs with Rosemary's initial. When Daisy had tried to thank her, her grandmother had dismissively waved her gratitude away.

"It isn't as though your poor mother can be much help to you," she said, and Daisy, still thankful, realized she had once again become a pawn in her grandmother's battle with her daughter. Daisy's mother didn't need pawns or hostages since she was, most of the time, actually or tactically unaware of her mother's barbs.

Sarah was now unwrapping her pig. Daisy's grandmother had taken fragments of pink and red, some of them patterned— checked and floral—from her patchwork bag and had fashioned them into a loosely stuffed pig. When Daisy had wrapped it for Sarah, she had found it mysteriously evocative. After a moment she had realized that some of the patches were familiar, and she sat down on her bed and looked carefully at both sides of the pig. She recognized a patch from a dressing gown she had worn as a small child, a hand-me-down from her sister; she had loved its pink warmth and the white bunny rabbits patched onto the small pockets. There was also a scrap from a slightly later velvet party dress and a summer skirt of her mother's. The other patches were less familiar, some not at all; her grandmother had cast a wide net in her quest for material for her pigs. She had completed the stuffed animal with a small tail made from strands of wool, and the eyes were covered buttons. The pig was soft enough for a little girl to put her head on as she went to sleep.

Her grandmother had knitted Daisy a pair of thick socks, the kind that came up to the knee. Rosemary had given her two pairs of fine stockings; stockings were now hard to come by and Daisy found it hard to imagine a circumstance that would justify her wearing them.

Rosemary was silent as she read her Christmas letters; she spent a little time and a sad smile on the two pages from her husband that she had, with admirable self-control, kept unopened for four days. Daisy thought perhaps George was capable of a little more sentiment in the written word than he appeared to be in person. He seemed, to Daisy, middle-aged and a little rough. At the end of a recent weekend leave, Daisy had been shocked that his parting endearment to his wife had been "old girl" and his last physical gesture an affectionate pat on the bottom.

Daisy opened the cards and letter from her family. There were two others; one from a girl with whom she had been at school, now a nurse in a hospital in the Midlands, and one that bore the stamp of a military origin. Inside the second was a card—a good quality reproduction on thick, stiff white paper of a portrait of a young Queen Elizabeth with a rather affecting little ermine, its neck circled by a small, ornate, gold coronet, on her lap.

Daisy opened the card. Inside was written:

This made me think of you.

Happy Christmas,
Patrick

Daisy laughed and Rosemary looked up. Daisy handed her the card.

"Ah, Patrick," she said, smiling also. "He's my favorite and also my most distantly related cousin. There's probably a connection that doesn't bear going into."

Rosemary, Daisy, and even Sarah were going to evensong, so

after breakfast, Daisy went up to her room. One of her presents was a copy of *Cold Comfort Farm* and she was going to read in bed and then sleep until lunchtime.

Apart from the faint sadness of being young and unmated, which Daisy often felt when she was alone and not engaged in physical work, and the itching of her chilblains, she was happy.

"Marmalade," she murmured happily, just before she drifted off to sleep.

AT ANY GIVEN moment of the day Daisy had a reasonable expectation of being able to picture her family, or at least her parents and grandmother—her sister Joan's life, since she had enlisted in the WRNS, was a little harder to imagine and not one evoked by Daisy during her rare moments of homesickness—going about their everyday lives. They were creatures of habit and her father's parochial duties provided milestones of obligation throughout the day and week. Christmas Day was easy to imagine. Daisy could be reasonably sure that her mother's domestic ineptitude and lack of interest would have, as it had even before the shortage of many of the imported ingredients of a traditional Christmas lunch added to the problem, produced an overcooked and unappetizing meal; that her grandmother's disapproval had been voiced or mimed; that her tired father was attempting to maintain his Christmas spirit until evensong.

At that moment in the afternoon, though, she could have been reasonably sure of accurately picturing the greater part of the population of England; they were listening to the King's Speech.

The King's Speech; just a trace of his stutter. Daisy imagined him and the rest of the royal family, the Queen, the little princesses, Queen Mary, at Buckingham Palace. Their subjects drew more and more comfort and reassurance from the presence and example of the royal family, and newspapers and magazines were full of photographs and accounts of their life. A mixture of intimacy and example, the little princesses engaged in minor war work, their mother visiting wounded sailors, the family spending Christmas Day together, while sharing some form of deprivation with the rest of the populace.

Daisy dozed in front of the fire, when she woke up she realized that she had missed the end of the speech. It was an hour later and tea was being brought in. The wireless was still on; Rosemary was knitting and half listening to the seasonal programming of the BBC.

"Tea," she said.

"Sorry," Daisy said, "I must have dropped off. The fire and overeating at lunch."

Nevertheless, Daisy allowed Rosemary to cut her a large slice of the Aberneth Farm Christmas cake with her cup of tea. Since rationing was imminent, the heavy cake, with its rich and exotic ingredients, might be the last they would eat until the war was over. Soon even tea would be scarce. Eight eggs had gone into the cake; Daisy was grateful and a little guilty.

The afternoon concert ended and the news began. Both Rosemary and Daisy increased their level of attention; Rosemary sat forward a little in her chair. The news was, in the main, good. More about the *Graf Spee* hunted by British cruisers and scuttled off Montevideo. The Finns valiantly pushing back their Russian invaders. Daisy did not underestimate the importance of the news she was listening to, but she sometimes had difficulty remembering where specific places were located, or their comparative strategic importance. The third news item was easier to understand since it required no geographic knowledge and felt a little like gossip. Sir Guy Wilcox, a founding member of the British Union of Fascists, had fled the country, just hours before he was to be arrested for treason. The whereabouts of Lady Wilcox was not known.

"I was at school with her," Rosemary said.

"You were? Really?"

"She was in the sixth form, just about to leave when I arrived as a very small new girl, so I wasn't the recipient of any girlish confidences. But there weren't any visible indications that she would marry a Fascist and become chummy with Hitler."

"So what was she like?"

Rosemary closed her eyes for a second, remembering.

"She had a cruel streak," she said after a moment, "—at least if the rumors that circulated her last summer term had some basis of truth. There was a curate who took some kind of responsibility for the spiritual well-being of the school, like preparing the girls for confirmation. He used to come to lunch on Thursdays and we were given a somewhat better meal that day. He was very handsome, or at least we thought so. Looking back I can see that he was unsure of himself in lots of ways—the school was rather grand and full of little snobs and he hadn't quite managed to lose his suburban accent. He was the object of giggling but not serious admiration—it was rumored that he got a special delivery of post on St. Valentine's Day. Anyway Emily Haverley set her cap at the poor curate. First she developed some religious doubts and he was consulted. They had long discussions and at the end of it he was in love with her. She apparently led him on for the remaining few weeks of the term, then school broke up. She went on to be the most beautiful deb of her year while he had some kind of nervous breakdown."

"Where do you think she is?"

"The same place that he is, I imagine, having traveled there by a more comfortable route."

"Christmas Day seems a strange time to decide to arrest him—them—Were they after her, too?"

Rosemary leaned over and turned down the wireless, now broadcasting the weather forecast.

"What could be a better day to disappear?" she asked. "The day on which no one is really paying attention."

"The best day for him to escape, but not the best day for them to catch him, surely?"

"Not completely an accident, I imagine."

Daisy looked shocked and Rosemary smiled, with the pleasure most of us take in a display of greater worldly wisdom or justified cynicism.

"He wasn't the only Englishman to believe that fascism was the political system that would save the country. And he did, you know, attempt reforms as a member of another party and other political organizations. It was just that when it became clear what Hitler and Mussolini were up to he didn't revert to the poetic heroism and self-sacrifice of the generation who perished in the Great War. There are plenty of former Fascist sprigs in the Foreign Office who would rather see him spend the rest of the war out of harm's way than in a prison cell."

"Where do you think he's—they've—gone?"

"It'll be interesting to find out. It'll give a pretty good idea of how much help he had from the top. I hope it's Germany."

Daisy looked surprised. The wireless was now playing popular music, unheard by either woman.

"It would serve him right. Just imagine—he'd have burned his boats here and it isn't as though he'd be of any use to the Germans or that they'd trust him. During the last war there were a few Irishmen who thought of England as the enemy and so regarded Germany as an ally."

"What happened to them?"

"They were used and discarded—sick, lonely, and unhappy. Some of them tried to get back to Ireland—most of them died. Casement, of course, was hanged."

Something in Rosemary's voice made Daisy say, "But he was a traitor, wasn't he?"

"Not everyone in Ireland thinks so."

But Daisy still saw things in black and white. Traitors were shot or hanged—you felt sorry for their families, provided they weren't traitors, too. Although it was horrifying to execute one of your own countrymen, there wasn't any choice.

"How about another slice of cake?" Rosemary asked.

CHAPTER 3

"THERE'S POST FOR you, Miss. Two letters," Elsie said as Daisy used the step outside the kitchen door to prize off her muddy gumboots. Daisy came inside and hung up her jacket, wet from a warm early summer shower. "On the hall table."

Elsie had not been instructed by Rosemary on how to treat the two young women who now lived in the house. Had it only been Daisy, it would have been easier for the staff. They could place her socially—Daisy's father was a country rector, her grandfather landed gentry. Her family's lack of affluence or her position as paid manual labor did not affect the attitude of household employees at Aberneth Farm. They thought of her as employed by the Crown, rather than by Rosemary. And she had a uniform; she was part of the War Effort. Lunch in working clothes, in the kitchen; dinner in the dining room. But the presence of Valerie clouded the issue. Elsie and Mrs. Thomas knew that, in peacetime, Valerie would be unlikely to sit at the dining-room table at Aberneth Farm—which didn't mean she would have belonged in the kitchen, either—and felt that she did so now under false pretenses. Daisy sometimes wondered what would have happened if a working class girl had been stationed at Aberneth Farm. And why one never had been. Was it by chance or were such things arranged? Fixed? And if they were, how was it done? What code, what euphemisms or words were employed? "She'll be good with animals; she has experience with horses and fox-hunting"? Was it possible that the Land Army was as hierarchical and class con- scious as the world to which Daisy, in the now seemingly remote pre-war past, had belonged?

Stocking-footed, Daisy walked along the corridor from the kitchen to the polished wood of the hall, the surface beneath her feet changing from scratchy to smooth wood, from wood to the tightly woven Turkish carpet and back to polished wood.

Daisy was twenty years old; letters had associations only of pleasure and excitement. Bills, taxes, appeals, and obligations were not yet part of her life. The post brought letters from home and occasionally news from friends. It was her only personal commu- nication with the outside world; the wireless connected her with the world in general, the post with people she knew. Now, of course, Daisy would sometimes hear on the six o'clock news about bombing raids on places where family and friends lived or were stationed.

There were two letters, and the envelopes were larger and thicker than those Daisy was now used to. Pre-war stock. She did not recognize the handwriting on either envelope. She opened the larger first. Inside was a stiff white invitation card. Daisy was puzzled; she seemed to have been invited to a dance. Quite a smart one, by the looks of it. A pre-war dance. Daisy did not recognize either the name of her hostess or the location of the dance. With- out wasting too much time puzzling over it, she opened the sec- ond envelope. As she had imagined, the letter cast some light on the invitation. It was from Lady Nugent, who introduced herself as James Nugent's mother and hoped that Daisy could stay for the weekend of her eldest daughter's coming-out dance. Lady Nugent went on to say that James, as well as she, hoped Daisy would be able to come and that she would arrange for someone to collect Daisy from the nearest railroad station.

Valerie entered through the front door and took off her boots. She tended to avoid going through the kitchen unless she was wet or dirty. In a general way, Valerie did not get as dirty as Daisy did. Her work was no less hard, but it tended to be cleaner. Valerie went to some lengths to avoid working in "blood, shit, and mud," as the girls called it. Daisy was not squeamish and was very much aware that cow manure and rabbit blood were not what Churchill had been referring to when he had told the English people that he had only "blood, toil, tears, and sweat" to offer them. But since it was all she had to give her country—since she had arrived at Aberneth Farm, Germany had seemingly effortlessly invaded and occupied Denmark, Norway, Holland, and Belgium—she did her work cheerfully and as best she knew how.

"You've got blood on your invitation," Valerie said with unconcealed disgust.

Daisy looked down; a faint bloody thumbprint now sullied the pristine whiteness of the invitation card.

Valerie loitered.

"I've been invited to a dance. In . . ."—Daisy glanced at the letter—"Near Ambleside, in Westmoreland."

"When?"

Daisy glanced down; the date was some weeks ahead. For reasons she did not quite understand, she felt relieved there was so much time.

"It's a whole weekend. I don't know if I'll be able to go."

Valerie looked at her with the pity and scorn she reserved for those unable to keep their priorities straight.

"I'll ask Rosemary," Daisy said, intending to ask her employer a good deal more than permission to take a clump of her days off all at the same time.

Among the first questions—and there would be others—were why had she been asked, should she accept, what should she wear, how would she get to the North of England? And an implicit unspoken question: How did Rosemary feel about Daisy's accepting an invitation to stay with Rosemary's relatives, to respond to interest shown by a male member of that family? Daisy felt that such a question was not premature; if Rosemary disapproved, or if she even had reservations, to refuse the invitation now rather than to beat a social retreat later would be simpler for all concerned. Even though the prospect of a house party and a ball and the attention of a handsome young man was a treat and adventure more thrilling than Daisy had ever before been offered. Even in peacetime.

Rosemary's reaction was flattering. Daisy silently and gratefully compared it with the conversation she would have had with her mother had she still been living at home. Girls serving in the Land Army apparently weren't asked questions containing words like "chaperone."

"Of course you must go. It'll be an outing for you and you've been cooped up on the farm for far too long. It's just a matter of logistics and even they aren't so very complicated. You'll have to look up the train connections and make sure you have what you need to wear. I'll help you. It's not the warmest house in England, and I'd better fill you in on the family eccentricities before you go. The thumbprint, I take it, is yours, not Aunt Hilda's?"

"My thumb—rabbit blood."

"How many did you get?"

The cows were milked twice a day. The washing of the dairy and milking machinery took place afterward. Then there was a longish stretch of time when Daisy had no regularly defined duties. Work, changing with the season, was found for her. Now, once a week, she and the shepherd picked up a couple of ferrets from the gardener's shed and carried them and a large net up to the rabbit warren on the hill.

If the day was warm, despite a certain sympathy for the rabbits and a reluctance to cause pain, Daisy enjoyed these outings. Frank was English and friendlier to Daisy than most of the Welshmen who worked on the farm. They were suspicious of strangers and although they could, when they had something to say to Daisy, speak perfectly good English, while conversing among themselves in her presence they usually spoke Welsh. They let her know, without resorting much to either language, that a girl had no business working on the farm. Her position was not simplified when one day a small dark woman, her face contorted with vituperation, screamed abuse at her. It took Daisy some time and a grudging, embarrassed partial explanation from one of the milkers to understand that the woman was accusing Daisy of having seduced her husband. Even after asking Rosemary which of the farmworkers was husband to the shrew, Daisy did not immediately understand that the woman suspected, or claimed she suspected, Daisy of carrying on with the painfully shy dairyman with the slightly twisted spine. Rosemary and Valerie were sympathetic, but Daisy suspected they thought the incident, on some level, funny; Daisy did not. She knew it to be ridiculous but so sad and squalid she would not have been amused even if it were not she who had been humiliated. Daisy was snubbed, ignored, or put in her place, but Frank, the shepherd, was a pariah. He was an Englishman, a foreigner. He came from Herefordshire, a county that shared a border with Wales. Rosemary reminded Daisy that historically the Welsh—and the Irish and Scottish—had more often considered England the enemy than they had Germany.

When Daisy and Frank reached the warren, they would spread the net over the entrances, then Daisy would take a ferret from the sack in which it had been carried, muzzle it, and send it down a rabbit hole. Rabbits would shoot up the other tunnels into the waiting nets, where Daisy would grab them and, with one swift movement, break their necks. The ferret would be caught in the same manner—its capture requiring more skill since it was wirier and had to be reincarcerated without damage to its person—and replaced in the sack. If everything went well.

"We got twelve, but we're short a ferret. The small female got laid up in the wood at the end of the long pasture. We left the nets—I'll go back later and see if she's surfaced."

Occasionally a ferret, inside the burrow, would disembarrass itself of its muzzle and catch an unwary or slow rabbit. It would eat the rabbit, curl up, and sleep off the substantial and unexpected meal. Short of digging out the burrow—hard work that also risked the loss of the well-fed ferret—the only solution was to leave the nets over all the possible exits and return later to retrieve the missing animal. Daisy knew that although she was not responsible for the predatory animal going AWOL, she was accountable. "It wasn't my fault" was not a wartime excuse. Nevertheless, she did not burden herself with a fruitless feeling of guilt. She had done nothing wrong. The ferret had been properly muzzled when it had been pushed down the rabbit hole into the warren.

A little later, after they had listened to the six o'clock news, Daisy walked back up the hill. The summer evening was warm and after a little time she was able to push away the fear that she felt listening to the BBC's increasingly grim news. She had for the first time been afraid when a Sunday in May—just before the evacuation of Dunkirk—had been designated a Day of Prayer. Every church in England had been full as an entire nation prayed. Prayed for victory. Prayed for peace. England stood alone and the German bombing raids had become more frequent and intense. The possibility of invasion was never far from anyone's thoughts.

CHAPTER 4

DAISY WORE HER uniform on the train. Uniforms were a great leveler. When she had been at school, Daisy had complained as energetically as the next girl about the navy blue gym slips, the gray kneesocks, and the mandatory lace-up brown walking shoes—and in truth the uniform was aesthetically unpleasing and not particularly comfortable—but she was, as were, she suspected, many other girls from the less affluent families, often grateful to be relieved of the competitive aspects of clothing.

At school, the uniform had concealed from the critical eyes of her fellow pupils that in winter both her skirts had once been her mother's and were cut down to fit Daisy. Clothes rationing had recently been imposed and already it was changing attitudes about clothing; few girls Daisy knew would now be ashamed to wear a hand-me-down skirt. The evening dress she packed to take to Westmoreland was Rosemary's. Even if it were recognized as such by another guest, there was now little shame attached to it being borrowed.

Daisy wore her uniform with some pleasure and pride. It was not by chance that Daisy had enlisted in the Land Army. Like many another girl, she understood at the outbreak of war that more than the future of Western Civilization was at stake. Daisy was not lacking patriotism, but her upbringing—as the younger daughter of a Church of England rector and his quietly desperate wife—had made her at once cynical about the civilization at stake, and utterly determined that she should never again be one of a group. A girlhood in which she had escaped neither the Girl Guides nor the choir and had watched her mother—a woman with a good degree in English Literature from Lady Margaret Hall—preside over the Women's Institute and separate the appalling from the merely worn for the church jumble sale had made Daisy strong and stubborn. Two qualities that would not have saved her had the world not suddenly been thrown into chaos. Daisy consciously saw herself as one of the cards tossed into the air and was fairly sure that wherever she landed she would prefer it to the life she watched her mother lead.

Daisy was grateful to belong to the Land Army. Unlike Valerie who, had her mother been a fraction less alert, would be driving senior officers around London, provocatively dressed in an ATS uniform, Daisy had sacrificed the possibility of a wartime romance for the countryside, the unlikelihood of being shouted at, long periods of silence, and her own room with a warm bed and the window open.

Her uniform still had a certain novelty value. She did not wear it for everyday work, depending rather on practical gum-boots with two pairs of socks, corduroy trousers, and a couple of heavy sweaters. Daisy was excited to be traveling to a dance and what was, she supposed, a house party; but a little out of her depth, she was very glad to arrive in uniform.

She had brought *Lorna Doone* with her for the long journey. Although she was happy looking out the window at the unfamiliar countryside or occasionally sleeping, she was grateful to have a half-remembered novel with lots of story and not too many characters, in the chilly railway station waiting rooms when she twice changed trains.

Daisy could see that people tended to read what gave them comfort. Since the outbreak of war, her mother had upped her intake of Smollett, drawing on the hardmindedness, the energetic sense of life, the bawdy lack of sentimentality, to help her get through days which had had, even before the war, an element of restriction, rationing, regimentation. Daisy, too, avoided sentimentality in any form; as a child firmly avoiding novels whose heroes were orphans or animals. *Lorna Doone* was perfect: the heroic aspect of farming, the masculinity of the farmer, enough familiar references to the history of the late seventeenth century to fix the story in a time and a place, and a certain timely suspicion of high life; Daisy felt it all. She regretted only that the train took her through Crewe and Lancaster to Windermere, and not by way of Exmoor.

Mrs. Thomas had packed sandwiches for Daisy. The train, full leaving Crewe, emptied out at the next two stations, the first a market town, the next an insignificant stop that seemed to serve a military camp. There remained only one other traveler in the railway carriage: a middle-aged, gray-haired, gray-faced woman knitting a ribbed sock on four fine needles. She looked like one of Daisy's father's parishioners. Daisy was sorry not to be alone; she had hoped for a stretch of the journey by herself, and would have liked to put her feet up on the seat, lean back, and eat her sandwiches while she read or looked out the window.

They sat, on opposite sides of the railway carriage, in silence. Although she never looked at Daisy, the woman managed, using only her expression and the occasional sniff, to convey her disapproval. It was an attitude with which Daisy was familiar, the assumption that youth and healthy beauty were the innocent exterior that covered rampant animal sexuality. This woman perceived Daisy as the enemy. Less threatening than Hitler, of course, but geographically more imminent.

When Daisy finished her chapter—John Ridd's harrowing quest into Monmouth's battlefield—she got up and took her sandwiches from her bag on the overhead rack. She was aware that every move she made was being watched. Daisy unwrapped her generous wax paper package of sandwiches and offered one to the woman opposite. She watched her hesitate and then take one.

"Thank you," the woman said. "I'm much obliged."

Daisy saw her look at the sandwich. Homemade bread, freshly churned butter, farm-cured ham, and plenty of strong mustard. She saw the surprise on the woman's face and watched her look more closely at the sandwich.

"It's well for some," the woman said.

"I work on a farm," Daisy said. "We're allowed to kill two pigs a year for ourselves." She waited until her companion bit into the sandwich. "Of course, if you'd rather not."

"I didn't mean that," the woman said, embarrassed, and Daisy wished she hadn't spoken. At the next station the woman gathered her things and left the compartment as though she had arrived at her destination, but when Daisy got off the train at Lancaster she saw her sitting, knitting, in another compartment. They pretended not to see each other.

The evening papers were for sale at Lancaster; the headlines on the board read: LADY MOSLEY ARRESTED. Daisy bought a paper and read it while she waited for her train. She felt sorry for Lady Mosley; despite Diana Mosley's open and enthusiastic membership in the British Union of Fascists, it was hard to believe she was really a traitor or a security risk. Daisy couldn't believe that Lady Mosley was wicked; she paused and asked herself why she had been pleased when Sir Oswald Mosley was arrested and shocked when his wife was imprisoned. It was perhaps the baby that made his mother appear innocent; how could a woman with a ten-week-old baby be evil? And even if she were, it seemed very cruel to separate the baby who, Daisy assumed, was breastfed, from his mother. Not only was Lady Mosley a mother, but she was beautiful and upper class; it was unimaginable that she should be in jail.

It was late evening when Daisy arrived at Windermere. James was waiting with a pony and trap.

"At last," he said, taking her suitcase and putting it in the trap. Then, before he opened the door for her to enter, he took Daisy's upper arms in his hands and looked into her face.

"Even more lovely than I remember," he said. "Of course, last time you weren't wearing that fetching khaki hat."

"There are," Daisy said, "long periods of the day and night when I don't wear it."

James sighed and Daisy laughed, although as she clambered into the trap she rather wished she had omitted the "and night" from her rejoinder.

Daisy had never been to the Lake District before. Soon they left Windermere and turned off the main road onto one narrower and poorly maintained. Mist concealed the tops of the hills on either side. On the sparse verges beside the road and on the hills, damp sheep grazed. Daisy, who felt affection for some of her cows, didn't much care for sheep.

"Lots of sheep," she said.

"Pretty well all of Westmoreland that isn't actually paved is ankle-deep in sheep shit," James said, twitching the reins to encourage the pony. "I'm glad you're a country girl; I'm tired of apologizing and telling girls to look where they step."

"And it's still light," Daisy said, with pleasure.

The longer the evenings were, the happier she felt. She loved to go for a walk after dinner, strolling through the woods at Aberneth Farm, listening to the birds settling down for the night in trees that made patterns of the yellowing light. She did not even wish for a companion on these walks, although she sometimes thought it would be very pleasant to have someone waiting for her at home.

"We'll be home before dark. At this time of the year it stays light until after ten and soon after there's a lovely slow dawn." From the way James spoke she knew he felt the same way she did about the long light months of summer. Daisy smiled at him. "And," he added, "in winter you can sometimes see the northern lights."

"The northern lights." Daisy could feel her eyes open wide, but she was not so young that she felt the need to conceal her almost childish enthusiasm.

"So you'll come back during the months of the long nights and I'll show them to you."

"I'd love to."

"Promise?"

Daisy laughed. "Yes."

"Promise."

"I promise," Daisy said happily.

Daisy knew that the words exchanged between her and James were identical to those that would have been uttered if James had been indulging in heavy-handed flirtation. But the feeling was quite different. It was as though he were doing her the compliment of not going through the preliminary skirmishes to any friendship—even one that was not flirtatious—between a young man and a girl. She was happy to take her cue from him and to bask in the pleasure of James's openly expressed admiration and the rare feeling of being with a kindred spirit. She loved not wasting time; and supposed his and her directness were the effect of war and its brutal suggestion that time was, even for the young, a commodity no one could afford to waste.

Bannock House was redbrick, early Victorian. Daisy was slightly disappointed and then ashamed of herself: disappointed because she had hoped for a castle, or a handsome Georgian house; ashamed of her disappointment since the house was grander than any she had so far entered as a guest. Around the house were tall, substantial, dripping trees and misty fields stretching away as far as she could see. Chinks of light showed at the front door, in a large room to the right, and at a couple of the upstairs windows.

"Staff crisis, traditional at this time of the year for some reason and, of course, the war doesn't help. My mother has already fed everyone except us. I've been detailed to feed you and billet you. You'll meet the family in the morning."

The traditional staff crisis did not prevent a boy—not a child but too young to have been called up—appearing from the dark shadows of the house and leading away the pony. James picked up Daisy's suitcase and carried it indoors.

The hall of Bannock House was paneled in dark wood, double height, and divided at the top of the stairs by a landing that ran the width of the room. As James carried her suitcase upstairs, Daisy could see that the landing formed one of three sides of a gallery around the inner half of the hall, the center of which was made lighter by a stained glass domed ceiling. Although it was midsummer, the house was not warm and dying fires smoldered in two fireplaces, one in each half of the hall below. Daisy, no stranger to drafty corridors and cold bedrooms—the rectory in which she had been brought up reached a pleasant temperature during only two months in the year—considered what midwinter at Bannock House might be like. Although the prospect of a return visit to view the northern lights was still an attractive one, it would entail warm socks and woolen vests.

"Here is your room. The bathroom is next door. Why don't you come down when you're ready and we'll have a drink and something to eat."

James put Daisy's suitcase at the foot of her bed and left the room. Daisy looked around with pleasure. The bedroom was larger than any in which she had ever slept, larger than any bedroom in her father's rectory. Daisy enjoyed feeling like a heroine in a nineteenth-century novel and for a moment felt mildly self-congratulatory about her literary association with her whereabouts; a moment later she realized that the heroine with whom she had most in common was Catherine Morland in *Northanger Abbey*. She was laughing out loud as she went through the door from her bedroom into the also large, old-fashioned, tiled bathroom that adjoined it. At the far end a second door led, presumably, onto the corridor. Daisy tried the door and found it unlocked. There was no key or bolt on her side or, when she opened the door, on the other side. Although, she reflected, suppressing a giggle, a lock on the outside would move her quandary from the mild inconvenience and the potential embarrassment of upper-class domestic arrangements to one of being the potential victim of some Gothic weirdness. Being unable to lock others out of one's bathroom seemed marginally preferable to being held a prisoner within it.

Gratefully using the lavatory—the ones on the trains had left a great deal to be desired—and washing her hands in tepid water, Daisy changed her clothes and went downstairs. James came out of a room that opened off the hall to meet her; he had a heavy glass tumbler in his hand.

"Let me get you a drink," he said, leading her into a large dark library. "Then we'll inspect the provisions. Whiskey?"

Daisy glanced at the drinks tray. Whiskey was not a taste she had acquired and it had, in fact, never been offered to her before.

"I'd rather have a glass of sherry, if I may," she said.

James raised one eyebrow.

"I was brought up in a Church of England rectory," Daisy said. "What do you expect?"

James laughed and poured her a sherry.

"Follow me," he said.

Daisy followed him through the halls, through a green baize door, along an uncarpeted wooden-floored corridor, and into a large kitchen, with a black and white tiled floor. There was a heavy tray, with settings for two people, on the kitchen table. Also a substantial slab of yellow cheese, a tin of biscuits, and a bowl of apples. Small, pink and gold; Beauty of Bath, Daisy thought.

James lifted the lid of a heavy saucepan and peered inside. He said nothing and after a moment Daisy joined him and also regarded the contents.

"Irish stew," she said, her tone unconvincingly enthusiastic.

"Bloody sheep everywhere. Would you like some?"

"I think an apple and some cheese is all I want," Daisy said. "It's late and I ate on the train. Sandwiches—from Aberneth Farm."

"In that case, we'll eat by the fire."

James loaded the tray and Daisy helped him carry their meal back to the library, doing her best to quell a suspicion that the meals at Bannock House might bear some similarity to those served at her boarding school.

Soon she started to feel a pleasant glow as her second glass of sherry warmed and relaxed every part of her body and lifted her spirits. The logs James had added to the smoldering embers in the fireplace began to burn brightly and he rose and switched off the overhead lights. The darkness made where they were sitting seem part of a festive, sensuous secret. As James returned to his seat— an armchair at the other side of the small table that held their plates—he paused by the large, round silver tray on which stood a selection of bottles.

"Ah," he said. "An open bottle of wine."

He pulled out the cork and sniffed the contents.

"Recent enough, I think," he said, "to suffice. Particularly since another glass of sherry will make you rather liverish in the morning. Enough here for a glass each to finish our cheese with."

Daisy had never before had three drinks on the same occasion, and she paused for a moment to be sure she wasn't becoming drunk. But she experienced only a feeling of warmth and well-being and felt no urge to giggle or show off, the only symptoms of inebriation she had so far witnessed.

"I should like to draw your head," James said. "Charcoal—or maybe chalk would do you more justice."

"I didn't know you were an artist," Daisy said, regretting her words as soon as they were out of her mouth. "I didn't know you drew" would have sounded less naïve. But James didn't seem to notice.

"Before the war I studied at the Slade. When it's over—well, what's the point of thinking about that? Time enough when—" And he raised his wine glass. "Peace."

"Peace," Daisy echoed, thinking that "Victory" was the toast she more usually heard, and that "Peace" sounded more thoughtful, more hopeful, less exclusively masculine. "I'd never thought it before, but I haven't made plans for when the war is over. I don't seem to be able to imagine it."

"Plans will be necessary only if we win," James said. "Although that's not why I don't make them."

"I know," Daisy said. "That's harder still to imagine. Losing."

"We won't."

And she believed him.

"One thing's sure," James said. "Whatever happens, those who survive won't take up where they left off. Everything'll be changed . . . forever."

They were silent for a moment. Daisy thought about what

James had said. She was too young to imagine that she would not survive the war. And, unlike James, she was in no danger—less, in fact, than many civilians. The idea that they—she—would emerge into a new, utterly changed peacetime world was an exciting one.

"So—you'll sit for me, when all this is over?"

"Yes," Daisy said happily.

James got up again, threw another log on the fire, and picked up the tray and put it on a sideboard. He pulled a large book from one of the shelves in the almost unlit part of the library—Daisy thought he must know its place, and that the room must be noticeably colder where he was standing—and came back and sat beside Daisy on the sofa. He set the book on the low table in front of them.

"May I?" he asked. Daisy nodded; she was not sure whether he was asking her permission to sit beside her or to show her the book.

James opened the book. Text and black and white illustrations, the lighter and finer lines suggesting paler or intermediary colors. James turned a few pages and then pointed to a sketch of a seated girl.

"Corot," he said. "You know, the prolific French nineteenth-century painter—landscapes, small leaves—lovely French countryside light."

Daisy nodded, not quite honestly. The name was familiar and she hoped that as James continued she would remember a little more. She looked at the reproduction of the sketch.

"Look at the base of the neck and the collarbone."

Daisy looked at where the collarbone would be and saw it, although it was not drawn; it was, rather, suggested, although she was not sure how.

"I don't know—quite understand—how much is him—I

mean actually drawn—and how much is me—my eye—filling in for him."

"Very good," James said. He picked up his glass and returned to where he had been sitting before.

"Look at the book, I'll watch you."

"And answer questions?" Daisy asked, pleased but a little embarrassed.

"Only if you show me your profile. Now."

Daisy turned obligingly.

"Hold your hair up so I can see your neck."

Daisy did as he told her, stretching her neck and straightening her spine. She could feel a blush rising, but for once did not feel doubly embarrassed by the evidence of her embarrassment. James's admiration made her feel beautiful. She was grateful, not only that he thought of her as a thing of beauty, but that his admiration was of her as she essentially was, not of an altered and idealized image of womanhood. It reassured her to know the world didn't always work the way Valerie said it did.

Daisy turned the pages. She had seen books as substantial before—in the library at school and the huge, leather-bound Bible with the brass clasp in her father's church—but she had never had one to handle or read for pleasure. The book seemed to be a broad history of drawing and sketching. The beginning sketches were reproductions of a medieval monks' pattern book. Daisy looked at the drawings of birds, animals—both real and fantastical—symbols, and emblems; she was aware of James watching her, but it did not detract either from her concentration or from the pleasure she felt. The drawings touched her in a way she did not quite understand.

"The cats are wonderful," she said.

"Aren't they? There must have been cats around the monastery or abbey to keep the rats and mice down. And some of the monks were amused by them, and some probably loved them."

"Sleeping beside the kitchen fires."

"Exactly."

Daisy turned over pages; the central pages were often of the Virgin and Child. She was surprised by the different ways artists had seen or imagined babies and small children. Some were drawn as though a child who Daisy herself might have held had sat for the sketch, some seemed to be miniature adults, some had heads strangely disproportionate to their bodies, others seemed a little too fat to represent the Christ child. Passing the original Corot sketch and some striking and slightly unsettling late-nineteenth-century self-portraits, Daisy found herself looking at an erotic drawing. It took her a moment to grasp the significance of the charcoal lines and to see the intertwining reclining bodies. It was the first time she had ever seen anything like it; she put her hand to the corner of the page to turn it, but hesitated, although she was keenly aware of James watching her.

"Schiele," he said. "That's his self-portrait on the other page. He was a friend of Klimt's—you saw his work a few pages back. They both died in 1918 in the influenza epidemic."

Daisy silently turned the page.

"What do you think?"

For a moment, Daisy considered replying, "About what?" But she knew the response would be coy, not quite honest. And that James, too, would know it. And surely the whole point—having been given the opportunities of the war—of escape from her father's rectory, an independent life as a Land Girl, her temporary incarnation as a guest at an upper-class house party, was to make the most of those opportunities, to ensure she would not have to return to the limitations of the world she lived in before the war.

"It's not what I—expected," Daisy said, waiting for James to ask, "What did you expect?" But he merely nodded, and she was grateful.

Daisy continued to turn pages and James watched her silently.

"Undo your blouse," he said after a moment or two. "Just a couple of buttons, so I can see your collarbone."

Daisy was excited by his request. Her limited experience with male admirers had, up to now, been the urgent groping and pleas of overheated youths, far too close to home; their awkwardness and their ignorance inspiring neither desire nor affection, their lack of control so clearly putting her in charge. Even so, Daisy sometimes, for a moment, could imagine how it might be with someone she loved. The assuredness of James's voice, the coolness of his request, was erotic. The distance at which he sat necessitated her keeping only her own actions and emotions in check.

She took a deep breath and started to unbutton her blouse, pausing when the top two buttons were open. She drew back the fabric from her neck and turned her head a little to one side.

"Lovely," James said. He came no closer to her, but his eyes did not move from hers and the slight smile never left his lips. He said nothing, Daisy said nothing, and the silence continued, not uncomfortably, until the door behind her opened and a male voice said, "So there you are."

Daisy jumped a little and dropped her hands from the neck of her blouse to her lap. She felt a blush rise to her face, and shame at the blush rather than the act that had precipitated it—which she still considered innocent—made her awkward.

"We thought everyone had gone to bed," James said easily.

Daisy turned a little; Patrick was now in the room.

"Hello, Daisy," he said, his tone pleasant, but without a smile. He made for the fire, turned his back to it, and addressed James. "I was in the billiards room. Driven out by lack of opponents and incipient frostbite."

"Drink?" James asked, again as casually as though moments before Daisy had not held her blouse open for him to admire the way her neck sat on her shoulders.

Patrick poured himself a glass of brandy and with a silent gesture ascertained that James wanted one, too. Neither offered Daisy another drink and after a moment she rose and said good night.

The bedroom seemed even colder than before; she put on a heavier pullover to unpack and hang up her evening dress. In the bathroom, the chill from the uncovered tiles rose through the soles of her bedroom slippers; she washed her face, brushed her teeth, set her hair for the night and postponed washing and further unpacking until morning. The same pullover on top of her nightdress, her feet tucked up and the fabric wrapped closely around them, Daisy curled up in bed and waited to become warm.

She wondered what else James might have said if Patrick had not come into the room. Patrick had seemed older than she remembered him. Older, tired, and grown-up. Perhaps it was just that he had seemed silently to convey disapproval. He had quite a nerve; her behavior had been completely innocent. But how delicately and skillfully James had handled the awkwardness of the moment. Her fingers, tucked between her arms and her breasts, relaxed although her toes were still cold as she fell asleep.

She was warm when she woke. The room was completely dark. Daisy was not disconcerted by the darkness; the blackout was faithfully adhered to at Aberneth Farm, the bombing of the oil tanks fresh in everyone's memory. Nor did she wonder where she was. Daisy woke every morning with a clear sense of where she had gone to sleep and what had happened the day before. She lay still and tried to work out what had awakened her. It was a feeling similar to that she had had after her mother's cat died. The old tortoiseshell had been in the habit of sleeping on Daisy's bed and, for some time after its death, Daisy used to wake up in the night sensing the absence of its inert weight at her feet. Now she was aware of a presence although the room in which she now lay was dark and silent; nothing stirred but somebody or something was close to her. Although James had been charmed by the drawings of the cats that evening, Daisy had seen no signs of a household pet. Without a sense of fear, she considered the possibility of a ghost. But a slight shift of weight at the foot of the bed and a faint smell of whisky suggested the presence was human— and most likely male. The probable maleness of her unseen companion did not add to Daisy's very mild alarm; she had no reason to consider James, or even Patrick, more alarming than a so-far-unmet, night-walking, whisky-drinking female alternative.

"James," she said tentatively.

"You're awake. I was listening to you sleep."

"What's the matter?" Daisy sat up.

"I didn't say good night to you properly downstairs."

And James came closer and took her in his arms. He did not move quickly or aggressively and Daisy allowed him to hold her for a moment while she thought about what she should do. Wryly aware of her famed common sense—she didn't think it the most admirable or romantic attribute for a twenty-year-old girl—she quickly considered the proper reaction to the presence of an attractive young man in her bedroom, sitting on her bed. A slightly drunken young man who was not only her host but her connection to the rest of the household. As a young unmarried woman, a virgin, what was the proper manner in which to deal with this unforeseen complication? Slightly to her surprise, Daisy found that she was also considering her own instinctive feelings, although she was well aware they should have little or no influence on how she now behaved. It seemed she could imagine James making love to her but, if such lovemaking did take place, it would not begin with her relinquishing her virginity in such a casual manner. She felt none of the desire she had experienced earlier, sitting fully clothed, a table between them, in the library. What had then seemed sophisticated and exciting had now become crass and presumptuous. What had then been flattering was now boorish. Before she had been in thrall to James; now she was embarrassed by him.

"James, I don't think you should be here. It's the middle of the night and you shouldn't be in my room."

James didn't reply. Instead he stroked Daisy's hair.

"How charming. You're wearing a snood."

That did it, and Daisy pushed him away. Her hair, thanks to one of Valerie's beauty tips, was rolled around a sanitary towel and held in place by a stout hair net.

"Daisy—"

Daisy felt a sudden and deep resentment for all the slightly disgusting procedures to which women were obliged to submit themselves in order to make themselves attractive to men. Daisy filed her fingernails out of earshot of the nearest man, spat guiltily into her mascara box, and rolled her hair up at night secretly and usually uncomfortably. Now it seemed she might be humiliated for choosing a painless alternative to sleeping on lumpy curlers.

James was not deterred by Daisy's rebuff, and his hands on her shoulders were stronger and more urgent.

"No, James, please." Daisy deliberately raised her voice.

"Shh," he whispered.

"Please don't!" She spoke a little louder, allowing—contriving—a note of panic in her voice. James let go of her shoulders and rose to his feet.

"Oh, very well. There's no reason to call for help. I'm not going to force myself on you."

Daisy felt a wish to placate him, but she knew that was what he intended and she remained silent. After a moment she heard him move toward the door, stumbling against some unseen object on the way. Daisy suppressed an impolitic giggle and a moment later saw his silhouette outlined against the dim light of the corridor. Then he closed the door and she was once again in complete darkness.

CHAPTER 5

DAISY STOOD IN front of a large, mottled looking glass. She held the diamond necklace up to her throat, holding the clasp together behind her neck without hooking it. The necklace was pretty, but sparse; a few perfectly respectable diamonds surrounded by diamond chips set into a band of dark silver, with some smaller stones set in strands that dropped from the neckband. Daisy thought it was probably several hundred years old.

"Trying it on for size?" Patrick's reflection joined Daisy's in the looking glass. Although his tone was light and amused, it lacked gentleness, and Daisy immediately felt defensive.

"I'm not trying it on, I'm just holding it up to see what it looks like."

Patrick raised one eyebrow and Daisy knew what he was insinuating. He thought she was imagining herself wearing the diamonds, having first married James and then killed off his mother.

"Lady Nugent asked me to unpick it; it was mounted on a frame so she could wear it as a tiara. It's been like that since the coronation."

Patrick laughed and if she hadn't been feeling offended and cross, Daisy would have laughed, too. But she was hurt by the insulting implication of his words and angry at the way she had been treated by James and his family that day.

"I don't know if this is an example of upper-class hospitality, or if your family is simply lacking in good manners, but I have been rudely and unkindly treated by everyone since I got here."

Patrick again raised an eyebrow, and Daisy once again read arrogance and pride in his expression. She would have liked to slap him, but though she was angry, her actions and even more important, her incipient tears, were under control. Daisy rarely cried, and when she did so, her tears were more often caused by repressed anger than by self-pity.

"You and James seemed to be getting along pretty well last night," Patrick said, his tone light, but his face in the looking glass, over the shoulder of her reflection, was cold and disapproving.

Daisy said nothing. She assumed—and hoped—Patrick knew nothing of what had happened later that night; it was, of course, possible that he knew that James had visited her room, and also, more horribly, that he believed that his cousin had done so by arrangement or had not been rebuffed were the visit a surprise.

Daisy's eyes met Patrick's; she had no idea what to say.

"Here, let me." And Patrick took the ends of the necklace out of her hands and held the diamonds high enough for them to be seen against the skin of her neck, rather than the hand-knitted jersey she wore.

Almost in spite of herself, Daisy looked again at her reflection. She nodded slightly as she saw for the first time the point of diamonds. It was not just that they were themselves beautiful, hard, sharp, brilliant, but they also lit up her face. Her skin, slightly brown from working outdoors, and lightly freckled, now seemed smoother and creamier; her eyes a deeper blue; and her hair, a pleasant but undistinguished brown, had developed richer, darker touches and a tinge of chestnut. She was aware of Patrick watching her.

"Can you see the northern lights from here? In the winter?"

"I shouldn't think so," Patrick said, blinking at this sudden change of subject. "I never have, anyway."

Daisy saw that her expression was thoughtful as she met Patrick's eye in the looking glass.

"Lovely," she said, "but as you can see, it doesn't fit." She took the necklace out of his hands and returned it to a flat worn leather box lined in dark red silk. She shut the box and hooked the flimsy metal clasp.

"Perhaps," she said, "you would like to return it to Lady Nugent. She needs it for this evening."

DAISY SNEEZED. THE bedroom was cold and she felt a slight pressure in her forehead and a tenderness on one side of her throat. She was getting a cold. Already treated disdainfully by the Nugents, when they weren't completely ignoring her, she would now be a pariah to the other guests at the dance that evening—a red-nosed wallflower, the other wallflowers edging away from her, alone and sniffling into a damp handkerchief. She wondered, for a moment, what kind of day she would have had, had she, the night before, whipped the "snood" off her hair, stuffed it under the pillow, and allowed James to make love to her.

She'd probably still have been getting a cold, but apart from that, would breakfast, for instance, have been different? Maybe not. But how much worse, she thought, it would have been, if having given her virginity to James—a man who knew her so little that the question of whether or not she were a virgin had not been raised—she had come down to breakfast and found he had already left for the day.

Lady Nugent had, at least, known her name; James's sisters apparently did not. Of the five people eating breakfast, Patrick was the only one whom she had ever met before. It would, Daisy now thought, have been better if her entrance had frozen a conversation. The lack of reaction to her arrival and apology for being late was even more disconcerting. It seemed as though no one quite registered her presence; one of the girls did not even look up from her plate.

"Which of the Treaty Ports will the Germans invade? Queenstown, Berehaven, or Lough Swilly?" a gray-haired woman was asking Patrick.

"Since, although I'm Irish, I'm an officer in His Majesty's Armed Forces, I probably wouldn't be the first person the German High Command would confide in."

Daisy hesitated, still unacknowledged and unwelcomed, at the door. Although their voices were not raised, and Patrick had replied with a smile, there could be no one in the room unaware that the woman was baiting him, that he was very angry but choosing not to show it. What was not so clear was whether the others were enjoying the woman's attack through patriotic conviction, sycophancy, or just because it was Patrick's turn to be bullied or teased.

Even though she was still standing awkwardly at the door, Daisy was curious about both the anger and the subject that had—ostensibly, at least—been the cause. And Patrick, with whom she felt quite cross herself for his cool and dismissive manner toward her the previous evening, would, she thought, probably be a good person, were the atmosphere less tense, to explain some of the more confusing aspects of Southern Irish neutrality. And it was confusing. She knew—or at least supposed—that Southern Ireland was behaving poorly, remaining neutral while Hitler threatened the future of Europe. And the IRA had exploded bombs in

London just before the war. But she also knew that many men from neutral Eire had enlisted in the British army. And why had England, only two years before, the shadow of war already over Europe, so casually handed back to Ireland the naval ports that they had held under treaty? The ports that the gray-haired woman was now taunting Patrick about?

"Good-morning-I-hope-you-slept-well-breakfast-is-on-the-sideboard," Lady Nugent said vaguely. Nothing fey about her vagueness; it was more that Daisy was an irritation that if given no more attention than deserved need not distract her.

"We call it Cobh. Queenstown's now called Cobh. It's spelled c-o-b-h, but it's pronounced 'Cove,' " Patrick said in a purely informational tone. "There's no v in Gaelic."

Daisy looked at the substantial remains of breakfast set out in two chafing dishes. One contained, in a shallow pool of warm grease, fried eggs, fried bread, and fried tomatoes. The other was half filled with thick, solid porridge. For the first time since Daisy had enlisted in the Land Army, she looked at a meal with no wish to eat any of it. A little to one side there stood a silver toast rack with some damp, caved-in toast. Daisy helped herself to a triangle and then, because it looked so puny on her plate, another. She poured herself some tea from a large silver pot. Very strong and not quite hot enough.

At the breakfast table, the others were eating methodically; the daughter who had partially acknowledged Daisy's presence glanced scornfully at the toast. Daisy sat down and, after slightly too long a pause, Lady Nugent introduced her to those present.

"My daughters, Lizzie and Kate. Patrick I think you have already met. This is my sister, Gladys Glynne."

Mrs. Glynne. Gladys Glynne. Aunt Glad. Her name had come up as a frequent visitor, an integral part of the household, when Rosemary was describing the inhabitants of Bannock House.

"Somewhere between Sergeant Cuff and the Grand Inquisitor," Rosemary had said. Adding, with the inflection that reminded Daisy that some part of Rosemary's family was Irish, "You'd want to mind yourself there. It won't do you any good, of course."

Mrs. Glynne now turned her attention to Daisy. In the background Daisy could hear the discussion, now openly tense, continue. The words "Black and Tans" spoken by both Patrick and Lizzie; Lizzie apparently standing in for the otherwise occupied Mrs. Glynne. Daisy would have liked to listen, but Mrs. Glynne demanded her full attention. In a kindly, interested way she drew Daisy out. Before Daisy had finished the first triangle of her soggy toast she had revealed her age, that she had been to boarding school, that she had one sister but no brothers, that her father was a rector—and a younger son—that Daisy's mother was well educated and from a perfectly respectable but not rich Norfolk family. Daisy knew that she was being placed. She also knew that this placing was only in the details; the Nugents would, without Mrs. Glynne's more vigorous approach—perhaps starting with Kate's glance at her meager helping of toast—have had no difficulty in knowing as much as they needed about Daisy's background and antecedents. Daisy knew there was nothing for her to be ashamed of; there was no suggestion that they thought her mannerless, ignorant, or vulgar. They saw her as she saw herself, as coming from what had once been minor landed gentry.

None of the others paid any attention to the interrogation; she was of no interest to them. Lady Nugent seemed preoccupied and, since the dance was to be held in her house that evening and Daisy had no reason to disbelieve James's assessment of the servant problem, she probably was. James's sisters were equally disengaged. Both were thin, pale; a reddish tinge to their hair suggested that freckles, rather than Daisy's golden brown, would result from exposure to the sun. Lizzie glanced at Daisy with an almost complete lack of interest; it was the first time she had looked at her since Daisy entered the dining room. Patrick's face was devoid of expression, although Daisy thought he was half listening.

Aunt Glad was rich, according to Rosemary, and had no children. There was a stepdaughter, but Aunt Glad was on record as considering the girl already to have more money than was good for her.

In return for her answers to Mrs. Glynne's questions, Daisy learned only that James had eaten breakfast early and left to fish. He might or might not be home for lunch. Daisy understood that she now occupied the position of an inconvenient pet adopted by an irresponsible child and left in the care of his exasperated and otherwise occupied family.

DAISY SNEEZED AGAIN; her feet were still cold and her eyes were beginning to feel puffy. She had time to spare—had had too much time to spare all day—and putting on her heavy jersey, she crept under the eiderdown. To avoid brooding over the far from satisfactory day, her thoughts returned to the scene at breakfast. While she was sure the Nugents and Gladys Glynne were capable of a full-scale row about as academic a subject as what fly James was, or should be, using best to catch a trout, she was not sure if what had passed between Mrs. Glynne and Patrick, watched expressionlessly by the female Nugents, was an indication of deeply held beliefs—fears?—or was merely a line of teasing that had produced results in the past. Ireland was not a country Daisy had thought about much, beyond having the sense, reading between the lines of her school history book, that they'd had a pretty raw deal from their English neighbors. They were a neutral country; did Mrs. Glynne really fear that they would welcome a German invasion of England via their ports? Were there Irish people angry enough actively to aid the Germans? Daisy didn't know, but thought it unfair to bait an officer, as Patrick had put it, in His Majesty's Armed Forces. And Sir Guy Wilcox—close enough to home for Rosemary to have known his wife— would his Fascism really have been extreme enough for him to betray his own country to the Germans? Was it possible that there were still members of the English upper classes who admired Hitler? And she thought again about the beautiful Lady Mosley and her new-born baby.

After breakfast she had asked if there was anything she could do to help, but despite the staff shortage, Lady Nugent seemed to have delegated all tasks to a small troupe of women press-ganged from the village. And Aunt Glad traveled with a maid who had done the flowers. Lady Nugent managed, not unkindly, to suggest to Daisy that the most helpful thing she could do would be to relieve her hostess of the responsibility of entertaining her. Daisy said she would love to take a long walk. "If you really want to make yourself useful, you could take the dogs for a walk," Lady Nugent said, her manner that of one ticking off two small items at the bottom of a very long list.

Daisy, wearing sensible shoes, set out with an overweight spaniel and an elderly Labrador. Since the dogs were both lazy and well trained, she stopped worrying about losing them by the time she reached the end of the avenue. Setting out along an unpaved road in the opposite direction to the one she had traveled the night before, Daisy followed the outer wall of the Nugent estate. Ivy-covered in parts, with glimpses of the woods showing through the broken-down bits, Daisy thought it beautiful. She also thought it a pity that James—the James who had met her at the station—was not with her. She wondered if she had, by rejecting him the night before, lost someone of great value, the only person with whom she had so far felt a complete sense of intimacy. Or had she merely been fooled by the charm of a practiced seducer, a practiced seducer who now couldn't be bothered to go through even the motions of good manners?

Lunch, while neither festive nor delicious, was not as silent as breakfast had been. The Nugents talked amongst themselves, largely about arrangements and guests for that evening. Aunt Glad had a few details she wanted to clear up with Daisy and asked how she was traveling back to Wales. Daisy told her, mentioning the time her train departed; she had, for the first time, the attention of every person present. Patrick and Kate, at the far end of the table, talked quietly. Daisy could not hear what they were saying. James did not appear.

During lunch, it started to rain. Afterward they drank weak coffee from small cups in the library. Patrick, and then Lizzie, left the room; Daisy, now desperate, asked Lady Nugent for some task. Either in response to Daisy's urgency or because she had just remembered that her necklace was wired onto a frame, Lady Nugent asked Daisy to unpick it carefully and had given her a small pair of sharp nail scissors with which to perform the operation.

The necklace had been professionally mounted. Sitting under a good light, Daisy had carefully edged the tip of the scissors under the thread that, tightly wound several times, held each strand in place. The thread was coarse and strong and had a stiff, wirelike quality. Daisy suspected she was causing irreparable harm to the scissors but wished neither to interrupt her hostess at her tasks, whatever they might be, nor to appear to question her judgment. She knew only that her own mother would have had a fit if Daisy had ever treated *her* nail scissors like that.

As Daisy cut the mounting away, the necklace grew pliant in her lap and a sprinkling of snippets of thread lay at her feet. She wondered where the necklace had been kept since the coronation. She didn't imagine there was a safe in Bannock House, and it seemed unlikely that an object so old and so valuable would just have been stuffed in a cupboard. It had probably been kept at the bank; but would the local bank—presumably small and modest—have a procedure for storing jewelry, or would they make an exception for the Nugents? Daisy was considering the probabilities and details of the arrangement when she snipped the last thread. Then she stood in front of the looking glass to see what diamonds would look like. Then Patrick had come in.

Becoming gradually warm under the slippery eiderdown, Daisy now remembered that she had not picked up the small, stiff fragments of thread she had let drop onto the carpet. She felt irritated at herself, but did not consider returning to the library to tidy up. Her throat was tender and she suddenly was not looking forward to wearing the pretty, expensive, and low-cut dress Rosemary had lent her.

Her neck ached and her head was uncomfortable, possibly because she was cold, huddled, and unrelaxed and partly because she had put her hair in curlers. Reluctant to further interrupt Lady Nugent with irritating questions and becoming, by the hour, less concerned with the convenience of the Nugent family, she had run a shallow but hot bath and while she washed—soaking was not a possibility—she had kept her head close to the steam to encourage her hair to set. She crouched in the bathtub until the water cooled, listening all the time for steps in the corridor outside the unlocked bathroom door. Time and the occasional drip from the large brass taps had left an orange and green stain on the white enamel of the high tub. Daisy thought that when the war was over she would celebrate by lying, for an hour, in a bath as large as this one, filled to the top with hot water. Or, on a beach, until the sun became too hot to bear. The Mediterranean maybe; somewhere other than the North of England.

———

LADY NUGENT WORE the necklace at dinner. Her dress was black and, it seemed to Daisy, not new. The necklace was effective, even at the distance of the table. It had made Daisy prettier; it made Lady Nugent regal; the diamonds had lit up Daisy's skin, they added authority and a suggestion of history to Lady Nugent's erect posture.

Lady Nugent caught Daisy's eye and smiled.

"My necklace is courtesy of Daisy, James's little friend. She spent all afternoon unpicking it from its frame."

Although it was toward the end of dinner, conversation was spasmodic and not animated, so most heads turned toward Daisy, some perhaps wondering why, if she were James's friend, little or otherwise, she was not sitting closer to him. He was seated between a pretty girl Daisy had not been introduced to and Mrs. Glynne.

"I don't suppose you're interested in gardening?" the slightly deaf neighbor of the Nugents, sitting on Daisy's left, asked.

"I am. Very," she said firmly. During the course of the evening she had been forced to admit to him, and to a captain in the Fusiliers on her right, that she did not ride, fish, shoot, play bridge, and was not acquainted with any relative or friend of the Nugents not present. "I don't know much about it, though."

"A middle-aged pleasure, *faute de mieux,*" her companion said, a little sadly.

"Do you have a garden?" Daisy asked him, determined not to let another conversational gambit lapse.

"Wartime, strictly wartime," he said, with another sigh. Daisy thought of the rectory garden, efficiently planted with rows of the less interesting vegetables, and wondered why it seemed less patriotic to plant artichokes and *mange-tout* than it was to cultivate cabbages and Swede turnips.

"I don't know how well you know this part of the world?" he ventured, when Daisy failed to respond, dutifully embarking on another conversational tack. Daisy, who would have dearly loved to give her nose a good blow, was becoming guiltily aware that she was very heavy social weather for the men seated on either side of her. She could see that she and they ranked low in Lady Nugent's placement. Since Daisy carried approximately the social weight of a governess brought down to avoid seating thirteen at dinner, the men on either side of her, though not perhaps quite so devoid of qualification, were unlikely to find themselves seated beside a Nugent. She wondered when Lady Nugent had reworked the placement and what James had said to her.

"Not at all, I'm afraid," Daisy said.

"Perhaps the Nugents—"

"I have to go back to Wales tomorrow," Daisy said, nipping in the bud the assumption that any Nugent would be prepared to go an inch out of his way to entertain her. "But," she added a little desperately, "we did do the Lake District poets at school."

There was another pause and Daisy realized that poetry was not the direction in which her companion had been hoping to steer the conversation.

"Yes," he said at last. "Wordsworth and . . . ah . . . Coleridge . . ." his voice trailed off. Then, "And of course there's Beatrix Potter."

Daisy was attempting to formulate a not too discouraging sentence that suggested that while Beatrix Potter was not, strictly speaking, one of the Romantic poets, she had a certain lyrical enthusiasm for nature, which made the error a very understandable one, when she was distracted by James's voice, quite loud, from farther up the table. He was speaking to Patrick.

". . . great sport, we missed you today."

"Why didn't you go?" Kate asked. The note of teasing in her voice might have been flirtatious.

"I don't think I'll ever voluntarily kill anything larger than a horsefly again as long as I live," Patrick said.

Apart from Daisy's dinner partner, there was a silence around the table, the silence that follows an extreme lapse in taste, a silence that no one wished to take the responsibility of breaking.

". . . *The Tale of Jemima Puddle-duck* and, of course, *Tom Kitten*."

Every head at the table was now turned toward Daisy and the man attempting to engage her in conversation. Kate's supercilious smile was followed by a disbelieving shake of her head; Daisy would have given a great deal to be able to smack her.

"You don't seem to have any difficulty polishing off the salmon on your plate," Lizzie said to Patrick in a tone that suggested to Daisy that she was less fond of him than Kate seemed to be.

"I didn't say I was a vegetarian—in fact, I imagine I'm essentially a carnivore."

"So?"

"If, after the war—and it seems more than possible I'll be happy to have it—a butcher's shop is my lot, I'll be capable of slaughtering my own meat. And eating it. I won't, however, be doing it socially. Or for sport."

The exchange did nothing to lighten the gloom now spread fairly evenly over the dinner table; two maids cleared the plates, unnerved by the sudden interest the guests seemed to have developed in their every movement. Daisy now seemed to have the most enviable placement and her dinner partner had never had a more rapt audience.

"She lives at Near Sawrey; she's an old lady now, of course."

Daisy nodded mutely. The Nugents seemed even more dangerous to her than they had a moment before. She would have liked to say something that showed solidarity with Patrick, but didn't know how. She had a pretty good idea that not only would he not welcome her support but a declaration of similar feelings would not have surprised her hosts. They would see her commonsense attitude toward the killing of rabbits and chickens and her distaste for blood sports to be a manifestation of her inferior birth.

"The inn is in the background of one of the illustrations in *Jemima Puddle-duck*," her companion finished triumphantly.

But Daisy was thinking that as much as she disliked Patrick, his aversion to spilling blood when the war was over was rather more admirable than her own determination to wallow chin high in a bubble bath.

ON WET AFTERNOONS at Daisy's boarding school—an old, academically distinguished, and even rather grand establishment that offered generous scholarships to the daughters of the clergy— there used to be country dancing in the gymnasium. No one enjoyed it. The games mistress, who was in charge, was well coordinated but had a poor sense of rhythm, and the music available was limited to three gramophone records, none of them new: an English country dance whose name Daisy had forgotten, "The Walls of Limerick," and a Highland reel.

Daisy had been not only bored but embarrassed by these afternoons. She was not graceful and felt ridiculous dancing with other girls, linking arms and spinning around, hopping up and down in her short, boxy, navy blue gymslip. Occasionally she would be sent out of the room and would while away the afternoon standing in the corridor, daydreaming and listening to the scratchy and repetitive music from the gramophone. Daisy tried not to spend too much time outside the door not because there was any further punishment involved—punishments and rewards at this high-minded school were largely theoretical—but because any visit to the headmistress's study would involve the always unspoken reminder that Daisy, as the beneficiary of a scholarship, was expected to provide a good example to the more privileged girls.

Daisy remembered these afternoons as she watched the dancing and could now see the point of learning the steps. She thought her former headmistress would be too fine to say "I told you so," either in words or by facial expression, but—as with the reduced fees—the thought would fill the room. The games mistress hadn't been nearly so fine, and Daisy could imagine her satisfied smirk.

So far no one had asked Daisy to dance. While this might prove useful ammunition if either of these bygone school-day figures were to materialize, Daisy was embarrassed and humiliated. She wasn't bored, and if no one could see her, she would have been content to watch the dancing. She liked the music; the tunes, familiar from the old gramophone records, now played by the small dance band were alive and energetic. Young women in long dresses, creamy whites and pinks—some of the men wearing kilts and the various traditional accoutrements—danced in the large, high-ceilinged, shabby room. The kilts reminded Daisy that they were not so far from Scotland; many of the guests must have traveled great distances. Bannock, she had the impression, was the only grand house in the neighborhood, and yet the room was full of young men and girls who had come from as far away as London. The gaiety and the carefree, noisy atmosphere of the ball were the result of complicated travel and logistical arrangements—of leave and of lodgings and hospitality provided by friends and neighbors of the Nugents. It explained why Lady Nugent might resent Daisy taking up a guest room but not why half a dozen other such rooms remained empty. Daisy and Mrs. Glynne—Lady Nugent's sister—were the only house guests. She started to wonder why Lady Nugent would have chosen to add the burden of a difficult middle-aged woman to the hard work and arrangements of a dance, and then remembered that the Nugent children were apparently Mrs. Glynne's heirs. It was not only a hastily reworked placement that had seated James beside his aunt.

Daisy had never before been in a house that had a ballroom; she didn't imagine that many still existed. It was a ballroom that could have done with new wallpaper; the original intricately designed colors had faded not unpleasantly into a subdued blended pattern, and the curtains, long, wide, threadbare, had once, it seemed, been a rich, dark brown velvet. Daisy rather liked the yellowish tinge they had now assumed. The gold cord sashes that held the curtains back had fared less well, as had the cords of a similar material that had once held in place the tired draped velvet on the pelmet. Daisy thought Lady Nugent would have done well to have removed the frayed, sad, gold bindings—rather as she, Daisy, had freed the diamond necklace from its frame—and given the curtains a good shake. In the meantime, the reel had ended and dancers were leaving the floor. After a moment the music started again; this time a waltz. No one asked Daisy to dance; no one had spoken to her since the family had finished their coffee and entered the ballroom. Feeling conspicuous and being ignored, Daisy reflected, were trials that should not be imposed simultaneously. Even making small talk with a friendly dowager—there was no shortage of dowagers seated, as was Daisy, at the end of the ballroom and in the adjoining anteroom—would have made her situation more tenable.

Daisy stood up; it seemed important to move with a purpose, and she drained the almost empty champagne glass that she held. She knew it was pathetic to have to fetch herself another drink, but she preferred to appear to lack a mannerly escort than to sit, smiling wanly, as the others danced. Especially since it seemed that she could remain there until the band went home without anyone even speaking to her.

The champagne that the waiter poured for her was cooler than that she had just finished, but not really cold. It was the one thing in the chilly house that should have been colder. Although the large vases in the hall and drawing room were, thanks to Aunt Glad's maid, filled with summer branches and tall flowers, a fire had been burning all day in the ballroom to take the damp chill off. Now, as the crush of energetically dancing bodies heated the room, it had been allowed to die down, presumably to prevent accidents caused by swirling inflammable dresses or the horseplay of drunken and overexcited young men as the evening wore on.

Sipping her fresh champagne, Daisy strolled into the hall, her gait more casual than she felt. Several men glanced admiringly, but none of them made a move toward her. Daisy might have paused to allow one to overcome his reserve, pluck up his courage, and compose a self-introductory sentence, had not Lizzie, surrounded by admirers, been holding court close to the door. That afternoon Daisy had wondered if there had been an expedition to a local hairdresser from which she had been excluded. But at dinner she had seen that Lizzie had done her own hair; reddish and tightly curled, it looked much the same as it had at lunch, except that a fine old jeweled comb held one side off her face. Her shoulders were bare, pale, and lightly freckled; she wasn't very pretty: on a London street she would have turned few heads. But, in some way Daisy observed but didn't understand, the Nugents believed, and seemed to have made others believe, that they were the criterion by which all excellence was measured.

Daisy kept moving and, since she was reluctant to double back to the ballroom, she found herself ascending the staircase. As she went, she glanced back at Lizzie. Lizzie's dress was very pretty: limp, pale satin, the plain white bodice suspended by narrow straps over her thin shoulders, the color gradually, almost imperceptibly, becoming a warm pink and then, as the smooth line of the dress became an undramatic ruffle about eight inches above the ankle, a shade of deep, but not dark, raspberry. She wore it casually. Daisy's dress, too, was pretty and probably had cost as much as Lizzie's had, but she wore it as though it were—as it had been—borrowed. How had all the Nugents developed this impressive, almost shocking, level of self-assurance? Lizzie was only eighteen years old. And why did no one seem to question this superiority?

Halfway up the staircase there was a landing lit, during the day, by a large window that overlooked a shrubbery. It had stained glass borders and an ornate carved frame. To one side of the window, the landing extended into a small sitting room with another window, a fireplace, a small sofa, and two boudoir-sized armchairs. It was here that Daisy thought she might sit for a few minutes before again going downstairs.

The fire was blazing cheerfully, but the room was not empty. Although Daisy did not crave solitude, neither did she wish to act as a chaperone to the adolescent couple on the sofa. As she entered the little doorless room, they separated. The girl's hair was untidy and her lipstick almost completely rubbed off. The boy's face, now turned enquiringly toward Daisy, was flushed. Daisy, no expert in these matters, thought the flush a combination of drink and sexual arousal.

Daisy smiled vaguely and withdrew; she continued up the staircase and along the corridor to her room, thinking that she might as well use her own bathroom, apply fresh lipstick, and see how her hair was holding up. And blow her nose; the threatened cold had not yet arrived, but it was on its way and Daisy's insubstantial dress had no pocket for a handkerchief.

Once inside the bedroom door, however, she sat down in the solitary armchair beside the unlit fireplace and considered her situation. It was already becoming chilly in her bedroom and after a moment or two she unhooked her dress, put her dressing gown on over her underclothes and stockings, tucked a fresh handkerchief into the pocket, switched off the light, made her way carefully across the dark room, and slipped under the eiderdown. She laid her head down carefully on the pillow, since she assumed she would, a little later, dress again and go downstairs.

Lying back and gazing upward into the darkness, Daisy tried not to weep. The last time she'd cried had been Christmas morning when her chilblain had burst. Then she had wept, not over a man, not over a slight, but from physical misery and pain. Her more than slightly puritanical streak—integral to her nature, not the influence of her father—considered the suffering of others to be the only proper reason to weep.

Her primary feeling during the day now drawing to a close had been one of embarrassment. Good nature, common sense, and a rectory upbringing had served her well since she had left home and joined the Land Army. Although she knew James had behaved badly, and the Nugents, aristocratic or not, had been unmannerly and inhospitable, she was not sure to what extent she was, if not to blame, responsible for what was clearly a misunderstanding.

Slowly and methodically she went over every moment of the afternoon she had met James, the invitation and letter from his mother, her conversation with Rosemary, her own conduct, limited conversational opportunities, and the way she had dressed since arriving at Bannock House. She found no clue and was once more embarrassed. Embarrassed and disappointed. It seemed a waste of saved money and days off. Daisy quickly nipped this self-pitying thought in the bud; again, while it might have pleased her father to think that her behavior had been guided by his precepts, more often it was Daisy's wish to avoid some of the more

egregious lapses of his parishioners. She checked her tears with the
memory of Mrs. Hill, who was in the habit of making a perfectly
legitimate complaint about some slight or disappointment and
then diminishing the sympathy of her listener with some additional details along the lines of: "I took the 8:10 to King's Cross,
three and fourpence round trip, and when I got there she wasn't
even . . ." Daisy knew that the three shillings and fourpence was
probably quite a lot of money to Mrs. Hill and didn't quite understand why she, Daisy, despised her for making it part of the complaint. She just knew it was awful.

After lunch that day, when James had not returned, and she
knew that something had gone very wrong with the visit, Daisy
had thought about leaving Bannock House. Had the railway station been closer, she might have packed her bags, carried them to
the station, and taken her chances on catching a train and making
a connection that would take her back to Wales. But this simple
if unambiguous course of action was not possible; she would have
had to ask for transport and that would have forced a conversation
that no one wanted. And a premature return would have been
awkward to explain to Rosemary when she arrived at Aberneth
Farm. Her affection and respect for her employer, who was
related to this cold family, was an inhibiting and deciding factor
in Daisy's decision to stick it out.

It was profoundly, uncompromisingly dark in the bedroom;
Daisy's watch was on the dressing table and she had no idea what
time it was. It felt a little after ten o'clock. She put her hands
behind her neck and made a plan. Ten o'clock and her train left
at quarter to eleven the next morning; were she Cinderella there
would be time enough to change her life but, since her expectations were fewer and more mundane, it was merely a manageable
number of hours. She would lie there for a while and in an hour
or so either she would undress completely, brush her teeth, and go

to bed properly or she would put on her dress, return to the dance—very faint sounds of music from below alternated with the silence—circulate for a few minutes, drink another glass of champagne, return to her bedroom and then go to bed. Breakfast the following morning, she imagined, would be a subdued affair—the Nugents silently shoveling down quantities of bacon and eggs, strong tea, and nursing hangovers, except, perhaps, for Lizzie, who might be radiant, triumphant, even in love—and she was quite sure that her one need, a pony and trap to take her to the railway station, would have been anticipated.

After a little while it became quite cozy under the eiderdown. Daisy told herself there would be other opportunities; her complete failure that weekend did not guarantee a lonely old age. Except for what she read in the final pages of novels, Daisy had no examples of what she did want; she knew she did not want to be an old maid or a lonely and defeated wife. The war had given the girls in her generation more freedom than ever before in the history of English womanhood, but it threatened a whole generation of young men. Innocent and twenty, Daisy was prepared to be a young widow but she was not prepared to submit to a life of utter and hopeless dreariness.

There was a tap at the door. Daisy did not know how long she had been in her room; she would have guessed three-quarters of an hour.

"Who is it?" she called a little awkwardly. Taps at the door were not part of her plan.

"It's Patrick."

"What do you want?"

"I want you to open the door."

"It's not locked."

"I'd still like you to come to the door." His voice was slightly testy.

"Just a minute."

Daisy got out of bed, pulled her dressing gown modestly around her, belted it, crossed the pitch-dark room, and opened the door. Patrick stood outside. There was a short awkward silence.

"I had a headache. I was lying down for a moment."

"Oh, I thought perhaps you were sulking."

"I never sulk," Daisy said coldly and very nearly truthfully. "What do you want?"

"I want you to put your dress on and come back downstairs."

"Why?"

"I want to talk to you and then, depending on how it goes, we might dance."

"I don't need to put my dress on again to talk," Daisy said, not feeling obliged to make it easy for him.

"Yes, you do. We can't stand like this in the corridor—of course, if you wait until I find a maid or someone's aunt as a chaperone, I could come and talk in your room. Better put your dress on."

Daisy looked at him coldly for another moment, then nodded and closed the door. Without hurrying, she went into the bathroom and arranged her hair and powdered her face. Then she brushed her teeth and put on fresh lipstick. She rolled her stockings, which had become a little baggy at the ankles and knees, straightened the seams, and made them taut, reattaching them to her suspender belt. Then she put on her dress, stepped into her shoes, and joined Patrick in the corridor.

"You might just do up the two hooks at the top," she said, turning her back to him.

He was, as she had imagined he would be, a little clumsy with the tiny hooks and eyes. The lighting in the corridor was dim and she suspected he made himself slower in his desire not to be found doing up her dress by someone coming upstairs. But they met no one until they were halfway down the staircase. Then, a neatly uniformed middle-aged woman carrying a salver with empty glasses came out of the little sitting room off the stairs. She bobbed her head to Patrick; the gesture, Daisy thought, some kind of racial memory of a curtsy.

"Mrs. Parsons," Patrick said. "The very woman I was looking for. Could you bring us up a couple of glasses of champagne."

The woman nodded and hurried away before Daisy had a chance to tell Patrick that the little sitting room might not be the ideal place for a quiet talk. He entered confidently, Daisy trailing a little behind him.

"Ah," he said, apparently pleased to see the young couple. Daisy noticed they were rather more disheveled than when she had last seen them. Patrick apparently noticed nothing.

"Lady Nugent is keen to set up a bridge table in here. I wonder if you would be interested in making up a four."

As soon as they left, Patrick gestured toward the sofa just vacated, and Daisy sat down. The cushions were still warm. Patrick sat in the small armchair on the other side of the fire. It was not quite large enough for him and he sat forward in it, resting his arms on his knees and looking at her.

"What's going on?" he asked.

"I told you—I had a headache and I thought I would lie down until the aspirin started to work."

He looked at her silently, not bothering to voice his disbelief. Daisy said nothing; she had no intention of appearing defensive.

"Lover's tiff?" he asked after a moment.

"No. I don't have a lover and apart from the words you and I exchanged this afternoon, I haven't had a tiff with anyone in this house."

"I can't help noticing that you and James seem—well, I haven't seen you exchange a word all day."

"Except for Mrs. Glynne, no one has had much to say to me all day. And nobody has spoken a single word to me since the dance began."

"I would have asked you, you know. As soon as I had taken care of a couple of duty dances." And then, as Daisy said nothing, he added, "Your dress is very pretty."

"It belongs to Rosemary."

"I wondered—"

Daisy raised her eyebrows, ready to be indignant or offended all over again. Patrick laughed.

"Don't look like that—your dress is pretty; it suits you perfectly and it has a look of Rosemary. It also clearly was expensive, but not like a major investment for, say, a coming-out dance."

Daisy nodded. Patrick was right; the dress was the choice of a young married woman with good taste, not what one of the dowagers might have ordered from a couturier for a seventeen-year-old girl. She wasn't sure what material it was made of, but it felt silky; it looked as though thousands of tiny diamond-shaped snippets had been attached to one another to make the fabric. Each diamond contained a pale green, white, and pale pink. Daisy could not decide if the pattern suggested Columbine or Lamia.

"And I'm not saying it's too old for you," Patrick added. "As always, Rosemary got it just right."

"Rosemary thought it all right for me to come and stay here— I asked her."

"You did?"

"Of course: not only if I could take the time off—I do work for her after all—but when Lady Nugent sent the invitation and asked me to stay, I asked how she felt about me accepting; all of you being relatives and in-laws of hers and George's."

"Aunt Hilda wrote and invited you to stay?"

"If you thought I was a gatecrasher, it goes a good distance toward me understanding why you have been so unpleasant," Daisy said, but her heart wasn't in it. She suspected there had been a misunderstanding although she could not imagine what it might be.

"Last night, when I went up to bed, I saw James coming out of your room."

"So you assumed he had been there by my invitation," Daisy said flatly, hurt and this time deciding not to let him off lightly. "And even if he had been, is that a good enough reason for the way everyone has treated me today? What did you think when James disappeared for the day and when he didn't speak a word to me at dinner?"

"I didn't—" Before Patrick could continue, Lizzie came into the little sitting room, slightly ahead of a young man with a flushed face, who held the hand she extended behind her. Both were laughing; Lizzie saw Daisy and Patrick first and stopped in her tracks. She stopped laughing and her companion, slightly behind her both geographically and in awareness of the room's other occupants, stopped abruptly on her heels. For once, Daisy saw a Nugent at a momentary disadvantage.

"Oh," Lizzie said, recovering herself. "We were looking for—"

"He's downstairs. In the hall." Patrick said, cutting in on her hesitation, a not entirely warm smile on his lips.

"Oh," Lizzie said, suddenly looking very young. Then, with an irritated glance at her companion, whose hand she still held. "Come on, Ian."

They turned; as they went through the door, Lizzie attempted a face-saving final remark.

"James was looking for you," she said, choosing not to address anyone in particular and, therefore, leaving it a little ambiguous whether James was looking for Daisy or for Patrick.

"Now you know where Daisy is, if he asks you again." Patrick did not raise his voice, but Daisy was pretty sure Lizzie heard him. Once again they were left alone.

"You're quite good at defending your territory," Daisy said, and laughed. The first time, it felt, that she had laughed during the past twenty-four hours.

"I come from the Irish side of the family," Patrick said; he seemed to feel no further explanation was necessary.

"How are you all related? You and James and Rosemary?"

"I don't think we are really. Purely an affectation based on some very loose connections. Rosemary's husband is a second cousin once removed of James's. James and I are actually cousins, but very distant, fourth generation probably. At some stage a late-eighteenth-century Nugent married a Scottish heiress who brought Bannock into the family. He had managed to get through most of his own money, but there was still a house and a little land in Ireland left when he died. It went to his second son, from whom I'm descended. In other words—"

"Don't," Daisy said faintly. "I'm sorry I asked."

She realized she'd imagined them to be more closely related than they were, not only because of the shared surname, but because they had been together on both the occasions she had seen them.

"If you're not twins, how do you manage to get leave at the same time?" she asked. The question was a little disingenuous since what she really wanted to know was how they had managed to get leave to come to a dance, and she was prepared to be disapproving of his answer.

Patrick looked surprised; then he laughed.

"James and I weren't on leave when we first met you. I was giving him a lift. I was on what might be called official business—running an errand for my commanding officer—and it wasn't far out of my way to take James where he wanted to go and to drop in and see Rosemary. The war hadn't really started then—except for the navy—and we all had a fair amount of time on our hands. This weekend James had some leave coming to him before he's off to wherever he isn't supposed to tell us about, and I'm on a training course that allows for flexibility. We were lucky; the army isn't really the non-stop party it seems to be."

They sat in silence for a few minutes. The part of the room near the fire was warm; Daisy gazed into the embers and felt reasonably content. Sitting beside a fire in a pretty dress was not what she had come all this way for, but it did make her failure less humiliating. After a moment the maid came back with two glasses of champagne and shortly afterward Daisy thought a gesture of grace on her part would be only fair.

"I liked my Christmas card," she said.

"To ferrets," Patrick said, raising his glass.

"I like them, you know," she said, laughing at the toast, but meaning what she said.

"I know."

"I feel rather like a ferret in this house."

"I think I already mentioned I come from the Irish side of the family."

Daisy smiled, feeling the delighted leap of her spirits she always experienced when talking to someone with whom it was not necessary to bridge parts of a train of thought. Then she hesitated and was silent.

"What's the matter?"

Daisy hesitated again for a moment before deciding, more for her own sake than for Patrick's, to tell him what she had been thinking.

"Yesterday evening I had just as cozy a chat with James—in the library."

"We're a family famous for our easy charm and treachery. Historically it was the principal reason the main branch survived; that and an ability to convert from one devoutly held religious belief to another—overnight, if necessary."

"I was thinking more of the ease with which I succumbed to the effortless charm of the aristocracy."

Patrick didn't respond. Then, after a moment he asked, "Do you know what the Sargasso Sea is?"

"This isn't going to be a geography quiz, is it?"

"No."

"It's where eels—all eels—go to mate." As she spoke, it seemed to Daisy one of those beliefs, like old wives' tales, that don't bear too close examination. It seemed also as though Patrick had skipped—or skipped articulating—part of the thought that had taken their conversation from her susceptibility to masculine Nugent charm to some not yet revealed but distant area. "Somewhere in the middle of the Atlantic?"

"Rather closer to America. Think of Bermuda. It's a sea, comparatively warm, named for sargassum—you know, the kind of seaweed you find on beaches after a storm. The Gulf Stream moves huge islands of sargassum around in a large drifting circle. Things live in the seaweed islands."

"Yes?"

"Those clumps of seaweed are small maritime universes to fishes and snails. Complete with cycles of revolution and, I imagine, evolution."

Daisy thought about it for a moment; the image was pleasing. She considered the endless repetition of day and night, the hot sun warming the salt water, the clear star-filled nights, and she had a crude but pleasing comprehension of eternity. It seemed easier to imagine than her father's devout belief in a more conventional but less easily described afterlife.

"I am a minor fish—imagining I have choices or reactions

when all I'm doing is living in an island of seaweed itself dependent on an ocean current," Daisy said.

"The seaweed is more substantial and longer lived, but it
hasn't more control over its own existence. Every now and then
there is a storm a little more powerful than the ones that particular cycle of nature has come to expect. And the island is thrown out
of the circle—the loop—its own version of what it imagines to be
perpetual motion."

"And the fishes and things die."

"Or move on to another island. Everything goes on as before.
Then, once in a thousand years, say, there is something that doesn't
fit the pattern. Or maybe it does, but it's too large a pattern for us
to see. A volcano, an earthquake, an ice age. What are you smiling at?"

"I was admiring the way you kept your metaphors in place,"
Daisy said, not untruthfully, but concealing the real reason for her
smile. She was thinking of the educational opportunities she had
had since she had arrived at Bannock: a lecture on art, another on
ocean currents, and a glimpse of the social structure of the English
upper classes at play. How much she had been told and how little
her opinion had been sought.

"All right. Sorry. The war isn't a storm—it's the equivalent of an
ice age. What's so strange is that no one else seems to see that when
the war's over nothing is going to be the same. The Great War got
the vote for women and altered the social fabric of this country
forever; do they imagine the Tommies will go back to the mines
or unemployment lines as soon as there is peace? Are you planning
to go back to whatever you were doing before you joined up?"

"I'd just left school, so in a sense I'll be back where I was—trying to decide what to do with my life. Of course, that in itself is a
change—the idea that I might decide instead of just accepting
what happens."

"And the choices will be different."

"Lord, I hope so. So, you see, I *am* an example—to your family—of the less affluent middle class forgetting its place. My father's a rector—to them, I suppose, a sort of grown-up chaplain. No wonder they're so snooty with me."

"You'll find it much harder to get me on the defensive. The main bunch of Nugents, this lot here—my family can't afford to be so picky—look down on the royal family as a little too recent, too German. Of course," he added thoughtfully, "in terms purely of blood-lines, they can make a case."

They both were laughing when James came into the room; Daisy could not have chosen a better moment for his entrance and she, an all too frequent victim of *l'esprit d'escalier,* felt a triumphant surge of delight.

"Daisy, I've been looking for you everywhere. Dance with me—" James said, his arms invitingly open.

Despite the triumph of the previous moment, Daisy felt her feet press the floor with an involuntary movement toward rising.

"Daisy has promised this dance to me—and I think a few young bloods of the neighborhood are ahead of you. Get in line, Nugent."

Patrick rose and took Daisy by the hand. Daisy glanced back as they left the sitting room. She achieved a glance of amused helplessness, tinged with only the slightest suggestion of regret. It was not hard for her to simulate the lack of reproach; at that moment she had forgotten the humiliating events of the day.

Daisy glanced at Patrick as they descended the stairs, very much aware of her hand in his.

"James has always been very competitive. He was rather a spoilt little boy."

"Gulls," she said. "Do you think seagulls circle the island of weed and the tiny fishes? Or would it be too far from land?"

ALTHOUGH DAISY FELT a lot warmer toward the North of England and those who lived there than she had the previous morning, she thought when it came to singing hymns, they couldn't hold a candle to the Welsh. Otherwise, matins was familiar.

The Nugents occupied two pews toward the front of the church on the right-hand side. Originally, Daisy thought, these pews would have been theirs, not only because the pews nearer the front were "better seats" but so that the Nugents would be visible to a larger proportion of the congregation to whom they provided an example. Since the Crimean War, their right to the second and third pews were further established by a memorial, on the wall above the pews, to a nineteen-year-old Nugent slain in battle.

Daisy spent most of the rather dull sermon thinking about the boy killed in the Crimea, the slaughter of young men, and a generation cut down before they could procreate. An officer, of course; that was to be expected, a product of his class. He would, Daisy imagined, have accepted the privileges of rank as his due. Gold braid, better food, greater privacy, a servant to keep him clean and polished—all that would seem an extension of his public school education. He would have been used to deference and obedience, but in a society with rules adhered to and actions having largely foreseeable consequences. To take responsibility for men, many older than himself, in a disastrously mismanaged campaign in an alien climate and to die there—what had he thought during his last moments? Assuming, of course, he had not died instantaneously. But Daisy, remembering descriptions of hospital tents, dying soldiers, Florence Nightingale, and of wounds cleaned with salt water for want of a better disinfectant, wanted to know whether the young captain had questioned his fate, his country, the values and beliefs of his family and class, as he lay dying.

Daisy was wearing her uniform as were, on either side of her, Patrick and James. On Lady Nugent's dark, no-nonsense hat was pinned a small brooch with her absent husband's regimental crest, and her black coat had a functional and almost official, although not military, cut. Daisy could imagine her wearing it as she performed organizational duties pertaining to the war around the neighborhood.

The pony and trap that carried them to church had continued to the railway station, where the boy who'd held the reins was to leave Daisy's suitcase in the care of the stationmaster.

After the service ended, while the congregation loitered, chatting, in the churchyard and enjoying the mild, sunny day, Daisy thanked Lady Nugent for her hospitality and set out on foot for the railway station. Both young men walked with her. Daisy thought that James was accompanying her because Patrick was there, but she thought Patrick would have come with her had she been alone.

The stationmaster greeted them deferentially. The train was already in the station. Daisy wondered if he would have held the train had they been late, and she would have asked Patrick, were she alone with him. But Patrick had followed the stationmaster to retrieve her suitcase from the left-luggage room. James was silent while left alone with Daisy, but she didn't ask him. They had danced together twice the night before but had not had a conversation since James's late-night visit to her room.

Patrick returned with Daisy's suitcase, and she and James followed him along the platform until he found an empty carriage. He stepped up onto the train and hoisted the suitcase onto the luggage rack.

"Window seat, facing the engine," he said, leaning out the open window. "With some tasteful views of Torquay."

After a moment, he rejoined them on the platform. The stationmaster, holding his green flag and a whistle, glanced at them expectantly and Daisy turned to James and Patrick to say good-bye.

James, stealing a march on Patrick, took Daisy loosely in his arms.

"Bon voyage," he said, and kissed her lightly on both cheeks.

Patrick merely took her hand, but he held it for a long moment.

"May I write to you?" he asked quietly.

Doors were slamming all down the train; Daisy released his hand and climbed on board. She closed the door behind her and answered him through the window.

"I'd like that," she said, as the stationmaster blew his whistle and the engine hissed a cloud of steam. In case Patrick had not heard her, she smiled and nodded.

The train started to move and Daisy went to her seat. By the time she had gained it, the tracks had curved away from the station and both men were out of sight.

CHAPTER 6

DAISY SAT AT THE kitchen table, peeling potatoes. Her mother, glasses slipping down her nose, was trying to find enough lean meat on the remains of the Sunday joint to make a shepherd's pie.

Daisy waited until her mother had tightened the screws on the sturdy metal mincer, so that it gripped the end of the kitchen table cruelly, before she spoke.

"Patrick is talking to Father," she said.

Her mother concentrated on the mincer, her right hand turning the stiff handle, the left adding small chunks of pale brown beef and steadying the machine. A strand of graying hair escaped from her bun.

"Your father was going to show him the churchyard. I'd have thought the grass would still be too wet. Did Joan go with them?"

Joan, Daisy's elder sister, had joined the WRNS at the outbreak of war, cheerfully embracing the discipline and physical hardship of the naval docks at which she was stationed, unfazed by the foul language, appearing to enjoy the heavy-handed flirtation of the men she worked with, and revealing a hitherto-concealed, unsubtly dirty mind.

Daisy didn't imagine her mother really thought Joan would

have accompanied Patrick and her father to the graveyard, and even spent a moment wondering what would be the minimum inducement necessary for her sister to form part of such a tour. That her mother seemed to be playing for time meant she sensed something was in the air. Something with which she would rather not cope. Daisy recognized her mother's plea not to involve her in any unpleasantness, any embarrassment, conflict, moral stand, or unpopular decision, but time was running out. Patrick had to return to his unit that night and Daisy herself needed to be back in Wales for milking the following evening.

"He is," she said, trying to keep her tone light, and not altogether succeeding, "asking for my hand in marriage."

Her mother flinched; she did not release her hold on the handle of the mincer, but her expression showed she expected to be told something that would throw her already difficult day further into disarray. Mrs. Creed never asked questions; Daisy always had the impression that she was just trying to get through the day and return to some other private and, presumably, more satisfying existence. A rich dream life perhaps—a generation before, one might have suspected laudanum.

"We want to be married next month."

Her mother darted a frightened glance at her, and Daisy was grateful to be able to reassure her.

"No, nothing like that. There has," and she laughed, "been nothing 'improper' in our relationship. Patrick is a man of principle."

After she had spoken there was a pause. It might, Daisy thought too late, have been more comforting for her mother to think her daughter's principles, rather than her apparently betrothed's, the foundation of the chaste nature of their relationship. But that kind of reassurance would not serve the argument she was about to make.

"Surely you should take a little more time. An engagement—"

"The war. Who knows how much time anyone has?"

"But—if anything happened to Patrick—"

"If anything happened to Patrick, I'd rather be a young widow than an old maid."

The argument was almost, but not quite, unanswerable. Daisy knew what her mother was thinking, but would never ask: *What if he survives the war? What if you find yourself married for the rest of your life to someone you chose without really knowing him? What if he comes back from the war crippled? Or maimed?*

Instead, her mother said, "Yes, but . . ." and her voice trailed off. She fed what was left of the lunchtime parsnips into the mincer to stretch the meat a little. Her unspoken question left, also unspoken, Daisy's answer: *Do you think I haven't thought of that?*

Instead, Mrs. Creed poured hot water onto a teaspoon covered with Bovril in a chipped white cup and stirred it thoughtfully. Daisy thought how much simpler and more helpful had been a similar conversation with Rosemary three nights earlier at Aberneth Farm. She knew her parents would unhappily agree to a marriage they were, in a changing world, unable to prevent. But that wasn't going to make dinner any easier.

THE SHEPHERD'S PIE—there hadn't really been enough left on the joint—was almost saved by the green tomato chutney. Daisy's grandmother, at the end of summer, scoured the greenhouse and bartered with their neighbors for the small green tomatoes that had grown too late to ripen. The kitchen had smelled pleasantly of the chopped tomatoes and simmering rationed sugar (there was an additional ration for jam-making, and the family feeling was that chutney came under the spirit of that heading) and spices as Daisy's grandmother made the chutney that would render palatable the cold beef or mutton—rationed, but rarely a luxury. Her grandmother, in the same spirit, made capers from the pickled seeds of the nasturtiums that bordered the caterpillar-ravaged vegetable garden behind the rectory.

Supper, that evening, was a meal that showed no member of Daisy's family at his—or in this case her, since her father was a reliable known quantity—best. It was as though each were determined to play a caricature of herself. Daisy's grandmother sighed during grace. Her mother was particularly, as Daisy and Joan had in childhood deemed it, "hen-brained." It took her several harried trips to the kitchen to produce the pie and the Brussels sprouts and several more to bring in the junket—which surely she remembered both her daughters had, from childhood, loathed—and stewed plums.

Daisy's grandmother watched this domestic ineptitude silently, allowing pursed lips and the speed with which the chutney was being ingested to speak for her. Not for the first time Daisy wondered whether her mother's inadequate housekeeping skills were partly a manifestation of her dislike for her own mother. If this were the case, Granny Cooper had a lot to answer for. Especially since she ate only breakfast and lunch with the family; supper, always a light meal, she ate on a tray in her warm room. When she moved into the rectory she had embarrassed Daisy's father and enraged her mother by installing a separate, coin-fed, electricity meter in her room, where she supplemented Mrs. Creed's cooking with small delicacies she kept in invitingly decorated tins. As a small child Daisy had spent many winter afternoons there, drawn by the heat of the electric fire and her grandmother's supply of biscuits. These afternoons infuriated Daisy's mother, thus presumably justifying her grandmother's expenditure of electricity and sugar.

A bottle of not terribly good wine had been produced to celebrate the engagement, but the atmosphere was far from festive.

Her father's reservations about the marriage were many and not unreasonable. Daisy hardly knew Patrick; she would, after her marriage, be living among strangers in another country and worshiping at unacceptably low Church of Ireland services. Daisy was his favorite daughter, and he could have seen the now often unnervingly coarse Joan move farther from home with fewer qualms.

"Of course, one marries earlier in wartime," her mother said, addressing one of her husband's unspoken reservations, "or during a plague."

Patrick, who had been performing the delicate task of separating, with his fork, a piece of gristle from the more edible vegetal matter on his plate, shot her a startled glance. Granny Cooper closed her eyes briefly.

"You know, like Dr. Munthe and the nun—in Naples during the cholera epidemic."

Daisy was the only one of her listeners who knew what Mrs. Creed was talking about; it had been to Daisy that Mrs. Creed had introduced *The Story of San Michele*. However, since no one at the table thought Axel Munthe had actually *married* a Neapolitan nun, they all pretty well got the gist of it.

"More sons born in wartime," the rector murmured, attempting to drag the conversation back on track without offering too obvious a non sequitur.

"What Mother means—" Joan started, the note of truculence in her voice doing nothing to ameliorate the tense embarrassment around the table. Daisy wondered if the change in Joan's nature was—like more males being born in wartime and her mother's euphemistically vague point—itself an illustration of some natural law.

"I think, Joan, we all take your mother's point," the rector interrupted mildly. "We are now, I think, moving on to practical arrangements, probably best decided by your mother and Daisy herself."

"As long as you don't expect me to be a bridesmaid," Joan said, not planning to be so easily subdued.

"Nothing was further from my mind," Daisy said lightly, but with absolute sincerity.

The practical arrangements could hardly be simpler. A wartime wedding at short notice: a wedding dress, flowers, a service performed by her father, a reception, champagne, some food, a wedding cake. No bridesmaids, no wedding presents, no honeymoon. Nothing that couldn't be decided that moment—if Joan could be held at bay.

Two years older than Daisy, but less pretty, Joan was sullenly unhappy that her sister should marry first. She had learned to assert herself in the company of her fellow Wrens and the men with whom she worked. She had learned to curse and drink, but she had not learned to sit at her parents' table and behave like an adult. There had been an awkward moment before supper when she had accompanied Patrick and Daisy to the pub in the village. Daisy, a reluctant social drinker, had asked for a half pint of shandy and Joan, who really needed a drink, asked for a gin and orange. Patrick had looked at her kindly and had said in a mild, almost amused voice, "I'll get you a gin, *or* an orange juice—or even a glass of gin and a glass of orange, but I won't order a gin and orange."

"Why not?" Joan had asked, not sure that there mightn't be a moment of flirtatious playfulness to follow.

"It's a tart's drink," Patrick said, his tone purely informational. "It's like ordering a port and lemon."

Patrick and Daisy had been alone for a moment before supper and Daisy, who thought he might have waited a little longer, at least until after the wedding, to embark on her sister's social education, had instead, with most uncharacteristic weakness, found herself apologizing for her family's eccentricity.

Patrick had looked at her for a moment, puzzled, and then had laughed.

"Wait until you see mine," he said, when he finished laughing.

Even so, Daisy wished it had been possible to accept Rosemary's offer and that the wedding would take place at Aberneth Farm.

CHAPTER 7

THE GREAT WESTERN Hotel. Convenient to King's Cross. Maybe too convenient, Daisy thought, touching the ring borrowed from Valerie, unfamiliar and unconvincing, on the fourth finger of her left hand. King's Cross, gritty, damp, smelling of engine smoke and cheap tobacco; thinly coated with the smaller feathers and droppings of the resident pigeons, and the residue and debris of troops and tired travelers; did she really want to lose her virginity in the atmosphere of a railway station?

It was Patrick's next leave and—Daisy's time off delicately orchestrated by Rosemary, the clandestine aspects advised upon by a pruriently sympathetic Valerie—the betrothed couple were in London for what Valerie insisted on referring to as "a dirty weekend."

Patrick had gone to take a bath; it seemed to Daisy he had been gone a long time. It took her rather longer than it should have, and threw her into a deeper state of ineffectual nervousness, to realize there had been a slight emphasis in the announcement of his bathing plans. Clearly she was supposed to—allowed privacy to—what? To wander about the room, to look at herself in the dressing-table mirror, to apply lipstick, and, on second thought, to wipe it off, to pull back the curtain and look out the window to find black-out material depriving her of further evidence of pigeons and grimy red brick. The bed she avoided, and she was sitting at the dressing table looking at her unconfident reflection when there was a knock at the door.

"Come in," she called, her heart pounding, imagining a hotel detective. As she turned toward the door, she saw in the mirror that her face was white. After a short moment, the knock was repeated, this time a little louder and with a brisk impatience.

She rose and crossed the room, wondering if hotel detectives really existed or whether they were merely a convention of the comic novel; the possibility of being confronted by one an aspect of clandestine trysts unmentioned by the otherwise informative Valerie. Daisy wished Patrick were there to confront this one as she opened the door, and feared suddenly that his absence was hotel detective related.

Patrick, wearing a camel-colored dressing gown and looking at her quizzically, was standing outside. He held his sponge bag in one hand and his uniform, folded neatly with no socks or underclothing showing, over the other arm.

"I thought for a moment you weren't going to let me in," he said affectionately.

"I thought you were the hotel detective," Daisy said breathlessly, standing in the doorway, a hand on the knob.

"May I come in now?"

"Oh. Sorry." And Daisy stepped back to let him in.

She closed the door, Patrick set his things down on a chair and looked back at her. Daisy did not meet his eye.

"Were you scared?" he asked.

"A little," she mumbled.

He took her by the arms and looked at her gently.

"You needn't be," he said. "Look at me."

Daisy reluctantly raised her eyes to meet his.

"Trust me," he said, and looked at her kindly until she nodded.

"I'm not sure there are such people as hotel detectives," he added. "I've never seen one."

"That wouldn't prove anything unless you spend a lot of time in hotel rooms with girls of dubious chastity."

"That is not the kind of question girls are supposed to ask," Patrick said just as kindly as before, but quite firmly.

Daisy was sorry to hear it. She understood that Patrick was behaving like a gentleman and also protecting both her and himself against the possibility of a sooner or later jealous scene, but she was more curious than jealous. She had hoped he was somewhat experienced; surely one of them, at least, should know how to proceed now.

During the silence that followed, Patrick took her in his arms and held her close to him. Her evening dress left her arms and shoulders bare and she felt the comforting warmth of his dressing gown against her skin. One hand on her waist and one on the naked part of her back pressed her closer; Daisy began instinctively to draw away from him.

"Trust me," Patrick repeated, and Daisy willed herself to melt into his embrace.

They had had few opportunities for physical intimacy and none in which Daisy had been so lightly dressed. The greater part of their courtship had taken place by letter. Since their engagement they had written letters every second day. These letters were difficult to write for Patrick, because he was not allowed to describe his daily routine at the training course in a country house outside London; for Daisy, because she knew so little of her fiancé's life. She had not—apart from the Westmoreland Nugents—met any member of his family. The letters served to emphasize how little each knew about the other, and neither had developed a knack for exchanging the small, telling details of everyday life, or developing intimacy through the written word. And an awareness of the censor's eye was an inhibiting factor not to be discounted.

"You're so beautiful . . . I love you," he said before he kissed her.

Daisy closed her eyes and felt, for a moment, a dreamy pleasure in his kiss before her body stiffened, not only in fear of the physical act so close at hand, but at his words. She knew she wasn't beautiful; she was young, healthy, maybe even pretty. And how could he love her; they hardly knew each other.

This was the fifth time they'd been in each other's company. There had been the day the *Royal Oak* had been sunk, when she had stood, stocking-footed, in the library at Aberneth Farm, holding a ferret in one hand as they listened to the BBC. And then the visit to Bannock when she and James had disappointed each other. After a self-conscious exchange of letters, on a wet Sunday afternoon, in a teashop with rain streaming down the windows, he had proposed to her over weak tea and sandwiches made with margarine. And after the briefest of hesitations, she had accepted him. Then there had been the awkward day when they had told her parents of their plans; and now, the commitment she had made so casually, so lightly, was to have its first consequence.

"I love you, too," she said, knowing the words were necessary if they were to make love, sleep together, marry. She felt as though the war had taken time from its normal pattern and sequence and flung it into the arbitrary rhythm of a dream.

Patrick, without loosening his embrace, had one-handedly unfastened the first button on the back of Daisy's dress, when the siren sounded. Daisy had just felt the first twinge of desire—occasioned, she noticed with surprise, by the adept manner in which Patrick was beginning to undress her—when the air-raid warning threw her sense of time further into the random, formless swirl she had felt a moment before.

Daisy had never been in an air raid before. She had watched the oil tanks in Wales light up the night sky, but she had never been the victim or the target of an enemy attack. Her fear seemed to be diluted by her inability to feel that anything was real. Patrick, who was not experiencing so many things for the first time, seemed calm. But, since he was an officer and a gent, she hardly expected him to panic; it was hard to tell how much danger they were in. Patrick was dressing quickly, getting back into his uniform.

"Get something comfortable and warm; this may take all night."

A few minutes later they joined the crowd of hotel guests streaming down the stairs. Patrick, handsome and impressive in his uniform; Daisy, a little crumpled in the coat and skirt in which she had traveled. They carried his overcoat, dressing gown, and a couple of pillows and a blanket from the bed.

Outside, the sky to the south glowed red through a dark haze; the clanging of fire engines, anti-aircraft guns firing in the distance, and, closer, a warden's whistle contributed to an atmosphere of resilient confusion.

"The docks," Patrick said. "Those poor bastards in the East End have no luck. Come on."

Daisy followed, scampering to stay close to him in the crowd, to the steps of the unidentified underground station. Beside her, a pale young woman with circles under her eyes carried a sleeping baby; a little girl, in pajamas, bedroom slippers, and a dressing gown, held on to her skirt. The child was not fully awake; Daisy took her other hand to help her down the steep, metal-topped steps, and soon they were all on the platform.

Underground it was quite light; there was noise but different from the one they had heard above. The sounds of sirens and gunfire were fainter, replaced by human voices, the grizzling of a sleepy child and, at the far end of the platform, singing. The wall sign with the name of the station had been removed, and Daisy did not know where they were. Daisy felt as she had as a new girl at school—wide-eyed at strange rituals familiar to everyone else.

"Let's find a place—as far as possible from what looks like quite a jolly party," Patrick said, and Daisy followed him along the platform to the darker, quieter end. Once there, he spread out the blanket on the concrete floor and propped the pillows against the tiled wall. Daisy stifled a protest at the casual way he was treating hotel property, and sat down beside him.

"What happens now?" Daisy asked, surprised by how quickly her fear was being replaced by a feeling of how inconvenient it all was.

"This goes on for a little while, then when everyone is in, it gets quieter and people go to sleep until the All Clear. Most of them have got it down to a routine."

"Even the children?"

"Look." Patrick gestured at the little family who had come down to the shelter with them. The young mother, her baby, and little girl were already asleep. They lay in an uncomfortable nest of coats and blankets, the baby in its mother's arms, the little girl snuggled into the small of her back.

"Londoners," Patrick said. "They can adapt to anything on their home ground. Rosemary's evacuees didn't last long, did they?"

"In and out in two weeks. Rosemary couldn't have been kinder—when they went she felt guilty but relieved."

"They could get used to bombs, rationing, noise, and danger, but they couldn't deal with the horrors of fresh air, cows, and meals not wrapped in newspaper."

"They missed their homes and their families and friends, and they probably couldn't get used to being looked down on or condescended to," Daisy said, surprising herself with a sharp note of defensiveness in her voice. "I think it's somewhat to their credit."

"So do I," Patrick said, smiling. "I shouldn't like to live somewhere that when I left, the best of them felt guilty but relieved."

"What would it be you couldn't manage without?" Daisy asked, after a moment. The platform was filling with bodies, but it had already become a little quieter. She spoke in a lower tone.

"Someone like-minded to talk to, I suppose. And you?"

"Kindness," Daisy said, feeling a little silly. "It's less lonely."

"So we both depend on other people to get through this— through anything, I suppose."

"My mother depends on books, silence, and privacy."

"Privacy is quite a usual one, I imagine. It's probably one of the worst things about being a prisoner."

"Lack of privacy. And no control over noise. Or having the window open."

Patrick nodded; it went without saying that they were talking about aspects of imprisonment other than death, physical pain, fear, or starvation.

"Music seems to be the main—the essential—comfort for an extraordinary number of people. People who didn't seem to pay it much attention in peacetime. Any kind of concert is packed out. There's a fellow in my regiment who sits by himself every evening and reads music. He doesn't even hum; every now and again he nods as though acknowledging something. No one ever disturbs him."

"Tea."

"Tea and teddy bears and the BBC," Patrick said, laughing. "Lie down, we're probably going to be here all night."

Daisy, a little awkwardly, wriggled herself forward until she was lying down. Patrick lifted his dressing gown and spread it loosely over her.

"You might want to take off your coat," he said.

Daisy sat up, took off her jacket, and lay back on the pillow. Patrick took off his shoes and lay down beside her.

"Teddy bears," he repeated thoughtfully, and put an arm over her body and drew her to him. "How little I know about you, my sweet Daisy. Are you afraid?"

"No."

He did not reply; instead he tucked her shoulder under his armpit and slid his other arm under hers, taking her breast in his cupped palm.

"Of course I'm afraid," Daisy said, her voice a little breathless.

"You'd be mad or unusually unimaginative if you weren't." Patrick's fingers gently squeezed her breast as his thumb, just as softly, stroked it. "What are you afraid of?"

"You know."

"I do, but it's—ah—helpful to name one's fears."

"I'm afraid of the bombs. I'm afraid of sleeping with you. I'm afraid of getting married. I'm afraid—although more often the idea gives me pleasure—of not having any idea of what it will be like after the war. If it ever ends."

"Very reasonable fears. And do you want reassurance and comforting meaningless platitudes?"

"No," Daisy said dubiously; a large part of her wanted exactly that, but she also thought Patrick might have something better to offer.

"What do you do when you're afraid? What do you hold on to?"

"What do you mean?" It was the most intimate question she had ever been asked.

"There has to be a thought, a memory, an image, that you invoke and use to supplant the fear. What is it?"

Daisy lay quiet for a moment; the feeling of Patrick's body against hers, larger, stronger, and, it seemed, protective, encouraged her to confide in him. It felt like an offering, a submission of her will to his.

"Poetry. The first two and a bit lines of 'Dover Beach.'

The sea is calm to-night.
The tide is full, the moon lies fair
Upon the straits.

It makes me feel calm and still."

"Yes," Patrick said, and nodded.

"And you?"

Patrick hesitated, but he did not simulate incomprehension. "I've never told anyone this."

"Did you think I had?" Daisy said, indignant.

"No. Of course not. Mine's just a memory. From when I was a boy."

Patrick paused a moment, Daisy imagined him concentrating before he started. "Hacking home from hunting—in the mist. With James. Tiny gray drops of water on our jackets, and the smell of autumn—leaves, the wet earth, smoke from a cottage chimney. I thought the rest of my life would be like that. The way my father had lived—he was already dead, killed in the Great War. The house, the horses, gun dogs, turf burning in the fire-places. I imagined James often there. We thought it would go on forever. Now I tell myself there could be moments of it again, if we were lucky. . . . That's what I hang onto when it all seems . . ."

"Yes," Daisy said softly, stroking his hand.

"Very Granchester I know," he said smiling, "but at least we had the grace to know we were happy. And now there's you."

They lay quietly together for a while. Daisy's body now relaxed, as she thought that she and Patrick were not strangers after all. When she had hurriedly changed out of her evening dress at the hotel she had put on, instead of her brassiere, a slip that was slightly gathered under her breasts. The fine, flimsy silk— Valerie had been very firm about the quality of what she called "lingerie" necessary for the weekend—although perhaps less inti-mate than the touch of skin on skin, was, it seemed to Daisy, sen-suous in a sophisticated way. Patrick was running the tips of his fingers so lightly over her nipples that she could not be sure what was the pressure of his fingers, the weight of the silk, or her own aroused imagination. She felt her body move against his and an involuntary low moan escaped her lips.

"Yes," he said, "it's going to be wonderful."

The other people in the station had become silent, except for a small group singing sentimental songs at the far end of the platform; even they were singing in lower voices and in a manner that suggested they were winding down. Behind Patrick's raised shoulder, the woman with the small children slept soundly, beyond them the lighted entrance to the platform.

Daisy heard the drunken laughter before the man and woman came through the archway behind her. She heard them hesitate as though deciding in which direction to go and a loud, not humorous, laugh suggested that the man had taken advantage of the pause to take what Daisy's family, lacking an adequate word in the vocabulary of their own class, called "a liberty."

She tensed, fearing they would come in their direction and, after a moment, they did. The woman stumbled over something in the dim light and laughed.

"Pardon," she said to the unseen object, and laughed again.

The man spoke a few words in a language Daisy did not recognize. The couple did not, as Daisy feared they would, stop next to her and Patrick. But they did not go to the far end of the platform where three men and a woman sat smoking and talking quietly. Instead, the man steered the woman, unsteady on her high heels, into a white tiled corner where the platform became a few feet narrower. Leaning his body toward hers, he trapped her with his weight, and Daisy saw his hand, pale against the woman's black skirt, run down her thigh, his fingers catching and pulling the material up.

"Polish sailor," Patrick said, "and, although perhaps I'm unfair to her, a tart. Time to turn over."

Daisy wriggled herself around to face him. She was relieved not to have to witness whatever brutish moment was now being enacted; at the same time, since she had never consciously seen a tart before, she would not have minded, had Patrick not been present, taking a closer look.

"It's said Polish sailors bite girls' nipples off," he said.

"No!"

"Probably not, but it's a prevalent and widespread belief. I've never met with any firsthand evidence or known anyone who has."

"That doesn't prove anything—you probably just don't move in the right circles."

"I imagine it's something made up by Cockney men to keep their women faithful while they're away at the war."

"Or tarts whose business is off because of the drop in wartime morals."

Patrick laughed.

"Maybe," he said. "It's been a long day. We should try to get a little sleep."

Daisy was tired but overexcited; she was not sure that she could sleep. Nevertheless, she sat up a little and carefully unhooked her precious stockings from her suspender belt, rolling each up, tucking it into its own thicker top to make a more protected package, and put them into the pocket of her jacket. After a moment she unhooked her suspender belt, which, no longer attached to her stockings, felt ridiculous. If Patrick were to run his hand up her thigh, she did not want him to encounter a lump of metal and rubber dangling on the end of an elastic suspender; that eventuality seeming more worrisome than his hand making the transition from her bare leg to inside her knickers.

She lay down again and snuggled beside him in a way suggesting sleep rather than an invitation to further intimacy. It had been a long day and Daisy wanted a little time to think about it. The train journey, the hotel, the theater, dinner at the Ritz—all were jumbled into one dreamlike image. Anticipation, awkwardness, childish excitement at sophistication and elegance, longing, love, and fear all seemed part of one continuous experience, an experience so intense she was unlikely fully to feel it until she had time to think about it later.

The train from Wales to London had been crowded and hot; Daisy stood in the corridor much of the way, her underwear becoming warm and damp and her hair and clothing absorbing the smell of tobacco and the gritty stale air of the railway carriage. Patrick, on the platform at Paddington, had seemed, for a moment, a stranger, barely identifiable in the sea of anonymous uniforms. Then his arms around her and his reassuring, although not yet quite familiar, smell made her feel safe and, best of all, not alone.

Then, again alone at the hotel, Daisy struggled to seem non-chalant as Patrick registered for them both. Once in the room, that nonchalance dropped and, her silence and tentative smile begging for reassurance, she became awkward and silent. Patrick's demeanor Daisy might, in the circumstances, have hesitated to describe as breezy, but she would have been hard put to come up with a better word. She understood that it was the approach to life that was supposed to win the war for England; even so, she would have been grateful if he could have dropped the almost brittle pretense that nothing remarkable or out of the ordinary was taking place. For the first time in her life Daisy felt a drink might help.

A drink did help. So did the theater; Patrick had bought tickets to a show rather than a play. An escapist bit of wartime froth, the early, wartime curtain, as well as the content and the audience full of uniforms, emphasized how temporary was the moment of frivolity. At intermission in the bar, there were not only British uniforms, but also those of the Free French and of the listless and frustrated Canadian airmen who had been languishing in their camps in the English countryside. Daisy had been told all London theaters were full, although she suspected the audiences for the Shakespeare, Wilde, Shaw, and Congreve productions were less raucous at intermission. Daisy found herself moved by the singers of patriotic and sentimental songs and, moments later, laughing at a low comic, then dazzled by the glamour of the chorus girls behind the footlights.

Afterward, walking along Shaftesbury Avenue surrounded by the overexcited, pleasure-seeking crowds of Londoners and the servicemen and -women, all with the sense that every moment remaining to them should be made to count for something and the feeling that all rules were suspended, Daisy thought this was an evening she and Patrick would, in later life, recall as a strange and almost unreal night—a moment of gaiety and respite in the middle of the war.

Every taxi on Shaftesbury Avenue was full; they were to dine at the Ritz, not too far to walk. They passed a series of London landmarks, each significant and symbolic—although not clearly visible in the growing darkness—to the elated Daisy. Piccadilly Circus, Eros protectively boarded up for "the duration"; the Royal Academy, showing an exhibition of firefighters' art. On the other side of Piccadilly, Fortnum & Mason, quiet, elegant, and expensive, inside the shelves stocked with sauces, relishes, and chutneys—the accompaniments to food rather than food itself.

Then the Ritz, another institution Daisy had encountered in novels but never before seen. Any hotel grander than a boarding-house had, since childhood, seemed to Daisy full of potential for drama and romance; the transient nature of such an establishment speeding up events and outcome, editing from time those long periods of uninterrupted boredom that largely comprise childhood. The transience suggested action, and if the stay turned out to be merely recreational, that in itself suggested a life unwilling to remain trapped in one location and with the resources to ensure that didn't happen. Those resources, Daisy imagined, were primarily financial, but wealth combined with a spirit of adventure or at least a need and desire for change. Daisy felt this way about every Grand Hotel facing a rainy promenade on the south

coast of England, so she was slightly surprised to enter the Ritz
and tread the carpet between the marble, palms, and uniformed
staff of the hotel without witnessing any acts of passion or intrigue.
The dining room was, however, all she could have wished. High
velvet curtains hid the blackout shades on the windows overlooking St. James's Park, and inside, the uniforms and the sounds of
diners determined to have a good time produced what seemed an
almost tangible sense of excitement.

Patrick ordered a bottle of red wine. The name of the wine
was not familiar to Daisy, but even she knew from the taste that
it was old and good. Wine was now increasingly hard to come by,
although George, Rosemary's husband, used every evening of his
leave to descend to the cellar and bring up a bottle of claret and,
every other evening, one of port.

The wine Patrick had ordered was, Daisy knew, expensive
and more so now that even the Ritz was bound by the new
rationing rules with limits to the price of a meal. The piece of meat
on her plate was no larger than it would have been had she and
Patrick eaten dinner at one of the new British restaurants,
although the vegetables were less pedestrian, better cooked, and
presented in a more ornate manner.

"If you were at Aberneth Farm this evening you would probably be eating a better meal," Patrick said.

This statement was unanswerable unless Daisy was prepared
to tie herself up in a longish and boring response. Was she supposed to deny the food at Aberneth Farm was better, although less
interesting, than that at the Ritz? To reassure him that this weekend was not, for her, primarily about food?

She did not speak; instead she raised her glass to her lips,
sipped her wine, and looked provocatively—she hoped—at him.
Valerie would have been proud of her. But now what? Or was the
ball firmly in Patrick's court?

He said nothing and smiled. His smile was not only affectionate but amused. He was, perhaps, smiling at her schoolgirlish attempt at flirtation. Daisy opened her mouth to say something to divert him, then closed it for want of inspiration. She could think of nothing to say that would not make her feel more foolish. After a moment, Patrick spoke.

"Daisy," he said, "are you—" He broke off as his attention was drawn to a disturbance—what Daisy's father would have called a rumpus—at a table two away from the one at which they were sitting.

"You bastard." The woman's voice was loud, angry, upper class, and, it seemed to Daisy, most likely drunken.

A section of the dining room, eight or ten tables surrounding the couple, became quiet, although no one looked directly at them. Daisy, without turning her head, could see them over Patrick's shoulder. The couple at the table between, somewhat elderly, who had been paying their bill in a leisurely way, now rose, in an unhurried but purposeful manner. With their departure, Daisy had an uninterrupted view of the quarreling pair.

Everyone within earshot listened; the man was now speaking in a low tone to his companion. Daisy could not hear what he was saying, but she could see him run a placatory hand down the woman's arm. She was one of the few diners with an uninterrupted view of the drama; no one else turned his head an inch in that direction. Daisy wondered if anyone else had the intensely embarrassing sense of being in some way—although she didn't know either of the parties involved and presumably, as a first-time diner at the Ritz, had even less connection with them than any of her neighbors—responsible for the behavior of the glamorous but uninhibited couple. The British diners probably, she thought, felt as she did, although perhaps the Blitz, bombs, death, grief, physical proximity with blood and fear, the camaraderie of patriotism and rationing had diminished the English sense of each man being an island. Or, probably, not.

"Don't touch me. Take your hands off me, you—you unspeakable cad." Daisy could see the woman withdraw her hand—lovely red nails and a big diamond ring—from that of the man, who was wearing a uniform with a fairly impressive strip of ribbons on it. Quite a lot more than Patrick's, anyway.

The man, older than his companion and, it seemed, considerably less embarrassed than was Daisy, laughed. The woman, who appeared to be maddened beyond words, opened her mouth once or twice and closed it again. Her manicured hand was now on the bodice of her dress, elegant and sophisticated against the gathered crêpe de Chine. The color of her nails and that of the dress— crimson, but soft, as though a touch of blue had been used to dilute the intensity of the color and make it more, but less obviously, dramatic—did not match but, instead, blended and complemented each other.

"What's happening?" Patrick asked.

Before Daisy could answer, the woman pushed her chair back violently and stood up. A waiter, who had been discreetly eyeing the table, stepped forward, swiftly and deferentially, to help with her chair, and found himself close enough to be splashed by the contents of the almost full glass of red wine that she threw in the man's face.

Half the dining room was now silent, heads were turning and even those at the farther end of the room, who could neither hear nor see the source of the drama, became quieter. An elderly woman, presumably deaf and unaware of both the sudden silence and the volume of her own voice, continued to confide in her companion some details of the trouble she was having with a new a set of dentures. After a moment, she, too, fell silent.

The woman in the crimson dress, ignoring the waiter, snatched her evening bag from the table, turned abruptly, and seemingly unaware of the eyes of the entire room on her, strode toward the door. She met Daisy's horrified eye as she came abreast with their table, but Daisy knew herself unseen. Then she paused, and for a moment—Daisy registered the possibility with a jolt of fear in her stomach—it seemed she might speak, or appeal, to her or Patrick. Then she turned and, as abruptly as she had left the table, returned to it. A waiter was mopping the apparently unperturbed officer with a napkin. He had dealt with the wine on the man's hair and face and was now attempting to blot the front of his uniform. At the woman's return, the waiter shifted himself almost imperceptibly away although his face remained expressionless. The officer rose an inch or two from his chair.

"My dear—" he started, but stopped as the woman, combining scorn with speed, swept her cigarette case—shagreen and silver, Daisy noticed, impressed and a little envious—from the table, turned again, and apparently unembarrassed, head held high, left the dining room.

Her former companion watched her for a moment, then waved away the waiter holding the wine-stained napkin. He caught the eye of the headwaiter, hovering at a discreet distance, and nodded. Then, thoughtfully, he lifted and drained his own glass; the other diners, recognizing the show was over, began again to murmur and then to talk.

Daisy, a little flushed, was explaining what had happened, behind him, to Patrick, interrupting herself to comment on subsequent events as they took place: "—then she went back and snatched her cigarette case—now he's paying the bill—without so much as looking at him. Who do you think she is? What did he do? He's standing up and taking a cigar out of a case and—he's—oh—"

"An altogether nicer type of girl—where do you find them?"

To Daisy's horror, the man was now standing beside their table, looking—as were, she felt, most of the other diners—at

Daisy, and speaking to Patrick. Daisy, helpless and now scarlet, looked at Patrick; she would have been on firmer ground had she not so obviously been talking about the incident just before the man she was describing paused at their table.

Patrick looked over his shoulder at the new arrival; Daisy noticed, with respect and relief, that he was holding up rather better than she was. But, before he could speak, the officer continued. "Mind if I join you? There should be some wine left—" And, drawing a chair one-handed from a neighboring unoccupied table, he sat down, rather heavily, with them.

Even as completely out of her depth as Daisy now was, she noticed with amusement the flicker of desperation on the face of the headwaiter, now moving toward them, and his qualified relief as Patrick smiled.

"I should have known," he said. "Daisy, this is Major Sir Ambrose Sweeney, M.C., my neighbor in Ireland and a desperate character. Ambrose, this is my fiancée, Daisy Creed."

Ambrose Sweeney, without taking his eyes off Daisy, gestured with one outstretched arm, and a waiter brought the unfinished bottle of wine from the other table. Daisy assumed the service at the Ritz, already excellent, would now become nervously instantaneous.

"Fiancée?" he said. "My congratulations. Has she met your family yet?"

"Ambrose! You don't feel you've caused enough trouble tonight?"

"You're right," Ambrose said, and turned to Daisy. "They're perfectly all right once they get to know you. In the meantime, push a chest of drawers across the door each night when you go to bed."

Daisy laughed and relaxed. Ambrose had not been the maker, although he might have—probably had—been the cause, of the scene, and his presence at the table made her own evening easier. It dispelled or at least postponed the, however exciting, however eagerly awaited, awkward moment when she and Patrick had to acknowledge the reason they were in London. That they had traveled here to anticipate their honeymoon. Although Daisy had become aware of Ambrose Sweeney's existence not more than five minutes before, she was pretty sure he understood what was going on; that he was at least as aware of their silent drama as he was of the more visible one in which he had just taken part.

"Daisy's a Land Girl in Wales—on my cousin Rosemary's farm."

Ambrose looked at her with interest.

"George ever get any joy with those grouse he tried to introduce on his moor?" he asked.

"I don't know," Daisy said. It was the first she had heard of grouse at Aberneth Farm.

"Didn't think so. Told him it wouldn't work. Grouse won't breed if they're nervous." He paused for a moment thoughtfully. "Unlike humans." Another pause. "Whole family pretty highly strung," he said, his gesture indicating the table where he had dined with his erstwhile companion. "Mother was a Chatfield— you know what that means—this unfortunate girl is the daughter of the old boy who put most of his money into Russian bonds in 1915. Enough to make anyone touchy."

"Touchy?" Daisy asked, both amused and hoping for further comment on the scene they had just witnessed.

"You can see she's overbred—beautiful and hysterical—like an Afghan hound."

Patrick and Ambrose exchanged banter, the subject of their conversation moving back and forth between regimental matters, friends in common, horses, and sport. The men spoke lightly and, it seemed, freely of their military duties, but it was in a uniformly self-deprecatory manner; had a German spy been concealed beneath their table, he would have come away with nothing to interest him—unless, of course, he cared about the population of foxes in Tipperary and West Waterford.

Although Daisy contributed little to the conversation, she was not excluded. Both of the men addressed an occasional observation in her direction and from time to time would appeal to her with a rhetorical question.

Eventually, Ambrose straightened his back, glanced at his watch, and remarked, "Evening's still young, might as well drop in at the old Kit Kat. Don't suppose—no, of course not." And he was gone.

"The old Kit Kat?" Daisy asked.

"Generic term for any club he might drop into after dinner. Covers most of Soho *and* the Guards Club."

Patrick called for the bill. He paid it in a less casual manner than Ambrose had his. Daisy, watching him, was sure the tip was neither too little nor too much; she was also sure that the Ritz was not where he usually ate his dinner in London, and it was not a place they would frequent after they were married.

Moments later they were on Piccadilly and, shortly thereafter, in a taxi on their way back to the hotel. There Patrick had taken a bath, embraced Daisy, and instead of making love to her had taken her to the air-raid shelter where she was now falling asleep.

CHAPTER 8

Despite Valerie's heavy-handed innuendo, there was no connection between Daisy's decision not to wear white for her wedding and the weekend she had spent with Patrick in London. She had returned to Aberneth Farm—thanks to the air raid, Patrick's early morning chivalry, and both their exhausted states—as she had left it, a virgin. She was, she thought, glad this was the case but didn't have the heart to tell Valerie.

Daisy had refused her mother's offer of her own wedding dress, suitably altered by her grandmother, and had spent the greater part of her saved wages on a pale lilac dress and a small, subdued pink hat. Both could and would be worn later.

After the weekend in London, Daisy and Patrick had returned to their wartime duties. Daisy to the late-summer, hot, hard, but not unpleasant routine of Aberneth Farm; Patrick to the training course near London. The next time they would see each other would be the evening before the wedding.

Daisy wondered if every bride felt at least a little ashamed of her family. Her parents' shortcomings could, at a pinch, be dismissed as eccentricity, that useful catchall excuse allowed to anyone whose family originated as minor landed gentry or better. Joan, whose stock was identical, could not be so easily explained;

from the moment she had enlisted she had assumed the vocabu-
larly of a dock worker. Barring criminal activity or relentless
promiscuity—and Daisy wasn't completely sure the latter was not
included in Joan's self-cast role—she could not have found a more
efficient way of revenging herself for the real or imaginary defects
of her upbringing. Joan's coarseness and Valerie's refinement were
equally embarrassing. Valerie: another reason for Daisy's heart to
sink. Daisy wanted and needed Rosemary at her wedding and it
would have been both unkind and awkward to exclude Valerie,
who, as stage manager of the London weekend, had now in her
mind expanded her role and felt responsible for the match.
Valerie's overwhelming advantage was that she was not a blood
relation and Daisy had no reason to feel responsible for her.
Though, of course, she did.

None of which should have been insurmountable—Patrick
already knew what he was getting into—had it not been for his
choice of best man.

"What a good idea, darling. I was worried that none of your
family would be there," Daisy had said, her heart sinking.

Patrick's parents were dead and none of his surviving family
were coming to the wedding; Daisy wasn't sure why not and
wasn't able to frame the words to ask. When her parents had
asked vague, not very pressing questions, Daisy had cited distance, short notice, and anything else that came to mind. Privately
she suspected lack of interest, both on Patrick's part and that of his
brother and sister. So when Patrick suggested James should be his
best man, Daisy simulated enthusiasm.

The conversation had taken place on the telephone; the telephone call a rarity, their slightly awkward letters a more usual
form of communication. Daisy thought Patrick had already asked
James and that he was not so much seeking acquiescence as
employing a polite form of telling her.

She sought out Rosemary. She had not, since James was Rosemary's cousin, told her of James's attempt to seduce her at Bannock. That memory no longer made her ashamed; but since she knew he was not well disposed toward her, this occasion would present an opportunity for him to sneer at her family and to revenge himself on her.

Rosemary, for the first time, disappointed Daisy. She had always seemed the personification of tact and common sense; now she seemed not to notice that Daisy was awkward, embarrassed, and inarticulate. She seemed unable to infer the problem from the words that Daisy did and did not mumble. The unsatisfactory conversation ended with the understanding that Daisy, like most young brides, was nervous about her wedding and that Rosemary would be helpful in any way she could. Daisy retired to her bedroom to consider what had and what had not taken place.

It didn't seem possible that Daisy had imbued her employer with a subtlety and delicacy that she did not possess, that she might have misunderstood the level of unspoken complicity between them at certain moments; Rosemary's responsive reaction to the eye met, the unspoken word, the moment's hesitation, belied that. Daisy had to assume Rosemary did not want to concern herself with this problem, or that she was, perhaps, in the other camp if everyone had to ally himself either with the Nugents, who Daisy assumed thought Patrick was making a mistake, or the Creeds, who as usual weren't paying much attention. Or, maybe, Rosemary was taking the view that now Daisy was engaged to be married, and had given notice to her employer, she no longer took responsibility for her, that Daisy should now stand on her own two feet. Daisy was quite prepared to be independent and decisive, starting the moment she was a married woman; it was the interim period that she worried about.

Patrick, Rosemary, and Valerie arrived at the rectory the

evening before the wedding. Dinner was exhausting. As on the only other occasion Patrick had eaten a meal with her family, each seemed a parody of his worst self. Daisy was far too nervous to feel hungry, but she noticed that her mother served a meal that was simultaneously burnt and cold; that her grandmother's sighs were louder and longer than usual; Valerie asked one question too many about James, so far unmet by her; and, most horribly, Joan seemed to have assumed the role of best man at a bachelor dinner, allowing no possibility of a double entendre to pass and, although stopping short of an after-dinner speech, managing to tell several coarse jokes that left Mrs. Creed genuinely bewildered and Daisy cringing. Daisy, her stomach constricted with outrage and embarrassment, was at the same time grateful that James would not arrive until the next day, shortly before the wedding. Not that she thought that anybody would be behaving any better; she imagined James, playing Darcy to Patrick's Mr. Bingley, drawing him to one side and whispering that it was still not too late to extricate himself from the clutches of this impossible family.

Daisy awoke, the next morning, to the most beautiful day of the year, cool, dry, and sunny with the warmth of Indian summer and the promise of autumn crispness. And to a feeling she could not immediately have described or defined, a mixture of confidence and determination and an awareness that if she allowed anyone to spoil her wedding day she would have no one to blame but herself. Confrontation, quarrels, and hurt feelings were not the solution; the only way to continue in her happy mood was to rise above the self-centered behavior of her family and Valerie. Or, better still, to isolate herself from it. She stayed in her room, allowing Rosemary to bring her a cup of ersatz coffee and, it having been established that she had first call on the hot water, took a bath and put on the dress she was to be married in.

Rosemary came in with two glasses of champagne.

"What's happening downstairs?" Daisy asked.

"Organized chaos," Rosemary said. "Lunch and—well, you don't need to think about that—it's your wedding day."

Daisy put on her hat; Rosemary stood behind her arranging her hair and tugging the shoulder seams of her dress to make it sit properly.

"You look lovely," said Rosemary, and Daisy, seeing herself in the looking glass, knew that she did.

"Thank you," she said, resisting the instinctive disclaimer.

They stood there for a moment, each smiling at the other's reflection; Rosemary broke the silence.

"Everything's all right. Your grandmother is putting the finishing touches to your bouquet, your mother is in fact getting food ready for later and it'll be fine, James is chatting with your father, and Joan—"

"James—" Daisy almost yelped. "What's he doing here?"

"He came over to get something Patrick had forgotten—the ring, his trousers—and now he and your father—"

"And Valerie?" Daisy interrupted again.

"She's sitting quietly in her room, reading a magazine and waiting for her nail varnish to dry."

"Has she—ah—met James yet?"

"Just in passing. I believe your grandmother introduced them."

Daisy looked at Rosemary in a manner that expressed disbelief or, at least, a need for elucidation.

"Last night, after dinner, for all our sakes, not least Valerie's, I told her that James—appearances to the contrary—was not the answer to a maiden's prayer."

"You what?"

"She looked as startled as you do now. So I added, meaningfully, that he was 'not the marrying kind.' "

"Rosemary, you didn't?" Daisy was shocked and amused. And grateful. But mostly shocked.

"It's true," Rosemary said, laughing. "He's not my idea of the answer to a maiden's prayer and so far as I know he's not looking for a wife until he's finished sowing rather too many wild oats."

"Rosemary, you're a genius."

"It's time to go downstairs. Finish your champagne. I told you—everything's going to be all right."

And it was all right. As far as she could tell. The next hour or so seemed as though observed by her from a distance; she tried to remember as much as she could in order to feel it all more deeply the next time she found herself alone. Which would not be for some time. She had a sense of faces swooping toward her, like parent birds protecting their nest from a predatory cat, then veering away. The faces spoke words that she committed to memory but did not understand at the time she heard them.

Daisy had not, since early childhood, done as she was told by either of her parents without evaluating the validity and wisdom of each instruction. It was not their motives but their worldliness that she mistrusted. Now, on a day when anyone might be out of his depth, she allowed her distracted father and flustered mother to bundle her, a posy of pale garden flowers in her hands, out the door, across the road, and into the little church. She was aware, without glancing up at the sky, that it would probably rain before the afternoon was over, but felt it was for once someone else's responsibility to remember the umbrellas. Joan's, Rosemary's, and Valerie's faces entered her vision and swam out of it. Her grandmother said something that seemed to require a reply but, although she could hear the words, they had no meaning to her.

And then, with no sense of time having passed, she was at the altar, Patrick at her side, repeating words that she seemed to know by heart, and she was married. Patrick gravely and decorously kissed her and they walked together down the aisle. The rain did not begin until they were again in the rectory, her mother making tea and her father reviving the smoldering fire in the sitting room.

She, it seemed, blinked her eyes and found she had a glass of champagne in her hand. She felt as though she were waking from a long sleep during which she had apparently promised to love, honor, and obey, until death did them part, the gentle and handsome stranger who stood beside her. She glanced around the room; the atmosphere was rather more that of the aftermath of a christening or of a family tea party that was going quite well than that of a wedding. Now that she seemed to have woken up, she became once more aware of the possibility—probability—of one or more members of her family doing something shaming, embarrassing, and completely in character. She looked from face to face, without seeing anything untoward. Valerie was sitting beside Rosemary, smiling in a preoccupied manner that suggested she was planning how she should spend the remainder of her leave. Her mother, no longer burdened with the practical arrangements of the wedding, was now free to start worrying that her daughter, married to a man they hardly knew, was going to live in another country with a family they had never met. Her father looked tired. Her grandmother was rearranging plates and glasses on the tea table. Joan was sitting quietly on the sofa, knees together and hands primly resting on her lap. Daisy wondered, for a moment, what magic Rosemary had wrought before she remembered an exchange she had heard but not comprehended just before they had left for the church. Without being able to recall the exact words, she had gained the impression that Joan's commanding officer—not her immediate superior, who was presumably a woman, but the person responsible for the whole operation in which Joan was an insignificant part—had been James's best friend at Eton. Daisy was considering whether this was in fact the case or if it was another convenient fabrication of Rosemary's—she didn't much like the idea of James taking it upon himself to sub-due or neutralize the less acceptable elements of her family—when her father opened another bottle of champagne for drinking toasts and cutting the cake.

Daisy stood beside Patrick, his hand on hers; the tip of a not quite sharp enough knife frozen for an instant on the undecorated cake—the ordinance against iced cakes begun a few weeks ago—while James took a photograph.

Champagne. The cake—eight eggs sent home with Daisy from Wales and butter and sugar saved from the family rations. Photographic film. Minor wartime miracles.

The pressure of Patrick's palm on the back of her hand increased as Daisy cut the first slice of cake, and she felt a wave of desire. Although she had spent nearly a year engaged in manual labor, his strength was and always would be much greater than hers; the feeling excited her. There had been a moment, in the hotel in London after the air raid, lying in bed beside Patrick, when she had taken his hand and held it up, palm against palm, to measure it against hers. She had been moved by the broad capa-ble hand, the strong straight fingers, and by simultaneous feelings of helplessness and trust.

The cork of another champagne bottle popped. Daisy and Patrick cut the cake. Photographs were taken. It was as though time were now moving at twice its normal speed. Daisy had just started to wonder what Patrick was feeling and whether he was as bemused and confused as she was at the momentous step and solemn vows they had, less than an hour ago, taken together, when all faces turned toward James.

The best man's speech. James, a glass in his hand, stepped for-ward half a pace—the size of the rectory sitting room did not allow for dramatic movements—and without any apparent nervousness began to speak. Daisy, after a moment, reminded herself to breathe; her strongest emotion embarrassment—for them all, including, surprisingly, James—rather than fear of what he, with the license implicit in a best man's speech, might say.

But it seemed to be all right. James, easily and amusingly, recounted a harmless anecdote of his and Patrick's childhood; said the conventional things about her family; about how happy his— completely absent—family was to have Daisy as one of their own, and ended, his voice as light as before, but his eyes only for Daisy.

"We both saw Daisy at the same time, but I was too stupid to see what a jewel she is. The better man won, the one she deserves, but I shall always think that if I were a better man than I am that Patrick might have been making this speech and I might have been standing proudly beside her."

Daisy's fingers on Patrick's arm tightened. She understood that she, with her family, although not necessarily Patrick, was being charmed. But she thought that, in order to be so charming, he must recognize some special quality in her. The thought was flattering until she understood that that was what charm is. Even so, for a moment, she found herself wondering what it would have been like if James, rather than the better man, had won.

CHAPTER 9

D AISY WOKE WITH an early morning breeze from the open window playing on her face. She lay, eyes closed, holding on to the feeling of intense pleasure and a sense of well-being. This, she thought, might be what heaven is like.

Patrick lay beside her; they had spent the night in the spare room at Aberneth Farm. Daisy listened to his even breathing and knew him to be asleep. She did not open her eyes, and lay still and relaxed, aware of the texture of the sheet lying lightly over her naked body. Birds were chattering in the gutter above the open window.

I am happy, she thought. *I am married and I love my husband and I am happy. Remember this moment.*

Patrick shifted slightly, drew in a deep breath as though he were about to wake, expelled it and sank into a deeper sleep. Daisy slipped quietly out of bed, wrapped herself in her dressing gown, shuffled her feet into her slippers, and silently padded to the door. She opened it with exaggerated care; the doors and floorboards at Aberneth Farm tended to creak, and it was her intention to be back in bed, bathed, with clean teeth and brushed hair before Patrick awoke. Closing the door carefully behind her, Daisy became aware of a small, still presence at the end of the corridor.

"Sarah," she said. "Good morning."

"Mummy said I wasn't to disturb you," the child said. "Why are you sleeping in the spare room?"

"Because I am married." Daisy knew this was explanation enough for Sarah, that the child only wanted to confirm, to her own satisfaction, that Daisy and Patrick now shared a bedroom.

"Is Uncle Patrick going to live here, too?"

"No, he's a soldier; he has to go back to his regiment, and now I am his wife I'll go and live in our house in Ireland."

Sarah nodded. She had been told all this before, but since she didn't really understand or accept the changes around the small world of Aberneth Farm, she tended to ask the same questions, hoping for a different or, at least, more comprehensible answer. Daisy sympathized with the child and wanted to give her an explanation she could understand; failing that, she was prepared to repeat the information until it was accepted, if not understood.

"Are you coming down to breakfast?"

"No. I'll come when Uncle Patrick wakes up."

"You have to wait for him because you're married now?"

"Yes," Daisy said firmly.

"I already had my breakfast. There's a letter for Uncle Patrick."

"A letter? Did the postman bring it?"

"A man rang the doorbell."

"I'll come down when I've washed my face," Daisy said. She went into the bathroom and closed the door behind her. Without even a passing thought of rats—or ferrets.

A telegram. Rosemary's heart must have dropped at the sight of it.

Daisy knotted the cord of her dressing gown more tightly as she left the bathroom; she had never gone downstairs before in her nightclothes. How clear it was sometimes, she thought, as she descended the stairs, how one was meant to behave. To have appeared in the dining room, fully dressed and with lipstick, half an hour later, would have been cold and vain, but to have dashed downstairs with sleep-filled eyes, wild hair, and a full bladder would have been overdramatic, hysterical, impractical, and, well, not English. The appearance of calm and order was next best to order itself, as if knowing what one was expected to do made possible continuing one's life in the chaotic, frightening, and lonely times of the war.

Rosemary was still at the breakfast table. In the same way that Daisy had instinctively washed her face before coming downstairs, Rosemary had remained in the dining room. Ready to welcome Daisy or Patrick and ready to commiserate over the contents of the telegram.

"Good morning," Rosemary said.

Daisy leaned over and kissed her on the cheek.

"Good morning," she said. "Sarah told me there's a telegram."

Rosemary hesitated, a little off balance, her prepared words no longer necessary.

"Have a cup of tea before you take it up," she said.

Daisy sat down.

"He has to go back?" she asked.

"I imagine that's it," Rosemary said. "So unfair."

Daisy shook her head. She knew what Rosemary must have thought when the telegram arrived. Any telegram that didn't notify the recipient that a next of kin was dead or missing had, now, to be counted a mercy.

"Have you ever met any of Patrick's family?" Rosemary asked. Daisy understood she was not referring to James or any of the Westmoreland Nugents.

"Not one of them. Now might be the time to tell me the worst."

"I only meant—you can stay here as long as you like. If Patrick has to go back, there's no need to go to Ireland on your own."

"Thank you." Daisy smiled, and repeated her words to Sarah, "But I'm married now.

FISHGUARD TO ROSSLARE. Daisy caught a train at Crumlin and made a connection to the train originating from Paddington and ending at the dark, cold, damp port. It was raining and windy when she got off the train and dragged her luggage to the boat. An overnight crossing and then a train journey on the other side. Would someone have come to meet them had Patrick been with her, she wondered.

She wasn't alone in the cabin. Two women had come in after Daisy was already in her bunk. She had turned her face away and pretended to be asleep, wanting to avoid the false intimacy of travel.

Daisy felt the gentle swell of the boat leaving harbor become a slower, stronger rhythm; there was no reason to imagine this rougher motion would abate—the contrary far more likely—before they reached the shelter of the Irish coast. She was afraid of being seasick; she was afraid of becoming tearful. Even as a child, Daisy had not wept easily.

Now, as then, she attempted to divert herself. The trouble was that almost anything she thought about increased her feeling of being alone, abandoned, bereft. There was little in the not uneventful past few weeks that did not concern someone not now with her. Primarily, of course, her husband of four days, now with his regiment and, Daisy imagined, on his way overseas. If she could fall asleep it might be possible to wake up the following early morning as the boat docked at Rosslare. She allowed herself to think about Patrick, about the three nights they had spent together. Such thoughts were rationed; she did not know how long they would have to last her, to console her. In her darker moments she knew it was possible it could be forever. But like women all over England, she banished, as best she could, such thoughts from her mind. Patrick's body on hers, the feel of his skin—warm, alive, an intimacy beyond anything she had ever imagined—against hers; his hands, with the same restrained strength as when he had helped her cut the wedding cake, holding her head as he kissed her. The weight of his stomach against hers. The feeling of being not alone, of being part of him, and the pleasure, the newly found and barely explored pleasure, of sexual love. And more even than love or pleasure, there was a feeling of relief.

Daisy knew, but chose not to dwell on it, that this love had developed after Patrick had taken her to bed; that love had followed sexual pleasure, in the opposite order to that prescribed by conventional morality and literature.

Eyes closed, she lay on her bunk in the airless cabin, melting with love and gratitude. Patrick would come back, safe and whole, and in the meantime she would hold the thought of him close to her and try to be brave.

PART TWO

Autumn 1940

CHAPTER 10

WHEN DAISY WOKE, the sea was calm. The small cabin was stuffy and smelled of unwashed bodies and clothing. Putting on her shoes and carrying her handbag, Daisy quietly left the cabin; it seemed important she should do so without waking her companions.

The air in the bathroom was foul; the floor, basins, and lavatories filthy. Daisy held her breath as she relieved herself and hastily brushed her teeth. All other washing would have to wait for cleaner surroundings.

The deck was wet and, apart from a couple of seamen, deserted. It had rained during the night and although the boat itself was redolent with the squalor of travelers—cigarette ends in the scuppers, beer bottles rolling with the mild swell, and a distressing smell of vomit—the wind from the Irish Sea was fresh, smelling of salt and rain. Daisy made her way to the bow and watched the gray outline of Rosslare harbor forming through the lighter gray mist. She watched small fishing boats setting out and listened to the shrieking gulls overhead. Although she was hungry, dirty, and tired, she felt her spirits rising.

This is it. The place I was always meant to be, Daisy thought, her feeling more of recognition than of pleasure. The thought so

clear that for a moment she thought she had spoken the words
aloud.

RAIN BEAT AGAINST the windows of Maud Nugent's bedroom,
the par. es a little thinner than they had been when the house was
built a hundred and ninety years before, eroded by exposure to
storms blowing in from the Atlantic. The wind rattled the window frames but the sounds, familiar to Maud, did not disturb her
sleep. Nor did the rhythmic clicking of Philomena's knitting
needles impinge on her dreams. It was not until an oak log, burning since just after breakfast, broke in two and slid down in the
grate that she sighed and turned toward the sound. She had been
dreaming of Princess Yusupov's black pearls and was once again
eighteen and in St. Petersburg. She was wearing a ball gown that
had been passed down from her eldest sister, and was waltzing
with an undersecretary. He was neither good-looking nor charming; nor did he perform this social duty with much real or simulated enthusiasm. Her father was the ambassador; the ambassador
had five daughters; if one of these daughters were short of a partner at a ball, the undersecretaries were obliged to dance with the
wallflower. At least once.

Maud did not, in either her dreams or her memory, romanti-
cize her place at these balls. She was there as a guest, but any
pleasure she took was the pleasure of a spectator. The Yusupov
black pearls adorned the princess's throat; around her own neck
was a necklace of coral and seed pearls. Life at the British Embassy
had been no more comfortable than it was here at Dunmaine; the
beds had been no softer, the rooms rather colder, and there had
always been the fear and possibility of rats. Maud had been
awoken more than once by a rat running across her bed. She had
not even been happier then. The past was not better; but it was
more real.

Reassured by the glow of the fire, the soft light casting shadows of the fireguard onto the rug, the anticipation of the cup of tea and biscuit that Philomena would soon carry up from the kitchen, Maud settled down again to sleep. She had gone to bed at the outbreak of war and had no intention of getting up again until peace was proclaimed.

THE TRAIN JOURNEY was as pleasant as the channel crossing had been nasty. Daisy had a carriage to herself. Although she suspected were she to beat the cushions on the upholstered seats, clouds of dust would have risen, train grime, after the squalor of a rough crossing, seemed cozy and cheerful.

She ate breakfast on the train and from the first sip of tea and mouthful of Irish railway bacon and eggs, she felt stronger and even more cheerful. The countryside outside her window was green and damp. The mist in which Rosslare had been shrouded had lifted a little, but enough of it lingered to soften the outlines of the hedges and fields, the overgrown ditches and stonefaced banks, the hills covered with gorse, the cattle on the road heavily plodding toward a farmyard to be milked. Coming into one of the many stations at which they stopped, Daisy had time to look at a pond in a field beside a road. It was surrounded by reeds and willows, rooted in the water. A moorhen with two chicks was making her way around the edge of the reeds, moving with sudden darts, ducking her head into the water. At the other end of the pond, water lilies were in bloom.

MICKEY NUGENT PROPPED a folded copy of an old *Illustrated London News* against the garage window and pushed a spanner against the bottom of the page to stop it sliding off. The corners of the window were darkened by rags of old cobwebs, but the dead flies on the sill seemed to have died of old age or starvation. A fine coating of barnyard dust covered both window and sill.

The shower outside dictated an indoor task, but Mickey would have preferred to potter in the garden shed, prodding the damp earth around seedlings, smoking and thinking, or even rearranging pots and tools into a semblance of order. He planted living things in the potting shed and they thrived; the dry dust of the garage, even without the desiccated bluebottles supine on the ledge, gave a less encouraging message. And Mickey mistrusted machinery. Still, the imminent arrival of his brother's new wife predicated embarking on this task, even if—and Mickey's life was full of unfinished tasks—he did not complete it that day. "The motor car is out of commission for the duration" would do the trick, although "up on blocks" made the possibility of meeting Daisy at Clonmel absolutely out of the question. Mickey had squirreled away a couple of gallons of petrol, not with any specific objective in mind, but he was sure that before the war ended he would find a better use for it than meeting a stranger at a railway station.

Wash, especially under wings and running board. Polish. That part was clear enough, and Mickey, who liked simple repetitive tasks that allowed him to think about other things, had done the job thoroughly.

Grease and oil all chassis lubricating points, road springs, brake operating mechanism, and engine controls. Mickey wished there was someone helping him. He knew in theory what a chassis was, road springs were presumably the things that prevented spine jarring and teeth grinding when the car went over a bump; the terms "brake" and "engine" did not present a problem, but "operating mechanism" and "controls" seemed to be rather blithely thrown in. Perhaps he should come back to that part later. He returned to the window ledge and read the next instruction.

Run engine until warm; drain radiator and cylinder block. The irony was that this information was not from a government pamphlet but part of an advertisement for an expensive motorcar. The manufacturers, who had no means of selling another car until after the war, kept their name in the public's mind with instructions on how to care for the model they had until a later one came on the market. After the war, Mickey thought, advertisements would hardly be necessary in order to induce any member of the British public with two coins to rub together to buy the now unavailable goods they hankered after.

The elegantly framed advertisement was for a Hawker Siddeley. Mickey had assumed the same principles would hold true for the modest Ford Standard that stood, gleaming, in the garage; now he was not so sure. He felt the need to consult another person; he didn't want assistance and he probably wouldn't take any advice proffered, but talking it through with somebody else often clarified his thoughts. In the meantime he would consult the encyclopedia in the library.

DAISY DOZED; OUTSIDE the window, fields and trees sped by. She had been delighted by them and enchanted by glimpses of castles and ruined mills standing, in silhouette, on distant hills. Closer, old stone bridges crossed small rivers and streams and Daisy had admired them all, loved them with the mysterious feeling of recognition she had felt at the moorhen's pond. The feeling of coming home.

I am coming home, she thought contentedly. *A new home, but my home now.* After a while she slept, tired from the uneasy night on the boat and the strain of the previous days. Her sleep was, not unpleasantly, interrupted by stationmasters' voices calling out the names of the stations at which they stopped—Wellington Bridge, Campile, Waterford, Mooncoin, Carrick-on-Suir, Kilsheelan—

followed by the slamming of train doors, and the *che-che-che* of the engine leaving the station, and then the rhythmic click of the wheels on the tracks, lulling her back to a deeper sleep.

PHILOMENA FINISHED A row and reversed her needles. She was warm, comfortable, and a little sleepy in the armchair by the fire. She was older than Maud, but did not think in terms of retirement, nor did she think it particularly unfair that her employer slept while she worked. The room in which she now spent most of her days was larger, warmer, and more cheerful than her own kitchen and seemed like the nursery that she had both worked and lived in when she had come to Dunmaine as a fifteen-year-old girl. The light that she knitted by was dim and strained her eyes, but since she did not have electricity in her cottage at the gate, she did not feel the lack of adequate light. Two more rows and she would go down the back stairs to bring up the tray with tea and biscuits for elevenses.

The terms of her employment had never been fully spelled out. She took full charge and responsibility for Maud Nugent, but the Nugents did not imagine she spent every moment in the chair beside the fire. They understood she would delegate the duty to a daughter or even a granddaughter, and no one was surprised if there was a not quite familiar face on the body in the chair. Even Maud thought of her nurse or companion—although she did not think of her by either not quite accurate description—as Philomena or one of Philomena's daughters. Preoccupied and self-absorbed as she was, Maud did not bestow on any of them an identity other than being an extension of the person of the old nanny.

———

WHEN MICKEY RETURNED—the encyclopedia had been very helpful; it was old and the description and illustration of a motor car was basic, uncomplicated, and assumed no prior knowledge on the part of the reader—he found his sister standing outside the garage.

Corisande was wearing a light tweed coat and skirt and her hat was small, fashionable, and sported a small wispy veil. Over one shoulder she had her binocular case, tags of different colors and degrees of fadedness attached to one worn, brown side. She looked elegant and very pretty, but Mickey did not for a moment consider telling her so.

"What are you doing here?" he asked, his question, as was so often the case, a play for time. Mickey was not quick thinking—the slowness of his thought caused by neurosis rather than stupidity—but even he had no difficulty in guessing what Corisande, with binoculars and a hat, was doing standing by the motor car.

A lifetime of being Mickey's sister, rather than any inherent good nature, stopped Corisande from pointing out that all the evidence of her intentions was before her brother's eyes. Any interruption to Mickey's train of thought caused a momentary startled look, followed by his return to the beginning of the conversation or monologue. Sometimes, when Corisande was bored and waspish she would tease him by setting him in motion before sending him back to go. It always took Mickey a while to realize what she was doing; when he did, he would silently leave the room and not be seen until the family reassembled for the next meal.

"Clonmel," she said briskly. "Our new sister-in-law is arriving and coincidentally there's racing this afternoon."

Mickey regarded Corisande silently for a moment while he assembled his arguments in order of validity, then effectiveness, self-interest, and moral indignation—the last two overlapping—and eventually he said, "You want me to drive you to Clonmel so that you can go racing?"

"I'd like you to take me to Clonmel, where I would, in fact, go racing, while you meet what's-her-name and bring her home. I'll come to the station with you, if you like."

"We don't have enough petrol," Mickey said, weakening already at the prospect of Corisande taking the responsibility of welcoming this new and, to him, very unsettling addition to their family. It didn't mean he had to make it easy for his sister. As he spoke he became aware of a faint smell of petrol and, simultaneously, of the two-gallon can at Corisande's feet. There was also, he noticed irrelevantly, on the garage floor a small patch of oil, possibly of his own making, and a sprinkle of very old sawdust.

"I've thought of that."

"Where did you get it?" Mickey asked, his voice rising as it occurred to him that his sister had discovered and raided his tiny stash.

"You know."

"What?"

Corisande did not repeat herself; she knew, and she knew that Mickey knew. He had heard her. Instead she waited until he had thought her reply through.

"I borrowed some from the farm," she then said.

"Borrowed?"

Corisande chose not to dignify this quibble with an answer. They both knew that the green-tinted petrol was designated by the government for farm machinery and vehicles.

Aware that he was all but defeated and suddenly bored by the process, Mickey extended a hand to the petrol can.

"All right. Just this once."

Corisande did not move. She had expected a longer battle of wills with her brother and had budgeted time for it.

"I said all right. I'll bring the car round to the hall door when I'm ready."

Corisande glanced at him sharply. He had given in too quickly and some piece of information was missing. Then, remembering she had more important things to do than score points off her brother, she smiled and turned to leave.

"The car is lovely and clean," she said.

Mickey said nothing; he was waiting for her to leave so he could substitute the green farm petrol for one of the cans of legal petrol in his secret stash. He couldn't that moment imagine the circumstances in which he would use the green petrol, but he had no intention of being had up for using the green either on the way to collect his new sister-in-law or, worse still, with her as a witness and without Corisande to charm the garda on the return half of the journey.

CHAPTER 11

DUNMAINE, ALTHOUGH NOT similar to any of the architectural fantasies Daisy had entertained about Bannock House, drew from her the reaction she had anticipated there. This house was smaller, plainer, but a hundred years older. Three floors in gray stone; a small parapet concealing the roof and accentuating the straight lines, the lack of decoration, and, it seemed, the refusal to charm or seduce the eye. A Venetian window on the second floor, over the hall door, widened the proportions, allowing a narrow window on either side of the front door. Inside, the additional light alleviated to some extent the gloom in the center of the large symmetrical hall. The principal reception rooms, the dining room and the drawing room, led off the hall, their windows overlooking a long expanse of meadow sloping away from the house, uninterrupted by any fence, with trees at the bottom. Each room had a gentle bay at the farther end with two windows that overlooked lawns, allowing rather wider views to the east and the west. When Daisy had been shown, fairly briskly, over the house by Corisande, she had not at first realized that the top floor, originally nursery and nursery staff quarters, was accessible only by the back staircase; the front one leading no farther than a large landing, lit by the Venetian window, off which lay the principal bedrooms at the front of the house and, to each side, longer, narrower corridors that led toward the back of the house and additional bedrooms and dressing rooms.

Daisy had, until that day, thought the gardens at Wallinghurst—the estate that had once included not only Daisy's father's rectory but the village on whose outskirts the rectory stood—the ultimate in taste and beauty. Now she compared Wallinghurst's contrived vistas, gravel walks, clipped hedges and topiaries, to Dunmaine's overgrown herbaceous borders, neglected lawns, and lazy streams, and found them lacking. At Dunmaine nature had begun to reclaim the work of man. The hidden aspects of the overgrown grounds, of landscaping almost eradicated, made Daisy think of hidden treasure. It excited her, promising surprise and delight.

And she was—she realized, fingering the silk cord border on the once purple cushion now faded to a tired pink on the equally faded sage green damask slipcovers of the sofa on which she was sitting—thinking in terms of years, of life, and even, she supposed, death. This house seemed her home, not only in the literal sense that she was now the wife of its owner—one of its owners? to whom did Dunmaine actually belong?—but the place she had been, unknown to herself, searching for all her life.

Sitting on that sofa, in that library, in that house, surrounded by her new family and friends, filled Daisy with delight. The whiskey had something to do with her feeling, she knew, but it seemed as though the simultaneously confusing and clarifying effects of the spirits allowed her to glimpse some distant but profound truth. A truth occasionally dimly apparent when she read poetry whose beauty was strong, intellectual, and unsentimental; recently, she had also felt not far from that truth when she and Patrick had made love.

There were five of them in the library. A moment—or perhaps an hour—ago there had been six.

"Where's Mickey?" Daisy asked, when she realized he had
been gone for long enough for her not to seem to be questioning
a call of nature.

Edmund, tall, languid, Corisande's friend—boyfriend?
fiancé?—the man who had returned from Clonmel with her, sat
closest to Daisy, and it was to him that Daisy addressed her question. Although Edmund was only informally connected to her
new family, Daisy was eagerly gathering any information she
could and indiscriminately forming impressions. There would be
time later to sort them out, to think about them, to try to fill in
some of the gaps.

Edmund's suit was similar to that worn by the other men, but
his shirt was crisper and newer; although he was not the oldest
man in the room, he had an air of authority and confidence. The
confidence—and the shirt—made Daisy assume that he was, if not
rich, well-off in comparison to his neighbors. Neither clue was
necessary to convince her he was wellborn: that was apparent at
first glance.

Edmund answered, but a burst of laughter, Corisande's, loud,
raucous, full of whiskey, cigarettes, lipstick, prevented Daisy from
hearing his reply. "Bats" was the only word she caught.

While she could see that Mickey might thus be described, he
was her brother-in-law, and this was her first day as part of the
Dunmaine Nugent family. Daisy didn't feel like concurring with
this non-Nugent and, she thought with growing, whiskey-fed
indignation, she wasn't sure she wanted to allow this slur to pass
unchallenged. But before she could compose a suitably loyal and
chilly reply, Edmund spoke again.

"Bats," he said, laughing, "literally."

As Daisy opened her mouth to ask Edmund to explain further,

she saw Ambrose Sweeney—she had believed him when he had
said that evening at the Ritz they would meet again soon, but she
had not expected it to be her first evening in Ireland—without
interrupting his conversation with Corisande, shake his head at
Edmund.

Bats, Daisy thought, repressing her question but putting the
subject on one side for consideration later. The list of things to be
considered was long, fascinating, occasionally worrisome—was no
one interested in food?—but definitely for later; it was all she
could do to keep up with what was going on around her.

Ambrose, having silenced Edmund, rewarded him with a dol-
lop of whiskey and then turned his attention and decanter toward
Daisy. She shook her head and, for insurance and emphasis, put
her hand over her glass. While seeing clearly that alcohol would
play a large part in not only the social life but in the culture of
which she was now part, for a variety of good reasons she had no
intention of becoming drunk.

Ambrose grunted and turned his attention to the silent—dozing or possibly dead—girl in a red dress slumped in a large armchair near Edmund's end of the sofa. She had, earlier in the
evening, when she had first seated herself, sat down heavily in a
manner that had scooted the armchair back far enough effectively
to separate her from the group. Daisy, herself listening more than
talking, had not heard her utter a syllable.

"How about you, sweetie?" Ambrose asked, pouring a little
more into the girl's empty but securely held glass. The girl, seemingly comatose, did not respond.

"Are you sure she wants another drink?" Daisy asked nervously, aware her question, like her motives—proprietorial protection of the carpet; of the, in England, virtually unobtainable
whiskey; an end-of-a-long-day reluctance to deal with a suddenly
drunken girl—was hopelessly bourgeois.

"Absolutely," Ambrose said, adjusting slightly the angle of the heavy cut-glass tumbler in the girl's hand.

"Literal bats?" Daisy asked, turning back to Edmund, determined to get some satisfaction in her own—her own?—house.

"Patrick didn't tell you?"

"No. What bats?"

"And what about Granny? Have you met her yet?"

Granny. Ambrose had asked the same question. Another subject on which Edmund might cast some light. Daisy was not sure, however, that she wanted to put herself in the position of questioning a comparative stranger about her own family. In a general sort of way Daisy tried not to ask questions; she had noticed it was among the less efficient methods of gathering information. To say nothing of it lacking dignity.

"Bats?"

"I would have thought Patrick—"

"Edmund!" Daisy said, attempting the she-who-must-be-obeyed tone she had noticed Corisande from time to time using with Edmund.

"You're not afraid of bats, are you?"

"Of course not," Daisy said scornfully, and not quite truthfully.

"The largest colony of long-eared bats in Europe lives at Dunmaine. Mickey rather makes pets of them."

How would you go about making a pet of a bat, Daisy wondered. And, rather more important, *where* does he engage in this pet-making.

"They live in the attic at the north end of the house. Mickey doesn't like them to be disturbed. They're quite rare."

"And he's gone to visit them now?"

Edmund laughed. "I expect he's just gone to bed."

How would one go about making a pet of a bat? Daisy imagined little saucers of milk balanced on pillars, Mickey climbing a tall stepladder. She stifled a giggle.

Edmund glanced at her; it was as though her giggle, mild as it was, marked a moment in the evening. He glanced at his watch.

"Bedtime for me, Partlet," he observed, putting his glass down on the small round table beside his chair.

Partlet? Daisy suddenly felt completely exhausted. She, Corisande, and the comatose girl, who had surely been introduced as Agnes, were the only females in the room. She glanced around for a parlormaid—there had been no evidence of domestic staff since they had eaten a light and not quite satisfying supper many hours ago, but—Partlet?

"Bachelor's quarters, *comme d'habitude*?" he appeared to be asking Corisande.

Simultaneously, Ambrose seemed to become aware of the lateness of the hour. Without looking at the girl in the armchair—her head back, her mouth slightly open, her knees touching but her feet splayed, her now empty glass clutched in a death grip—he patted her shoulder with firm affection.

"Time to go home, sweetie," he said.

The girl—Agnes—without quite opening her eyes, obediently rose to her feet and stood, not quite steadily.

"All right if she uses the gents' cloakroom?" he asked Corisande. "I don't want her roaming about upstairs."

Edmund cleared his throat and Corisande, who hadn't necessarily been about to reply to Ambrose, turned her full attention to him.

"Your sheets are on the bed from Saturday," she said, crossing to Edmund, and putting a hand out to him affectionately. Daisy had the impression that the quietly cleared throat was a call to order. "Come with me and we'll find you a hot-water bottle."

They followed Agnes out of the room and Daisy was left alone with Ambrose. He sat heavily on the sofa beside her; she could see one of his eyes was slightly bloodshot and there were small broken veins on the upper parts of his cheeks. Ambrose was not quite as she remembered him from the evening at the Ritz. His clothes seemed to sit a little differently and Daisy noticed that his speech was subtly different. He looked and sounded more Irish.

"End of your first day at Dunmaine," he said. "What do you think so far?"

Daisy's head was buzzing with fatigue, alcohol, and unanswered questions. How were Ambrose and the drunken girl going to get home? Was Edmund engaged to Corisande? What was the significance of the Granny allusions? Just how large was the largest colony of long-eared bats in Europe?

"Who or what is Partlet?" she asked.

"It's a nickname Edmund has given Corisande. She doesn't much like it and he knows it."

"Partlet?"

"*Canterbury Tales*. It's a Christian name for a hen. I'm not sure she knows that."

There was a short silence during which Daisy remembered the exact inflection Patrick had used when he had said, during the night they had spent in the underground station, of Ambrose: *"He always has beautiful girlfriends—he takes them to parties and neglects them—other men marry them."* Other men, Daisy reflected, might have a job marrying Agnes; they'd have to wait for her to regain full consciousness first.

Daisy and Ambrose, at the same moment, became aware it was some time since Agnes had stumbled from the room.

"I wonder—would you ever—Daisy—"

"Of course."

"You know where the gents' cloakroom is?"

Daisy didn't, but she smiled and nodded her head. Dunmaine was a large house, but it wasn't Versailles; she was sure she could find the gents' without directions from one of her own guests.

She opened the door into a study, and a large, cold, and sparsely furnished billiards room before it occurred to her that all she had to do was to look along the corridor until she saw a crack of light under a door. The light was weaker than she expected and when she tentatively pushed open the door she saw why. She found herself in a large and well-equipped gun room, at the farther end of which was a cubicle of dark brown wood and ridged opaque glass, the door slightly ajar. On the lavatory, fast asleep, sat Ambrose's girlfriend—if that was what she was—the girl Ambrose had sent her to fetch.

Daisy cleared her throat. She rapped on the glass panel of the door. She called out to the girl, feeling more than foolish as she did so. Eventually, she shook her gently by one shoulder. There had been no reaction to the sounds she made, but to the touch on her shoulder the girl reacted with a low growl. Daisy stepped back, with a vision of the girl coming out of her reverie—or possibly coma—and leaping for Daisy's throat with bared teeth.

"I'm afraid," Daisy said to Ambrose, on her return to the library, "she's asleep—I can't wake her."

"Oh, for Christ's sake—" And he rose to his feet.

Daisy felt vaguely and resentfully apologetic. She was not quite sure whether he was irritated that she could not complete the apparently simple errand he had sent her on, or whether he was lumping all women together as incompetent, difficult, and more trouble than they were worth. She saw, for a moment, that life with Ambrose could have its less amusing moments. At the same time she knew that as soon as he smiled, as he now did, that she would be charmed all over again.

"Sorry, darling," he said. "She's a dear girl, but she can't hold her drink."

Daisy followed him along the corridor and stood in the doorway of the gun room as Ambrose advanced on the cloakroom door. The cubicle, although large enough to contain a washbasin as well as a lavatory, was narrow and wood-paneled. The drunken girl, now snoring gently, lolled with her head against a framed photograph of a racehorse being led in by a woman wearing silver fox and a, to Daisy's eyes, old-fashioned hat. Ambrose regarded the girl for a moment, then clapped his hands.

"Pull your knickers up, Agnes," he said briskly. "Time to go home."

To Daisy's impressed amazement, the girl, without opening her eyes, slowly rose to her feet and did as she had been told. But Ambrose had already turned and was looking at a large salmon mounted on a dull wooden board on the wall. He was peering forward, hands clasped behind his back, in the dim light to read the small plaque beneath it.

"And so to bed," Daisy said, under her breath.

It had been a long and interesting day.

"WHO ARE THE Black and Tans?" Daisy asked.

"A hunt on the Limerick and Tipperary borders," Corisande said, her attention visibly not on Daisy.

There was a yip of laughter from Edmund.

"I think Daisy means 'Who were the Black and Tans?' " he said.

Corisande's face was expressionless as she buttered a piece of toast, but Daisy sensed she would not quickly be forgiven for making her sister-in-law look foolish.

"English people," Edmund said, "often say, rather defensively, that the Irish hold a grudge forever. And then they say something about Cromwell. The Black and Tans are a little harder to laugh off. They were twenty years ago."

"They were a supplementary police force," Mickey, sitting at one end of the dining-room table, said. "Pretty rough types—it wouldn't be inaccurate to call them mercenaries—recruited in England during the Troubles. With an unofficial charter to give the IRA more than a taste of their own medicine. Brutal, drunken, trigger-happy, and out of control."

At least Daisy didn't have to ask what the Troubles were. She knew it to be a euphemism for the war of ambush, assassination, and house burning waged by the IRA against those who represented English power in Ireland. That war had taken place before Ireland had become a Free State in 1921. The official euphemistic term for the war now being fought in most other parts of the world was the "Emergency."

"A completely indefensible moment in England's uneven relationship with Ireland," Edmund continued. "We might as well try to make you feel guilty your first morning. Why do you ask?"

Daisy had descended to breakfast after a wakeful night during which her head had spun with a multitude of unanswered questions. Most of them—the more important ones—either because those present at the breakfast table were ignorant of the answers, or because the questions required a delicate approach, would have to wait. In the meantime, she was trying to fill in some of the enormous blanks and frightening gaps in her knowledge of Patrick and his family.

"Patrick said something about them—staying with your cousins—and I forgot to ask him afterward," Daisy said, thinking about the overheard breakfast conversation at the house party in the Lake District. The courtship had been so brief and so urgent that she had never asked Patrick for an explanation of the ostensible—but clearly not actual—reason for the flare-up between him and Aunt Glad. And she had not asked him later about the real cause of the row. The spats between Patrick and the Nugent sisters she thought were the manifestation of invisible tensions—

sexual or romantic—but the animosity between Patrick and his honorary aunt seemed deeper and more mysterious.

Edmund laughed and even Corisande and Mickey smiled knowingly. Daisy looked to Edmund for an explanation.

"The usual trap. We all fall into it in England. Someone says something stupid or provocative and you find yourself defending positions that would be completely contrary to the ones you would hold in Ireland. The little I know of the Nugents, I would probably become an honorary Sinn Féiner in their presence," Edmund said, adding, as Daisy still looked mystified, "The extreme Irish nationalist party."

Daisy would have liked to question Edmund further, but Corisande sighed, so she crossed the room to the sideboard and helped herself to a large plate of bacon and eggs—breakfast apparently intended to be a more substantial meal than dinner at Dunmaine—and sat down. There was silence until Edmund put his napkin beside his plate, stood up, kissed Corisande on her forehead without any reciprocal gesture of affection on her part, and left the room.

Corisande seemed happy enough to allow Daisy to finish her greasy eggs and to chew her soggy toast in silence. The tea was hot and strong, and Daisy had enough to think about to be content to eat without talking. Nevertheless, she wondered a little at Corisande's lack of hospitable conversation; her sister-in-law had not even asked if she had slept well. It seemed that there was a similarity in manners between the Westmoreland and Irish Nugents.

She had slept deeply rather than well—her mind had been racing even while asleep—not only exhausted but heavily sedated with alcohol. Perhaps Corisande was hung over; Daisy glanced sideways at her and decided this was not the case. She recognized the look—less than an expression—on Corisande's face. It was one her mother habitually wore. Just getting through the moment, the day, until she could get back to and concentrate on whatever it was that held her entire interest. Which was? There were more important facts to be uncovered, but Daisy thought they all tied together, and that she was unlikely to be given any answers before breakfast was cleared away.

Daisy's mother was tired, defeated, and disappointed; none of these descriptions fit Corisande. But the bored, irritated, sealed-off, intensely preoccupied look was the same. Corisande's complete lack of interest in Daisy suggested the preoccupation did not pertain to family or home. Nor did it suggest—it was not soft enough and far too restless—a life ruled by love or sexual passion. Daisy recalled Corisande's response to Edmund's quietly cleared throat the night before and knew Corisande was determined to marry him. She also knew, with absolute certainty, that Corisande wanted to marry Edmund because she needed to be married. She needed to be married, and she had no alternative suitable man in her sights and no plan for how to live out the rest of her life if she did not marry. It also seemed quite possible that Edmund was aware of this.

"Who is Agnes?" Daisy asked, both to break the silence and as a preliminary to a further question about how Ambrose and the drunken girl had got home. Petrol, other than the farm issue, Daisy had learned the night before, being available only for doctors and priests.

During Corisande's silence it occurred to Daisy that Corisande might be jealous of any girl Ambrose brought to the house.

Corisande sighed again—there had been a long enough pause for Daisy to assume that Agnes was not the cause of the sigh—then she got up and crossed to the side table where the remains of breakfast were being kept warm in two chafing dishes. Turning a small knob at the base of the wicks, she extinguished the squat blue flames. On her way back toward the table, she reacted to something, unseen by Daisy or Mickey, outside the window.

Mickey got up and left the room. Shortly afterward there was a hollow metallic sound similar to the one made by the car the evening before when it had driven over the grid of hollow pipes that prevented cattle in the unfenced pasture from wandering up to the house. Soon there came the crunching of a bicycle on gravel.

A moment or two later, Mickey came in.

"Post," he said.

Corisande's eyes followed Mickey as he handed two letters to Daisy and tossed the rest—thin, buff envelopes—onto the sideboard where a pile of perhaps ten or twelve similar missives lay. Daisy could see that the arrival of the post was an important moment in the day for Corisande. Not because she expected a letter from Edmund—he had left Dunmaine only minutes ago—but because it was the moment most likely to offer surprises, opportunities, invitations, and news from the outside world.

Daisy's letters were addressed to Mrs. Patrick Nugent. She was for a moment startled; it was the first time she had seen her new name on an envelope. Both letters bore English stamps. One was in Patrick's handwriting, the other in her father's small, elegant scrawl. If Corisande and Mickey had not been looking at her with uninhibited expectation, she would have taken both letters back to her bedroom, settled herself comfortably in the armchair and, after a moment of concentration and readying herself, she would have slowly opened Patrick's envelope and even more slowly read the letter. Now she found herself having unceremoniously to tear open and read her husband's letter under the scrutiny of strangers—even if those strangers were his brother and sister.

She read through the letter swiftly, resentful that the moment should be taken from her, skimming, so that she could read an edited version to Corisande and Mickey and then take her letter upstairs to read in the manner it deserved. But the letter, although affectionate and long, contained nothing she could not have read aloud. There was no reminder of passionate or tender moments shared, no extravagant declarations of love, no longing for the moment they would once more find themselves in each other's arms. Wordlessly, she handed the letter to Corisande; her father's letter, at least, she could read privately.

Patrick's letter sounded quite different when read aloud by his sister; Corisande caught his tone in a way her own reading of it had lacked. Corisande's inflection made it sound conversational, but conversational in a way that addressed the whole family; the letter had not been intended solely for Daisy.

Daisy felt angry and jealous, and when Corisande read, " 'last letter for a while that I'll have the luxury of writing without the censor peering shortsightedly over my shoulder and breathing adenoidally in my ear,' " she realized all future letters she received from Patrick would not only have been read by one more person but have been written in even more inhibiting circumstances than had this one. Perhaps next time, she thought, already composing her reply although she had not yet read his letter properly, he could enclose a separate missive for her. But surely that possibility would have already occurred to him. Or would it? How little she knew of him. Maybe he had decided to give all members of his family equal attention. Maybe he was right to do so. Daisy's time—it might be years—at Dunmaine without him would pass more smoothly without dissension, jealousy, and perceived favoritism. And if he never came back? Daisy brushed that thought from her mind and started to compose a numbered list of questions for her own letter as she half listened to Corisande.

" '. . . training we thought we would be sent to France. I'm looking forward to seeing the vineyards with incongruous Irish names and the trees with clumps of mistletoe.' "

Do you love me? she would write. *Is the house haunted?* Would that really be her second question? France—not France, of course—but where? That it was not a safe posting she had inferred from his complete silence about where he was going. *Why is everyone so curious about whether I've met your grandmother yet?* Probably it would be more efficient to ask only questions with a yes or no answer. Or ones with a choice of possible answers composed by herself; he could finish his letters with a series of numbers. Or would the censor cross out anything that seemed to be—that was—a secret code? Maybe one question a letter; she was now unbearably impatient to take her letter and go up to her room. At that moment Corisande stopped reading and Mickey put down his teacup and got up.

"Back to work," he said, rubbing his hands.

Work? Another question. Mickey seemed to work outside; his clothes were earth-stained and Daisy noticed he had left a small lump of fairly dry mud from his boots on the dining-room carpet. But it seemed to be something he was pleased about, so it was probably not a chore. Daisy was confident this, at least, she would have had explained by the end of the day. She imagined it was a subject he would be happy to discuss, although no doubt Corisande's eyes would glaze over while Daisy was being enlightened.

Taking her letters in her hand, Daisy went upstairs. Her bed had been made and the room looked tidy. One of the two bedrooms separated by the landing with the Venetian window at the front of the house, it seemed to have been the best spare room. Now, she supposed, it was hers and Patrick's. The evening before she had found Patrick's old room with its simple bed, some photographs, worn silver-backed hairbrushes, some mementos meaningless to Daisy, and a saucer with keys, buttons, and low denomination coins—their design still unfamiliar. She had opened the door of the wardrobe and sniffed the tweed jackets and solitary, worn gray suit, hoping for a trace of his smell, but there was only the camphor scent of old mothballs. She'd wondered who had put them there.

Their new room was large, with a big bed and an inadequate reading lamp. There was a chaise longue, Edwardian, a little lumpy but designed for the bedroom or boudoir of a married woman.

Daisy took a pillow from her bed and settled comfortably with her letters. A couple of cushions and a shawl would make the chaise a place she could happily recline and read. A window behind it provided enough light, at least during the day, and presumably she was meant to spend her evenings downstairs with the family. Against the wall between the two windows overlooking the fields—park?—there was a small, rather pretty, writing desk. All it needed was a chair. She assumed no one would object to her making small changes in this room although it would probably be polite not to turn it into a bed-sitting-room; she imagined for a moment a gas fire and a hot plate, and it occurred to her that during a southwestern Irish winter such additions might not be unwelcome.

Wriggling herself comfortable, Daisy opened her father's letter, saving Patrick's to read again a little later when she had settled herself enough to read it at her own pace and to try to have a sense of Patrick as she did so. Her father's letter covered both sides of a single sheet. She wondered how he had filled so much space; she had left home only four days ago. Her life had changed immeasurably but, as most children do, she imagined not much happened when she wasn't present.

> *My dear Daisy,*
> *By now you will be in your new home, and we are eagerly awaiting a letter from you telling us you arrived safely and giving us some sense of Patrick's family.*

I imagine for a little while now your letters will be full of interesting news and descriptions of your new life and ours will be full of the dull and familiar. That won't stop me writing, however. I don't want you to be homesick and I miss you less when I am writing to you or planning a letter to you.

Daisy paused to see, in her mind's eye, her father at his desk in his study. The door, of course, closed. When at home, she was on the other side of that closed door. From the time she had gone away to boarding school, and during her year as a Land Girl, she had enjoyed a closer relationship with her father through the written word than she had since she had been young enough to sit on his knee. It did not make her happy to know that he required distance in order to express his affection, but it was one of the reasons she preferred to read his letters in private.

On a practical matter, loath though I was to forgo the traditional prospective son-in-law interview with Patrick, the war and your wishes seemed to make such a conversation irrelevant. So I have no way of knowing what your or, indeed, his circumstances are in the way of material things, money, and property.

Daisy paused and blinked, she knew no more than her father did. She had, during the course of the previous night, waking from an anxious dream—in which she had gone to a race meeting in a strapless cocktail dress—wondered about clothes, money to buy them, and then about her responsibilities as Patrick's wife. She assumed Corisande kept house after a fashion, but who, for instance, paid the bills? And then she wondered how her own— since her wedding—tiny savings would be replenished when they were spent. She had about five pounds left; although she imagined her day to day expenditure would be modest, she would have the normal small needs for money: postage stamps, toothpaste, the collection in church on Sunday morning, and presumably, in time, the occasional present. She and Patrick had never spoken about money and she felt he should have asked her if she had, for instance, enough money for her journey to Ireland. The conversation that had never taken place between him and her father would presumably have touched on Patrick's ability to support a wife, the peacetime questions of prospects and expectations being suspended for the duration. Daisy thought perhaps her father would have been inhibited by the likelihood that Patrick's family were rather better off than he was.

So money was another matter to be, perhaps, touched on lightly in her letter; although a difficult one for Patrick to respond to, if the letter were to be read first by the censor and then, as a group, by the family. Daisy sighed; it was the first sigh of her marriage.

I have been for some years the trustee of a very small bequest made to you by my mother just before she died. There are several reasons I have never mentioned it to you. You became a wage earner soon after you left school and joined the Land Army; although she did not specify it, I always felt your grandmother intended it for you on your marriage; and, most important, she chose to leave some money to you but not to Joan.

Daisy's father was the only person she knew who used semicolons in a letter. She was amused by his precision and at the thought that her life was, at last, shaping up the way she, as a faithful reader of the nineteenth-century novel, thought it should. Marriage, an old and beautiful house, now a will.

At the time I remonstrated with my mother, but she was a stubborn woman, at an age when she could take an unreasonable dislike to a two-year-old child not on her best behavior and disinherit her in favor of a baby with a sunny disposition. She was, nevertheless, of sound mind in the legal sense. It seemed foolish to cause trouble between you and your sister and I am of two minds—although we should not, of course, resort to deceit—as to when or even whether we should mention it to Joan. It seems more than a little unfair that one unfortunate moment should have so influenced my mother.

Her father should not worry about his letters from the rectory being uninteresting to Daisy. She would now demand a full and complete account of how exactly Joan, at the age of two, had managed to get herself disinherited. Although the wording of her father's letter betrayed nothing, Daisy suspected him of not being devoid of humor about this as yet undescribed event.

The income from the bonds has, of course, been reinvested over the years. At present it comes to about forty pounds a year. Not a fortune, but what used to be called pin money. Unless you wish it to the contrary, I propose to draw last year's income and send you a check for forty pounds and will instruct the bank to credit the quarterly payments to your bank account as soon as you let me know where you have opened one. If you have no use or need for this money, it could be left to grow and would in time make something useful for a daughter or younger son. Please let me know what you decide.

The heroines whose adventures Daisy most enjoyed reading all had private incomes. It wasn't necessary for them to be rich: too much money, for example, made Emma Woodhouse a little unsympathetic. Daisy read accounts of Dickensian poverty or of the lives of Mrs. Gaskell's Industrial Revolution mill workers with sympathy and pity, but not with the pleasure she experienced knowing that Catherine Morland had set off for Bath with ten guineas in her reticule. Now she, too, was a woman of means, however modest. She felt grateful to her unremembered grandmother, and to her father for his well-timed letter and for his thoughtful decision to start her off with a whole year's income. She would write to him and walk down to the post office after lunch. Taking, of course, a letter to Patrick.

"GRANDMA, IT'S CORISANDE."

Maud was half asleep. Every bone in her body felt loose and warm; her bed held her as comfortably as though she were floating in warm water, the pillows on which her head rested soft and comforting. Last night the rheumatism in her leg had been acting up and her sleep had been intermittent and restless; now she was dozing, in the ideal state between sleep and wakefulness, her body free of pain in a way it never was while she was fully awake, her mind able to steer her thoughts, avoiding unhappy memories in favor of the half-dreams in which she now chose to live.

"Grandma, it's Corisande," she heard again, a long moment after the now almost forgotten interruption. "I've brought Daisy to meet you."

Daisy. There had been a Daisy—a daughter of the consul in Copenhagen—or Berlin—a girl with curly hair and freckles, but the young men had liked her. The third secretary, a young man from Norfolk, had danced attendance—*What was his name? Never mind*—and at the embassy picnic by the lake . . .

"Daisy," the voice, probably her granddaughter's, repeated, "Patrick's new wife?"

A short silence and then she heard a door close quietly and she sank further into sleep.

———

MAUD NUGENT, DAISY thought, must once have been beautiful. Her hair, now thinning, was a pure white. A whiteness devoid of the yellowish tinge usual in gray hair, or of the tint of blue employed to counteract that yellowness. Her nose was thin, straight, distinguished, and her skin pale and unmarked. Since Maud's eyes were closed, Daisy could not see what color they were, but she imagined they were clear and blue. One hand, long-fingered, slender, heavily veined, lay across her neck; the fingernails were short and buffed.

Daisy could not tell whether the old lady was asleep or whether her lack of consciousness had some other significance. No one had told her anything about Mrs. Nugent, but they had all managed to suggest there was something unusual that Daisy would see for herself. But all she could see was Patrick's grandmother asleep and failing to react to Corisande's thoughtless interruption. And she could think of no reason other than rudeness or apathy that had caused Corisande to wait almost a week before attempting this surely no more than ritual introduction.

What did the hints, the half sentences, signify? Was Maud—and even here Daisy hesitated. What was she supposed to call the old lady? Mrs. Nugent, she supposed. But normally there would be a response asking her to call her—what? Grandma, like Corisande had? Surely not. Was Maud—Mrs. Nugent—in a coma? Terminally ill? Senile? And who, in heaven's name, would tell her? Another question for Patrick? Or Ambrose? Or should she first ask Patrick if she could question Ambrose about his—their—family? Daisy followed Corisande out of the room, by far the warmest in the house, holding back a silent, interior fit of hysteria. As they crossed the landing, an old woman carrying a tray came out of the corridor that led to the back stairs.

"Ah, Philomena," Corisande said vaguely. She did not intro-duce Daisy. Corisande started downstairs; Daisy had the impres-sion that her sister-in-law had forgotten about her. She went to her own bedroom for a Nugent-free half hour before lunch.

What, if anything, did they think of her? Of the sudden mar-riage? Of this stranger parked with them for the duration of the war? And Patrick, what had he thought? Why had he married her? She felt that he loved her, but with a love that would in peacetime have been the preliminary to a courtship. A courtship, during which, as they grew to know each other better, their love would have grown into something more mature or, if it didn't, they would have gone their separate ways and avoided a terrible mistake. She didn't ask herself why she had married him. She had made a choice—not quite consciously—between marrying Patrick and a future in which she had not married Patrick. A future that would not necessarily offer many choices. She would be part of the second generation left short of men by two world wars. Daisy knew that the idea of girls having much say about the direction their lives were to take was a relatively recent one. And that choice—for men or women—tended to be inextricably entwined with privilege.

What choices, if any, had Maud Nugent made to end up thus?

"WHY DO THE vineyards in Patrick's letter have Irish names?"

Corisande stared at Daisy for a moment; her expression, as usual, lacked warmth. Daisy, although she would have welcomed a greater feeling of affection from her sister-in-law, did not take her coldness personally.

"Because of the Wild Geese."

The wild geese? Daisy waited, but Corisande's mouth had closed in its usual discontented line and her eyes looked at something far away; it was as though she were listening for the telephone, a knock at the door, the sound of hooves on cobblestones. Daisy glanced toward Mickey and found him leaning forward in his chair, in the manner of a shy child who knows the answer to a question posed, perhaps rhetorically, by the teacher. After a moment, and a flick of his eye toward his tensely daydreaming sister, he began.

"The Wild Geese were Irish exiles—after the Treaty of Limerick—well, actually the first Wild Geese were the Earls—the Flight of the Earls after the Battle of Kinsale in 1601?" He paused to see how much of what he was telling her was familiar to Daisy. None of it was and she felt ashamed.

"I went to school in England; we didn't really learn any Irish history."

"Why don't you find her something in the library after lunch?" Corisande asked impatiently. She glanced with distaste at the uneaten remains of the rhubarb crumble on her plate, and stood up. "God, I'd kill for a cup of real coffee," she said under her breath and, apparently oblivious to the other two, left the dining room.

The library was darker than the dining room. Mickey switched on the overhead light, a heavy chandelier; Daisy noticed, as she had not the night she'd arrived, that two of the bulbs were burned out.

"I don't know how much history—English history—you know," Mickey said.

"Just what I learned at school. I remember most of it pretty well. We tended to do some parts more than others. The Tudors and Stuarts seemed to get a lot of attention."

"Good, good." Mickey's animation made her feel slightly uncomfortable. Surely history, unless of course one was living in it, as she supposed they all were, was a dryer subject than Mickey apparently considered it?

"If you take the Reformation as a starting point—I know it's impossible to draw a line in history and say it all starts here; but if you could, the Reformation is the place to do it."

"All right." Daisy was thinking back to fifth-form history. Henry VIII, six wives, taking on the Pope, England becoming Protestant.

"As soon as there were two religions, it was all over for Ireland," Mickey said. "Until then the conquerors and colonists became enthusiastically Irish in about five minutes. There was a banal phrase in our history books about how they 'became more Irish than the Irish themselves' and most of the old families in Ireland, the pre-English families, are Norman. But as soon as there were two religions instead of intermarriage, you got slaughter."

"And the Wild Geese? The Earls?" Daisy asked. "They were fleeing religious persecution?"

Mickey paused, for a moment distracted, he gave his head a little shake before he started to speak again. How old, Daisy wondered, was Mickey. Corisande, she thought, might be twenty-eight, twenty-nine, a year or two older than Patrick. Mickey, despite an eccentricity of manner she associated with middle or old age, could not be more than three years older than she herself was.

Daisy missed the first part of Mickey's explanation. She was realizing that Mickey wasn't considering what path in life he would take, preparing—perhaps a tad lethargically—to spread his wings, deciding what his future would be. This was it. Mickey's plan, or lack of it, for the rest of his life, was a continuation of what was in front of her eyes. This was Mickey's home. They would grow old together. And Corisande—Daisy put off thinking that one through. She was not, under any circumstances, going to live out her life in the same house as Corisande Nugent.

"As soon as there were two religions instead of intermarriage you got slaughter. Henry VIII was stuck with being a Protestant;

Edward died before he could do much harm; Bloody Mary was a Catholic; Elizabeth I a fierce Protestant. Religion was brutal but unambiguous. Then came the Stuarts—mixed marriages, favorites, conflicts of private and official beliefs, and no one knowing quite where he stood. Cromwell and the Protectorate were clear enough, of course, but the Restoration, Charles II, and the Roman Catholic James II really did for Ireland. When the Protestant William of Orange beat the Catholic James at the Battle of the Boyne in 1690, Sarsfield—do you know who he was?"

Daisy shook her head.

"Patrick Sarsfield—one of our more satisfying patriots. The first Earl of Lucan?"

"Same family as in 'The Charge of the Light Brigade'?"

"Hm. Well, more or less."

Mickey's usually expressionless face lit up and Daisy was encouraged to add a thought she had had before but never clearly enough to put into words.

"I imagine that's what a good—a really good—education feels like. That you can see how everything connects. For me it's only these odd threads that join and hint at a pattern I can't see."

But she had gone too far. Mickey was looking at her nervously although she could see he was reluctant completely to let go of someone who might share his interests. Daisy wondered if this might be a good moment to ask about the bats.

"Yes, well—Lucan is close to Dublin. Soon after the Battle of the Boyne and the sieges of Limerick—you'll find all that in this history book—" and Mickey took a battered and worn book from the bookcase, "Irish soldiers went to France and later all over Europe. Some of them made good, although most of them ended sadly. So you get the occasional Irish name on a French vineyard."

Daisy crossed the room and took the book. There were traces of a partially erased name on the flyleaf; an ill-formed hand had written the words "third form" deeply into the paper; the book seemed to have belonged to more than one person before it had become Mickey's. Unless he was in the habit of treating his books very shabbily.

"The local priest, Father Delaney, and I have talks about history and politics. He gave me this. It's a textbook taught in the national schools all over Ireland. If you start with the accession of Elizabeth I—"

"I'll start at the beginning, and then I'll try and connect it to the English history I learned at school."

"You may be surprised how differently they read," Mickey said. He was moving toward the door. "Some of the Irish in France were successful enough to get themselves executed during the French Revolution and there were some Nugents who did well in Austria—probably distant relations. Very distant."

And he was gone. Daisy, still holding the shabby book, stood at the window looking out. At the end of the graveled area in front of the house, there was a chain looped between four stone pillars. Behind there was a steep drop, too deep for Daisy to see from where she stood; apart from the chain, presumably to prevent someone driving a car over the small cliff, there were no fences, hedges or visible barriers of any kind for as far as her eye could see. Mickey, now wearing muddy gumboots, crossed her line of vision. She watched him go around the end of the house and out of sight; he did not look up at the library window.

The library was cold; a fire had been set in the fireplace but Daisy hesitated to light it. Not only because there probably was some traditional time for fire lighting at Dunmaine, but because she suspected there might be a knack to opening the flue or warming the chimney and she feared filling the house with smoke. At home her father had firm opinions about how fires were set, lit, and maintained, and he did not encourage females—the rest of his household—to fiddle with his handiwork.

Daisy felt forlorn. Reminding herself her husband was away

at war and the feeling perfectly natural but not to be indulged, she crossed the room and sat at the desk at the far end. A letter to Patrick and one to her father, then a walk to the village and the nearest post box.

Seated at the desk, aware of a draft about her ankles, Daisy drew a sheet of writing paper toward her and put it on the blotter. The blotting paper bore traces of previous letters, Daisy wondered if any of them had been written by Patrick. For a moment she considered taking the blotter to the looking glass over the fireplace and reading in the reflection the words and phrases from past letters, but instead she reached for the ornate stamp that impressed the address on the paper. Then the pen and the inkpot, but the nib was encrusted with dark blue rust and the ink dried out. She looked at the writing paper, the disused implements, and knew a moment of fear. As though she were Sleeping Beauty and the last in the palace to fall asleep.

Daisy pushed the chair away from the desk and got to her feet. She reminded herself of her exultation on the train traveling through Ireland, of the excitement of her first evening, spent in that very room. She told herself she was English, had been a member of His Majesty's Forces, that she was the daughter of a Church of England rector. That was a new one, and it made her smile. She would write her letters upstairs. She would commandeer a chair for her desk. She would explore the house, have some questions answered, and if no one was willing to introduce her to Patrick's grandmother at a time when the old lady was not asleep, she would take the law into her own hands, find her new relative, and introduce herself. She did not consider Mickey, or even Corisande, hostile, but that did not prevent them being dangerous to her. She could feel apathy, like the damp draft at her ankles or the Virginia creeper on the front of the house, ready to subsume her, freeze her, bind her, deaden her, and render her passive.

"No," she said aloud. "I'm too young, too healthy, too English, too much in love." The first two, at least, sounded convincing. She took most of the writing paper and all of the envelopes and went upstairs to her room.

AFTER LUNCH EACH day the household retired. Daisy didn't know what the servants did, but they disappeared until shortly before tea was brought in. Mickey went outdoors, Corisande and Daisy to their rooms. The house was never completely silent. It creaked as the wood expanded and contracted with the seasons; the wind shook windows and whistled in the chimneys on stormy days. But no sound was made by a human between two and four o'clock.

Corisande, Daisy assumed, was resting. But what did that mean? Neither she nor Daisy was young enough or old enough to need a nap. Maybe Corisande slept to shorten the day, to reduce the time she had to wait until her real life began. Daisy wrote to Patrick and then lay on her bed reading until it was time to go downstairs for tea. Sometimes in the mornings she went for a walk: sometimes it seemed too great an effort. She was aware of a lassitude creeping over her. She, too, was marking time, waiting for the war to be over and for her husband to come home.

The afternoon of the day she had been to some extent introduced to Maud Nugent, Daisy thought it was time to make a more extensive tour of the house than the one Corisande had taken her on when she arrived at Dunmaine. Leaving her room quietly—tell herself as she might that this was her house, the exploration felt clandestine—she tiptoed across the landing.

She knew which were Corisande's and Mickey's bedrooms. Corisande had indicated them with a casual hand toward the closed doors as they had passed. It was the other closed doors that now interested Daisy. She opened the door to a schoolroom, a box room, a bathroom—all containing nothing that would suggest any of them had been used, or even entered, by anyone in the recent past. The rectory in which Daisy was brought up was Victorian and large. Even so, she was startled by the amount of unused and wasted space. It would have been different if the rooms had been completely empty, or clean, or if the contents were neat though sparse. But each room seemed to have been used as a depository for pieces of damaged furniture, battered suitcases with missing locks and handles, or basins with chipped jugs standing in them. Objects that a person more energetic than any of the Nugents would have thrown away. Daisy suspected that, although damaged, most of the furniture was to some extent functional, and she could imagine Corisande saying vaguely that perhaps one could be mended, another would do in a pinch, and that any amount of them might come in handy someday. And relegating them to somewhere outside her view.

Daisy felt discouraged and depressed. The future was hard to imagine, so much depended on events outside her control, on history, but it seemed reasonable to suppose she and Patrick would, one day, live at Dunmaine and that she would be mistress of this house and its spirit-sapping contents. She tried for a moment to imagine what she would do. In her mind's eye she emptied the room she was looking at, ruthlessly dispatching everything in it to the rubbish heap. Then what would she have? A large room with a cracked windowpane; peeling paint; a patch of damp; drooping and dirty curtains, all lit by one overhead lightbulb partially shaded by a cheap and dusty shade. It could be pretty—the windows were large and graceful, despite the cracked pane and the knob missing from one of the shutters—if someone spent quite a lot of money on it. Which brought her back to the question of how well off was the family. Were these rooms of broken and worn objects a symptom of comparative poverty or was it merely lack of energy? Or both?

Although now understanding Corisande's reluctance to show her over the house properly, and with a suspicion that she'd be well advised to return to her bedroom, Daisy opened the door to another room.

She stood for a moment, surprised, in the doorway. Then she stepped into the room and, sensing she had now come upon something private and secret, she pulled the door almost closed behind her. But not shut; it seemed, by some rule or instinct drawn from the fairy tales that had frightened her as a small child, important to draw a distinction, should anyone come upon her, between someone who had chanced upon something private, perhaps not understanding what it was, and one who was concealing herself in order to pry.

The room was small, Spartan; it contained a bed, a chest of drawers, a chair, and some shelves. The bed had a plain iron frame, the kind Daisy had slept on at boarding school, and on the shelves were some worn books. G. A. Henty, Rider Haggard, *The Just So Stories* and *Kim,* the Bible, and, Daisy noticed with pleasure, *Lorna Doone.* But it was not only a boy's bedroom. By one of the two windows there was a stand that suggested that at some time the room had become also a man's dressing room. The top was shaped to hang a jacket on with a press below for a pair of trousers; on a narrow shelf in front were a shoehorn and a buttonhook, and at the base a pair of hunting boots, a man's size, carefully polished.

Daisy looked around the room. It was spotlessly clean. The sheets on the bed were fresh and crisply starched, the pillow plump, and the blanket at the foot of the bed neatly folded. No personal objects were visible and Daisy didn't open the wardrobe or look inside the drawers. On top of the chest, in an open, silk-lined box, lay two medals, their striped colored ribbons flat and parallel behind them.

It didn't take Daisy long to understand that this room was kept as a shrine to Patrick's father who must have died in the Great War. It took her a little longer to realize that the room she now occupied—the room that should be hers and Patrick's—had in all likelihood been that of his parents.

CHAPTER 12

"DEAREST PATRICK," DAISY wrote, and paused.

It was the twenty-first letter she had written to him from Ireland, the twentieth since she had received his last and only letter. Each letter was a little more difficult to write than the one before; very little happened each day, what happened tended to be the same as what had happened the day before, each time she described her impression of something new she was aware of describing something familiar to him, and each day it was a little harder to have a sense of her absent husband. And she was worried and trying not to show it in her daily letter; each one carefully dated since it seemed possible to her that he might receive a week's worth all at once. Then she would think of how repetitious her letters must be and it would be harder still to embark on a new one.

She looked out her bedroom window, seeking inspiration in the unfamiliar view. At least this letter would be a little different; the writing paper had a different address. Corisande, Mickey, and she were staying at Shannig, Edmund Crighton's house. They had just finished a late tea and Daisy had come upstairs to write to Patrick before she changed for dinner. The house was smaller than Dunmaine and quite a lot warmer; a fire burned in the small grate in her bedroom. She wrote quickly, describing the slow train journey and the drive in the pony and trap at either end. Daisy knew the journey must be familiar to Patrick, but it had taken most of the day to travel between the two houses and there was little else, apart from telling him which of her two dresses she planned to wear for dinner, to write about.

She had begun, during the past ten days, to fill a paragraph with a description of what she was reading. There seemed to be no book in the library at Dunmaine that had been bought during the past fifteen years; prior to that time, a sprinkling of novels of the period—*The Green Hat, Of Human Bondage, The Constant Nymph*—had been added by, Daisy imagined, a female Nugent. Among the older books were Dickens, Hardy, military memoirs, and the complete works of Charles Lever. Daisy rationed herself, reading the lighter, more romantic novels for an hour before she went to bed, and during the empty hours of the day reading the heavier, darkly bound, seemingly more masculine classics. For an hour every afternoon she read history and this most often filled her daily paragraph to Patrick.

Every day she read a chapter of the history of Ireland that Mickey had lent her. She began the unfamiliar story full of admiration for the country and people with whom she was now allied, and read it unquestioningly until she came to the sixteenth century, when some of the events described seemed familiar but different from how she remembered them being taught at school. During her exploration of the house, she had seen a copy of *Our Island Story* in the bookshelf of the empty and uninviting schoolroom. She now brought down the old illustrated English history book and read it in conjunction with the Irish version. Side by side, they made interesting reading. Elizabeth: the Virgin Queen, Sir Walter Raleigh laying down his cloak so that she shouldn't dirty her shoe; the Spanish Armada; the tragic although possibly necessary execution of Elizabeth's cousin, Mary, Queen of Scots— as a child, Daisy had been unable to read this passage without tears, mainly for the unfortunate and treacherous queen's little dog. A parallel reading of the period in the Irish primer described the Ulster and Munster plantations and the Elizabethan scheme for wholesale extermination of the native Irish.

Our Island Story Daisy now saw as brilliant, but not necessarily cynical. Although she was only twenty-one and it was no more than ten years since she had last opened it, she knew that the stories and the dramatic and colorful illustrations were part of her memory and would be for life. And it was only because she had become part of another nation—living in another country would not necessarily have done the trick—that she questioned the truth of the images portrayed. The Irish history book—less interestingly illustrated in black and white and mostly maps—recounted an Irish version of the history of that period. Daisy had no way of gauging the truth, but knew the books accurately to reflect each nation's attitude toward its own history. The Irish history book presented the Irish people as heroic and high-minded, crushed by the superior forces of a brutal invader, intermittently rebelling, often with no real hope of success but as gestures of brave, principled self-sacrifice. The English version, and this was what most interested Daisy, felt no need to justify any action. The emphasis was on the dramatic moment, often further impressed by effective, colorful illustrations: King Alfred, lost in thought, allowing the peasant woman's cakes to burn; Henry I, told that the Black Prince had drowned, "never smiled again"; Drake finishing his game of bowls as the Armada appeared in the distance; Charles I on his way to the scaffold; Mary's claim that the word *Calais* was engraved on her heart. The reader was not expected to, and probably wouldn't, question the morality or motivation of the English people or their rulers.

Then Daisy filled a short paragraph telling Patrick how much she loved him and how much she missed him. She had written these sentiments before, every day for three weeks. They were less true than when she had first written them, when she could remember with more emotion how his body had felt touching hers. Now these memories had worn out and her words seemed to her, unconvincing. She wondered if his letters to her—the ones she had not yet recc·ved—were equally threadbare. Whether he regretted their hasty marriage, if he couldn't always remember what she looked like. These fears preceded the one she struggled to keep at bay; what if there were no more letters, what if he were dead? She finished her letter quickly, addressed it, but left it unsealed; maybe there would be something further to write after dinner.

She stood for a moment, looking out the window, before she changed into her evening dress. Her room was at the back of the house and looked over a field running down to a river. Fat red cattle grazed slowly on the still-lush grass; two horses—one bay, one chestnut—stood, heads sleepily lowered on the dusty, hoof worn patch under an oak tree. Already the days were becoming shorter. Daisy thought of the long, silent winter ahead of her, and felt desperate.

"WHAT IS MRS. GLYNNE doing here? Why is she staying with Ambrose?" Daisy whispered to Corisande after lunch the next day, during a moment when Edmund was diverted by a letter brought in by a maid.

"It's what she does. She travels around, staying with people." Corisande didn't whisper. "I'm not sure she has a home of her own."

"But why does Ambrose have her to stay?"

"God knows. It's a sort of tradition. When she's making a tour of her heirs she always stops with him for a day or two. And now she's coming to tea and it's your turn to entertain her."

"Shouldn't you be protecting your interests?"

"Aunt Glad would never leave her money to a woman. And, anyway, James has always been the pet. He can do no wrong."

Daisy remembered Mrs. Glynne seated beside James at dinner at Bannock House and the way she had laughed when he teased her.

Two hours later she was sitting in front of the fire, being once again questioned by Mrs. Glynne. Daisy, putting a good face on her allotted task, had seen this as an opportunity to have a few questions answered. Unfortunately, she had been sidetracked into the "milk in first" question and was already regretting her own stubbornness in refusing to concede that a woman's social future, if not her entire worth and character, should rest on the order in which she poured liquids into a teacup.

"Suppose I put the sugar in first?"

Aunt Glad looked interested but did not seem to make a connection to the subject under discussion.

"Suppose I put the sugar in first, then the tea, and then the milk, would that be all right?"

"Why would you want to do that?"

"I don't, but suppose I did. Would it be"—and Daisy hesitated, trying to find the exact word that would make her question clear to Aunt Glad—"common? Awful?"

"No, it would be unusual, eccentric, perhaps a little clumsy, but not social suicide."

It seemed to Daisy that she had succeeding in making Aunt Glad consider her point. Although it was far from the most important question Daisy had to ask, she had been determined to get to the bottom of one of the vague conventions that surrounded her, although it might mean postponing the solving of some of the larger mysteries. Her instinct told her there was a stronger, although invisible, connection between the two than the evidence would suggest.

"Let me put it another way. Given that we don't pour the milk in first, what is it that causes those who do to do so?"

"I suppose," Aunt Glad said after, for the first time in Daisy's experience, pausing for thought, "they pour it in first because they're frightened of staining the cups."

"Yes?"

"And"—Aunt Glad's face brightened, and her words came a little quicker and with the pleasure of making a clear point—"it shows they aren't used to good things; they don't know they should seem to take them for granted."

Daisy nodded, not because she concurred with Aunt Glad's explanation, but because she had been given one; the word "seem" might warrant some later consideration. They were quiet for a moment; Aunt Glad broke the silence.

"Do you play bridge?" she asked.

Daisy had been running through her list of unanswered questions—the mysteries she tried to solve in her head each night before she fell asleep—trying to find one she could ask Mrs. Glynne. When did Patrick's mother die? Was it she or Maud who had made a shrine of his boyhood bedroom? What makes Corisande tick? What's wrong with Mickey? Does Patrick love me?

"No. Tell me about old Mrs. Nugent. Does she know who I am?"

Daisy had worried, ever since she had come to Dunmaine, at the reluctance her brother- and sister-in-law had shown to introducing her properly to the bedridden old lady.

Aunt Glad glanced at Daisy with more interest than she had shown during any moment of her previous cross-examinations. It didn't prevent her answering Daisy's question with another question.

"Have you met Maud yet?"

"Yes," Daisy said. Aunt Glad had answered one of her unasked questions, the significance of days elapsing before Corisande had taken her to old Mrs. Nugent's room to introduce her. "Corisande took me to see her, but she—Mrs. Nugent—didn't say anything. She seemed to be asleep, but I wasn't sure if she really was."

"Sometimes she can surprise you."

"SOME OF THE Wild Geese—some of the ones who settled in France—the ones with Patrick's vineyards—the vineyards Patrick was writing about—were, in fact, going back to where they had come from originally. Although I don't expect they, or anyone else, thought about it like that." Mickey paused, looking at Daisy.

"They were originally Norman, you mean?" Daisy was having a harder time understanding why Mickey imagined they—he and she—should now continue a conversation that had begun in the library at Dunmaine almost three weeks before. Especially since everyone else at the table was weighing the merits and disadvantages of the current master of the local pack of foxhounds.

"Three daughters," said Fernanda, a dark, well-dressed woman with a slight accent, whose surname Daisy had not heard clearly when Edmund introduced her and her husband.

Her husband, Hugh, as clearly homegrown as his wife was imported, looked at her as though she had said something in poor taste. But Aunt Glad nodded sympathetically.

"So unfair. Three girls, all of them pretty, all of them with money of their own. And no son."

Fernanda opened her mouth as though she were going to protest that her own daughter—daughters?—was devoid neither of charms nor fortune nor likely to pursue the son—had there been one—of the MFH, and then changed her mind. Aunt Glad. Daisy thought that if she had married James, rather than Patrick, she would now be sitting in Westmoreland, in similar circumstances, with his family, rather than the comparatively friendly Irish Nugents, and was, once again, grateful for her lot.

"All of which has no bearing on his inability to exert any kind of control over horses, dogs, hunt servants, or the field. Or to get on with local farmers," Corisande said crossly. She was looking lovely and was, as always, beautifully dressed, but she had been edgy all evening and Daisy thought it would not take much to reduce her to tears. Daisy found herself crying far too often; not only because she was separated from Patrick and feared for his safety, but over novels and, sometimes, minor frustrations.

Edmund laughed; Daisy was, as usual, curious about him and what he and Corisande were to each other. During the weekend, as on the only other occasion Daisy had spent time in his presence, Edmund seemed to allow himself to be bossed around by Corisande and to be sent on little errands for her. Before dinner he had gone upstairs to fetch her cigarette case. During his absence the room had been silent, no one pretending that Corisande's request was anything other than a test of her power over Edmund. Aunt Glad's silence had been disapproving. Ambrose had whistled quietly, lying back in his chair, looking at the ceiling, his face devoid of expression. Corisande had been defiant and a little pink-faced. Daisy embarrassed and, as usual, feeling some responsibility for the tension. Mickey, only, remained oblivious. He had offered his sister one of his own Senior Services from a crumpled pack; her only response had been a look of silent dislike which Mickey, again, showed no sign of noticing. When Edmund returned he had given Corisande the slender silver box and kissed the top of her head.

"There you are, my little Partlet. Happy now?"

Watching Corisande and Edmund, as a maid cleared away the plates on which had been served bread-and-butter pudding—flavored with kirsch and dotted with raisins worth their weight in rubies in England—Daisy wondered about them. Corisande was unhappy; Edmund was aware of it but seemed only amused. And yet he had not struck Daisy as being cruel. If he were, would she not herself have been an easy and novel target? But to her he had been kind, polite, thoughtful, and hospitable.

"So in one column," Ambrose said, "we have a master who is at best a mediocre horseman, lacking in charm, authority, and sons of a dancing-partner age. In the other column, we have a substantial bank balance, albeit derived from what our grandparents—or, in the case of an old geezer such as myself, parents— would have called 'trade.' I'm not sure I see your problem."

Edmund laughed. He, Ambrose, and Aunt Glad looked amused. Mickey seemed to be thinking about something else; Daisy was alert, watchful; the others—Corisande and Fernanda and Hugh Power—angry, Corisande to a degree that made Daisy uncomfortable. Watching Ambrose and Edmund working in concert, she thought they were like sophisticated schoolboys. Then she realized that it was more than a similarity; they were two men who had never grown out of a taste for teasing someone smaller and weaker than themselves. Edmund was simply teasing Corisande. No wonder he had been willing and amused to run upstairs for the cigarette case; it allowed him to make more of a fool of her later. In front of the same audience.

"Beggars can't be choosers. He who pays the piper calls the tune," Aunt Glad said cheerfully.

Daisy couldn't tell whether Aunt Glad was joining in the men's teasing of Corisande or if she was operating as an independent agent. Or maybe Aunt Glad just meant what she said; she was rich enough to be allowed to mouth banalities with impunity.

"I don't see why you don't hunt them yourself," Corisande said, her voice unsteady. "It's not like you have to join your regiment or anything."

Edmund laughed; the rest of the table was silent and aghast. Even Mickey—for that matter, why had Mickey not enlisted in the English army as his brother had?

"The white feather," Edmund said, and laughed again. "I don't hunt the Lismore hounds because I don't want to, and so far as enlisting in the English army, let me remind you I am a citizen of a neutral country. Even Ambrose here is a neutral volunteer."

"One of the reasons I'm usually on leave," Ambrose said lightly. "I really only serve until cubbing begins, and I have time off for major race meetings."

"Cubbing is the beginning of the hunting season," Mickey said to Daisy. "*The Four Feathers* is a novel by A. E. W. Mason. It's about—"

"Shut up!" Corisande screamed, pushing back her chair. And she ran out of the room.

Once again a silence descended. Despite her embarrassment, Daisy wondered whether Edmund and Ambrose felt satisfied with the outcome of their teasing, or whether they felt they had gone too far. Did Ambrose really have a part time arrangement with his regiment? He must have been less casual than he seemed to have earned his Military Cross. And again she wondered about Irish neutrality: she strongly disapproved of it and of the stance of the Irish government; the attitude of the average Irish citizen was mysterious to her, incorporating, it seemed, both those fighting— or the families of those fighting—in the British Army; and those who hated England, seeing her as the enemy as long as the six counties in Ulster were not part of the Republic; now she began to see that even the attitudes of the Anglo-Irish varied, were unclear and inconsistent. After a moment, Aunt Glad rose heavily to her feet, as did Fernanda. Daisy thought, for a second, that the women were following Corisande in sympathy, and then realized they were leaving the men to their port. She got up, a little too quickly, and followed them. Ambrose smiled, although not unkindly; he knew she had missed her cue.

When Daisy entered the drawing room—she had gone upstairs less to answer a call of nature or to powder her nose than to take a deep breath and compose herself—Aunt Glad was talking intensely to Fernanda.

"An operation for goiter!" she said. "She always wore a pearl choker like Queen Mary to cover the scar. But Kate said she knew it for a fact that she'd tried to—"

She paused, aware she had lost Fernanda's attention.

Fernanda raised an eyebrow slightly and Daisy shook her head. Fernanda had assumed that she would have knocked at Corisande's door while she had been upstairs, but Daisy had not even considered it. She had no intention of playing a minor role in the drama Edmund and Corisande were enacting: a slave to Corisande's exquisitely garbed Cleopatra, a drab governess to Corisande's enchanting—

The door opened and the men rejoined them before Daisy could find a suitable play or Fernanda had a chance to reassure Mrs. Glynne; evidently the presence of Mickey had discouraged a too long lingering over port. Corisande did not reappear.

THE NEXT DAY Corisande sulked. The sulking was constant but the form it took varied, adapting itself to the occasion. At breakfast she was simply absent. Edmund inquired and was told by the maid who had taken up early morning tea that Miss Nugent was resting and would not be coming down to breakfast.

She was, however, in the hall, ready for church, when Daisy came downstairs. Daisy was wearing for the first time since her wedding the dress and jacket she had been married in. Corisande was dressed in a pale coat and skirt and another of her small hats with a veil that covered the upper part of her face. Her skin was pale and lightly powdered and her lips were moist and colored a light cyclamen. Her delicacy made Daisy feel like an overgrown schoolgirl. How strange it was that Edmund should appear to see Corisande as a teasable younger sister while others saw her as a delicate piece of porcelain.

Edmund ran downstairs tugging at his waistcoat and shouting for Mickey, who had been ready for some time and was now outside, hands in pockets, kicking gravel. Edmund seemed not to notice that Corisande didn't look up from the glove she was buttoning. He hurried them outside to where a groom stood, holding the bridle of the shaggy pony harnessed to the trap.

"Why don't you girls take the trap? Mickey and I will walk across the park and meet you there. How pretty you look, Daisy."

Corisande did not speak as they rattled down the avenue. Daisy hoped Corisande did not know that she, Daisy, was wearing her wedding clothes—so much less smart than what Corisande had put on to go to church and out to lunch in the country—and rather suspected she did. Daisy knew she was supposed to say something sympathetic and tentative to Corisande. That she should allow her sister-in-law the choice of remaining coldly and rudely silent or of breaking that silence to complain. Instead, Daisy said nothing, looking about her at the scenery with a cheerful expression, leaving Corisande stuck with her sulk.

On either side of the avenue were well-clipped laurels and yews and, a little farther on, fields and then more laurels as they passed between the large, open gates and their substantial stone pillars. As the pony turned downhill into a narrow lane, Daisy noticed the public road was not only less wide but less well maintained than Edmund's avenue. On their left, the whole way to the village, was the high stone wall that surrounded his property; on their right, a tall hedge with trees growing out of it.

A few minutes later they passed what Daisy imagined to be the boundaries of Edmund's land, since there were signs of other habitations. An avenue, little more than a cart track, led from two plain stone pillars to an equally plain, but not insubstantial, slate-roofed two-storey house. Daisy would have liked to have asked who lived there, not seeking a name or the anecdotal gossip that seemed to be how such questions were usually answered, but to understand a little more of the social structure of the society in which she now lived. Mickey might have told her all she wanted to know, and probably a good deal more, but he was strolling over the fields with Edmund, and Daisy, as was so often the case, had to answer her own question as best she could with a mixture of guesses, observations, and generalities. It probably belonged to a farmer. The house appeared to be nineteenth century; the land was fully farmed, a field with some red and white cattle on one side of the stony track and on the other a low green crop that Daisy did not recognize. It was not, she understood, a farm whose owner Edmund would meet socially, although if the farmer were Protestant he would, like some of the shopkeepers and trades-men, worship at the same church. These Protestants were part of a society that Daisy knew less about than she did the poorer Catholics who were employed by Edmund or the Nugents, or the inhabitants of the small cottages that were becoming more frequent as they neared the village. Whitewashed, thatched, a half door between two small windows. Behind, a field—over-grazed, with a few thistles and some ragweed—and a shed. Daisy knew that, unlike the farmhouse which would have indoor plumbing, these houses depended on a tap in the yard, if they were fortunate—she was already used to the sight of shawled women carrying buckets of water from the pump—and a privy; they were, as was the farmhouse, lit by oil lamps and candles. The cottages stood back a few yards from the road, with small gardens, a few flowers by the door, or fuchsia growing over a stone wall by the gate.

The church bell was still ringing as they arrived in the village; Edmund and Mickey were already there, talking to a very old man. The church bells had been silent in England since the evacuation of Dunkirk. The next time they rang would be to warn of invasion or to celebrate victory.

Edmund still refused to acknowledge that Corisande was sulking, although she had apparently not spoken a word to anyone since telling the maid she would not eat breakfast.

"There you are," he said lightly, addressing them both. As they approached the church, and just after he had stood back to allow Corisande to enter ahead of him, he added, "I hope you're not going to faint, Partlet, singing hymns on an empty stomach."

The church was cool inside. Outside it was sunny and there was no breeze, but there was, nevertheless, a cold draft around Daisy's ankles. Corisande followed the service with commendable attention, sitting upright, standing, singing, kneeling, praying, and listening to the conventional but short sermon, without taking her eyes off the vicar. Even while Edmund read the first lesson; particularly while Edmund read the first lesson. While he stood at the lectern, Daisy was free to look at him as long and as carefully as she wanted. He was younger than Ambrose, probably in his late thirties, a handsome man but now carrying a little more weight than he should. He was what Daisy's grandmother called "a good trencherman," and it seemed likely that as he got older he would become heavy. She wondered why he had not yet married.

During the service, Edmund glanced at Corisande once or twice, but she did not acknowledge his attention. Her face seemed attentive and serene, her profile flawless.

After church there was the usual brief gathering on the graveled area in front of the church door. Parishioners loitered, greeting one another and exchanging banalities. Without food, drink, or the imminence of blood sport, this could not be considered a social occasion, but it was a time and place where the small Protestant community found themselves gathered and many of them were reluctant to hurry away. There were somewhere between twenty and thirty people—ten or fifteen families—and it was unlikely that there were more than a couple of additional members of the congregation not present. Daisy wondered if the farmer whose house she had been curious about was among them. Even the members of this small community did not automatically meet one another socially; perhaps five or six of the families were Anglo-Irish, the others middle-class Protestant merchants and shopkeepers. For the latter, this was their opportunity to mix with the gentry; and even the landowning, or formerly landowning, classes were often isolated and starved for company.

Edmund's groom was waiting with the pony and trap. It had been arranged that Edmund and his guests would eat Sunday lunch with the Powers before the Nugents caught a train back to Dunmaine. Edmund took the reins from the groom, who would walk back to Shannig while Edmund drove them to Corrofin, where the Powers lived, closer to the next small town, about five miles away.

Daisy sat in the front of the trap beside Edmund. She would have enjoyed the drive more if she had not been uncomfortably aware of Corisande's silent presence behind her. The countryside was pretty, the day fine, and the road busy with other horse- or pony-drawn vehicles taking local farmers home from Mass.

"Corrofin used to belong to Corrofin Court," Edmund said. Daisy had noticed he tended to give her a full description, both historical and architectural, of any house mentioned in conversation, but that he rarely added much detail about the families that lived in them. "Corrofin Court was ten miles away, on the other side of Stradbally. It was burnt down in 1920. The family took the compensation, such as it was, and Corrofin Lodge was sold to Hugh Power's father. That's its real name but everyone now calls it Corrofin."

"Lodge?" Daisy asked, imagining the neat, well-built, but undeniably small lodge beside the main gate at Shannig that she and Corisande had driven past earlier that morning.

"Lodge in the sense of a hunting lodge. Although that wasn't what the old marquess used it for. What it really was—" and Edmund laughed, "was a gardening lodge. The old boy was childless—part of the reason they didn't stick it out—and what he was interested in was growing vegetables. There were, of course, gardens at Corrofin Court. Properly laid out in, I think, the mideighteenth century, around the time Corrofin was built. But that wasn't what he wanted. He liked to grow asparagus and sea kale and all kinds of unusual potatoes, and he built the lodge overlooking the river and only a mile from the sea. Seaweed and silt from the river, that's what he put on his gardens. And he used to give famous picnics; my father was taken to one when he was a small boy."

They were now driving along a dirt road beside a wide river. Daisy could see, on the other side of the water, tall reeds growing out of the dark mud. She could imagine old-fashioned carts, drawn by donkeys, carrying loads of dripping mud to the gardens, and others, their wheels digging into the sand, as men with pitchforks loaded seaweed at low tide. The images, in her mind's eye, were pale; the thin watercolor of the past.

Soon they turned in at a gateway, smaller, less imposing than that at Shannig, but the stone elegantly carved and the wrought iron delicate and ornate. The avenue was straight and not long, the house directly ahead, elms on either side. Moments later, the wheels of the trap crunched to a halt in front of the hall door.

Corrofin was not what Daisy had imagined. From Edmund's use of the word "lodge," she had imagined a compact building, but the house was low and graceful. Only the center, directly above the hall door, was built two storeys high, and on one side a conservatory added to the impression of glass, openness, and light. A house built for the spring and summer months, not as a permanent residence.

Hugh Power and a couple of golden retrievers, came out to greet them and he led them into the conservatory and introduced them to the other guests. Although Corisande had smiled and shaken Hugh's hand when she had arrived, she still had not spoken a word. Daisy wondered if she planned to remain silent for the entire visit; even if Edmund were at fault—it was certainly possible the scope of his teasing had exceeded what Daisy had seen at dinner the night before—it put an unfair strain on her and on Mickey. The idea that Mickey might be seen as picking up the slack and shouldering more than his share of the social burden made Daisy want to laugh. She bit the inside of her lip and looked at the ground to steady herself. When she raised her eyes, she found herself looking at a handsome middle-aged man with the most charming smile she had ever seen.

"Daisy, this is Sir Guy Wilcox—Guy, this is Mrs. Nugent. She is married to Patrick Nugent, one of our neighbors. Sir Guy and his wife have taken a house a couple of miles farther up the river."

Sir Guy Wilcox. Taken a house. Sir Guy Wilcox. The traitor who had fled England nearly a year ago. On Christmas Day.

Daisy's mind raced. She felt as though she were a child who, dressed up in her mother's clothes, had suddenly been called upon to assume adult responsibility. She would have liked to have had an explanation of what was happening, to have been told how to act, react, but she found herself unable to flicker her eyes away from Sir Guy's almost hypnotic smile. She could feel herself being charmed and she now understood what the word "charming" meant; Sir Guy's charm made her feel like a snake, devoid of a will of its own, slowly rising out of a woven basket, obedient to the sound of a pipe's thin music. She found herself smiling and reaching out her hand in response to his.

He held her hand a moment longer than was usual—to emphasize and increase his power? What would Patrick have done? Daisy thought that he would refuse to shake a traitor's hand and that he would have left; but if she were to emulate what she imagined he would have done, where would she go? How would she get home? Or even as far as Shannig? And what were the others doing? She could hear Edmund's voice, loud and jovial, and someone laughing. Corisande seemed to be silent, but there was no reason to assume her silence was patriotic. And patriotism wasn't the correct word; Corisande was not English, but the citizen of a firmly neutral country.

Irish neutrality. A subject on which Daisy had, thanks to the *Irish Times* and Mickey, most of the facts, if not all the nuances. Eire, the Republic of Ireland, at the beginning of the war, had existed for only three years. Barely time for Ireland to settle her internal differences and to design and agree on a method of government. Eamon de Valera, the Taoiseach—the Irish equivalent of Prime Minister—and Minister of External Affairs, had in 1916 been jailed and sentenced to death by the English following the Post Office Rising. Revolutionary turned statesman, his vision was of a self-sufficient, intensely Roman Catholic country, emphatically separate from England. And neutral. Daisy had to this moment assumed that the Irish who weren't actively fighting the Germans as part of the English army were neutral in a pro-British way, and that the Anglo-Irish were entirely sympathetic to the Allied cause. So what were they all doing here, smiling and laughing and shaking hands with a notorious Fascist?

Now she was being introduced to Lady Wilcox. Tall, graying hair, no longer the beautiful young girl she had once been, now a handsome, elegant woman and, like her husband, a presence. She wore a black knitted coat and skirt that might have been made in Paris or one of the grander London houses. On the collar, an old-fashioned ruby brooch glowed dully. Country house jewelry.

A not unpleasant smell of roasting meat accompanied the glasses of sherry Hugh Power was now handing his guests. It blended with the unsweet scent of geraniums and a hint of mildew. The sun, warm through the glass of the conservatory, the domestic smells, and the view of cattle grazing in the field by the river made the atmosphere hospitable, benevolent, innocent. Daisy felt outraged, confused, then for a moment seduced into a sense of well-being, followed, as such a thought often was, by one of Patrick, and she found herself again outraged and confused. Mainly confused. Was Edmund, who seemed to operate under a more conventional set of rules than did either Corisande or Mickey, as surprised as she was to meet the Wilcoxes? Their presence in the neighborhood must have been general knowledge, so why had it never been referred to in her hearing? Because she was English and would feel differently to the way they did? Had the treacherous Wilcoxes been welcomed by the Irish Government, the native Irish, and, just as warmly, by the Anglo-Irish? Some of the Anglo-Irish? And was Sir Guy actually a traitor? He was a Fascist, and that was surely a dangerous and morally reprehensible political belief; but since he had flown the coop before he could be arrested, she couldn't know if he would have been interned, or—like the Mosleys—would have gone to prison. But that didn't necessarily make him a traitor. She remembered Rosemary suggesting not everyone shared Daisy's black and white view of the execution, during the Great War, of Roger Casement for treason. Feeling uneasily disloyal and confused, Daisy took a glass of sherry, smiled, and accepted the fact that none of these questions could be asked or answered until the Shannig party left Corrofin.

Daisy sat between Edmund and Sir Guy at lunch. Corisande had been seated on Hugh Power's left, between him and Sir Guy, with Lady Wilcox—Emily—on Hugh's right. Then Mickey and Fernanda Power and back to Edmund to complete the circle. Corisande was now quite cheerful, smiling and chatting; some-thing—the glass of sherry, the placement, sitting next to a new face—had cheered her up. Edmund caught Daisy's eye as she turned back from observing Corisande and winked. Daisy smiled weakly.

They sat down to a prewar English Sunday lunch: a sirloin of beef; Yorkshire pudding; rich, smooth gravy; and roast potatoes. The vegetables presumably came from whatever remained of the famous garden. French wine in Irish cut glass. Daisy was fasci-nated by the pocket of cosmopolitan sophistication in this remote corner of the former British Empire. She knew that between these isolated instances of worldliness, of education and architectural distinction, lay the cultureless world of the landowning, fox-hunt-ing Irish squires; the market towns, twice a month ankle deep in manure and the sidewalks hazardous with lurching, red-faced drunken farmers; and the relentless poverty of the rural poor. Between the Sunday lunch tables where salsify or purple sprout-ing broccoli was served, there were a lot of families to whom veg-etables were cabbage and boiled potatoes, with an occasional carrot for variety. And many for whom potatoes were the greater part of their diet. And over it all lay, almost invisible, the remains of an old and completely separate culture. And a complicated and, to Daisy, obscure political present.

Sir Guy was entertaining Corisande—and since Daisy also sat next to him, he probably considered her part of his audience too—with a description of his and his wife's domestic life.

"We both agreed it was terribly important not to let the side down, so we looked up our Somerset Maugham for hints about how not to go native and we change to eat our sardines on toast for dinner. I understand you're English, too, Mrs. Nugent—Emily could give you some pointers, if you like. Otherwise you'll wake up one morning and realize you've stopped washing your hair."

The description was funny because it was true. There was something enervating about Ireland—the climate, the cultural gaps and lonliness, the tolerant attitude toward eccentricity, the lack of an imaginable future—that caused Englishwomen to sink to levels of disheveled despair they could never have previously envisioned.

"Corisande feels as you do," Edmund said. Daisy had not realized he was listening to their conversation. "She wants to see me in uniform. Either in a pink coat as master of the Lismore Hunt or in khaki; she doesn't much mind which."

There was a moment's silence while everyone looked at Edmund. *Why*, Daisy thought, *oh, why couldn't Edmund leave well alone?* Even the Wilcoxes, who had not been present for the scene Corisande had made the night before, looked startled.

"Corisande thinks Edmund should join up," Mickey said helpfully.

"On which side?" Fernanda Power asked with a smile.

"Since my brother—Daisy's husband—is serving in the English army, it would probably make some sense for us to break the habit of a lifetime and all fight on the same side."

Daisy was impressed by the lightness of Corisande's tone; she had been expecting another outburst, another chair pushed back, another door slammed, more all round embarrassment. Not that the air was now clear of tension.

"My brother, who wore the Italian uniform, is missing in action," Fernanda said, although without rancor. Again there was a moment of silence.

"I'm sorry to hear it," Corisande said. "It must be terrible for you."

"It is," Fernanda said, "and worse for him." She paused, then shrugged and smiled. "But—what can I do? And, anyway, here we all are."

It seemed the storm had been avoided, or at least a corner of it weathered. Daisy turned toward Edmund with no idea what she was going to say. She was willing to embark conversationally on any safe subject, however banal; even those her mother considered the bane of parochial life, poultry and the servant problem. Or she could regress further and ask him how old he was, and if he had any brothers or sisters; anything to stop him teasing Corisande or forcing his fellow guests to declare their colors and personify a different protagonist and fight the war out over the unusually delicious apple pie.

"The accident of origins, the irony of war," Sir Guy said, drawing her attention back from Edmund. "Mrs. Nugent, may I call you Daisy?"

It didn't seem possible to say no—as a guest not only of the Powers, but of the mysteriously complaisant Edmund—but Daisy was damned if she was going to say yes. But before her silence could become uncompromisingly insulting—and Daisy was very unsure of what would happen once it did, though Sir Guy would clearly come out of the confrontation the winner—they were interrupted by the first voice raised in anger, that of Hugh Power. He was standing, having started to refill the wineglasses from a bottle he now held like a potential weapon. His normally ruddy face was dark.

"Sympathy for my wife and her brother, who is a very decent chap, doesn't make me pro-German. I was born in Ireland, I am an Irish citizen, and I can't think of a reason in the world why I should fight on either side. Enough Irish blood has been spilt fighting for England, and even more fighting against her for our freedom. Hitler's a dangerous madman and Mussolini—Fernanda knows how I feel—is not much better, but neither of them is likely to behave worse to Ireland than England has already done."

Daisy thought about the atrocities being perpetrated by the Germans even as they spoke, but then she remembered the Irish history book she had been studying. She thought Hugh Power was wrong but was not sure she would win an argument if she were to take him on. Anyway, shouldn't one of the men be making her point? She glanced around the table. Edmund appeared calm and mildly sympathetic. Mickey—who knew what he might be about to say? Sir Guy was a Fascist, dangerous enough for the English Government to want him interned, or even imprisoned, for the duration of the war, but that did not necessarily make him pro-German. Surely the point of a British Fascist party was that it had a different vision for the future of England; any connection with Fascism in Germany or Italy would have ended with the out-break of war. Or would it? Now would be the moment for the Wilcoxes to state their position, to make their case. But both Sir Guy and his wife were silent, and both completely expressionless.

For a moment no one spoke. No one moved; even Hugh Power seemed frozen in his semiheroic pose. The silence only lasted an instant and was broken by the person least likely to defuse the incipient explosion.

"Power—Poer, probably de la Poer at some time," Mickey said. "Norman in origin and Hugh here is a good example of what I was talking about. More Irish than the Irish themselves."

"I am one of the Irish themselves, Goddamn it," Hugh said, but his anger seemed to be already less dangerous. "My family got here five hundred years before yours did, and there are about eight of what you think of as the original Irish left."

"Who themselves came—"

"Mickey!" Corisande's tone was its most elder-sisterish, and Mickey stopped in midsentence. He seemed content enough with his performance, although whether it was because he had ridden his hobbyhorse a little farther than he had expected or because he had diverted a full-scale row, it was impossible to tell.

Fernanda Power was the one who broke the brief but significant silence.

"Ireland," she said, "the history is so—" and she paused as if searching for a word.

"Sad," Lady Wilcox said. She seemed grateful for an opportunity to rejoin the conversation with a sympathetic observation provocative to no one at the table.

"Depressing," Fernanda said firmly, but it was her husband, not Lady Wilcox, that she was having a go at.

"Goodness," Corisande said, glancing at her wristwatch. "It's dreadful, but I think we should leave in a moment if we're going to make the ten to four."

"She thinks we live in a country where the trains run on time," Edmund remarked, but his heart wasn't in it.

DAISY COULD HARDLY wait for the pony and trap to take them out of earshot of the Wilcoxes and the Powers, who stood, waving good-bye, on the steps of Corrofin. She was unable to imagine how Edmund would explain and excuse the circumstances that had led them to sit down to a delicious friendly lunch at the same table as the Wilcoxes, as though most of the world was not engaged in bloody combat. Surely affiliations in the largest and most savage conflict in history was not something on which even the most polite could agree to differ.

The pony's hooves crunched the gravel and then clip-clopped down the avenue; the trap had passed through the gates and out onto the winding country road before Edmund spoke.

"Hugh had to put down that old retriever of his; turns out she was sloping off to kill sheep."

Silence greeted this remark. Corisande seemed to have resumed her sulk. Edmund's eyes flickered toward her and his lips twitched with a suppressed smile. Mickey was quiet also, but Daisy knew his thoughts could be about anything and that there was no reason to attribute significance to his gloomy and preoccupied air. That he and his sister had remained mute for almost five minutes was probably coincidental. Daisy supposed the equanimity with which she was beginning to regard long, loaded, gloomy silences meant she was settling into Patrick's family, becoming a Nugent. Nevertheless, she required some kind of explanation from Edmund.

"Is this the first time you've met the Wilcoxes?" she asked, giving the question no particular weight.

"Yes," he answered, his tone matching hers. "They took what was the dower house for Winter Hill. Winter Hill doesn't exist any longer; the Moores sort of let it fall down around them—it took less time than you might imagine—but the dower house is very pretty. It's on a good stretch of river."

"Did you know, ah, that they were going to be at lunch?" Daisy kept her voice as pleasant and her words as unemphasized as before, while making it clear she wasn't going to let the subject drift off in another direction.

"No—Hugh didn't mention it. But I think the Powers helped them find their house when they first came over—"

"They did arrive"—Corisande now broke her silence—"rather unexpect—"

"I thought you were sulking, darling."

Corisande stopped speaking and pressed her lips firmly together.

"What Corisande was about to tell you," Mickey said, leaning forward, "is that the Wilcoxes got out of England about five minutes before he would have been arrested. If they were lucky, they'd have spent the rest of the war in an internment camp on the Isle of Man. Or else in prison, like his pal Mosley."

Edmund's expressionless silence prevented Daisy asking him a direct question; she felt as though she had forfeited that right by approaching the whole subject of the Wilcoxes in such a tentative manner. That she might engage Mickey on the subject in the presence of the stiff silence of Corisande and Edmund seemed equally impossible.

As they approached the station, the road crossed the railway line. The barriers that prevented traffic, such as it was, from crossing the tracks were down, and the pony stopped and danced, as far as the constraints of the shafts of the trap would allow, nervously.

"Damn," Edmund said. "She's not mad about trains."

At that moment, a man appeared on the steps of the very small but solid brick house beside the crossing. He glanced at Edmund, laughed, glanced quickly up and down the line, and went back into the house. A moment later the barriers lifted and they drove through. Daisy looked back, carefully avoiding the eye of either Nugent, and saw the barriers come down again behind them.

"Mosley, you know," Mickey said, "was one of the people who took a stand against the organization of the Black and Tans."

No one spoke the rest of the way to the station. Mickey had said his piece and settled back into silence. Corisande continued sulking and Daisy felt herself effectively silenced. That Edmund had chosen to describe one more crumbling Anglo-Irish house rather than discuss the presence of an eminent Fascist—two eminent Fascists?—at the lunch party, suggested that he, for his own unimaginable reasons, did not want to discuss it.

Daisy, sinking into the Nugent silence, wondered if Edmund was embarrassed that he had brought them to meet such a person.

It was hardly his fault since he couldn't have known the Wilcoxes would be there. And the Powers? They were apparently on good terms with the Wilcoxes. Fernanda Power's nationality and Hugh's anti-English feelings might well account for such a friendship. Which left Daisy wondering about Edmund's acquaintanceship with the Powers. It occurred to her—especially after his "citizen of a neutral country" speech of the night before—that he might not, as she had assumed, share all her English views and feelings. But Ambrose and Patrick were officers in the English army, so surely Edmund felt as they did. Or did he?

At the station Edmund busied himself retrieving their luggage from the stationmaster's office and made small talk to Daisy until they could hear a vibration on the rail. All eyes looked along the track and soon they could hear the engine, then see smoke above the small stone bridge that crossed the cut into the side of the hill, and the train chuffed into the station.

"You know, Daisy," Edmund said, as the train hissed to a halt, "I'm really very pleased with Partlet. The way she behaved at lunch. You know, I think any man might be proud to have her as his wife. I know I would myself, but unfortunately I have no way of asking her. She doesn't hear me when I speak to her and I'm no great hand at writing letters."

Before Daisy could answer him—she would have liked to slap him and, while she was about it, give Corisande a good shake—the stationmaster blew his whistle and began slamming doors farther down the train. Corisande mounted the step; Daisy followed her and stood on one side to allow Mickey to take their luggage from Edmund.

"I don't think this is the sort of thing you should joke about," Daisy said, with uncharacteristic severity. "It's not kind and later on it'll seem like a—like a waste."

But Edmund was looking toward the window of the first

compartment. Irritated, Daisy sighed and followed Mickey through the narrow door, past the grimy windows of the corridor, to join Corisande.

Corisande was standing by the open window. She was still silent, but from the angle of her head Daisy thought she was looking at Edmund. He was certainly looking up at her, his head a little on one side and with a small closed-mouthed smile. As the train lurched, a preliminary to drawing out of the station, Edmund nodded. Corisande remained immobile for a split second, then turned, and pushed her way past Daisy.

"Get out of my way," she snarled at Mickey, who was trying to put her suitcase onto the rack, and dashed out into the corridor.

"Don't you want your—" Mickey dithered with the heavy suitcase and then carried it to the window.

"Give it to me," Edmund said to him and reached up to take the suitcase. "What about her dressing case?"

Mickey turned back to the rack where the rest of the luggage was stacked, but the train was gathering speed and Edmund only just managed to catch Corisande as she threw herself into his arms.

CHAPTER 13

A LTHOUGH DAISY WAS not averse to becoming the head of her own household, she would have been grateful to have someone show her the ropes.

Corisande sent a list, surprisingly short, on Shannig writing paper, of things to be packed—she suggested by a maid—and announced that it would be easier all round if she were to marry from Shannig. Clearly this was true; were she to be married from Dunmaine it would be up to Daisy to arrange the wedding. Equally clearly, it was out of the question for the housemaid to pack Corisande's clothing and effects. Daisy would not have expressed this opinion aloud—she knew that being mindful of what servants might think was bourgeois; she also suspected that there was little in Dunmaine that was secret from the kitchen and, were she the sort of woman who gossiped with servants, she could have learned much of what she wanted to know from them.

Mickey took his sister's departure—elopement?—with equanimity; it was as though, after a day or two, he had forgotten she once lived with him. Daisy found herself grateful for his presence, although his contribution to mealtime conversation was minimal. After a couple of attempts she stopped asking him even the most innocuous questions about his family; he became inarticulate and sullen and his replies, such as they were, were not to the point. History was a bond between them; any question about Ireland's past caused Mickey's face to light up and made his voice full of energy. Daisy was still eager to learn about her new country, although sometimes she would set Mickey in motion and allow her thoughts to wander. Mickey would have made an excellent teacher, but Daisy knew better than to ask him why he had never considered life as a schoolmaster.

Instead, Daisy tried not to imagine what her life would have been like if Mickey weren't there and she had to live out the war, and an indeterminate period afterward, in the company of old Mrs. Nugent and the maids.

Daisy waited until the end of the week to begin her reforms. The kitchen seemed the obvious place to start. Armed with what she thought of as a preliminary list, starting with a suggestion about the amount of time vegetables need to be cooked, she arrived in the kitchen about an hour and a half after breakfast had been cleared. The cook, Philomena, and the two maids were seated at the kitchen table drinking tea. Daisy recognized elevenses and withdrew, telling them she would come back a little later.

She retreated to the library, the warmest room—other than old Mrs. Nugent's room, the kitchen, or the linen closet—all, in a sense, out of bounds to her. Already she could feel some of her first enthusiastic energy draining away. Seating herself at the desk, she started a new column of her list, things that needed taking care of around the house. She began with the burned out lightbulbs on the chandelier in the room where she was now sitting, the cobwebs in the corners of the hall ceiling, the tarnished rods that held the carpet in place on the front staircase.

When she returned to the kitchen she found Philomena leaving by the back stairs, carrying a tray, on it a cup of milky tea and a plate of oatmeal biscuits. The cook was still sitting at the kitchen table; she did not rise as Daisy entered. Daisy, who had intended to start as she meant to continue, wondered if she should say something, found herself unable to frame the words for a reproof, and instead, took a seat at the other end of the table.

Mrs. Mulcahy seemed to be about the same age as Daisy's mother. She was heavy, her breath came in a wheeze, and Daisy imagined her feet gave her trouble. On the table in front of the cook were two slim paperbound notebooks, one older than the other and both stained with kitchen grease.

"The baked apples at lunch yesterday were delicious," Daisy said. It was not how she had intended to start, but Mrs. Mulcahy's massive presence unnerved her.

"Herself is partial to a soft baked apple; she wants one for her tea tonight." When the cook spoke, her whole bosom, covered by a striped and not particularly clean apron, heaved. It seemed even breathing was a conscious and draining exercise for her.

There was a little pause. Daisy had planned to follow her compliment about the baked apples with some gentle but firm amendments to the set weekly menu and a question about the cold beef on Monday tradition having been adhered to even though everyone who might have eaten it hot on Sunday in the dining room had been away for the weekend. Now she could answer the question herself. Corisande had not countermanded the standing order; old Mrs. Nugent was entitled to her roast beef for Sunday lunch whether she knew what day of the week it was or not, and there were the unspoken but always implicit rights of the servants. Daisy also paused before speaking about the over-cooked vegetables; it now seemed possible that soft vegetables were an accommodation to Mrs. Nugent's teeth or digestion. It also occurred to her that the cook was not the person to speak to about lightbulbs and cobwebs. Mrs. Mulcahy broke the silence.

"You'll be wanting the messages," she said, pushing the newer of the two notebooks toward Daisy. Her bosom prevented her from reaching even half the length of the table. Daisy rose and took the order book. She had been reading, along with Irish history, for balance and light relief, the works of Somerville and Ross. Now she felt like one of the foolish and ineffectual English characters from their novels. Without voicing a complaint or asking a question—she had, in fact, limited herself to a compliment—she had been bested. No contest; holding the order book, she did not sit down again. But Mrs. Mulcahy had not finished with her.

"There's one other thing, madam."

Daisy soon learned that to be addressed as "madam" by anyone who worked for the Nugents was a precursor to a request or demand, rarely unreasonable, for money.

"Miss Corisande didn't pay the wages before she left last Friday."

"Oh," Daisy said faintly.

Mrs. Mulcahy held out the second notebook. Daisy took it; who paid the wages was a question she had not asked herself but had assumed that the grown-up in charge paid the running expenses of the house. It suddenly seemed important not to allow a silence to develop.

"I'll go to the bank when I go into Cappoquin for the shopping," she found herself saying. Mrs. Mulcahy nodded, and Daisy, dismissed, left the kitchen.

Lunch was minced beef, with snippets of toast stuck into the top; apart from an overliberal addition of salt, it was unseasoned. Two pounds of minced beef, to feed kitchen and dining room, might be almost priceless in England, but here it was merely unappetizing. And expensive.

Outside it was sunny and cold. Daisy and Mickey sat at a small table beside the dining-room windows. Soon, Daisy thought, it would be time to move the table closer to the fire. Mickey ate his way through lunch with no indication of either pleasure or disappointment.

Shortly afterward, the whole meal having taken no more than twenty minutes, he went outside again. What, Daisy wondered, did he do during the winter? What, for that matter, would she herself do when the weather got colder and the days shorter and darker?

Daisy was about to leave the house when she realized she didn't have the ration books. Aware that the bank closed before the grocery shop, and with the image of Mrs. Mulcahy's truculent face before her, Daisy, with an anxiety beginning to border on panic, searched the desk in the library without success. For a moment she considered leaving without them; it would be humiliating as well as inopportune to return without money. Then she thought that returning without tea would be a failure only slightly less unacceptable to the kitchen than leaving the wages unpaid. After a moment of frustration and resentment, reflecting that doing without the odd cup of tea or sugar to sweeten it was far from the worst thing happening to those suffering all over Europe, she went upstairs to look for the ration books in Corisande's bedroom.

Daisy had only once before entered Corisande's bedroom, when she packed a suitcase of her sister-in-law's clothes and possessions to send to Shannig. Now she opened the door, aware that not only was she unlikely to be observed—it was the hour after lunch when Dunmaine seemed as uninhabited as the *Marie Celeste*—but that the search she was about to engage in was legitimate and necessary. The room had the dead feeling of one that neither fresh air nor a living creature had entered for some time. Crumpled scraps of tissue paper lay on the bed, left there from when she had packed. The wastepaper basket had not been emptied; at the bottom of it lay small wodges of cotton wool, stained with lipstick and nail polish. No maid had entered the bedroom since Daisy had last been in it. No one had dusted, tidied, or changed the sheets on Corisande's bed. Daisy felt surprised and betrayed; with a glimmer of humor she now understood what her grandmother meant when she complained of being "let down." But had she been? Was the neglect of Corisande's bedroom part of a lazy and cynical reaction to a new and inexperienced employer—as Daisy supposed was now her role since she was being held responsible for the wages—or had Nelly, the housemaid with the untreated adenoids, assumed that without instructions no action was expected?

Corisande's desk was closed and locked. As were the drawers beneath. For a moment Daisy was unsure what to do. She had been brought up in a family where it would be unthinkable that any member would invade the privacy of another. The locked desk made her feel both guilty and insulted; nevertheless there seemed no choice but to persevere. Looking now for both the key and the ration books—not necessarily behind the locked lid of the desk—Daisy sat down at Corisande's dressing table and opened the drawer. The drawer smelled of Corisande; face powder mingled with scent that had leaked or been spilled from a small, pretty, now empty bottle; there was an open mascara box, worn down in the middle, the brush caked with dried mascara and spittle; a broken eyebrow pencil; the stub of a lipstick in Corisande's everyday color; all of which seemed, like the wood of the drawer itself, to have absorbed, and contributed to, the essential smell of Corisande herself.

At first Daisy did not see the key, then she found it concealed by a bottle of solidified nail polish and a crumpled lace handkerchief; she picked it up and closed the drawer, a little uneasy at this unnerving glimpse of her sister-in-law's toilette.

The inside of the desk was, in contrast, neat and orderly. On one side of a leather-bound blotter with a pristine sheet of blotting paper stood a large box of chocolates, on the other, a framed photograph of Ambrose. No sign of the ration books. Daisy opened the shiny, black chocolate box with the red tassel. Four cups of crenulated dark brown paper in the center of the box were empty. On the inside of the top of the box was an illustrated chart of the contents; Corisande had eaten the ones that contained nuts. Daisy smiled and carefully lifted one edge of the paper separating the layers. Two chocolates were missing from the center of the second layer. After a moment's hesitation, she took a chocolate filled with marzipan. She picked up Ambrose's photograph; in it he was wearing a tweed jacket and knickerbockers, one foot on a stile, a game bag over his shoulder and a double-barreled shotgun broken open over his arm. A dog stood beside him, looking up expectantly. Ambrose, a few pounds lighter than he now was, smiled at the photographer.

Thoughtfully, Daisy put the photograph down and opened a drawer. Inside were three packets of nylon stockings. In the second drawer two pairs of unworn gloves, made in soft thin leather. Opening the third—Daisy was beginning to feel like the heroine in a fairy tale—she found the ration books. They were held together with a thick red rubber band. Replacing Corisande's book in the drawer, Daisy wondered whether Corisande had forgotten that she would need hers or if she had been unable to ask for it since that would entail allowing someone to go through her desk. Daisy had so far uncovered evidence of selfishness, an attachment to a man other than her fiancé, some miscellaneous black market goods; who knew what else might lie in the other drawers?

Daisy helped herself to another chocolate, closed and locked the desk, and returned the key to its place in the dressing-table drawer. As she did so, she heard the pony and trap arriving at the front door and crossed to the window. On the other side of the landing from her own, Corisande's room looked out not only over the field in front of the house, but a little way down the avenue. Mickey was making his way past the overgrown laurels and rhododendrons to an area where the shrubs were lower and seemed to have been clipped. Leaning her face against the window, Daisy could just see the edge of a small grass clearing. A moment later, Mickey had passed out of her vision.

THAT AFTERNOON WAS the first time Daisy had driven the pony and trap by herself, although she had occasionally taken the reins in Wales when she and Rosemary were going to church or when they, on a warm summer evening, took Sarah for a drive and a dolls' picnic. The pony, Prudence, simulated terror at the sight of a couple of sheep looking bleakly through a gap in the hedge, but Daisy was in no mood for that kind of carry on. She had done some simple arithmetic with a pencil and paper before she left the house and she was running through the figures again with some alarm. Two pounds for the cook, thirty shillings for the parlormaid, twenty-five shillings for the housemaid, twenty-five shillings for Philomena. Six pounds. Twelve pounds if she were to pay them this week's wages also. Daisy had fifty pounds—the income for a year and one quarter from her small trust—in the bank at Cappoquin; there seemed something shocking about withdrawing almost a quarter of it to pay two weeks' wages. She felt worried and resentful. This was a problem that should not have been landed on her. She was uncomfortable about the prospect of telling whoever it was that she was owed twelve pounds and requesting that some more efficient method of weekly wage paying be put into practice. It was only since her father had sent her the trust fund check that she had had a bank account and a checkbook. What would have happened if she had not had her grandmother's money to borrow for the wages? She wasn't even quite sure how to find out who was responsible for household finances. It certainly wasn't Mickey, and she didn't look forward to extracting the necessary information from him. She supposed, hoped, that vague as he was, he would at least know who was in charge. And if he didn't, she asked herself, panic rising and then receding as common sense reasserted itself—and if he didn't, then she would telephone Corisande and have the necessary, if embarrassing, conversation.

Daisy tied the pony's reins to a telegraph pole; it didn't seem quite satisfactory but it was what other people were doing, and she could see no alternative. Corisande and Rosemary appeared to have the ability to summon up a small boy who, in return for sixpence, would hold the pony's bridle until they returned. The men in their families always seemed to have a groom or stable lad close at hand. Just at that moment, Daisy was far from sure she wanted to part with a sixpenny bit and the idea of adding another person, however temporarily, to the Dunmaine payroll made her shudder. She patted Prudence firmly and, she hoped, reassuringly, and went into the grocer's.

The shop was one of the most cheerful places Daisy had been in since she had come to Ireland. Two large windows onto the main street of Cappoquin let in daylight and the shop was better lit than most houses Daisy had visited. The floorboards were bare, unpolished and uneven; the softer parts of the wood had worn down in the areas most often trodden. A counter ran the length of the shop, on it a cash register and an accumulation of brown paper packages and bags belonging to the other customer, a woman in a brown coat with permed hair. Daisy did not recognize her but thought she might be a schoolmistress or housekeeper for the local parish priest. Mr. Fleming, the grocer, Daisy knew; she had seen

him in church. Mr. Fleming took around the plate on Sundays; he
had a strong baritone voice and often kept the trickier hymns and
duller psalms on track.

"Mr. Fleming, I'm Daisy Nugent, from Dunmaine. My sister-
in-law—" Daisy could tell, from Mr. Fleming's expression of
respectful interest, there was little she could tell him about
Corisande's affairs he didn't already know; all she could add to his
complete familiarity with the progress of Corisande's life and
courtship was the party line taken by those of the Nugent family
remaining at Dunmaine.

"I'll be ordering the groceries now that Miss Nugent is getting
ready for her wedding."

Mr. Fleming took the order book and glanced at it.

"I'll have it ready for you in about fifteen minutes." He set the
book on the counter, pressed it down to encourage it to stay open
at the right page, glanced at it again, and started moving up and
down behind the counter, taking packages from the shelves and
setting them down beside the order book.

At the bank Daisy withdrew twelve pounds in pound notes,
ten-shilling notes, and half-crowns. It was more money than she
had ever had in cash before.

The grocer was slicing rashers of bacon when she returned.
The machine hummed and whooshed back and forth, each return
dropping a fatty rasher onto a sheet of thin, white greaseproof
paper. When Mr. Fleming had finished, he ripped a sheet of
brown paper from a roll beneath the counter and neatly wrapped
the bacon in a small flat package.

"That's it," he said. "We'll carry it out for you."

He picked up the order book from the counter but hesitated
a moment before he returned it to her.

"Mrs. Nugent," he said, and Daisy's heart sank. Something—
the directness of his look, the lack of embarrassment, the respect-

ful tone but concealed irritation in his voice—made it clear this was going to be a demand for overdue payment of an account.

"Yes, Mr. Fleming," Daisy said brightly, appalled to find herself playing for time, simulating an innocence that had, just a moment before, been genuine. It crossed her mind that she had taken another step toward becoming a member of the Anglo-Irish. In the next two minutes she took two further steps: she made a six-pound payment on a thirty-pound overdue account and, robbing Peter to pay Paul, she did not write a check but took the money from the wages envelope in her handbag.

Minutes later, the boy from Fleming's loaded the groceries into the trap, and Daisy untied Prudence and set off for home. She had intended to stop at the ironmonger's—lightbulbs for the chandelier—but thought better of it, fearing a similar confrontation.

AS TIME PASSED Maud experienced less and less difference between being asleep and awake. Between day and night. One hour led to another and light and darkness seemed to alternate more quickly than they used to. Most of her dreams were pleasant and she had, during the past two years, learned to exert a degree of control over them. Tonight she was reliving a summer afternoon in 1890, a hot day during her first pregnancy, and a picnic on the strand at Woodstown. The pony, head down and drowsy under a tree, sandwiches and smoky tea on the plaid rug, the flattened beach grass underneath making small bumps, the perfection of the moment tinged with the beginning of a backache. Charles—long since dead—insisting she should take off enough of her clothing to accompany him into the sea. The ridged sand under her feet, the shallow water warm from a tide that had, as they watched, crept in over a mile of sun-warmed sand. And Maud, her young husband's hands supporting her, had floated, at first a little embarrassed by her protruding belly, then, with pleasure and relief, feeling weightless and relaxed, happily aware that her hair was wet and the sun and salt water were soaking into her body, refreshing her and, it felt to her, nourishing her child.

The dream started to slip away and memories of uniforms, letters from the front, and—Maud steered her dream, her thoughts to safer and happier memories and they floated, the past and present not being clearly delineated, to that afternoon when a young woman with a pleasant voice had arrived in her room, greeted her warmly in a not overfamiliar manner, and had sat beside the fire and read to her. *Evelina*—the first chapter. When she had finished, the girl—Maud did not know her name but felt that she lived in the house and seemed to be in some way attached to the family—had sat quietly in the shabby armchair, looking into the glowing, slowly burning turf for a few minutes. Then she had left, announcing she would return the following afternoon. Maud remembered it, without curiosity, as being strange; the present generation was not of much interest to her.

She could see a silhouette against the pale light from the fire. *Thomas,* she thought, but she could no longer see the image. Sometimes she imagined his presence and sometimes she knew that he was close by.

Her dream shifted to 1917, to the Troubles, the Civil War, to English uniforms until it came too close to Thomas's death. Instead of waking herself, she sank a little deeper into sleep and back to pre-revolutionary St. Petersburg.

MICKEY PADDED QUIETLY along the corridor off which lay Maud's room; he was wearing his dressing gown and bedroom slippers. He carried an old blanket over his arm. Carefully avoiding the creaking board outside his father's room, he quietly opened the door and, without turning on the light, closed it after him. He opened a window, lay down carefully on the bed that had last been slept in in 1918, pulled the blanket over him, and waited. The curtains were undrawn and there was enough light from the moon for the old ash tree on the lawn to be visible in silhouette. One or two stars could be seen intermittently as a light west wind from the Atlantic pushed rain-filled clouds across the sky. Soon a bat flew in through the window and circled the room.

My dear Daisy,

You are often in my thoughts these days. So is Patrick and I know that as soon as you have news of him you will let us know. We pray, at every service, for the armed forces and their families. It gives me, at least, some comfort.

On Sunday morning we celebrated Harvest Thanksgiving, rather belatedly because of the weather, and not quite as festive in recent years as it was when you were a child. Stooks of corn on either side of the front pews, a mound of fruits and vegetables at the baptismal font, and flowers at every window. After the evening service everything was taken away and nothing wasted. Your mother managed to distribute the fruit and veg discreetly and fairly—and so generously that the rectory ended up with a vegetable marrow and no grapes. The marrow is to be made into jam, rather to my relief since it was a large one and stuffed with rationed meat and minced leftovers it might have lasted for a week.

Your mother and your grandmother have had a difference of opinion and I am sorry to say. . . .

Daisy sighed and put down the letter. She was sorry for her father and thought her mother and grandmother, fond of them though she was, selfish and self-indulgent if they could not control their bickering enough to keep it from her father.

There was a second envelope, the stamp also an English one, and the address in her grandmother's handwriting. Daisy opened it, glanced at the first few lines, then scanned the page.

> *. . . I can only assume she is having a difficult change of life . . .*

Although Daisy was not in the mood for any letter of complaint about problems of the writer's own making, she was for a moment amused that her own new status as a married woman allowed her grandmother to make a reference to menopause. She skipped a few lines.

> *. . . so I feel I can no longer live under the same roof. I wonder if you would be good enough to look out for a pleasant, not too expensive, residential hotel, preferably close to the sea, and a church with an educated vicar, not too Low . . .*

Daisy shook her head. A residential hotel. Even her hotel fantasies could not encompass an Irish seaside hotel out of season. Or her grandmother in such a setting. She supposed she was meant to invite her grandmother to visit her at Dunmaine, but she wasn't going to take the hint. What if her grandmother asked her straight out? She shook her head again to dismiss the thought; she had other problems closer to home.

VALERIE HAD ONCE told Daisy a story she would never forget. It was a tragedy Daisy had not read about in any newspaper; she didn't ask anyone else about it, not wishing to know more than she already did. It had happened in Hyde Park, when a group of young and inexperienced WRACs were anchoring a barrage balloon. Daisy was not even sure whether the story was news when Valerie told it to her, or whether it was a rehash of a past disaster, or even apocryphal. The girls were attempting to anchor the balloon to mooring pegs on the ground when a gust of wind, or perhaps the buoyancy of the gas that filled it, had lifted it a little off the ground. The girls, about twenty of them, according to Valerie, had tugged at the ropes, trying to pull it down with all their strength and weight. But they were not heavy enough and the barrage balloon continued to rise; the WRACs clung on to prevent it from escaping and soon it was high enough for the girls to hesitate to let go. A moment later it was too late, and the girls clung on for their lives. The balloon rose over the park, caught the wind and was blown away. There was nothing any of the appalled witnesses to the disaster could do to help them and they watched as the girls, clinging to the ropes, drifted away and out of sight. According to Valerie, not one of them was ever seen again.

Toward the end of the summer, Daisy began to dream of the terrified girls drawn upward by the huge, silent, canvas monster. When she woke, her heart pounding, she would sit up in bed, force herself to take deep breaths, remind herself she wasn't in any physical danger and, after a while, she would try to go back to sleep. In her dream, as in her imagination, the tragedy took place on a sunny day and the barrage balloon was silhouetted against a blue and cloudless sky, the beauty of the day making the incident even more horrible.

The dreams had started a little after Corisande had moved out of Dunmaine, and they had increased in frequency after a letter arrived letting Daisy and Mickey know that Corisande and Edmund would be spending the next few weeks—until their wedding—visiting friends in Meath and shopping in Dublin. The letter mentioned neither where they would be staying nor how to get in touch with them in the event of an emergency. The letter had arrived the morning of Daisy's visit to the family solicitor.

Mr. Hudson's offices were airless, slow moving, and full of papers. The papers were tidy and lacked a sense of immediacy.

Daisy sensed wills and the management of small estates and the occasional renewal of a lease or sale of a parcel of farmland. Nothing pressing, nothing that entailed a sudden or decisive move, nevertheless the kinds of procedures that once set in motion would move, however slowly, inexorably toward an eventual conclusion.

As with her conversation with the grocer, Daisy had the feeling there was not much she could tell Mr. Hudson that he did not already know. Nevertheless, she explained who she was, spoke of Corisande's impending marriage, answered as best she could—not very well—questions about old Mrs. Nugent's health and about Patrick, from whom there had still been no second letter. Mr. Hudson—Mickey had referred to him as Hudson, but Daisy could not imagine doing so, even when not in his presence—nodded as though he were registering each new item of information in some dusty but neat pigeonhole in his memory.

"So you see, with Corisande gone and Patrick not here and Mrs. Nugent and Mickey—you see?"

"Quite, Mrs. Nugent."

"I thought I should come and ask you about the day-to-day management of Dunmaine. Wages and—" She broke off, aware that wages were not the only expense in running a house and remembering the small but suddenly sinister pile of thin buff envelopes on the hall table. And the couple of envelopes Mickey had tossed on the sideboard the morning of Patrick's letter; more than three weeks later they still lay there unopened.

Mr. Hudson nodded, his expression attentive, courteous, and apparently unaware that Daisy was asking him to pick up her cue, to volunteer some helpful information, to give her some hint of how the domestic economy of Dunmaine worked.

"Who is supposed to pay the bills?" she asked at last, a little desperately.

"Mrs. Nugent. Mrs. Nugent senior."

"And when—how does she do that?"

"I post her a check at the beginning of each month."

"Mr. Hudson," Daisy said firmly, "Mrs. Nugent is very old. She is bedridden. I have not heard her speak since I came to Dunmaine. I doubt very much whether she is in any condition to write a check or pay a bill."

"I think perhaps Miss Corisande Nugent deposits the check in her own account and pays the wages and bills."

"In that case you had perhaps better write the check to me and I'll pay the bills."

"I'm not sure I—" Mr. Hudson looked as though he had no intrinsic objection to what Daisy proposed but that he was not prepared to accommodate her in any way that could conceivably later cause him inconvenience or embarrassment.

"You have been writing the checks to Mrs. Maud Nugent?"

"Yes."

"And Corisande has been depositing them in her own account."

"I imagine so."

"Very well. From now on I would like you to write the checks to Mrs. Nugent, and—I will take it from there."

There was a pause while Mr. Hudson considered Daisy's proposal, then he nodded.

"Very well," he said, "but I shall have to consult the other trustee. The executor of Colonel Nugent's will."

"Colonel Nugent?"

"Mr. Pat's grandfather. His executor is Sir Ambrose Sweeney."

Having invoked Ambrose's name, Mr. Hudson seemed to feel himself not obliged to divulge any more information. Daisy needed to know, if she were to find herself the grown-up in charge, how much money there was, to whom it belonged, and how much of it was needed to keep Dunmaine running; it seemed she would have to address those questions to Ambrose.

THE FIRST TIME Daisy visited Maud on her own, she introduced herself and announced her intention of reading to the old lady several afternoons a week. In the afternoon, after the time she imagined Maud rested, before tea. She intended to make the visits part of her routine and knew that if she attempted and failed to make conversation with Maud these visits would become short, sticky, and pointless. Instead, Daisy settled herself by the fire—usually the warmest place in the house—and read a book that gave her pleasure. If Maud chose to listen—was capable of understanding—so much the better; if not, she could interrupt if she had anything to say to Daisy, or she could doze while Daisy read.

Daisy did not, during the first few weeks, form an opinion of how much Maud understood—of what she was told, of who Daisy was, of the story and wit of *Evelina*. After a little while she thought it didn't matter. Maud was Patrick's grandmother and it seemed natural that Daisy should behave as a member of the family, even if Maud, as it seemed entirely possible, didn't know, or perhaps did know but forgot between visits, that Daisy was Patrick's wife.

Soon, Daisy found herself understanding what the others, it seemed to her, had so inadequately described—Maud's mental state or capacity: sometimes Maud understood what she was told, sometimes she didn't, but the difficulty was to engage her interest since essentially she didn't care very much. Although Mrs. Glynne had once remarked, "Sometimes she can surprise you," Daisy was still waiting to be surprised.

———

AMBROSE CAME TO tea on Saturday. Tea was usually served in the library, but Daisy had asked for tea and the drinks tray to be brought to the study and for a fire to be lit there.

"I'll just pop up and have a word with Maud," Ambrose said after he had greeted Daisy, kissing her on both cheeks and giving her a brief but hearty hug.

Daisy waited in the study. The desk, to the right of the fireplace, was in the darkest part of the room. A tall desk, with drawers below the writing surface and with doored shelves above, it had been, when Daisy decided to use it for household accounts, closed and locked, but with the key, a yellowed ivory oval disc attached, in the lock.

After her interview with the solicitor, Daisy had taken the unopened bills into the study and opened the desk. A Christmas card and its envelope, with a postmark from just before the war—and the desk in the library, with its rusty-nibbed pen and dust-filled inkpot—led her to assume it had been some time since any Nugent had devoted much energy to writing letters or adding up household accounts.

Daisy took the top sheet of writing paper, too discolored from time and dust to use for correspondence, and opened the envelopes. Soon she found herself crossing out items on the list of money owed; the total of one account was often included as a previous balance in the next bill and the new total carried, intact, to the following month's bill. The butcher had not been paid in three months.

Daisy was shocked by the length and range of debt incurred. It seemed that Corisande had not paid, or even opened, the majority of bills in some months. Daisy copied out her first list with the changes and corrections. Although the totals shocked her, she felt as though having neatly listed them was the first step to straightening out the messy finances of her new family. There seemed something almost familiar about the feeling that she had achieved some goal and she remembered how responsible Pip, in *Great Expectations*, had felt after listing his debts.

Nevertheless, when Ambrose came down to the study, she was waiting for him, efficient and businesslike.

"Would you like some tea?" she asked.

"I had a cup with Maud."

Daisy tried to imagine Maud sitting up in bed, wearing a soft, lacy bedjacket and holding a teacup in her hands, having a cozy chat with Ambrose.

"You had tea with Mrs. Nugent?" she said, asking a good deal more than the redundant question.

"She eats and drinks, like you and me. Specially tea, and of course she doesn't understand rationing."

"And you had a little chat? What does she talk about?"

"She doesn't say much, but every now and then she can surprise you."

Now Daisy knew that her grandmother-in-law was not in a coma and that she enjoyed a cup of tea. It added, although not much, to her knowledge.

"So, help yourself to a drink."

Ambrose poured himself a small whiskey and added quite a lot of water; Daisy assumed he was going to give her his full and serious attention.

"Corisande has gone and soon she'll be married and anyway she seems to have shrugged off any responsibility for the running of Dunmaine."

Ambrose said nothing but managed, nevertheless, to confirm Daisy's supposition that Corisande's new domestic arrangements were common knowledge.

"She seems to have left the household accounts—well, there aren't, as far as I can see, any household accounts per se—but the bills haven't been paid. For some time."

Daisy hesitated; Ambrose was wrinkling his nose, his head a little quizzically to one side.

"What?" she asked.

As Daisy watched he opened a drawer in a table behind him and smiled.

"Look," he said.

Inside the drawer was a large and perfect pear. There was a faint scent of fruit and unpolished wood. Daisy felt as though she were Alice in Wonderland, the pear huge since it came up almost to the height of the drawer, and magical. She looked enquiringly at Ambrose.

"Conference pear. Corisande must have put it in the drawer and forgotten about it."

Ambrose opened the other drawer; in it there were two smaller pale green and speckled golden pears.

"Why are they in the drawers?"

"You mean is it some Irish eccentricity? It's how you ripen them. The trick is to remember where you've put 'em."

"So," Daisy said firmly, "Mr. Hudson said I should talk to you. I seem to be the one people are asking for money and the one who orders things from shops where we have accounts."

"*Faute de mieux.*"

"So I suppose I am in charge. Old Mrs. Nugent—and I don't suppose Mickey—"

"Quite."

"So I thought I should know what the situation here is—and, as Patrick's wife I suppose I have—"

"Some rights and responsibilities. Obligations."

Daisy paused; Ambrose sipped his drink and looked encouragingly at her over the top of his glass.

"Damn it, Ambrose, stop being so cagey. I'm the only one here who doesn't know what's going on. Every time I make a move I come up against some new and chilling fact and I have to start all over again. They know that I don't know and they wait until I ask a question or make a request that is a cue for them—I can see it in their eyes."

"What do you want to know? Most people think a little merciful ignorance is a blessing."

"Everything."

Again a moment of silence. Daisy drew in an aggressive lungful of air, and Ambrose seemed to become alert.

"Fire away."

Suddenly Daisy found herself afraid. There were things she needed to know and, entangled with them, probably things she would rather not know. She could see the wisdom of Ambrose's willingness to answer questions rather than relate the family history piecemeal.

"Who does Dunmaine belong to?"

"Maud," Ambrose said. He sounded surprised and Daisy could see, as she now so often did, that the answer to this, and probably many other questions that bothered her, could not have been other than what it was.

"Maud. And, of course, the bank."

"The bank?"

"The bank. The whole place is mortgaged to the hilt."

If Daisy could have had her way—and she knew that, having dragged Ambrose to Dunmaine on a wet afternoon, she could not—she would have asked him to come back in a day or two when she had digested the information he had just given her.

"So who pays the bills?"

"In theory, Maud. They come addressed to her and the accounts are in her name."

"But she has abnegated responsibility for them?"

"Basically she's given up. She's old and tired and sad—her only son is dead and she's outlived most of her friends—and she's gone to bed and closed her eyes and closed her mind. She's had enough."

Daisy wanted, now that Ambrose had given her the opening, to ask about Patrick's parents, but she knew she had to deal with the more immediate point.

"Isn't there some legal thing that one does when an old person is no longer capable of looking after her affairs?"

"Power of attorney. Yes, Maud would be a prime candidate for such a procedure. She would welcome it, I imagine—if you got her on a day when she could understand."

"But?"

"But—there's a pretty good case to be made for letting sleeping dogs lie."

"And it is?"

Now Ambrose was the one to draw a deep breath.

"I don't much like landing you with all this stuff at the same time. The rest of us have had years to get used to it. The house is mortgaged; Maud is very old; I am the trustee. We all know this can't go on forever, but it's probably better if it can go on until Maud dies and the war is over. We're not talking about a long time, in either case."

"We haven't heard from Patrick, you know."

"I know."

"What does it mean?"

Ambrose was silent; he looked helpless.

"This is your afternoon for answering questions."

"I really don't know," he said after a moment. "Obviously it's not a good thing. But if he was known to be a prisoner or dead, or even officially missing, you would have been informed, of course. He could be—he may have been doing something a little more complicated."

"Complicated? You mean like spying?"

Ambrose looked startled and then laughed.

"Patrick a spy? Try and imagine it. No, I think what he was doing—he went, you know, on that course—was training to be part of the second wave after a Commando landing force. Anything like that could hold his letter up for months. Sometimes families get six or seven at a time. Really, I don't know. If I did, I would tell you."

"So, what should I think?"

"Cautious optimism and courage." Ambrose spoke gently.

"I see." Daisy drew in a deep breath. "And about Dunmaine?"

"I feel that as trustee I should try to keep the spirit of what Charley—Maud's husband—intended rather than act as a sort of financial policeman."

"For as long as possible—until the war ends and Maud dies?"

"If we can struggle on until then."

"Can we?" Daisy asked.

"Probably. It's in almost no one's interest to speed the process along. The bank isn't going to make a sudden move; they're no better equipped to take on Dunmaine than anyone else. They'd sooner wait until the war is over."

"And then?"

"Well, I suppose the place will be sold up, the bank and the other creditors paid, and—there'll be, ah, death duties and—well, everyone'll get on with their lives as best they can," Ambrose ended lamely, not quite able to meet Daisy's stricken gaze.

"Does everyone except me know this? I mean, am I the only one this is news to?"

"Everyone concerned—Maud, Corisande, Patrick, and Mickey—has this information. To what extent they have thought it through and come to a logical conclusion is another matter. Maud isn't interested in the present, and less so in the future. Corisande has extricated herself; what she thought or knew, I couldn't say. Mickey—who knows what he thinks, but since he is planting a maze or something on the grounds that will take ten years to mature, I have to assume he hasn't quite faced up to facts."

A maze? Surely not. Daisy did not allow herself to follow this new distraction, although she added it to her mental list of unanswered questions.

"And Patrick is—missing. That leaves me."

Ambrose shrugged lightly, sympathetically, but said nothing.

"Well, now I have the broader view, but we still need to deal with some of the day-to-day practicalities. What we're talking about is surviving until—things change. I paid last week's wages myself and I have a stack of bills here. Where does the money come from to pay them and—ah—how much is there?"

"There is some," Ambrose said apologetically. "It's just not quite enough. There is Maud's pension—colonel's widow—and a few shares that send a dividend once a year. Some of the land is let—but you shouldn't think of that as cash; it goes straight to the bank against the mortgage."

"Against?"

"It pays part of the mortgage."

"And the rest—of the mortgage payments?" Daisy could feel the beginnings of a headache, and she felt very, very tired.

"They sort of get added to the overdraft. As I said, the bank is helpful because in a way, their interests are not so different from ours."

"And the bills and wages?"

"That's a kind of juggling act. You'll always be a bit short at the end of the month, but in the end everyone knows they'll get paid. Probably."

AFTER AMBROSE HAD left, Daisy returned to the desk. Again feeling a little like Pip, she set out the new financial facts of Dunmaine as best she could. She had no knowledge of bookkeeping, but since she had a logical mind and the facts themselves seemed to fall into easily recognizable separate categories, she set out the figures on three separate sheets of paper.

The weekly wages; the total of the monthly bills for the household; the bank overdraft, mortgage, rates, taxes, and other not yet identified expenses connected with Dunmaine.

Then she set the income that Ambrose had described against those figures, setting, as he had, the rental for the land let to the farmer against the bank column, and the other income against wages and bills. The result was illuminating; in every category Dunmaine was sinking further into debt, but not by much. Daisy could see why the bank was content to wait; why the shopkeepers understood that they had to take turns being paid, and never in full. It was an example of the principle set out in *David Copperfield*—the one that supposes an annual income of twenty pounds, and defines happiness as being an annual expenditure of nineteen pounds, nineteen and sixpence, and misery as one of twenty pounds, ought and sixpence. Daisy did not find it reassuring that Dickens was the author who again came to mind when she was pondering her financial affairs.

There were two overdue bills that Daisy did not include in her accounts. One was from a milliner's in Dublin; Corisande's appearance was not apparently only the result of an innate elegance, but required considerable expenditure. Daisy firmly marked it "opened in error" and, putting it in a new envelope, forwarded it to Corisande at Edmund's address. The other, almost as substantial and also dating back six months, was from a nursery garden and largely for shrubs. Mickey's maze? Daisy thought she might leave it to one side and deal with it another time.

She fell asleep that night thinking that if she were to contribute her small income to the Nugent housekeeping and find a way to reduce expenses a little, she could make that economy settle at no greater an indebtedness than had existed at her arrival. She awoke—from a dream in which Maud had become a heavy ornate clock with a loud, ominous tick, her life span and the distant war predicating Daisy's life and the future of Dunmaine—to the sound of someone stepping on the gravel outside. Daisy leaped out of her warm bed, her heart pounding and adrenaline rushing through her body, and moved quietly and quickly to the window. She carefully drew the corner of one curtain back to see outside.

At first she could see nothing. Then the hollow sound of the cattle grid into the pasture on the side of the house led her eye to a man setting off down the field toward the village below. Daisy could tell from the time elapsed during which she had heard him cross the gravel that he had come from the avenue rather than from the house, and she thought he must be someone taking a shortcut home. There was, at any rate, nothing clandestine about his bearing; he seemed, rather, oblivious to the house—as though he were an animal that would avoid humans during the day but followed at night the path his ancestors had since before the house had been built.

Daisy returned to bed, but not to sleep. It occurred to her that she had not allowed any kind of contingency or reserve in her calculations of the housekeeping economy of the Nugent family. Nothing for repairs or medical bills. Nothing for clothes, veterinarians, entertaining, presents, or charitable contributions; as a rector's daughter, Daisy knew well that the latter were not always completely voluntary.

Next, she wondered how Corisande had paid her previous dressmakers' bills. Did she have some money of her own? Had Maud Nugent paid them? Had they come out of the housekeeping money? If old Mrs. Nugent had paid, was it the same as them coming out of the housekeeping? What was going to happen to her, to any of them? Was she responsible for Mickey's long overdue bill for the shrubs? If not, who was? Did Mickey have any money of his own? Or did he just charge anything he needed to the estate? How did they all manage to live in a world in which realities were never addressed? Was her anxiety a sign that she was hopelessly bourgeois? Would she, in time, become like them and waft through life disregarding her obligations? She rather thought she would not; it seemed possible that she might be unable to meet those obligations, but unlikely she would ever do so with the insouciance of the rest of the family.

What did Patrick think? Or did he, perhaps understandably, assume that the financial problems of Dunmaine were something he would consider after the end of the war. Which Ambrose had said would be soon. She had believed him, but was it because he was better informed than she was, or just because he had spoken with masculine authority? What would happen if Patrick never came back and she, apart from the devastation of his loss and the sadness of widowhood, were to live out her days at Dunmaine, in the company of Maud and Mickey, with the estate gradually sinking into the quicksand of irreversible debt.

For a brief middle-of-the-night moment, she even considered returning to England, making the pretense of being part of the war effort, and living with her family until Patrick, God willing, came home. Even with the war effort excuse, it seemed dishonorable. Daisy knew what "for better or worse" meant. She had made a commitment—taken vows, even—to throw her lot in with these frozen people. With this cold country.

Daisy was about to slide back into a sleep she knew would be troubled by anxious dreams, when a cry outside left her rigidly, wide-eyed awake. The sound was loud, painful, extravagantly sad, like a baby suffering dreadfully. It came again, more primitive— and louder. A cat. This logical explanation stopped her heart racing, but was otherwise little consolation. That the mating cry of a cat should contain such depths of devastation, loss, longing, and broken-heartedness suggested that human suffering could be infinitely greater than she had observed or imagined. That suffering could hardly find a more probable locale than among the victims and participants of the war being fought too far away for her to witness or be part of, but not so far away that it would not affect her life and those of everyone she knew or loved.

The cat stopped in the middle of an ambitious yowl; it had been interrupted by something in the dark. Outside it was now completely silent. Daisy lay, breathing slowly and deeply, trying to relax.

The silence was now broken by the creaking of a floorboard on the landing outside her room. The timber in the old house still settling after almost two hundred years? Mickey crossing the landing, as he often did at night, going to observe his bats? Or that unnamed and in no way frightening presence she often felt, and occasionally caught a glimpse of, in the upstairs corridors of Dunmaine? What would happen if they actually ran out of money? If the bank decided to cut its losses? When Maud died and her pension with her? If the creditors got together and forced the issue? If the staff became tired of wages always a little late, and left?

For all the discomfort of Dunmaine, its old-fashioned amenities required labor. Daisy's mind led her unwillingly down a line of questions, all of them beginning with "what if?" What if there were no staff? No cook, no maids? Not even the scarcely visible boy who acted as a part-time gardener and groom; so rarely seen that Daisy had not remembered to include him in her original calculation of household expenses. What would happen then? She would not, as millions of people all over the world even now did, face the four horsemen of the Apocalypse, nor would she or those around her experience hunger, cold, exhaustion, or fear on any level greater than extreme discomfort. Nevertheless, Daisy had difficulty imagining Dunmaine functioning without the help of what she had once thought of as an unnecessarily large staff. She could, she thought, learn to cook, and presumably she could learn to humor the vagaries of the old-fashioned kitchen range. But could she also look after the bedridden old lady upstairs? And the pony and old cob in the stables, their only means of transport? Could she also chop and carry the wood necessary to keep the house minimally heated and grow the vegetables and fruit that, with the hens and eggs, made up a large part of their diet? She could not. There might be a way to reduce the weekly wages, but she could not see it now. It was equally difficult to see how the monthly bills could be reduced; Daisy had got as far as rationing alcohol and introducing two vegetarian meals into the weekly menu when a fox, in the distance, began to bark.

A minute or two later, the fox barked again. Daisy had been listening for him; she was young enough and hopeful enough to find the sound pleasing. Without a thought for the henhouse, she took a deep breath and fell into a comparatively dreamless sleep.

THE NEXT DAY was sunny but cold. Maud could see the leaves on the Virginia creeper around her window had turned the golden brown of autumn.

She was aware of the changes of season outside although she did not favor one season over the others. She observed the progress of the year without preference or emotion and had learned to accept the small pleasures each brought. The blue skies of autumn, small white clouds blown briskly across her limited horizon. The dark storms of winter, the sound of wind and rain against the window, the fire glowing in the grate. Spring—in the warmer months she sometimes broke her silence to ask Philomena to open the window wide enough for her to feel the breeze on her face as she dozed. The sensation appealed to her dreams and memories, to the past rather than the old lady pleasures and comforts she sometimes enjoyed in her waking moments. During the warmer days of the summer, without her having to ask, Philomena would open the window and Maud would smell the pleasant and evocative scents of that season.

She looked at the vine and thought she would live to see the leaves become brittle and dead, to see them tear and fall in a winter storm and, perhaps, to unfurl and grow, a pale and then darkening green, the following spring. She knew she would live a little longer and she knew that Philomena and the maids thought she would die. Perhaps that very day. She had heard, as they had, the cries in the past two nights; the animal-like cries they, and she, thought of as the banshee, foretelling a death. Or two deaths. Maud didn't doubt there would be a death although she was sure it would not be her own. This war brought death to families of the young men who had gone to be soldiers, as the cold weather would kill some of the old people, as tuberculosis, rife in the damp valley below, killed men, women, and children. She did not doubt the announcement of death; she doubted only it would be her own. But she would know whose it was. Every one of her visitors told her what was happening in the world outside. Some, her family, thought she did not understand much of what they said; others, Philomena or a visitor from below stairs, knew she understood but imagined her more interested in what interested them. Ambrose was her most satisfactory occasional visitor; he tended to give her the headlines of world news and then would talk about the past. Sometimes he told her about people and events that, although the information did not interest her, she thought he was not meant to speak about. Neither he nor Philomena would mention the banshee. Although Philomena and she would listen again that night.

CHAPTER 14

THE DAY OF THE lawn meet began bright and sunny, the air cold and sharp. The traces of a light frost had disappeared by the time Daisy and Mickey set out for Ambrose's house.

As the crow flies, Dysart Hall was about five miles away, over some tall hills, or low mountains—Daisy could not decide which—and a river. By road, with the pony trotting briskly most of the way, it took them an hour and a half. Daisy had wrapped up as warmly as was compatible with the first social event since the weekend they had all stayed at Shannig, but by the time they had reached the end of the avenue her toes and fingers were aching. Mickey didn't seem to feel the cold; the top button of his overcoat was open and although he wore a scarf, it hung loosely over his lapels. An acquired Darwinian hardiness, Daisy wondered, or was her brother-in-law merely as oblivious to the natural elements as he was to the niceties of day-to-day social behavior? It wasn't that he was rude—he said please and thank you and good morning and stood up when a woman came into the room—it was just that preoccupation—melancholia? having been dropped on his head as a baby?—had made him seemingly oblivious or deaf to the tensions and subtext of most human conversation. Oblivious, too, to a greasy stain on his trousers that irritated Daisy.

Dysart Hall was larger than Daisy had expected, and in worse repair. The avenue was longer than at Dunmaine, but with bigger and deeper holes and puddles. On either side, behind railings, horses and bullocks desultorily grazed. The house itself was gray-stoned, early Georgian, the pleasingly plain lines of the front of the house emphasized by a wing, set back a little, on either side. At even a first glance, Daisy could see cracked tiles and sagging gutters and that all the windows of one wing were shuttered. There were similar shutters at Dunmaine: painted white, heavy wood, with a metal bar that slotted into place, the bar when swung up and attached made a distinctive sound, not loud, but one that could be heard several rooms away. Inside such a room it was heavily dark, the gloom only emphasized by the cracks of light between the folds of the shutters. Daisy knew that at least a wing of Ambrose's house was closed up; closed up, she suspected, in the sense of being shuttered and the doors closed on it, not sealed and secured against the day it would once again be opened. Damp, cold, and neglected, it would be deteriorating at an even faster rate than the rest of the house. The rest of their houses.

In front of the porched-in hall door, on the gravel and on the lawn surrounding it, horses shifted about nervously. Big Irish hunters; a pony or two with small, determined boys and girls on their backs; owners and grooms. It was an impressive sight: the sturdy horses, glossy bay or chestnut; the horsemen in black coats, hats, and boots, and cream riding britches; the brown of the grooms' jackets and flat caps; interspersed with the odd red coat that she knew she should call "pink." Farther away, and on the lawn, the hounds waited, kept in place by hunt servants.

The sweep in front of the house was large and generously covered with gravel. Daisy, who now knew how much a load of gravel cost, wondered that Ambrose had not, instead, invested the money in repairing the roof. The sweep might become bare and muddy, might even sprout the odd dandelion, but it was not likely to deteriorate to the extent that it infected the rest of the house.

Daisy and Mickey turned off toward the stables, around the back of the house, and down a short stony hill into the stable yard. Mickey unharnessed the pony and put it in a stall, and he and Daisy walked back up the incline, past some overgrown rhodo-dendrons, to the front of the house.

The first person Daisy recognized, and he was in front of her smiling before she knew how to—or even if she should—return his greeting, was Sir Guy Wilcox. He was dressed for hunting and a red poppy was stuck in his buttonhole. Armistice Day. His black coat, the stock tied at his neck, and his gleaming top hat made him seem even more distinguished than he had at the Powers' lunch party.

"Mrs. Nugent. Daisy—I hope I may call you Daisy?"

Daisy felt herself start to blush. She would have avoided Sir Guy if she had seen him first. Now, cutting him would be embar-rassing and ridiculous. Nevertheless, she had no intention of allowing their acquaintanceship to become less formal or more intimate.

"Oh," she said coolly. "Good morning, Sir Guy."

There was a moment's silence.

"Armistice Day," she said, her eyes indicating the poppy, made from a stiff red cloth around a black center. "I hadn't realized."

"Yes," he said, "the eleventh day of the eleventh month."

Daisy glanced at Mickey—they were surely close enough to matters with which he concerned himself for a small, not neces-sarily uninteresting, fact to be produced—but he was looking thoughtfully at the hounds at the end of the lawn. The hounds, quarreling among themselves, were exhibiting more excitement and tension than were the humans who stood about, holding cups and glasses in one hand and the reins of their mounts in the other, talking and waiting for the hunt to move away.

"I thought I might try and find a cup of tea," Daisy said at length, stamping her feet lightly to emphasize the cold. "Can I bring you anything?"

Somewhere on the way to the open front door, Mickey wandered away and Daisy entered Ambrose's house for the first time, alone.

Although the light in the hall had been turned on—a large opaque glass bowl coming to a metal-covered point in the center and suspended by chains from the ceiling—it was, at first, hard to see anything; the light outdoors had been hard and bright. When Daisy's eyes became more accustomed to the gloom, she saw that the atmosphere of the hall was completely masculine. Two old dogs, kept indoors because of the hounds on the lawn, were sleeping deafly by the embers of the fire. The large one looked like an old and lumpy black hearthrug.

The dining room, too, suggested that it had been many years since a woman had been mistress of Dysart Hall. Even the food and drink spread on the handsome and very long table seemed masculine: sandwiches, a visibly dry seedcake, decanters of whiskey and of a dark red liquid that Daisy thought might have been cherry brandy or port.

The older women were clustered around the fireplace, their tweed suits and thick stockings not warm enough for them to want to stand about outside. Some of them, Daisy supposed, were her neighbors; most of them knew who she was; none of them spoke to her. Daisy poured herself a cup of tea, drank it, and went back outside.

Ambrose, both hands free—his horse presumably still in the stables—stood close to the hall door. He was talking to a woman; their momentarily frozen silhouettes suggested a tableau vivant or, perhaps, a game. The woman held a tray supported by a strap around her neck. Daisy fumbled in her handbag for money.

"All right," Ambrose was saying as Daisy joined them. He was holding up a pound note in a way that suggested that a bargain

had not yet been struck. "If you'll buy a lily from me next Easter
Monday."

The woman tittered nervously, not quite sure how serious he
was. After a pause Ambrose put the pound into the box and chose
his poppy. Daisy, too, bought a poppy and the woman moved on.
Ambrose waited until she was almost out of earshot before he
spoke.

"Bloody sauce," Ambrose said, securing the poppy in his buttonhole. "English, of course."

Daisy raised her eyebrows, but Ambrose was undeterred.

"And an almost complete ignorance of history. Does she think
Ireland doesn't have her own fallen to remember?"

Daisy hesitated, not because she felt the need to remind
Ambrose she was English but because it seemed, if she could find
the right words, a moment when Ambrose might answer some of
her questions. How English was Ambrose? How did he manage
to spend so much time on leave? And Patrick? Did he, like
Ambrose, fighting in the English army, feel as strongly about Ireland as Ambrose seemed to? Or was Ambrose's objection to the
Englishwoman about manners? Form? And what, if anything, lay
beneath the apparent acceptance of Sir Guy Wilcox by the Anglo-
Irish?

"Is the lily the Irish equivalent of the English poppy?" she
asked instead.

"Yes, except in England you buy a poppy on Remembrance
Day, the day the Great War ended. Here you buy a lily on Easter
Monday, on the anniversary of a revolutionary beginning, the Post
Office Rising. Both in aid of soldiers' charities. The other differ-
ence—which is why that silly woman was confused—is that there
would also be a bit of a class thing. You see—"

They were interrupted by the arrival of a maid. A maid who,
Daisy noticed, looked more cleanly and neatly turned out in this

bachelor establishment than did either of those employed at Dun-maine.

"If Hugh Power shows up, see if you can get that woman to try and sell him a poppy," Ambrose said, over his shoulder, as he followed the maid back to the house.

Daisy rather hoped Hugh Power would come to the meet, but she suspected that he didn't hunt, that he thought of hunting as English, a decadent sport of a decadent former enemy. She thought it unlikely he would disapprove of it as a blood sport; she suspected, given the right circumstances, Hugh Power could shed blood.

Reluctant to search out Mickey, the only person, other than Ambrose or Sir Guy, familiar to her, Daisy strolled away from the front door to look at the horses.

The horses were nervous, anticipating the excitement of the hunt. They danced about, their weight crunching the gravel, and Daisy was careful to avoid being either trodden on or kicked by one of their cold steel-shod hooves. A hard-faced woman on an overexcited gray mare swore at her when she got in the way and Daisy, rather shocked, went to look at the hounds.

The hounds seemed undoglike and independent. Daisy knew that each, as a puppy, had for a time lived with a family, separated from the pack. Mickey, always reliable with hard facts, had told her that this was called "walking" a hound, and that hounds were referred to as couples even to the extent that a single hound was half a couple. Despite this exposure to humans and domestic life, they appeared to remain pack animals, aware of, but not sub-servient to, their human masters, obedient only when the rules were enforced by the hunt servant's whip.

Daisy was lost in thought when Ambrose came back. She was thinking about Patrick and what he had said about blood sports, about whether she would ever ride well enough to hunt, what it would cost to keep a hunter—a great deal, she suspected—and whether she would, in some distant postwar time, be among the frighteningly competent women on horseback that surrounded her.

"Daisy—"

"Patrick said he never wanted to indulge in a blood sport again as long as he lived," Daisy said, wincing inside at the "as long as he lived" bit.

"Did he?" Ambrose said thoughtfully. "He's a good chap—bit more imagination than I have."

"But it looks as though it must be exciting," Daisy said tentatively, even a little longingly.

"It is," Ambrose said firmly. "Daisy, I need—come with me."

He took her by the arm and steered her back toward the house. Two people tried to get his attention on the way but he waved them away. Daisy felt curious, then frightened, as she began to understand the urgency implied in his actions.

"Let's go into the study," he said, indicating a door on the other side of the hall from the dining room and a little past where the staircase swept into the hall. He closed the door behind them.

"Sit down, Daisy," he said, although he remained standing himself, his back to the unlit fire. From the corner of her eye, Daisy could see Mickey sitting immobile in an armchair; she was too agitated to acknowledge his presence.

"What is it?"

"Corisande just telephoned—" Daisy could see that Ambrose's ruddy complexion was paler than usual.

"Tell me, Ambrose. Quickly," Daisy said, her mind running through the full gamut of disaster. From the most terrifying, news of Patrick, through the possible illness of either of her parents, a domestic disaster at Dunmaine, to the most probable—news of Maud's sudden sickness or death.

"It's James Nugent. He was killed. Rufisque. Covering the re-embarkation. A hero's death—he's being recommended for a decoration."

It didn't seem possible. Although she was sad, her primary reaction was not one of grief; it was more one of incomprehension. James was someone she hadn't, when she lay awake at night, fearing and anticipating the deaths of others, ever imagined dying.

"James," she said. "Oh, his poor mother."

Pity now mingled with the dislike Daisy felt, to a degree that varied with her own mood, for every member of the English Nugent family and for the condescending, shabby, and humiliating way they had treated her.

"How did you find out?" she asked at last.

"Corisande telephoned," the first words that Mickey had spoken since she entered the room. His tone and face as devoid of expression as ever.

Corisande had telephoned Dunmaine and a maid had told her they were at Ambrose's lawn meet? Corisande had telephoned Ambrose, who was not related to the Nugents, before she had telephoned her own family? Corisande's first instinct on hearing of James's death was to use it to have Ambrose's complete attention in the form of sympathy? What difference did it make?

"I have—ah—there are people—the meet," Ambrose said, after a moment.

"Yes, of course," Daisy said. "Your guests, you must look after them."

"I thought I'd—ah—send them on their way. No point in telling them something like this—what good would it do anyone?"

Ambrose left the room, his hunting boots noisy on the parquet floor, and Daisy and Mickey were left alone.

He was rather a spoilt little boy. Daisy could hear Patrick's voice and his casual summing up of James as they had walked down the stairs at Bannock House to dance together for the first time. She remembered how aware she had been of his closeness to her, how his hand had brushed against hers, how she had glowed with his attention.

Then she remembered the plaque in the church at Bannock, the memorial to an even younger Nugent who had also given his life for his country. She started to weep softly. Weeping for the vague and formidable Lady Nugent; for her pale aggressive daughters; for James, who would never again shoot a pheasant or creep into a pretty girl's bedroom; for all the never agains; for Patrick; for herself; for all the poppies and the lilies; for the whole brave, lonely, and inarticulate bunch of them; for the hopelessness of it all.

She wept for James, then for families all over England who had lost husbands, fathers, children. For the Londoners bombed nightly. For those who, whatever the outcome of the war, had already lost the center of their lives, someone who could never be replaced. For mothers who could never be comforted. She wept for families in occupied countries, for parents no longer able to protect their children. She wept for all the horrors of war, and hopelessness of living in a world where men could do this to one another. She had been brought up with the assumption of happy endings; now she understood that anything was possible, that these horrors could happen anywhere to anyone.

She continued to weep quietly for some time, quietly enough for Mickey, slumped, blending into an old and shabby armchair, either not to notice, or to be able to pretend not to notice, her tears. Outside she could hear the hunt moving off, the crunch of gravel, a voice raised, the yipping of the hungry, eager hounds. After a while, Ambrose, now wearing an old and rather worn tweed suit instead of his smart hunting clothes, came back. He gave Daisy his handkerchief and rang for the drinks tray.

PART THREE

Spring 1941

CHAPTER 15

WHEN AMBROSE ARRIVED, Daisy was sitting at the desk in the library. She was trying to write a letter to her grandmother. He greeted her warmly, but he did not hug her as she had throught he might. She offered him a drink.

"It's quarter past three. To offer me a drink suggests either you have been brought up in a convent or consider me a dipsomaniac. So unfair when I came over to take you for a ride."

"I don't know how to ride—"

Ambrose looked at her with interest.

"You're not frightened of horses, are you?"

Daisy shook her head; it had never occurred to her that one might fear domestic animals.

"Good. Put on some old slacks and thick socks so your ankles don't get pinched, and I'll get that old cob of Patrick's saddled up."

When Daisy came downstairs, dressed rather as she had as a Land Girl, Ambrose was waiting in front of the hall door with his own mare and the reassuringly fat and unclipped cob.

"There are two good rides, one through the woods and one over the moor. Let's go over the moor today, so you can see where you are."

There was an awkward and undignified moment when

Ambrose gave her a leg up onto the sturdy Osbert. Daisy had imagined that his boost and her spring would land her gracefully in the saddle of the mercifully immobile horse; this turned out not to be the case and she was sliding back toward the gravel when Ambrose shoved her into position. He stood back, panting a little.

"Sorry," Daisy said; it was the first time she had ever thought of herself as heavy, but she knew she would not feel slim again until she had been reassured by a looking glass.

"You'll get the knack of it; it's harder than it looks," Ambrose said reassuringly, and then added, "There's a mounting block in the stable yard."

Ambrose led the way to the end of the avenue. Then, just before the gates, he turned along a narrow path between the high stone wall and the edge of the woods.

"Don't let him get too close; Cissy might give him a little kick to encourage him to keep his distance. They're so much bigger than we are that they can hurt you without meaning to. A little love nip from Cissy left me with a bruise that took two months to fade. Just remember that they bite and they kick, and don't let them fall on you and you're not likely to come to any harm—until we get you out hunting at least."

That was unlikely to happen in the foreseeable future, even apart from a lack of reckless courage and the new austerity measures Daisy planned for the household. There was, in a family photograph album, an image of Corisande seated sidesaddle on a sleek, fit, and clearly well-bred horse. Not only the contrast between Corisande's mount and the comfortable old armchair on whose back Daisy was now seated, but Corisande's posture, her elegant habit, her hat—with, or maybe Daisy had imagined it, a small veil—her hair, anchored safely but attractively, like a dancer's, made Daisy feel she had a long way to go, on many fronts, before she would make her debut on the hunting field.

She had no intention of appearing at a meet, mounted on a horse with a reputation as a nurserymaid, and floundering about like a bag of laundry on a day when her sister-in-law and Edmund made a vice-regal appearance.

"Don't let him do that," Ambrose said sharply, interrupting her musings. He was referring to Osbert's—it seemed to Daisy harmless and reassuring—new activity, the tearing of succulent greenery from the bushes they passed and his meditative munching as he plodded along, an exemplary distance behind the heels of Ambrose's mare.

Soon the path led them past a field, then through a wooden gate that Ambrose dismounted to open and close behind them, then uphill along a stony and deserted lane. Ambrose's mare showed signs of not quite convincing fear at arbitrarily chosen objects: a stone gatepost, a cow looking over a gate, a dog barking in a farmyard.

When they had ridden about a mile, all of it gently uphill, the thick hedges on either side of the lane gave way to low banks topped by a single strand of rusted barbed wire. The unpaved but hard surface of the road became cart track. Now packed-down earthen tracks ran on either side of a strip of rough grass and weeds, the height of the growth limited by the hooves of the horses and donkeys that pulled the cart and by the load they drew. But it was, however, high enough for Osbert to pause from time to time and lower his head to snatch a mouthful of the grass. Each time he did so, Daisy found herself grabbing hold of the pommel of her saddle to avoid sliding, head first, down his sturdy neck.

"Don't let him make a fool of you," Ambrose said quite kindly. "He doesn't know he's bigger than you are."

"I know it, though."

"You're going to have to learn to ride, so—"

They passed through another gate; Daisy realized she would

have to learn to mount and dismount without assistance if she were to take this ride by herself. The cart track continued, but now there was open moor to each side. The plants between the tracks were lower, coarse and prickly; Osbert didn't seem interested by them. For a long way there was nothing but stones, heather, and the occasional sheep. The heather was purple and dull green on top, below it was brown and dry and the roots seemed to have raised a small mound around each plant; Daisy had the impression that each winter the dying plant contributed a little to the earth in which it grew and that the soil beneath was veined with roots and more like the turf they burned at Dunmaine than the rich dark earth in the vegetable garden. The afternoon was fine and clear, the mild wind part of the quiet sounds of the moor. Daisy saw a skylark high above and, a little later, a hawk. She was filled with the unreasoning happiness that Ireland sometimes gave her.

"Make him come alongside," Ambrose said, and with new confidence Daisy pressed her heels into Osbert's fat, furry ribs. To her surprise he reacted obediently to her instructions—or maybe he just wanted to walk beside Cissy.

"You have to grip with the upper part of your legs," Ambrose said. "If you depend on balance you're going to spend a lot of time on your bottom in the mud. If you grip, you'll be ready if your horse shies or changes direction without warning."

"I've been thinking about what you told me the day I asked about Dunmaine."

Ambrose nodded, not apparently surprised by the change of topic; for a moment Daisy wondered if his last equestrian instruction had contained a hint of metaphor, then decided it was not likely.

"When I drew up some rough accounts, it seemed to me as though Dunmaine was a disabled ship drifting very slowly toward an iceberg—"

Ambrose laughed.

"Forgive me," he said, "I'm not unsympathetic, it's just I've often—usually in the small hours of the morning—drawn similar pictures for myself. A sluggish whirlpool, a waterfall around the bend of a slow-moving river. But I've never heard anyone voice these images. Perhaps everyone in the same situation, and that's practically everyone we know, thinks like that."

"With an image of water, do you think?" Again, Daisy had the impression that Ambrose was not much interested in metaphor. "But the point is that it is slow-moving and therefore not necessarily inevitable—in the case of Dunmaine, at least."

"It doesn't have to be, but it usually is," Ambrose said gently. "Everyone has a scheme for cutting costs or earning money; it's just that they don't usually work or they don't work enough to change anything. Which isn't to say there isn't fat that could be cut from most households; it's just the luxuries are often the last to go—they often feel like the only thing that makes existence bearable."

Daisy looked puzzled.

"My place is fairly uncomfortable, but I'm attached to it. I don't know how long I'd go on trying to make a go of it, though, if I couldn't have the occasional whiskey and soda and a couple of days a season with the West Waterfords."

"Why doesn't anyone get a job?" Daisy was surprised at the level of irritation in her voice. "Mickey, for instance, why couldn't he get a job as a teacher?"

"A knowledge of the Irish language is necessary to graduate from a school or college or to obtain most professional qualifications. I suppose there are a few Protestant schools that might employ Mickey, but nothing around here."

Corisande's clothes, Mickey's maze. Now was the time to ask Ambrose about the private finances of her new family, of her brother- and sister-in-law, of her own husband, but Daisy found herself putting off these questions for another occasion.

"Mild market gardening, keeping hens, they've all been tried," Ambrose continued. "Even PGs—that could work if it was done properly, but most people think of it as a last resort and combine it with cutting costs around hot water and edible food."

"PGs?"

"Paying guests. Five guineas a week is about what you can get. But you can't act as though there is something amusingly eccentric about taking in lodgers. And you can't think of it as a fiver clear profit and five shillings to be spent on the unfortunate guest. You charge someone five guineas and you have to spend some of it on food, heat, and making sure they have a comfortable bed, a warm room, and an adequate clean bathroom." Ambrose spoke severely; Daisy could not be sure if he was lecturing the impoverished Anglo-Irish as a class or telling her that Dunmaine had a long way to go before she could think of entertaining a guest, let alone making one pay for the privilege. Charging five guineas— it could be a way out of the quicksand, out of the end-of-week embarrassment of late wages, the end-of-the-month bills let slide by, the middle-of-the-night fears. The thought of it made Daisy feel energetic and somewhat excited.

"But where would one—where do they find paying guests? Do they advertise? And doesn't that cost a fortune?"

"I suppose the initial advertisement in, say, the Agony column of the *Times* probably sets you back a good part of a week's rent, but you don't necessarily have to invest an advertisement for each guest. You should get more than one response and if you do it properly you'll get most of your business by word of mouth."

"So, why don't more people try it—if everyone's in the same boat?"

"Lack of imagination, pride, a level of household disorder

they would be reluctant to show to a friend, let alone a stranger with some rights and expectation of comfort. Not enough energy or capital to deal with the leak in the middle of the spare room."

"And form? How about form?" Daisy asked, addressing what she suspected was the principal obstacle in such an endeavor. What would Patrick have to say if he came home and found his bride running a boardinghouse? But what would he say if he returned, exhausted, from Europe to find bailiffs in the kitchen? And if he never came home? Or if the war lasted another five years?

"Oh form—it's a little late for that," Ambrose said dismissively.

Daisy knew he could not really mean so lightly to renounce the creed by which he lived; that he had omitted form from the list of reasons the south of Ireland had not been converted into a series of uncomfortable lodging houses was an indication he approved of her as yet unarticulated plan.

"If you wanted to give it a try," Ambrose said casually, "a friend wrote and asked only the other day if I knew of a house in the country where a fellow officer could put up for a week or two. He's on medical leave and would like to be somewhere with fresh air, fresh vegetables, and plenty of meat."

The casual manner of Ambrose's suggestion did not ring quite true and Daisy wondered if Dunmaine were in greater trouble than her amateur calculations had suggested.

"What do you think Patrick would want me to do?" she asked after a moment's hesitation.

"I think Patrick would want you to use your judgment and initiative. And housing a wounded officer would surely be something he would approve of."

"Even if I was charging him for it?"

Ambrose shrugged; she was losing his attention.

"Now we're going to go a little faster. No one can teach you to post; it's just a matter of trial and error. In the meantime, it's pretty uncomfortable so you'll probably catch on quite quickly."

Without any, to Daisy, perceptible action on Ambrose's part, Cissy walked a little faster and then broke into a gentle trot. Daisy flapped her calves and heels against Osbert's sides and he lumbered into a gait that kept him close to, though not abreast of, Cissy. Daisy was jarred, awkward, bounced about by Osbert's changed stride. She tried to find his rhythm and after a while she found it for a moment and then lost it again. It was quite enough to keep her thoughts occupied until they turned and headed back to Dunmaine and tea.

CHAPTER 16

ANDREW HESKITH WAS tall, slight, and fair. His eyes were blue and cold; he walked with a limp. Daisy's stomach contracted when she first saw him. Desire made her stop breathing for a moment before she greeted him and showed him up to his room.

Daisy waited in the drawing room, but he did not come downstairs for tea. He must, she thought, be resting. His hair was a little too long and she supposed he had been recovering from his wound, or whatever made him limp, for some time.

When she went upstairs to get ready for dinner, taking a little more trouble over her appearance than she usually did, she opened the book of Yeats poetry on the table beside her bed. She found quite easily the poem that Heskith made her think of. The final two lines—

> . . . *his hair is beautiful,*
> *Cold as the March wind his eyes.*

When she had first read the lines, not unaware of the implication of their context, she had felt the same erotic shock as she had when, an hour ago, she had shaken her new guest's hand. *Cold as the March wind.* Patrick, she thought, trying to summon up an image of her husband; but he had been gone too long and she had worn out the memories of their three nights together. Every word, every touch, every sensation had been taken out and held in her mind until, like an old photograph, they were faded and cracked and there were times when Daisy was not sure she could accurately summon his image. Although she could still remember the hard warmth of his body against hers.

MAUD COULD FEEL there was someone new in the house. Not someone she could see or hear, not someone she knew. A soldier, she thought. Not Patrick, her favorite grandson, missing. Not James. How strange it was, she thought, as she sank deeper and even less communicatively into herself, that they kept information from her as though she would not be able to understand the horrors and implications of war. Why did they imagine Thomas's room was kept untouched since his last leave in the spring of 1918? Why, for that matter, did they suppose she had taken to her bed and more or less stopped talking when war had been declared? Not because she was old and senile and didn't understand what was happening, but because she was the only one who really knew. And because she knew she would not experience it twice.

The rhythm of the house, the subtle changes in the times and quality of the meals told her something had changed a little. She was not sure whether she smelled or imagined the distant scent of a cigar.

DAISY DECANTED A bottle of port before dinner and opened a bottle of wine; she was for the first time grateful that Mickey was oblivious to the greater part of what went on around him. He drank a glass of what Daisy now slightly nervously assumed to be the best wine in the cellar, and ate his Irish stew—did it always have to be so gray?—with his usual somnambulistic mealtime methodical lack of concentration. Heskith ate the stew as unflinchingly and largely silently, although he raised one eyebrow slightly in appreciation as he tasted the wine and shot a quick surprised glance at the label on the bottle.

The dining-room fire smoked. Daisy noticed, to her surprise and horror, that there was a small stream of dirty white smoke coming from just under the mantelpiece. It suggested a small outlet on the side of a volcano that occasionally emits threatening but not necessarily dangerous gusts of sulfur.

Heskith said little and his expression did not encourage small talk. He and Mickey seemed equally preoccupied and Daisy broke the silence only to offer food and drink. The former invitation was largely rhetorical; she had never seen anyone take a second helping of any food offered at Dunmaine. Heskith took some more wine and a glass of port afterward. Daisy felt a nervous compulsion to offer him something further and by the end of the meal it had been arranged that Osbert should be made available each afternoon for the week; Daisy blushed when she offered the cob, self-consciously aware that she might appear to be alluding to Heskith's wounded leg.

After dinner, the entire meal—even with the glass of port that Daisy had left the men to drink, presumably in total silence—taking less than an hour, Heskith went upstairs to his room. Daisy was restless, filled with nervous energy. What she really wanted to do was to have a stern conversation with Mrs. Mulcahy; dinner the following evening would be better, she promised herself, even if it meant holding a gun to the cook's stubborn, untalented head.

Instead she went to her room, lit the small fire, and sat at her desk in the nest she had made for herself in a corner of her new home.

First she wrote to Patrick; the letters now were not so hard to write. Form, ritual, superstition were invoked and drawn upon. They were written in a vacuum and sent into a void. She no longer believed he received them, but equally she believed if she stopped writing that she would allow him to float away from her, to die, that she would kill him. Dutifully she wrote a description of the day, of the weather, of the buds on the trees in the lane behind the walled garden. She described Heskith's arrival, and by alluding to his reserve, avoided much description. She told her husband that she loved him, that she was reading *Bleak House,* that his family was well, that there was a small patch of damp under the window in the library but she was keeping an eye on it.

She sealed the envelope; any afterthoughts she might have before she posted it would be gratefully included in the following day's letter. Then, quickly and without much consideration, she wrote to her grandmother. She wrote a letter similar to the ones she sent home each week: full of description, short on event, devoid of any reference to the doings of her new family. She was silent on the subject of her lack of news from Patrick, of her financial worries, of her grandmother-in-law's apparent senility, of Mickey's eccentricity, of her scheme to take in paying guests.

Then she got into bed and stretched her legs under the cold sheets until her feet found the now tepid earthenware hot-water bottle.

A SPRING DAY shone outside the landing window. Daisy gazed dreamily out, putting off the moment when she should go down the main staircase to the hall. She felt a reluctance to speak or to be spoken to. Words or, in fact, sound that was not part of the rhythm and pattern of the now largely silent natural world outside seemed an intrusion on her confused feelings and aroused senses. Gradually, she became aware of activity below. Distant but animated voices, oddly lacking the usual gloomy, almost sullen, sounds of morning. No sound of silver on china, no double clink of cup clumsily returned to saucer. Instead voices, urgency, the energy of emergency. Daisy was by now too well aware of the pleasure the bored servants took in any kind of drama to find comfort in the cheerful tone of the voices below.

Mickey and Heskith were already sitting at the dining table when she came in. Daisy was not hungry; she was pouring herself a cup of weak tea when Nelly came into the room. The housemaid stood for a moment, struggling for the words to explain her presence in the dining room and for maximum dramatic effect.

"Begging your pardon, Mrs. Nugent." She paused, apparently considering including Mickey and Heskith in her greeting, then deciding not to spoil the timing of her announcement. "They've gone and bombed Belfast." She had their full, shocked attention now. Mistaking their silence for incomprehension or a request for elucidation, she added: "Hitler's bombed Belfast. Last night."

Mickey and Daisy just stared at her, but Heskith rose quickly and left the room. After a moment, they could hear the wireless begin to hum as it warmed up, then a high-pitched atmospheric whine that quickly changed to crackling and then the reassuring, convincing voice of a BBC newsreader. An account, general and lacking in detail, of the bombing followed: the docks had been the target; the extent of the damage not revealed. Soon the news moved to the war in Europe, an encounter at sea. None of them moved. Daisy thought of the afternoon in Wales when they had listened to an account of the sinking of the *Royal Oak* at Scapa Flow.

"How do you get the Southern Irish news?" Heskith asked, his tone a little impatient.

"Radio Eireann"—Radio Eireann was the station the wireless was tuned to in the kitchen, the station on which the maids had heard news of the night's raid. The Nugents listened to it only for race meetings—"It's on the other band; let me." And Mickey, slowly but accurately, moved the dial until the station was clear. "Why do you want the Irish news?"

Heskith shot a quick look at Mickey; Daisy, who had been wondering the same thing, was grateful it had not been she who had asked.

"I wondered what the official Irish reaction was."

The wireless crackled, then a man's voice, speaking Irish. After a moment or two, Daisy picked up the word "Finisterre"—a weather report. While they waited, Daisy considered the implications of Heskith's thought. While Eire was neutral, the six counties of Northern Ireland—in a sense another country—had remained loyal to England and were at war with Germany. Ireland might be neutral, but Irish families—Irish although not citizens of Eire—had been victims of the bombing. De Valera's adamant neutrality would be tested; the hatred and distrust of a large part of the Irish for England, at whose hands they had suffered in the recent past, would be weighed against Germany, who had bombed the northern part of their own island.

She glanced at Heskith; he was alert, attentive, not so tense. Now she could see that there was and probably had been for a long time, beneath the surface tautness, a look of deep sadness, of a loss she could not imagine.

The newscaster continued to speak in Irish—farm prices, Daisy thought. She, Mickey, and Heskith continued to listen as carefully, struggling to understand. It was de Valera's goal, already implemented in the schools, for the country to revert to its native tongue. Would it be possible, in the unimaginable future after the war, Daisy wondered, that she would live in a country whose language she didn't speak?

"Do you speak Irish?" Heskith asked Mickey.

Daisy glanced at her brother-in-law and saw why a stranger might have assumed Mickey was following every word with rapt attention. As usual, Daisy had no idea of what he might be thinking.

"Only a few words. The news in English will follow in a minute."

And moments later they were listening to an account of fire-fighters, fire engines, and equipment from Ireland moving north toward Belfast, where houses near to the docks were still burning.

"Thank God," Heskith said under his breath. Daisy glanced at him and saw that he had tears in his eyes.

"Thank God," Mickey said, a little more loudly. Daisy thought he might mean it literally.

"Thank God," Daisy echoed silently; she, too, was close to tears. Grateful to de Valera for the spontaneous gesture of humanity and solidarity with the Irish families on the other side of the border, she felt a wave of love for the Irish people and less alone than she had been since she had arrived in Ireland.

A GUST OF WIND flung raindrops as loud as pebbles at the window on the landing as Daisy came downstairs. The storm had gathered speed over the dark surface of the Atlantic and was now meeting the west coast of Ireland, the first obstacle in its path.

If the gale continued, the next day also would be spent largely indoors. Some form of entertainment, as well as better food, warmer rooms, and hotter water would be required if Daisy were to depend on paying guests to keep the old house afloat. Maybe subscriptions to *Country Life* and *Punch* were part of the overhead in running a guest-supported household; she was nervously aware that the last issue of *Country Life* was from just before the war.

In the meantime, that day's copy of the *Irish Times* should be put in the library, the lights turned on, and the fire lighted. Daisy crossed the hall at the foot of the stairs, the central overhead low-wattage bulb, its light diffused by a dusty opaque glass shade, doing little to alleviate the gloom.

The library was almost as cheerless although a little lighter; wind rattled the windows and rain was now heavy and regular on the panes. Daisy switched on a lamp and was looking for a box of matches on the mantelpiece before she became aware of Heskith. He stood, immobile, with a small book in his hand, the dim light from the streaming window behind him, his stillness rather than the lack of illumination rendering him for a moment invisible. Daisy gasped when she saw him.

"I'm sorry, I didn't mean to startle you."

"It's so dark in here; I was just coming to light the fire," Daisy said, a little breathlessly. She knelt, struck a match, and set fire to a corner of the crumpled newspaper in the grate. A sprinkling of damp soot lay over the logs and kindling. The paper caught, flared and, after a moment, burned out. The sparks on the sticks that Daisy had gathered on one of her walks turned black and soon all that remained of the fire was smoldering ash and smoke. Daisy crumpled some more paper from the basket beside the fireplace and pushed it under the wood with a poker. She struck another match, pushed the poker between the logs, and lifted one to allow some air to feed the flame. Slowly the fire caught and, as Daisy continued to kneel by the fireplace, it established itself as a dull glow rather than a cheerful blaze. Heskith had not moved from where he stood by the bookshelf.

"What are you reading?" she asked at length, standing up and dusting off her knees.

He didn't reply and instead held the book out. It was small, red, clothbound. Even had the room been brightly lit, Daisy could not have read the title from that distance and she crossed the library to where he was standing.

"*Memoirs of a Fox-Hunting Man,*" he said when she was still five or six feet away from him. "Siegfried Sassoon."

"Patrick—my husband—likes his poetry," Daisy said. For an instant she could recall, with the full emotion of the moment, Patrick saying some lines from the poem walking along a damp lane the afternoon he proposed to her. " 'Everyone suddenly burst out singing,' " she added.

Heskith said nothing but, instead, nodded; a small nod of acknowledgment, recognition.

"I wondered if I might borrow it," he said. "Take it to my room."

"Of course," she said, "I'll have the fire lit for you."

"I can do that myself," he said, his tone polite but discouraging any further offers of hospitable solicitude.

And he was gone. Daisy remained by the bookshelf; she had spent a good deal of time since she had come to Dunmaine choosing books from the library but she had never noticed the small book in the poorly lit shelves. And yet Heskith had found it easily. She looked to see if there was another book by Siegfried Sassoon, but there wasn't.

MRS. MULCAHY, WITHOUT descending to the use of words, allowed Daisy to know she had once again picked a poor moment to visit the kitchen. But this time Daisy had arrived prepared for a battle of wills.

"Captain Heskith would like sandwiches tomorrow instead of lunch. If you could have them ready soon after breakfast. And we'd better give him a proper meal in the evening, with a pudding."

The cook's timing was off; she had chosen silence with which to cow Daisy and would now lose that advantage by questioning Daisy's instructions. And Daisy on the way to the kitchen had practiced not asking the instinctive question that would normally follow such an instruction: the modifying "I hope that won't be too much trouble" as well as the "Will that be all right?" plea for reassurance. After a short struggle with her own nature, Daisy strangled the apologetic confidence that only financial desperation would cause her to impose on Mrs. Mulcahy's good nature and, instead, she asked that when Nelly had finished making the beds she should join her at the linen cupboard.

She hadn't, of course, heard the last of it. Mrs. Mulcahy would even now be swelling with outrage, listing her arguments and complaints and preparing to bluster and bully. Daisy's hands were trembling when she left the kitchen. Transforming Dunmaine into a comfortable enough house to charge, with a clear conscience, for the pleasure of staying there might be an impossible task.

She had started off well: the best spare room in Dunmaine had been given a spring cleaning; a fire had been lit to dispel the constant hint of damp throughout the not regularly used parts of the house. The fire had had a tendency to smoke and Daisy had added a chimney sweep to her list of how the initial five guineas should be spent, ruefully aware that the total now came to just over sixteen pounds.

THERE WAS THE sound of hooves on cobblestones and Daisy, arranging flowers in the pantry, went to the window. Heskith, leaving the stable yard, had ridden Osbert up the short laurel-bordered incline and was now riding away from the house, down the avenue. His back to her, Daisy could gaze at him, moved by the straightness of his spine and the fair hair that curled just over the collar of his jacket. Osbert was moving at a rather more lively pace than he did when Daisy was riding him away from his stable. She watched, aching with desire, until the horse and rider turned the corner. Then she sighed and went along the corridor to join Nelly in the linen room.

Apart from a lack of oxygen and Nelly's silence—half defensive and half resentful that her afternoon had been commandeered—the atmosphere in the small room was not unpleasant. It had stopped raining, but the day was damp and cold. Now she found herself warm enough to take off her cardigan; even the tips of her fingers and toes lost the feeling of coldness to which she had almost, but not quite, become used.

Daisy had known what to expect since the morning, earlier that week, when they had searched for an adequate pair of sheets for Andrew Heskith's bed. She supposed, had she been Nelly, and had Corisande been her employer, she might have used the same method and, instead of rotating the use of the linen, have kept the least damaged at the top of each pile and have allowed the unmended and unusable sheets and pillow cases to stand in neat misleading stacks. When they finished, the linen cupboard did not look much different, but on the bare wooden boards of the passage outside the door now lay a small heap of material to be used as cleaning rags. There were plenty more that were unmendable, but Daisy thought she would save them for later. The largest pile was that of napkins and sheets damaged and torn but not worn out; they could be darned and mended, but by whom? Daisy knew her own limitations and suspected those of Nelly.

DAISY'S ARMS FELT the cold of the night room; they lay, wrists upward, on the pillow beneath her head. The second pillow was adrift somewhere under the sheets. The dark room, the darkness a little thicker in the corners of the high ceiling, lit only by the dying red of the lumps of turf, glowing in the small grate.

Heskith, asleep, lay on top of her, inside her. Some time had passed; Daisy, open-eyed and choosing not to think, breathed slowly and was conscious of every inch of her body where his skin touched hers. Her own body felt as though it had changed its shape. She knew herself to be strong, healthy and rounded; now she felt as though she were several inches taller, her legs longer, her shape remolded by the thrusting of Heskith's hard, tense body. He slept, breathing almost imperceptibly through his nose, still and relaxed. Daisy felt as though she had given him some desperately needed relief. Relief quite apart from the urgency with which he had made love to her.

Her eyes, as they had every ten minutes or so, glanced toward the window, fearing the pale light of the dawn. Heskith would not stay in her bed until it became light, and he would leave Dunmaine that morning. Daisy forced herself not to waste the moment in anticipation of its loss and breathed deeply, inhaling the faint masculine scent of her lover's fair, too-long hair. She ran a hand gently over the back of his head, stroking his hair, his neck. He shuddered and muttered, Daisy held him closely, reassuringly, both arms around him, and he sighed and fell once more into a deep sleep.

The evening before had been tense, the atmosphere of the house permeated with silence and danger. Heskith had returned from his ride and had spent a commendable amount of time in the stable, rubbing down Osbert and brushing him after their afternoon on the moors. Daisy thought he had, or before the war used to have, horses of his own. Alerted by the returning hooves on the cobblestones reentering the yard below, she had watched and waited, unseen, by the window on the landing.

She was loitering in the hall when Heskith came in, ready to offer tea. But he brushed past her, muttering that he would, if he might, take a bath. Daisy spent most of the next ten minutes by the copper cistern in the airing cupboard, patting its sides and hoping there was enough hot water. Heskith did not come down until it was time for dinner. Mickey was silent, preoccupied, but, Daisy thought, unaware of the tension that thickened the air of the dining room.

"How was your ride?" she had asked to interrupt a silence broken only by Mickey's ingestion of the thin soup made from the too-well-picked carcass of the pullet they had eaten for Sunday lunch. Heskith had taken a spoonful; when Daisy spoke he put the spoon down and looked at her blankly for several moments before he replied.

"Very pleasant," he said eventually.

Daisy found herself nervously continuing, although it was clear Heskith wished to be left in peace—perhaps she should offer paying guests the option of eating meals on a tray in their rooms.

"Where did you go?"

This time she had his complete attention. He gazed at her, apparently appalled, for a moment before he replied.

"Onto the moors, and then I just rode around. Looking at birds."

Birds could have been a topic to take them through the next two courses, but Daisy was unnerved by the moment of horror she had seen in his eyes. *Shell shock,* she thought. *I suppose it happens in this war, too.* A pity almost maternal served only to increase the painful ache of desire.

The lamb chops were rather better than Mrs. Mulcahy's usual effort, but Daisy was unable to eat. Heskith, who had not taken up his soup spoon after Daisy had interrupted his thoughts, did not even help himself to the second course. Mickey ate solidly, oblivious to the silence and to the solitary nature of his own meal. As soon as dinner was over, Heskith excused himself, rose, and left the table. Daisy and Mickey sat for a moment longer, the silence unbroken.

"Odd chap, isn't he?" Mickey remarked, and Daisy, eschewing a too easy rejoinder, merely nodded.

Muttering an excuse, and irritated that she felt the need to account for her movements to the completely indifferent Mickey, Daisy went up to her room.

There was a small fire, flaky and gray, still just alive in the grate. Over the winter, Daisy had learned how to rescue the embers and give the fire enough life for it to burn until she fell asleep. She took off her dress, hung it up, and put on her dressing gown. It was still early and she thought she should do something useful before she went to bed.

On her desk was the modified menu she was planning; repeated every two weeks, it would allow her to feed the household more economically and it could be adapted, with no additional expense or waste, when they had a paying guest who wanted a picnic lunch.

Daisy sat, rubbing one stockinged leg against the other, trying to generate a little warmth in her lower extremities. *Stewed apples,* she read, *baked apples, apple Charlotte. Suet pudding, canary pudding with red currant sauce. Chicken fricassee, chicken hash, chicken soup.* She made a note against chicken soup; the chicken soup needed a lot of work.

There was a gentle but firm knock at her door. Tying the cord of her dressing gown more tightly around her and slipping the foot with which she was massaging her calf back into its shoe, Daisy rose and crossed to the door. She felt suddenly tired and not able for the domestic emergency, minor she hoped, that a knock at that hour presaged.

Andrew Heskith, paler and more tense, stood at the door.

"I'm sorry," he said. "I am going to have to go back to England tomorrow. I'm packing and I wanted to give you a check and ask if you can arrange transport to the station."

Daisy looked at him for a moment. Had there been a telephone call? Or a telegram? Or was this not, more likely, the thin excuse of a man no longer able to bear the boredom and bad food of a stay at Dunmaine?

"I'm sorry," she said, scarlet with embarrassment, "I'm afraid I am a very poor housekeeper."

Heskith looked at her with, it seemed, genuine surprise. The landing outside Daisy's door was dimly lit and his silhouette was easier to see than was the expression on his strained face. Daisy realized that she, too, was only faintly visible in the half-light. Their proximity; the growing darkness; her cold bed, in the background, turned down for the night; Heskith's low voice, made it impossible for Daisy to continue. What would she have said, anyway? A reiteration of her previous apology, meaningless since Heskith had no choice but to deny the truth obvious to both of them.

"I have to go," he said. "It's nothing to do with not liking it here, I—"

He stopped, Daisy waited for him to continue.

"Mrs. Nugent," he said at last, and paused again. "Daisy—"

He stepped forward and Daisy almost involuntarily took a step backward. In one continuous movement, fluid and it seemed effortless, Heskith was inside the room, the door closed behind him, an arm behind Daisy's waist, drawing her to him.

"No," she said, "I—"

"Don't say anything," he said, and Daisy found herself instinctively obeying him, as though he had relieved her of all responsibility for what was going to happen.

"It's all right," he said, "it's all right."

Those were the last words they spoke for a time; he untied the sash of her dressing gown and opened it, pushing the shoulders back so that it slid down her arms and dropped on the floor. He stood back a little and looked at her. Cold and helpless in a satin slip she had bought for her trousseau, Daisy found herself moving closer to Heskith, not so much to touch him as in order not to feel so visibly undressed; he was still clothed as he had been at dinner, a meal that now seemed to Daisy to have taken place a week ago.

His hands resting on her hipbones, he held her away from him and continued to look, unsmiling, at her half-dressed body. After a long moment, still holding her waist, he drew her to him, supporting her and helping her to balance, while she stepped out of first one, then the other, of her shoes. His jacket felt hard and scratchy against her skin and Daisy felt smaller, shorter, delicate. Heskith crossed to the foot of the bed and sat down.

"Now take off your clothes."

Daisy paused for a moment, but she did not consider disobeying him. Slowly, awkwardly, even a little clumsily, she unhooked a stocking from her suspender belt. She felt fear, and slightly cold, but none of the excitement that she would have imagined, even an hour ago, accompanying the touch of his hand on hers. Heskith watched her, expressionless, and she undid her other stocking and slid it down over her foot. Reaching under her slip, she unfastened her suspender belt and dropped it to the floor. Still, Heskith remained expressionless, although his attention fully on her, his gaze unwavering. Daisy hesitated again, and he nodded a little impatiently; she pulled her slip up over her head, stepped out of her knickers, and scurried to the bed.

He watched as she slipped under the cold sheets, drawing them with both hands up to her chin. A belated and ineffectual protection from the man who was, even then, switching off the light, crossing the room, and approaching where she lay. The sheets chill against her naked skin, Daisy thought that she was still at an age and level of inexperience that should entitle her to a modicum of reassurance before seduction or lovemaking, although neither word began to describe what was happening. He undressed quickly, neatly, and efficiently and slid into bed beside her. She was aware that he still had not kissed her when she felt him spread her body out on the sheet and a moment later he was on top of her and then, urgently, painfully, inside her.

Heskith slept on, Daisy holding him, stroking the back of his head and his neck gently so that she made his sleep more peaceful without risking waking him. She knew that when he woke he would leave and she knew also she would never see him again. She knew that when he left her room she would continue to feel the warmth of his body, that the smell of him would linger, exciting and satisfying, until she got up. Good-byes in the chill of morning would be awkward, bitter with the taste of lost opportunities. And then he would be gone and the lonely, guilty suffering would begin.

ANDREW HESKITH LEFT soon after breakfast and Daisy, lonely as an abandoned dog, wandered the house. Cold with longing and lack of sleep, she huddled beside the dining-room fireplace, sitting on the rug and rocking her body gently to and fro. The fire smoldered and smoked slightly, tiny belches of paler smoke coming from the same crack under the mantelpiece. Daisy looked at it unseeingly and went upstairs to her room. On the low chair beside the dead fire lay the envelope Heskith had brought to her door the night before. It was sealed, and nothing was written on it. Daisy opened it; she had never seen Heskith's handwriting. Although he had mentioned a check, the envelope contained only the money he owed, banknotes and two half-crowns. Daisy set it down on her desk and wandered toward Heskith's now empty room, looking for traces of him. But Nelly, curious about her tip, had made an early start on the bedrooms and sheets and pillowcases now lay in a crumpled heap by the door. Daisy returned quietly to her room, closed her door, and lay on her unmade bed, burying her face in the pillows, searching for the smell of her lover.

THE FOLLOWING DAY Nelly again came into the dining room while they were eating breakfast. Again with the air of someone with important news.

The meal was silent; Daisy, although aware she should still be jubilant about the Irish firefighters in Belfast—and, indeed, when she thought about them she felt close to tears and knew her voice would break if she attempted to speak—was still shocked by the not yet quite understood night with Heskith. Shaken by the knowledge that she had, without it seemed a moment's hesitation, betrayed her husband, shaken by the tender places on her body and the bruise on her shoulder, shaken that the pale bruise seemed a small treasure and that she would regret its fading.

Nelly was sure of her audience and Daisy might have expected her to show some pleasurable sense of her own dramatic status, but the housemaid seemed, if not exactly frightened, unsure of herself, and as though what she was about to impart might have some not immediately apparent but unpleasant implications for herself.

"Mrs. Nugent," she said, and paused. "Mr. Mickey—"

Patrick, Daisy thought. *It's something to do with Patrick. He's dead and its all my fault.*

"What is it, Nelly?" Daisy was surprised by the calm of her

voice. Mickey was expressionless, but she suspected he too felt fear.

"It's Wilcox, m'am—they're saying down below he's been shot."

Shot? Sir Guy seemed an unlikely person to get shot. Daisy had formed the impression of him as careful, methodical, meticulous, and most unlikely to find himself accompanied by anyone so irresponsible as to climb over a fence with a loaded gun.

"Is he badly hurt?" Mickey asked. Daisy could see he was as puzzled as she was.

"He's dead, sir." Nelly now was puzzled, too. Daisy realized that "shot" to the housemaid meant an act of violence, not of carelessness. Or perhaps the shooting season was over and she was shocked at her employer's ignorance.

All three were silent. It was more Nelly's lack of pleasure in the drama than the fact of the death itself that suggested to Daisy there was something deeper and more sinister involved. Nelly looked as though frightening and painful memories and fears had suddenly been revived. English soldiers, unpopular landlords, the Black and Tans. Sudden deaths, acts of violence and revenge; more likely her parents' memories than her own, but Daisy had a quick glimpse of the troubled not so distant past of Ireland.

"It was, of course, an accident?" Mickey seemed to be firmly deflecting any suggestion of something awkward—suicide, perhaps?—before Nelly put words around whatever it was she was hinting at.

"He was shot," Nelly repeated patiently. "Killed. Someone murdered him."

This time the silence was a little longer, frozen with their fear and struggle to understand.

"When did it happen?" Mickey asked.

"They found him yesterday. He'd been missing."

So the news had traveled the distance from the Wilcoxes' house—the house on a good stretch of river—to Dunmaine by word of mouth; there would be nothing about the murder, if murder it had indeed been, in the newspapers until the following day's *Irish Times*. There might be something on the six o'clock news.

"I see," Daisy said eventually. "Thank you, Nelly. That will be all."

CHAPTER 17

EDMUND AND CORISANDE arrived late the following afternoon. They had been staying with his cousins in Westmeath.
Mickey went to meet the train; Daisy, lonely, lacking occupation,
though hardly bored, would have liked to accompany him, but
knew it would overload the trap for the return journey, some of
it uphill. Her own driving skills were still uncertain enough for
her to prefer them unwitnessed, least of all by Corisande.

Mrs. Mulcahy sent up an above average beef stew; the effort,
Daisy thought, less motivated by her own lecture of two days ago
than by the excitement in the air. First the feeling of pride that de
Valera had, spontaneously, without counsel or advice, sent firemen
north to fight the fires on the docks of Belfast; then the frisson and
uncertainty caused by a shooting that had connotations of a dia-
metrically different national mood.

Mickey had, on the way back from the station, told Corisande
and Edmund everything he knew about the death, the probable
murder, of their neighbor. Edmund was silent, thoughtful.
Corisande, after a longish absence and complete change of scenery,
had returned to the level of irritation with her brother that she had
apparently felt at the time of her departure.

"But why?" Daisy asked, addressing Edmund. Now, surely,

the attitude of the Anglo-Irish in general, and that of the Nugent family in particular, toward the displaced Fascist Wilcoxes would become clear or, at least, clearer.

"I don't know."

"Because he's English?" she asked. "It's not as though he was a landlord or anything. The Powers told us they'd just rented the house."

"They didn't even farm the land," Corisande said thought-fully. Daisy could tell that Corisande was uncomfortable with some unexpressed thought, some implication she wasn't going to explore, even at a family dinner. Daisy assumed that Corisande's discomfort related to the unaddressed question of the Wilcoxes' politics and why, if they were close to being considered the enemy in England, he should have become the victim of what seemed to be a belated nationalistic assassination. She wondered if Corisande would talk more frankly to Edmund about whatever it was in bed; they would have separate rooms, but Edmund had been promoted from bachelor's quarters to a spare room with a double bed.

"Is that why they didn't burn the house down?" Daisy asked. "Because it didn't belong to the Wilcoxes?"

Edmund shrugged.

"Probably whoever it was had learned something from the past. They tried to burn down Winter Hill in 1919, but it was too damp."

"What was he—were they—doing here anyway?" Daisy asked, feeling justified in pressing the question a little. Corisande's discomfort—embarrassment—might be based only on Daisy being English, but whatever it was, surely now was the time to drag it into the open.

"Avoiding rationing, I expect. All those little dogs." Corisande sounded surer of herself, as though she had avoided something unpleasant.

"But—" Mickey said, and earned a look of blank dislike from his sister.

"There'd been a spot of trouble in England," Edmund said, with a calmness that made Daisy think she might have been mistaken about Corisande, "a few of his friends interned and some 'detained as security risks' in actual prisons. So it was probably easier and less all round embarrassing for everyone if he left the country."

The ease that Edmund spoke with and his frank open manner seemed so natural that it took Daisy a moment to realize that he had only volunteered something known to them all and already voiced, on the way home from the Powers' lunch party, by Mickey.

"It's not as though these things don't happen," Edmund continued, after a pause. "Admiral Somerville shot on his own doorstep—probably because he'd written a couple of letters for local boys who wanted to join the English navy. That's four or five years ago and no one ever charged with the murder. It happens, although less often than it did; de Valera takes a pretty hard line these days. Still, I wouldn't count on anyone getting charged."

"Mickey tells me you've been taking in guests?" Corisande said to Daisy, giving her words no weight but coating them with a suggestion of mild amusement. It was an abrupt change of subject, but Daisy had the impression Corisande was following her own convoluted train of thought.

"We have," Daisy said calmly, giving a small emphasis to the first word. She would have been annoyed by the note of amusement had she not felt so guilty; the events of her first effort as a landlady representing a far stronger argument against the scheme than Corisande could have come up with in a month of Sundays.

"Keeping the wolf from the door," Mickey said cheerfully. "Surprised we didn't think of it years ago."

Corisande's eyes flicked nervously toward Edmund, and

Daisy, who knew her sister-in-law wouldn't really feel safe until after her wedding, thought her reluctant to have it pointed out to Edmund that he was marrying into a family of Johnny-come-lately lodging-house keepers. Mickey, of course, did not catch the nuance and seemed eager to continue to follow his subject until he had beaten it to death.

"Interesting chap," he continued, rather to Daisy's surprise since she couldn't remember Mickey and Heskith exchanging so much as a word. Perhaps they had had a fascinating, albeit brief, exchange over port the evening of Heskith's arrival.

"So long as he didn't pack the silver," Corisande's laugh was brittle and tinkly. That laugh, Daisy thought, might have proved a greater obstacle to marriage than her lack of fortune or her relatives. And Edmund and Corisande still weren't married. His proposal had not made her more secure; quite the contrary, she was now hopelessly compromised, unable to retreat and dependent on him to advance to respectability and position. Daisy now thought that her early impression of him and of Ambrose as teasing, or perhaps bullying, schoolboys was not accurate; Edmund at least, had a cruel streak.

"It was either that or hock the silver," she said lightly, for the first time asserting herself in the face of Corisande's habitual dismissal. "Bills to pay, taxes, overdrafts, mortgages." She paused significantly. "Wages."

Corisande blushed; Edmund laughed. Startled, Daisy looked up and caught Mickey shooting her a quick and, she thought, sly glance. From, it seemed, nowhere, she remembered a patch of wallpaper in the bedroom that was never used, the room that seemed to have belonged to a boy or young man, and to have been left unchanged, although clean and dusted, since the end of the Great War. The patch, centered over the neatly laid, but unlit, fireplace was rectangular, clearer, darker, fresher than the paper around it, and surrounded by a border of dust stains; the dust stains had rounded corners. Corisande had been selling off bits and pieces from around the house. Daisy's first thought was to wonder why she hadn't at least thought of that solution herself; her second was that if Corisande were trading in partially stolen goods—even after her grandmother's demise she would be entitled only to a third—it would have been better form if she had paid the household wages as well as her dressmaker.

During the silence that followed, prolonged by Kathleen clearing away their plates and bringing in the rice pudding, Daisy realized that Corisande had thought Edmund and her brother ignorant of her pilfering. And that she would never entirely forgive Daisy for innocently causing her ridicule.

DAISY LAY HALF asleep, her head buried in the pillow, dozing, dreaming, thinking of Heskith; reluctant even to have the linen on her bed changed. Soon he would exist only in her memory. His bedroom now housed, or seemed to house, Edmund. Or maybe Corisande was the one who padded across the cold landing. Heskith, she assumed, was now on the way back to his regiment; Daisy didn't know what regiment, let alone where he might be going. Into the void of war, to disappear as her husband had. Patrick, she cried silently, but she could hardly remember his face or his voice. His hands, the flat nail on the middle finger of his left hand the truest memory she could summon.

There was a creak from the landing outside her door. Edmund on his way to Corisande's room? Corisande visiting him? Mickey visiting his bats? Or the house protesting the damp spring air? Had the landing creaked in the same manner when Heskith had crossed it, coming to her bed, leaving her bed, two nights ago? If she felt this much pain and loneliness two nights after she had slept with a warm, hard body next to hers, how would she feel in a month? Another quieter creak, followed by a small crackle and the sound of soot falling from the chimney. And how faint the feelings of guilt compared to the pain of loss; she knew she would never see Heskith again. . . . *that his hair is beautiful,/Cold as the March wind his eyes.*

A little smell of smoke, as though Edmund had thrown the butt of his cigar into the fireplace after dinner and it had set the hard ends of the knotty wood alight again. Without enough upward draft, all the fireplaces at Dunmaine smoked. In fact, her own fireplace, no longer glowing, seemed to be smoking a little.

MAUD LAY HALF awake; she was not unhappy, day and night had little difference for her now.

During the day, although she rarely spoke, she listened to human sounds, sometimes comprehending the significance of the words or noises, sometimes not. Philomena alone understood that it was not senility, but a lack of interest, of relevance, that caused Maud to close her eyes or to allow them to glaze over while she was being told something of importance to the speaker, of interest to everyone else. She felt herself, more and more, a separate entity from the rest of the world, spinning as though she were in a separate slow orbit. She cared about the firefighters in Belfast. Although she had not spoken a word while Philomena recounted the day's news, she had blinked several times and made a gesture that only Philomena would have understood to be a nod. She cared that her grandson was missing, missing in a confusing, unofficial way; she cared that his cousin James—her great-nephew— was dead; she cared slightly less that soon she would die. But caring didn't make her interested—*It doesn't make any difference*, she half consciously thought, pleased to be able to find the words. Already incipient death was making her see all life, all humanity, as part of a precise but too large to comprehend pattern; already nibbling at the part of her brain that stored her vocabulary. There were times when she would have liked to say a word to encourage more details, to show a moment of affection, to correct a mistaken assumption, but more and more she feared her inability to carry the clearly thought reply or sentiment from her mind to the spoken word.

At night she listened to sounds that seemed as clear and easy to understand as many of the words spoken to her during the day. That night there was an owl and, in the distance, a vixen barking. The sounds made Maud happy and for a moment full of hope.

"Fox," she said, not able to find the sound for "vixen." She felt as though there might be someone in the room who could hear her. If not, it hardly mattered; it merely gave her an opportunity to try her voice and words.

"Fox," she said again, a little louder. The first attempt far too low for Philomena, her most probable companion, to hear.

There was no reply and Maud turned her head slowly, careful of her stiff and rheumatic neck, toward the armchair beside the fireplace. The fire had become so gray that it was difficult for her to make out the dark outline against the pale chair.

"Philomena," she said as loudly as she could, "wake up; it's the middle of the night. You should be in bed."

There was no reply; Philomena did not move.

"Philomena, wake up. And put some turf on the fire—it's almost out and it's smoking."

Philomena did not move. It occurred to Maud that it was possible that Philomena had died. She was more fond of Philomena than of most people, but the thought she might be dead did not seem sad. Soon they would all be dead, she herself sooner than most.

DAISY WOKE GASPING from a dream. In it Heskith had been killing her, holding her down with one hand, smothering her with the other. The hand that he held over her mouth was covered with the sheet and maybe the blanket. Daisy knew she was being killed and she was not struggling or contesting his right to extinguish her life. Then, it seemed, there was a moment of unsureness, of wondering why she could not feel the skin of his palm over her face, why the coarse linen sheet was between them, and a horrified suspicion that it was not Heskith, but Edmund masquerading as Heskith, concealing the essential taste and smell of him, who was killing her—she did not have the sense that it was a murder although she knew it must end in death—and she started to struggle.

She woke gasping for breath and sweating with fear; her heart was pounding and she felt the sick rush of adrenaline in her stomach. Sitting up in bed, she waited for the more extreme sensations to pass, and it was a second or two before she realized she was not able to draw in the deep breath of cold, clean air she had anticipated. The room was full of smoke.

Daisy jumped out of bed. Without thinking she might be wasting time, she slipped her feet into her bedroom slippers, wrapped herself in Patrick's schoolboy dressing gown—it had P. NUGENT embroidered in red on a name tag inside of the collar—ran across the room and opened the door onto the landing. The smoke was thicker.

"Help, Edmund, fire, fire!" Daisy's voice—she had not taken much of a breath—was not loud but should have been loud enough for either Mickey or Edmund, whose rooms lay off the same landing, to have heard her.

"Mickey," she shouted, more from good manners than because she thought him the one to deal with the crisis, as she pounded on Edmund's door. There was no reply, and understanding that her hesitation was ridiculous, she opened the door.

"Edmund, Edmund, there's a fire, the house is full of—"

But Edmund's room was silent. The curtains were open—Nelly had forgotten to draw them, or to turn down the bed—and there was enough moonlight for Daisy to see the bed had not been slept in. If Edmund was, as he undoubtedly was, in Corisande's room, then she should wake Mickey. Banging a little harder with her fist on his door—why did she assume he was a heavier sleeper than his brother-in-law?—and opening it a little more quickly since she had no reason to think Mickey would not be alone, Daisy found herself in another unoccupied room. Mickey's bed, unlike Edmund's, had been slept in, the sheets rumpled and the blankets hanging off the bed as though Mickey had had violent dreams. Or perhaps he, too, had been woken by the smoke. If so, where was he? What was he doing?

Daisy started toward Corisande's bedroom. Then she paused, thinking it likely that Mickey had gone first to rescue his grandmother before raising a general alarm. The choice illogical, but not out of character.

Opening the door to Maud's bedroom quietly, Daisy crept into the room.

"Mickey," she whispered, not wanting to frighten Maud before she knew what she was supposed to do.

"He's not here, I heard him go along the corridor about an hour ago," Maud said calmly; the first words Daisy had ever heard her speak.

Along the corridor? An hour ago? To Corisande's room? Had Mickey woken up, found the house on fire, and decided to alert Corisande and Edmund? And had the three of them decided to leave Maud and Daisy to perish? Or were Corisande, Mickey, and Edmund, oblivious to the danger, indulging in a midnight feast? Without her, she thought, with a little pang.

"I'll be back," Daisy said, keeping her voice calm and instinctively feeling no need to tender an explanation. Turning to leave, she saw, in the dim light—it was closer to dawn than she had imagined—the dark gray outline of a form in the armchair beside the fire. What was Philomena doing there at that hour of the night? Had she not gone home? Or had she come in early? If so, why hadn't she lighted the fire?

"Philomena?" she said tentatively.

"It's no use," Maud said, in the same calm articulate tone. "I think she's dead."

Daisy began to wonder if this were not part of an unusually vivid nightmare. For a moment she considered screaming, since that was the way she had, as a child, woken herself; the struggle to emit even the faintest sound usually enough to return her, terrified, to the waking world and her dark bedroom. Instead, finding herself in what seemed to be a deserted, probably burning, house, her only companions an old, dead servant and an invalid she had, up to a moment before, assumed to be partly or completely senile, she tried to act decisively.

"We need to get you downstairs," she said, crossing to the bed. "I think the house is on fire."

"Yes," Maud said, just as calmly. "It's a chimney fire. Smoke has been coming up all night."

"But, why didn't—sorry—" Daisy broke off, horrified that Maud had lain awake for hours, aware that the house—her house—was burning slowly, unable to move or call out loud enough to get help. Her own reassuring "I'll be back" didn't seem quite adequate now.

"Let's get you downstairs," Daisy said, crossing to the bed. "Then I'll find Mickey and Corisande, then I'll come back for Philomena. I think there's plenty of time."

It seemed important, now that she knew Maud was sentient, to explain exactly what was happening; at the same time, Maud's calm gave Daisy the illogical reassurance that she was in the presence of an adult. She paused a moment by the bed, looking down. Maud was frail, tiny-boned; she must have been a small woman even before she had faded and shriveled. Daisy was a strong girl; she had no doubt of her ability to carry Maud downstairs, but she was not sure how to do so without hurting or frightening her. She pulled the heavy, slippery satin eiderdown off the bed, better to assess her task, and Maud shivered. Knowing that now was not the time to try to dress the old lady, Daisy started to wrap her in the sheets and blankets in which she lay. She discarded the pillows and tugged at the undersheet and blanket in order to wrap Maud more fully, deciding that when she had brought her downstairs and possibly outside, she would return for coats, shawls, and blankets. The sheet came loose easily enough, but the underblanket caught on something as Daisy tugged at it. Letting go of Maud for a moment, she lifted a corner of the mattress to unhook the blanket from the spring that caught it. It took her a moment to free it; she was aware she was wasting time and it made her clumsy. The washed-out flannel blanket had caught because there was a solid object wrapped in it and pushed between two of the coiled metal bedsprings. Once she could see the problem, it was easy for Daisy to free the wrapped object and then the blanket.

Surprised to find herself with something apparently secret, and not belonging to her, in her hand, Daisy hesitated, confused. But Maud, quicker than Daisy could have imagined possible, whipped the flat package, loosely wrapped in a piece of old white silk, away from her. She unwound the silk, which Daisy had the impression was intended to keep the box she now revealed closed rather than to protect it. The box was flat, a dull worn black, the hook that should have secured it broken. Maud opened it a little, as though to make sure the contents were intact, and Daisy caught a glimpse of a strand of fat pearls before the old lady closed it again. Glancing slyly at Daisy, she tucked the case and the hand holding it under her shawl and waited to be rescued. Daisy continued to wrap Maud into a warm bundle so that she could carry her downstairs.

She was almost at the door of the room, Maud light and limp in her arms, her head, like a baby's, against Daisy's shoulder, when Edmund arrived.

"The house—" he said. "Well done, Daisy, I'll—" and his eyes flicked to Philomena's motionless form.

"I—Aunt Maud," Daisy said, the question of how to refer to the old lady solved by the urgency of the moment, "Aunt Maud thinks she's dead."

Edmund's expression did not change as he quickly moved to the armchair and lifted Philomena's face, pressing two fingers against her neck as he did so.

"Yes, I'm afraid she is."

Edmund hesitated, looking down at Philomena.

"Perhaps—" Daisy murmured.

"Yes, of course. Sorry," he said, and carefully took Maud into his arms.

Daisy preceding him, and holding up the trailing ends of the sheets he might have stepped on, they went quickly down the stairs. Daisy wondered what they would do with Maud once they got her downstairs; Edmund, without hesitation, carried her into the drawing room and set her on a sofa close to the French window that opened onto the conservatory.

"It's not the warmest seat in the house," he said cheerfully, "but it makes it easy for someone to break in and bring you out, if it's necessary. Not that that's going to happen, of course."

Maud, who to Daisy, didn't look as though she needed reassuring, looked about her.

"Corisande changed the slipcovers," she said. "No one told me."

Daisy thought Corisande might have quite a lot of explaining to do. She wondered if new slipcovers had been an overdue necessity or, like the dressmaker bills, an investment in Corisande's future.

"Good girl, Daisy," Edmund said. "Right, let's wake the others, and the maids, get help, and maybe take a few of the better things out onto the lawn. Why don't you telephone and I'll get the others up."

So Edmund went upstairs and Daisy, standing in the hall, lifted the receiver and wound the handle. No one picked up her call at the exchange, but since it often took minutes during the day for the postmistress to connect a call, particularly if one were so thoughtless as to attempt communication at times when Mrs. Crowe was cooking, feeding her family, or answering a call of nature, Daisy was not at first alarmed by the lack of response. She watched Edmund turn the corner on the landing and he was out of sight before she realized that the telephone exchange was probably closed for the night and she didn't know what time Mrs. Crowe got up in the morning.

Daisy went back upstairs. She asked herself where was Corisande while all this had been going on? Had Edmund left her catching up on her beauty sleep while he went to investigate the now quite thick smoke? Was she packing the contents of the locked desk in her room? And where was Mickey? She realized she had not told Edmund that Mickey was not in his room, and she hurried along the corridor toward the room she assumed Edmund was sharing with Corisande. She paused by the door to the room that appeared to have been frozen in time since 1918. Daisy pushed the door open tentatively.

"Mickey," she said, entering a little breathless, "wake up. There's a fire—"

But although the top of bed was rumpled, the room was empty.

"I woke Mickey," Edmund said from behind her. "He was asleep in here—I sent him—"

"The exchange doesn't answer—I think it's closed for the night."

It was cold on the lawn, and Corisande stayed in the drawing room with Maud. Dawn was breaking. As Daisy went back and forth into the house she could now see smoke coming up between the floorboards. The house, she thought, was a little warmer than it usually was early in the morning, but there was no sign of fire or sound of burning.

She passed Edmund on the stairs; he was carrying a painting. Daisy had never noticed it before and even now in the dim light, had Edmund not appeared to have thought it worth saving, she would have passed it by. She peered at it as they paused, a dark portrait of a far from handsome woman; it badly needed cleaning.

"Where—" Daisy asked, embarrassed that she had not asked the obvious question before, "where exactly is the fire?"

She had opened the dining-room door to take out silver a little earlier and had been faced with such thick smoke that she had been unable to enter, but the smoke had not been accompanied by flames or the crackle of fire.

"It's in the chimneys; they're all connected and it's probably been burning all night. Or longer." Daisy remembered, horrified, the small belches of smoke she had seen from above the fireplace in the dining room. "But it's going faster now, getting hotter—what happens is that when it reaches a certain temperature the whole thing goes up and—"

Edmund gestured and Daisy, reminded of the lack of time, continued more quickly up the staircase. It felt strange and almost dreamlike that she and Edmund were drifting around the burning house, making arbitrary and probably illogical choices of what they would save.

Daisy wandered—her lack of any kind of plan making her light-headed—into Maud's bedroom. What were the old lady's treasures? Philomena still sat, forgotten, in the armchair. She had to be taken downstairs, but where? Not to the drawing room to join Maud and Corisande. Not out onto the lawn, to be exposed to the dew and the increasing light of day. Maybe Mrs. Mulcahy and Nelly—Kathleen had disappeared sometime before—would go and tell her daughter, still asleep in the gate lodge.

Daisy swept the photographs off the dressing table into a large tapestry bag, which Maud must once have used to keep her needlework, and hurried on to find Edmund. Philomena would have been too heavy for Daisy to have carried herself, even if she had known how to carry the now perhaps stiffening body.

Holding the heavy but not large clock that sweetly chimed the hours and quarters from the landing table, Daisy ran downstairs. As she crossed the hall there was a sound—a whoosh—as though a rush of air was being drawn out of the whole large drafty house and expelled through the chimney. She fled through the hall door, across the gravel, onto the semicircle of lawn. The grass was wet under her feet.

Corisande and Edmund were helping Maud slowly out through the conservatory. Daisy slipped past them; looking back through the dusty, mildew-edged glass, Daisy could see that a light armchair for Maud had already been carried onto the lawn. Despite the whoosh, there were still no flames. It seemed foolhardy to go back through the front door into the paneled hall, but she thought it might still be possible to save a few things—silver, photographs, a small painting—from the drawing room. The conservatory would surely be one of the last places to catch fire.

On a wicker sofa in the conservatory were piled the valuable and random objects brought from upstairs or from the library and smoke-filled dining room, left there until the last moment to protect them from the dew. Corisande's fur coat had been tossed over one end of the sofa. Daisy picked it up; she didn't much care if it got wet on the dew-covered grass, and it might serve to keep someone—probably Corisande—warm during the next few hours. She was surprised, even at such a moment, by the softness of the fur. Squirrel, she thought. Underneath the coat lay Corisande's dressing case. Pale leather, with her initials on it. Daisy glanced out at the group on the lawn and unlocked the fasteners; she was curious to see what contraband Corisande had chosen to rescue from her room. Would, for instance, the photograph of Ambrose have been saved? As she opened the dressing case, releasing the sweet mixture of powder and scent, the soft leather of the case's interior changing and adding to the comforting smell. Inside there was a jewelry box and a flat case, similar to the one she had found under the mattress of Maud's bed. And a silk scarf loosely wrapped around an oblong object. Daisy picked it up; it was heavier than she expected. Unwrapping one end, she found that she was holding a gun. A revolver or a pistol, she thought, not knowing the difference. Not a kind of gun she had ever seen before. Not a gun for shooting birds or even one that she imagined soldiers using—this was the kind of gun a man could carry, concealed, in his pocket.

There was the sound of a footstep from the drawing room behind her. Daisy, shocked by what she held in her hand, remained frozen for a moment, then rewrapped the gun, and put it back in the dressing case.

"I think we should—" Edmund said, and then seeing Daisy replacing the gun, paused. Daisy, shocked and confused, looked at him silently for a moment. His face was expressionless and for a moment he didn't say anything. Then, "It's probably time to get out of the house."

Daisy picked up the dressing case and the fur coat and stepped out onto the lawn, followed by Edmund. Corisande and Maud were not far away but Daisy could hear nothing but the sounds of dawn. A cow, waiting to be milked, lowed in the pasture below the house; a blackbird, oblivious to the drama of the burning house, assured his mate on her nest that all was well with the world.

A lilac tree, mature, the blossoms wet, the leaves green and full of resilient presence, magnificent against the black horizon of incipient rain. Rain that would be hard and heavy, but probably not heavy enough or soon enough to drench the flames that would surely engulf Dunmaine.

CHAPTER 18

THERE WAS SOMEBODY coming up the avenue on a bicycle. At first, I thought he was coming to help—although I don't know what good a boy on a bicycle could have been. He'd been given the package of letters and told to bring them on his way home. Mrs. Crowe knew we hadn't had a letter from you since the first one. But he—it was never clear, he was evasive—I think had been to a dance in the other direction and was on his way home. I suppose he'd planned just to push them through the letterbox but when he saw us he didn't seem at all surprised. I took the letters and Edmund sent the boy off to the village.

Daisy, once again writing from Shannig, had already described the fire and the extent of the damage. Not in huge or depressing detail. She had told Patrick that Dunmaine was intact but uninhabitable. She reassured him that everyone had a roof over his head and that she, Mickey, and Maud were staying with Edmund and—leaving this bit out—a visibly less enthusiastically hospitable Corisande.

First, of course, we looked at the dates. The postmarks on the envelopes. The last one was addressed to me and was dated six weeks ago. Mickey said I could open it first if I wanted, that I wasn't to read it out to anyone, so that your letters could be read in the proper order.

She hadn't opened it first, although she had held the letter in her hand, her eyes focused on the blurred postmark. She waited silently as Mickey sorted the other letters into the order in which they had been sent; it was the first time she had seen Mickey take charge, or assert himself in any way that did not involve sullenness, withdrawal, silence. When he had sorted them, he handed them out. Some of the letters written over Christmas were addressed to the family as a group; these he handed out in order, as though dealing cards for a primitive game. They opened them and took turns reading them aloud.

Now that I know you get my letters,—or have been getting my letters—it is easier to write.

She paused; it was true that it was easier to write, but not true, as she had implied, that it was now easy. Six weeks was a long gap; she didn't know whether Patrick was still at the prisoner-of-war camp from which he had written.

Your last letter took six weeks to get here. Since they all came at the same time, that's probably longer than they usually do. When you next write please let me know how long this one takes to get to you.

Daisy no longer sent the questions she needed answered to Patrick. Too long without a letter back made them feel demanding, and the letters that had arrived, all at once, the morning of the fire, contained little information and no direct answers. Maybe he had not had all her letters. By now Daisy knew these questions would have to be answered, although gradually, by herself.

Through inference, instinct, and sometimes, as she understood more of the world of the Anglo-Irish, by a process of elimination.

I don't know how much Philomena meant to you. I gathered from Corisande that she had at one time been a nurserymaid, but she didn't go into details

No need to enlarge on that conversation; she had to assume that Patrick knew his sister better than she, Daisy, did. And that he knew Mickey to be a source only of information of his own choosing.

I am sorry another link to the past has been broken. At the very least she must have been a familiar face. It seems she died in her sleep. The fire had nothing to do with it, and she didn't suffer. Nor was she alone. Your grandmother is being looked after by the wife of Edmund's groom. She seems kind and quiet; it is hard to tell how Aunt Maud feels about her, but time will tell.

Still no one had speculated on the cause of the fire; it seemed to have been accepted as an act of God. But Daisy feared it had come from a spark in the dining-room fire, a fire lit for Andrew Heskith. She had lit it for the benefit of a paying guest, but her conscience made her feel she had burned Dunmaine to warm her lover.

"STRICTLY SPEAKING, IT'S not necessary for women to go to funerals," Edmund said, "but, in this instance, I thought we should perhaps show the flag."

"Which flag would that be?" Corisande asked sourly.

"Of course," Daisy said quickly, her mind already turning toward suitable clothing.

"A large turnout is going to look more like curiosity than what you call showing the flag—" Corisande added, "although that's certainly a better choice of phrase than solidarity."

Corisande was right, of course. Daisy was pleased that she was going to the funeral, her pleasure that of drama and curiosity, and she was well aware a funeral such as Sir Guy's could be one of the larger social events of the foreseeable future. And something she could write to Patrick about.

"You're right," Edmund said, his expression and voice pleasant, "of course. As usual, you're right. You probably shouldn't go, especially not from this house."

Since she had come to stay at Shannig, the spats between Edmund and her sister-in-law had embarrassed Daisy, less by their content than by the implied subtext. Edmund, every time he and Corisande exchanged verbal blows, was silently saying *I haven't married you yet and if you don't behave, maybe I never will* and she, in return, was suggesting that she was holding her punches until after she was his wife, but that then there would be a day of reckoning. Daisy watched, horrified, as Corisande from a position of weakness habitually overplayed her hand. But now Daisy was beginning to realize that, as was so often the case, everyone was doing exactly what he wanted. Not that it made it less embarrassing for those who witnessed these outbursts of malice.

No one was surprised when Corisande, exquisite in a black coat and skirt with a little gray hat and a long gray chiffon scarf was, uncharacteristically punctual, ready and waiting in the hall when the others assembled for the funeral. Mickey was wearing his usual Sunday tweed suit with the addition of a black tie. Edmund was dressed in his up-from-the-country-for-a-day-in-London dark suit. He, too, wore a black tie. It seemed possible to Daisy that elegance, as well as a love of good clothing, was one of the stronger bonds between Edmund and Corisande.

Corisande had made the wreath. The day before, the sink and draining board of what was still called the butler's pantry, had been piled with greenery and clumps of wet moss. Corisande had taken a piece of chicken wire and twisted it into a large circle. Then she had stuffed it tight with moss; Daisy watched, fascinated not only by her sister-in-law's skill but by the way her beautiful, pale fingers with their immaculate nails plunged into the cold muddy moss and forced it through the wire netting. Then she covered the moss-filled wire with larger, greener pieces of moss, binding them to the base with raffia. Corisande managed to tie the raffia so that it made a pattern and, at the same time, cut deep enough into the wet moss not to show. Next, tendrils of ivy were plaited and entwined, each piece pulled taut enough to remain a tight part of the wreath and for the leaves to appear to be growing from it. Sprigs of rosemary were pulled from their larger branch, the leaves at the base of the stalk stripped off, and the pantry filled with their evocative scent as Corisande threaded the rosemary into the moss and ivy. Once the base looked fat and solid and no longer even a little bare, Corisande added the flowers. She had a loose assortment in a bowl of water, white flowers of different sizes picked from the hedgerows between the fields and japonica from the garden wall. Daisy knew few of their names, though she was sure Corisande knew them all. Corisande, secateurs in hand, trimmed the stem or stalk of each flower and stuck it into the wreath, making sure it was securely placed and deeply enough embedded for it to stay damp. When the whole wreath was evenly, but not profusely covered, Corisande stopped.

"I'm going to leave it upstairs in the nursery bath," she explained, "with a couple of inches of water. In the morning I'll add a few last minute flowers and replace any that haven't lasted. The trick is to remember to take it out of the bath tonight and allow it to drain; otherwise we'll arrive at the funeral tomorrow with it dripping on our gloves and skirts."

Daisy had been the one who had gone upstairs after dinner with a plate rack to take the wreath out of the bath. The water had already drained out, the perished rubber plug another of the small factors and adjustments that Daisy was learning to remember and allow for while performing the simplest task. The bath plug that wasn't watertight, the doors that didn't close, the windows with broken sashes, the dripping taps, the smoking fireplaces, the temperamental stoves—and those, she thought ruefully, were only the inanimate objects. If she started to consider the human factors, most of them now relatives of hers—the mute grandmother; the silent but not necessarily mysterious brother-in-law; the untrustworthy, wreath-making sister-in-law; the gun-carrying future brother-in-law; the husband she hardly knew—she would feel like a tired Alice slipped through a dark looking glass.

Daisy assuming that although the water had drained from the bath that the moss was now sufficiently wet—the alternative to backing her own judgment going to ask Corisande who had delegated the task when she had gone up to bed right after dinner with a headache—set the plate rack in the bath and put the wreath on it to drain.

The wreath maker of the family, a strange role for Corisande to assume. Daisy imagined that Corisande was not unaccomplished; she was sure that she could dance and, if necessary, play bridge, but wreath making seemed to be her sole domestic skill. Daisy had eaten too many inadequate meals at Dunmaine to imagine that Corisande was qualified to instruct Mrs. Mulcahy, and the unpaid dressmakers bills did not suggest that Corisande spent her spare time running up her own clothes. But somebody, at some stage, had taught her sister-in-law how to make a funeral wreath. Daisy shook her head, once again astonished by her new family, as she went downstairs; she paused before she reached the hall, struck by an uncomfortable thought. She, Daisy, didn't know how to make a wreath, or strictly speaking—since she had watched Corisande carefully—she did know, in principle, how, but she had never, in practice, made one; so what was her own domestic skill? She, too, was unable to cook or sew or even run a household well enough to delegate such tasks successfully. What was she good at? She could milk cows, kill rabbits, but little more. She hadn't even succeeded in being a faithful wife. She turned round and went up to her room to write her evening letter to Patrick.

The following morning, when they gathered in the hall the wreath had been drained and Corisande had made the necessary last-minute additions.

"Forget-me-nots," she said, and smiled.

Now, she waited, in her still, unnerving way, holding a hand-bag Daisy could not remember having seen before, as the rest of them looked for gloves and prayer books. Mickey, presumably because a drop of muddy water, more or less, wouldn't make any difference to his suit, had been given the task of carrying the wreath.

Daisy was, as usual, reminded of her own worn handbag and aware that one of her gloves, not expensive in the first place, was coming apart at a seam. Her mother had bought them for her during her last winter at school.

"I've a letter for Patrick. I haven't sealed the envelope yet—" Daisy said, looking about her inquiringly.

"Send him my love," Corisande said, but not as though she imagined Daisy would take a fountain pen from her bag and add a postscript.

Daisy assumed she was not the only member of the family to write to Patrick, but supposed each did so, as with most other activities, in private.

"How did you learn how to make a wreath?" she asked, breaking a silence of several minutes. They were halfway down the avenue; Edmund held the reins and the pony was trotting briskly, its hooves clattering over the uneven stony surface.

"My mother taught me," Corisande said.

Daisy nodded, and the silence resumed. Corisande had revealed more information in that sentence than Daisy sometimes gathered in a week. It was the first time she had heard either Corisande or Mickey refer to their mother. Patrick had, slipping it between two other pieces of information, so that it need not be acknowledged or commented on, told her that his mother was dead. Corisande and her mother, the passing on of family skills and secrets. Wreath making could not be the only one. Daisy, now also silent, wondered what the others might be and if she would ever know; and what, if anything, had his mother taught Mickey? His love of history and plants? Or had he been too young? When had she died? If Corisande was three years older than Mickey and she had learned to make a wreath, then Mickey should have been old enough—or did his adult preoccupations owe more to the loss of his mother than to her influence while she was alive?

It started to rain soon after they reached the end of the avenue. Corisande pulled a mackintosh cape from under the seat, put it over her shoulders, and pulled the capacious hood loosely over her head, pushing her hair into place as she did so. Edmund, the reins in one hand, pulled another waterproof from under his seat and, after a barely perceptible pause, handed it to Daisy. After a longer, slightly awkward pause, Daisy, fully aware that it was Edmund's own waterproof she was taking, accepted it. It had a large, stiff collar that pulled up to protect the back of her head, but no hood. The rain was not heavy, but even with the partial protection of the mackintosh, Daisy could feel her hair becoming damp and curly. She pulled the heavy material gratefully over her knees and tucked her feet under the seat.

The funeral, despite the weather—gusts of wind were batter-ing the rooks' nests in the churchyard elms and shunting loosely shaped clouds across a paler gray sky—was well attended. Edmund effortlessly attracted the attention of a ragged ten-year-old boy, whose only protection from the elements was a too large flat cap, and handed him the reins.

Although the war had now entered its third year, Daisy had never before been to a funeral and her experience of Church of Ireland services was limited to morning prayer, either at the small church in Cappoquin, or as part of the congregation at the smaller and even less well attended church where Edmund sat in the front pew and read the lesson. The Church of Ireland seemed to Daisy close to the Church of England, the differences minimal and lim-ited, in practice, to the omission of the prayer for the king (few parishes having the means to replace their prayer books, his name still appeared on the flimsy printed page) and, from fear of find-ing themselves swept into the outstretched arms of Rome, a rigid determination not to indulge in any ceremony or tradition even slightly High Church.

The church was full, as always more crowded at the rear. Daisy, accustomed to making for the front, and seeing a half-empty pew, started up the aisle; Corisande nudged her and indi-cated a not quite large enough space in the back row. Daisy, slightly embarrassed, followed Corisande past a damp, muddy-shoed farming family to the end of the pew. Corisande had taken her mackintosh off as soon as they had reached the shelter of the church porch; she now looked pretty, neat, and elegant as she knelt in prayer, eyes closed, her perfect hands pointing upward, showing her engagement ring to advantage and obscuring part of her smooth and flawless face. Daisy was aware that her own hair, damp and curly, did not sit neatly around her hat and suspected that her nose was pink and shiny and her lipstick worn. Reminding herself that such worldly thoughts were not only out of place but unconstructive—she could hardly take out her powder compact—she composed herself for concentrated prayer. She had been taught as a child by her father that prayer should be confined to praise, thanks, penitence, and a desire for knowledge of God's will, but she knew, as did her father, that in wartime, prayer became more specific. Prayer rose like steam from grieving and frightened congregations all over England.

Daisy prayed for Patrick's safety, for the well-being of her family, for strength. She prayed, as she did nightly on her knees by her bed. She did not pray for forgiveness for her adulterous night with Heskith, for her breaking of a commandment, because, although she understood the gravity of her sin, she knew that were the opportunity again to present itself, she would not hesitate to take it. That such an opportunity would not again occur could make no difference to the imperfection of her repentance.

Corisande and Edmund prayed only briefly; Edmund leaning forward, one hand covering his face; Corisande's more devout posture, Daisy suspected, a reflection of her grace than the depth of her belief. Mickey was still praying when Daisy sat back and picked up her prayer book. He remained on his knees until the service began. It had been apparent, from the first time she had attended church with the Nugents, that Mickey had a deep and possibly morbid religious streak. She would not be surprised if, when he grew older and if he remained unmarried, he affiliated himself with some not too extreme religious order.

The service began; Mickey straightened himself up and opened his prayer book. Daisy was immediately moved by the beauty of the language; it seemed to her possible that the Church of Ireland, perhaps even more than the Church of England, was better designed to comfort the bereaved than to celebrate the betrothed. A culture a little embarrassed by joy and the celebration

of life was more comfortable—and hence more effective, comforting, and uplifting—when dealing with loss and restrained
grief.

Man that is born of woman hath but a short time to live, Daisy
thought, not of Sir Guy, but of James. James dead; Patrick a prisoner and wounded. Patrick's letters had been, in the main, unsatisfactory; with all but the first and last one addressed to her—the
one she had edited before reading aloud to the rest of the family—
Daisy had been well aware the letters were written by a Nugent
to other Nugents. Not quite evasive but lacking in detail; not quite
secretive but reticent. Even months in a prisoner-of-war camp,
part of it—how long not specified—in a hospital, either in that
camp or elsewhere, had apparently not tempted him to take a
more intimate tone in his letters. A wound, according to Patrick
not serious, and now completely healed, would leave him with a
slight limp. It was only in the letter that he had written on receiv-
ing the news of James's death that he sounded to Daisy like the
man she had married.

Despite the censor's pen, by putting together details and allusions from all his letters, his family thought Patrick had been
taken prisoner in North Africa.

> *I was so jealous of him and so angry with you. It was those
> feelings that made me see that I couldn't behave in my usual
> guarded way, that I had to move quickly and fight for you. Not
> only the war but James forced me to show my hand in a most
> uncharacteristic way. I suppose that out of a lifetime—I don't
> know if you even know that we were at prep school together—
> of memories of happier times it is the feeling of relief and tri-
> umph I felt when I knew that it was me you would love, that
> I will first think of when I remember him.*

Daisy closed her eyes briefly, shutting out the people and
sounds around her, hearing Patrick's letter with the rhythm and

intonations of his voice. She was overwhelmed with emotion, some of it love but most of it guilt.

Outside, a gust of wind slapped a sheet of hard rain against the stained glass window; the vicar, without pausing, flicked a glance toward the sound. What had been a light rain on the drive to the church was now heavy; there would be intermittent showers and heavy gray clouds blown in from the Atlantic for the rest of the day. Daisy's feet were wet and the church was cold—and damp. To the side of the window, bubbles had formed under the pale yellow paint and the uneven patch was fringed with a white growth that looked like frost.

The first Lesson. Then a hymn. "Abide with Me." As with the rest of the service, when the flat, emotionless tone of the vicar served to underscore the strength of the words, the hymn, not particularly well sung, and the organ taking it a little slowly, only emphasized the beauty and despairing sadness of the words.

"Abide with Me." A hymn that had been sung countless times since the war began. And, perhaps, even more often during the Great War. Those who had survived that war once again sang it, once again prayed. And those who had not, like Patrick's father, were commemorated on plaques in these small, cold, damp churches, with carved crests of regiments that were now, but hadn't been then, part of the army of another country. And the others who had neither perished nor survived? Maud, who didn't get out of bed, let alone go to church and, Daisy suspected, no longer put much faith in prayer. And why, Daisy thought, with a shiver, would she?

The second Lesson. The Collect. *God be in my head . . . and . . . in my understanding*—and then, quite quickly, it was over. The whole service had taken twenty-five minutes and had incorporated, as Daisy had known it would since the rattle of rain on the stained glass, some of the service that would usually have been read at the graveside.

The service over, there was a moment of shuffling, pews creaked as the congregation stood, someone sneezed, and then, tactfully orchestrated by the undertaker's assistants and the vicar, the coffin was brought down the aisle followed by Lady Wilcox, Hugh Power holding her arm. Fernanda Power was part of a small group that followed them, a discreet step or two behind.

The farming family filled the pew between the aisle and where Daisy stood, and apart from Mickey, who had been sent into the pew first to form a human buffer between the women and the damp wall, she and Corisande were as far as possible away from the coffin and the principal mourners. This allowed Daisy to take an uninhibited look as they passed. Lady Wilcox looked as quietly elegant as she had the only other time Daisy had seen her, at the Powers' lunch party again wearing a lovely coat and skirt— this one, of course, black—and a small black hat with a light veil that covered, but did not obscure, her face. Her face was immobile, expressionless, and the manner in which she held herself immensely dignified. Hugh Power, beside her, red-faced and glowering, seemed the more likely of the two to break down. He looked from side to side and Daisy found herself lowering her eyes, afraid of meeting his glance. A moment later they were past and Daisy was able to take a good look at the second wave of mourners, the one that included Fernanda Powers.

Fernanda Powers, eyes cast down, was also expressionless. But not expressionless as Lady Wilcox was expressionless; her lack of visible emotion suggested, rather than dignified grief, the ability to play a strong poker hand to the maximum advantage. With her were four men Daisy had never seen before. It was not impossible that there should be four men, apparently close to the Wilcoxes, who were unknown to her, but it was surprising. There was a small enough population of Anglo-Irish—and it did not seem likely that Sir Guy's coffin would be followed by members of the Protestant shopkeeper middle class—for Daisy to know, by sight, almost everyone not rendered invisible by extreme youth or age who attended any of the occasional local parties or who worshiped at either the Nugents' or Edmund's church. And, although Daisy had originally met the Wilcoxes while staying with Edmund, they lived a little closer to Dunmaine than he did. It seemed probable these men were strangers, family or friends from another part of Ireland or perhaps from England. All wearing dark suits, no uniforms, but that wasn't a clue, since wearing the uniforms of another country was not permitted in Ireland. As when she had first met the Wilcoxes, Daisy felt these men could not be fitted into any of the easily identifiable categories that defined almost everyone she had ever encountered.

A moment later, the coffin and the group behind it passed through the church door and the congregation slowly followed them. The farmer's family with whom they had shared the pew, visibly torn between waiting for the rest of the congregation to leave and a reluctance to delay Edmund and the Nugents, filtered awkwardly into the flow, but Edmund did not follow them. There was only an old woman kneeling in prayer, two younger women conversing in whispers, and a man who appeared to have some connection with the church behind them when Edmund led his small party out onto the churchyard gravel.

The rain continued, although it was no colder than it had been inside the church, and those who did not intend to accompany the coffin to the graveside were moving toward the tall wrought iron gates as briskly as they could without seeming to hurry. Something not immediately visible to Daisy had caused a delay, and the coffin and those who were to accompany it to the graveside were gathered to one side of the churchyard and on the small path leading to the graveyard. Daisy found herself only a couple of feet away from Lady Wilcox and realized, with a rush of self-consciousness, that some words were necessary. Good manners dictated that she murmur some words of condolence; common sense told her that Lady Wilcox would not have the slightest idea who she was. She moved slowly forward, hoping that Corisande or Edmund would step in front of her and allow her to express her sympathy as an echo of theirs. Surely they both had known the Wilcoxes or if they had met them at the same time that she had—she couldn't now remember whether Edmund and Corisande had been introduced to the older couple or whether they seemed to already know them—at least the Powers were people they both knew.

There was a moment of awkward hesitation, during which Daisy wondered what Corisande and Edmund, behind her, were doing, and then she stepped forward, holding out her hand. Before she could speak, Lady Wilcox, accidentally, it seemed, catching her eye, looked at her coldly for a split second before turning away.

"Keep away from—" Hugh Power, his voice raised and his face even more flushed than it had appeared to be inside the church, seemed to be speaking to someone behind Daisy. Lady Wilcox placed a gloved hand on his arm and he broke off in midsentence. In the same moment, Daisy withdrew her outstretched hand, turned to see to whom Hugh Power had been speaking, and saw Edmund close his mouth on unspoken words. The whole incident had taken only a second or two and, Daisy thought, had probably not been fully witnessed by anyone else.

Lady Wilcox and Hugh Power stepped onto the path toward the graveyard, and Corisande, touching Daisy's arm, indicated that they should move toward the gate.

They regained the pony and trap in silence, conversation not necessary as Edmund tipped the boy, wiped off the seats, and flicked the reins to indicate to the pony it was time to go home.

"What was that all about?" Daisy asked, breaking the silence when it became clear that information was not about to be offered. "Did I do something wrong?"

"It was nothing to do with you," Edmund said kindly.

It wasn't enough, but Daisy didn't ask a further question.

"Lady Wilcox is upset and irrational," Corisande said after a moment. "And Hugh Power always tended toward self-dramatization."

After this there was a long silence, then Corisande, speaking to her brother in an uncharacteristically encouraging manner, asked him about the arrangements for Philomena's funeral, which would take place the following day. His reply took them most of the way back to Shannig.

Daisy, hunched under Edmund's waterproof, thought about the scene in the churchyard. There was too little information for her to draw any conclusions, but she realized that her vague assumptions about Sir Guy's death were almost certainly inaccurate. She lacked information; although the murder had, of course, been headline news every day in the *Irish Times,* the reports—like the kitchen gossip that Daisy, although never soliciting, strained to overhear—not only lacked any new information but emphasized the mystery and contradictions surrounding the case. Daisy had assumed that the murder had been a random act of violence based on naïve nationalistic beliefs combined with inept larceny. She had also gained the impression, and the events in the churchyard did nothing to alter this belief, that it was in no one's best interests for the full facts to be disclosed. The government, with the strained relations between the two countries exacerbated by Irish neutrality, could hardly be happy that a well-known Englishman, however discredited in his own country, should be murdered on Irish soil. The local guards, although undoubtedly not wishing to appear incompetent, probably had mixed feelings about tracking down and arresting a local man for whose family the general population would feel more sympathy than they would for an upperclass Englishman. And the English authorities? They could hardly condone the murder, but surely it was far from inconvenient and with the daily desperation of the war, did anyone really care? Daisy remembered a story someone—probably Valerie—had told her. It had apparently taken place in London during the Blitz. A junior officer on leave, strolling back from dinner through Soho, is finishing his cigar; he lifts the lid of a garbage bin set out on the side of the street, stubs the end out on the inside of the lid and drops the butt into the bin. As he does so, he becomes aware that what seemed to be a bundle of old clothes is really a dead body, folded and stuffed into the garbage bin. He pauses, lid in hand, and as he does so, the siren starts to scream, and he carefully replaces the lid and makes his way to the nearest air-raid shelter. And in the case of Wilcox, even more than that of a minor London gangster, the authorities had more pressing things to think about.

Edmund, instead of handing over the pony and trap to the boy desultorily attacking the young dandelions in the gravel with a hoe, dropped the Nugents off at the hall door and continued around to the stable yard. Mickey, without even a murmured excuse, wandered off in the direction of the billiards room, although that, Daisy thought, was unlikely to be his ultimate destination. Corisande and Daisy silently entered the house. Corisande put down her gloves and prayer book on the side table by the front door and riffled casually through the post awaiting Edmund's attention.

Daisy waited a moment and then, as Corisande continued to ignore her, crossed the hall and started up the stairs. She had barely set her foot on the second step when her sister-in-law's voice stopped her.

"Daisy, just a second."

Daisy waited, one hand on the smooth wooden banister, as Corisande crossed the hall and paused at the foot of the stairs, looking up at her.

"Daisy, . . . I don't want you to be upset by what happened at the church."

"I don't understand. Lady Wilcox cut me—she saw me and she looked away. Quite deliberately. I was surprised she even knew who I was."

"It was because you were with us."

"I don't understand." Daisy paused, allowing her silence and her look to be almost a direct question. She could see that Corisande wanted, at least partly, to explain the incident.

"She thinks Edmund had something to do with her husband's death."

"But why should she think that? You and Edmund weren't even here when Sir Guy was killed." Daisy noticed that both she and Corisande had avoided using the word "murder."

"Not that he, ah, shot him. Himself. More that he knows who did and has some, ah, connection with that person."

"But why?" Daisy tried to sound as though she were questioning Lady Wilcox's sanity rather than asking for information; she sensed that Corisande didn't plan to tell her any more.

"Politics. Wilcox's Fascist connections—just the sort of thing that ass Hugh Power would be attracted to. Lady Wilcox thinks Edmund and Ambrose are outposts of the British army."

"Ambrose?"

But Corisande had said more than she had intended. Daisy was aware that her mention of Ambrose's name, almost certainly inadvertently, was the element of indiscretion that finally checked the confidence.

Corisande turned away and went into the small study that

Edmund used as an office. Daisy hurried up the stairs; she thought that Corisande was probably only waiting for her to leave so that she could go upstairs herself.

Once Daisy was in her room, she took off her hat, changed out of her damp shoes and stockings, and tried to subdue her hair before descending for lunch. Considering what Corisande had said would fill a good deal of time; apart from the content of the brief conversation, there were two mysteries unexplained. Why had Corisande, to whom it was almost a point of pride never to apologize, never to explain, felt the need to account for the incident outside the church? And what was it that had made her look so frightened on the way home afterward?

Her expression, had changed after she had mentioned Ambrose. It now seemed as though her own enunciation of his name had shocked Corisande not only by her indiscretion, but by a sudden realization of something that had caused her to curtail the explanation she had begun.

THE *ILLUSTRATED LONDON NEWS* was taken at Shannig. The day after she and Mickey had started their stay, yet to be determined in length, at Edmund's house, Daisy had sat on the sofa and idly leafed through the most recent issue. A month later the study of the magazine had become of central importance and took up much of her day.

Life at Shannig was comfortable although a little tense. Daisy was always aware that her presence was an inconvenience to Edmund and she tried to keep herself from under his feet, knowing that she would never see far enough beneath the layer of his good manners to know when she was intruding. She knew, also, that her—and Mickey's—presence was an irritant to Corisande and feared, even more, her sister-in-law's less inhibited reaction.

The days passed slowly; a chilly wet April became a mild May. Relieved of the pressure and anxiety of trying to run Dunmaine, Daisy found she had long empty hours, devoid of responsibility and containing only minimal planned activity. She ate more—the food was better than she had been used to—and took long naps in the afternoon.

It would have been very pleasant if there had been a clear plan for the future. Three weeks or a month at Shannig would have been a holiday, a welcome respite. Living there indefinitely made Daisy feel like a maiden aunt or, she thought guiltily, as Mickey probably did much of the time. Dunmaine was not inhabitable, but the damage was reparable and the house had—miraculously, it seemed to Daisy—been insured. When these repairs would begin was not clear; from time to time Daisy asked Edmund, a little awkwardly, aware that his future in-laws were rather more trouble than she would have wished. Each time it seemed to be a matter of waiting. Waiting for the insurance claim to be completed, for it to be submitted, approved, waiting for an estimate from a builder, waiting for him to finish another job.

The *Illustrated London News* came by post. It arrived two days after it had been published in England and, since it was a weekly magazine, some of what it reported or depicted could be as much as ten days after the fact. Daisy's imagination adjusted to remove the time lapse, and she opened each edition as though it were an illustrated bulletin from the BBC. For the first week or so she waited until Edmund opened the solid roll that came in the post, but by the time she began to become obsessive, she waited for the postman, tore open the tightly bound label, and took it somewhere quiet to read.

She would sit at a table so she could hold the magazine flat as she read it. The illustrations formed her images of war. Apart from the very occasional newsreels she had seen in cinemas in

England at the beginning of the war, until now she had had to rely on her imagination to picture the scenes and locations referred to but not described by the announcers on the BBC news. Between issues she would study the back numbers of the magazine that stood in neat stacks on the library table.

Some of the illustrations were photographs; others were drawings. The tone of each was different. The photographs were of the Queen, plump, soft, always smiling, comforting and reassuring, pearls, fur, and powder; the King, slight and sensitive; the princesses, a little embarrassed, awkward; factory workers doing their bit; bombed buildings, rubble, and shocked, brave families rising to the occasion or, at least, to the photograph; and portraits of those in the news that week.

The most dramatic pictures were the drawings, in shades of gray: battleships in the North Sea, steel and high salt waves, wind and the bitter cold, imminent death by drowning and freezing; interiors of ships and submarines, neat in a way only possible with men living in close quarters, totally lacking in privacy. Sketches by prisoners of war of their camps were among the most cheerful, small evidences of humanity, of the individual, of inner resources. They gave Daisy some comfort. Although she knew they had been drawn and reproduced with a view to keeping everyone's spirits up, she was also, at times, able to imagine Patrick in those surroundings.

The photographs of the war in North Africa, often bleached and yellow like old snapshots in an album, hot metal, sand, heat, flies, showed a world that Daisy could see was brutally hard, but it did not move her the way the pictures, in the old issues of the magazines, showing bitter cold, did. The photographs of the partisans in the Greek mountains filled her with horror, their flimsy shelters in the snow, their inadequate clothing, their frigid hands on cold weapons, and the distance and unlikelihood of survival.

The bombing of Belfast was not portrayed in the *Illustrated London News*. Daisy was disappointed; it would—although the event had taken place at some distance, and at the other side of a border—have made a connection between her own life and the world she so eagerly scanned once a week. And brooded over the other six days.

At the beginning of April, the magazine had reported Virginia Woolf's suicide. Although Daisy knew her name, she had never read any of her books. But her face, a small oval photograph on a page of such photographs, caught Daisy's attention. She tended to spend more time studying the photographs of women or the younger men, most, although not all, suddenly dead. And never again referred to: the following week their places taken by a fresh wave of news and fatalities.

At the beginning of May, again unphotographed by the magazine, Belfast was bombed for the second time. By then, Daisy was drifting around Shannig in a waking dream. Or two dreams, for she spent much of the day in bed, sleeping deeply. Day-to-day life at Shannig seemed no more real than the photographs reproduced in the *Illustrated London News*. She felt as though she were passing from one dream bubble to another, the only moments when she felt awake were those spent lying sleepless in the dark. While the rest of the household slept, Daisy, who had been resting and napping all day, lay brooding on her bed. Then she understood that her husband was a prisoner of war, that his last letter was dated eight weeks earlier, that she had betrayed him, that her life now consisted of little other than waiting. And, for the first time ever, she lacked the energy, willpower, or ability to do anything to alter her circumstances, even if she knew what she should do.

Later in May, Hess parachuted into Scotland and brought a new element—mysterious farce—into the news. For days Daisy found herself surrounded by others as fascinated by the news as she was; she even temporarily moved her focus to the BBC and the *Irish Times*. For a while it was all anyone talked about; four meals a day were accompanied by fruitless speculation. Then it became clear that the mystery would not be explained or, perhaps, that there was no rational explanation, that Hess, disappointingly, had acted in an impulsive, naïve, and almost random way. Interest faded and Daisy once again found herself alone in her preoccupation. And her lethargy.

The sinking of the *Hood* and, three days later, that of the *Bismarck*. The loss, fear, grief, and pity followed by drama, excitement, the chase, bloodlust. Daisy was astonished that anyone could pay attention to day-to-day life at Shannig while such events were played out on the world stage. She was overexcited, tired, and tearful: like a child, she would weep and then fall asleep.

Dublin was bombed at the end of May; thirty-four citizens of a neutral country were killed. On the fourth of June, the Kaiser died. That day Ambrose came to lunch, the first time Daisy had seen him since Dunmaine had caught fire. He was full of war news, teased Corisande, flirted with Daisy, and gave her a short history lesson about the Great War.

Daisy, by now, skipped some meals, preferring sleep or the long solitary hours she spent curled up in her warm nest of sheets, blankets, and eiderdown. After the meals she ate in the dining room, she would sometimes sit in the library or, if the day was mild and sunny, walk down the avenue as far as the gate and back again. Then she would return to her room to rest and dream again.

A MONTH WENT by at Shannig before Daisy started to read to Maud again; a month during which both settled into the new pattern of their lives: Maud adapting to life without Philomena, to the new bedroom, to better food; Daisy, fueled by the *Illustrated London News,* sunk into a dreamlike state. Then Daisy appeared one afternoon in Maud's bedroom carrying a copy of *Can You Imagine Her?* Daisy's demeanor was the same as it had always been, polite, respectful, not expecting a response, although her opinion of Maud's mental capabilities had changed substantially. The night of the fire, Maud had surprised her.

Four afternoons a week, all through the end of May and through June, Maud failed to acknowledge Daisy's presence in any way. Daisy was beginning to wonder if the shock of the fire had finally moved Maud's mind to a place from which it could no longer return, when one warm afternoon in early July, Maud laughed. It was not clear to Daisy whether or not the laughter was a response to the book.

The next afternoon she spoke.

"A Nugent ancestor was drowned, in a shipwreck. In 1782. He was crossing the Irish Sea—he was drowned, there was a storm and he was drowned. And his wife and son, and the coachman and the horses."

"Oh?" Daisy said encouragingly. But Maud, having nodded thoughtfully once or twice, closed her eyes. Daisy waited a long moment and then continued reading. The passage she was reading did not involve travel but it was not impossible that Maud's reflection had been caused by some association with the story of the book.

"If he had lived," Maud said, a little later, interrupting a scene where there was the first glimmer of hope that the novel would have a happy ending, "all our lives would have been different. There is no reason to suppose that either of us would have lived in this house."

Daisy thought about this for a moment. While she and Maud would have existed—they had, after all, been born independently of the Nugents—the Nugent family would have taken a different path. Maud had married into the line of a younger brother, a line that probably would not have existed but for the unexpected inheritance of the estate. And if Maud's destiny had been dependent on an eighteenth-century shipwreck, so had her own.

Daisy marked her place and closed the book. She sat quietly for a moment, watching Maud out of the corner of her eye and waiting to see if she said anything more. She was beginning to understand that Maud was not merely the delicate scale on which the legal and financial present and future of the Nugent family balanced so precariously, but that she was the silent force and will from which the life of the family emanated. And she felt that she, Daisy, was merely an agent and tool of that indifferent force.

After a little while, Daisy rose and made her way quietly to the door. Her hand was on the doorknob when Maud spoke again.

"Edmund always loved playing spies, even as a child. He'd do anything Ambrose told him."

Daisy felt her whole body stiffen. Then, slowly, conscious of every movement, she carefully released the doorknob, allowing the mechanism to slip quietly back into place, and turned toward Maud. But Maud, her eyes closed, drew in a deep, sighing breath, and turned her head and shoulder toward the window and the yellow late-afternoon summer sunlight.

Walking along to the corridor toward the landing and her bedroom, Daisy was unsure, because of Maud's uneven breathing, whether Maud had said "Edmund always loved playing spies. Even as a child, he'd do anything Ambrose told him," or if she had said "Edmund always loved playing spies, even as a child. He'd do anything Ambrose told him."

CHAPTER 19

ROSSLARE TO FISHGUARD. Daisy felt sick, and she felt cold. She considered the possibility that at the midpoint between Wexford and Wales, say directly south of the Isle of Man, it was always dark and always raining. She was not very cold, not even very sick; if she were to get out of her bunk and go up onto the wet deck she would begin to feel better. But the cause precluded the cure, so she huddled under her inadequate blanket and breathed in the stale air.

She remembered a moment, almost a year ago, during her first visit to Shannig. Aunt Glad, after Ambrose had, straight-faced, used the phrase "since we got our freedom" for the third time during the same meal, had glanced toward Daisy and had caught her not quite quickly enough concealing a grin.

"England," Aunt Glad had said, reproving her treacherous fellow countrywoman, "England. Where the Irish go when they're in trouble. When they need work, or get pregnant, or to find somewhere to hide. Then they forget about Cromwell and oppression and the talk of freedom; suddenly they're dancing to quite another tune."

Daisy had opened her mouth, ready to rush into an angry and not thought-out reply but, before she could disgrace herself, Ambrose had laughed.

"Rises like a trout, every time," he said to Edmund, and it was Aunt Glad who looked flushed and unsatisfied. And Daisy was left wondering at her own loyalty to her new country, a country where she was generally considered more allied to the former oppressors than to the oppressed. Unlike Edmund and Ambrose, she didn't feel she could have it both ways.

Now, sick, cold, and unhappy, she was recrossing the Irish Sea. The only feeling this voyage had in common with the one she had made as a newly married woman was the sense that she was leaving home for the unknown. Not, of course, the time she planned to spend with her parents, but after that. The England to which she was returning was more alien, threatening, unwelcoming, and harder than her worst imaginings of the unknown Ireland she had traveled to when she had first crossed the Irish Sea. However nervous and apprehensive Daisy had been, lying in a similar bunk, a year ago, she had at least been a bride and known herself to be loved. Now she felt utterly alone.

Alone, and without a cogent plan. She was to visit her parents and stay for a couple of weeks. That part was easy and required no explanation; her husband was overseas and her home was unhabitable. Less easy to explain would be her luggage; had anyone been paying attention, he might have asked whether she intended ever to return to the country she had so enthusiastically embraced as her own.

SAUSAGES AND MASH for lunch. The equivalent of almost a week's ration for each member of the family. Except for Daisy, who pleaded a slow recovery from a rough crossing. Her excuses were unnecessary; her family's attention was on the meat.

"You appear to have packed the better part of a pig in your suitcase," her father said. "For what we are about to receive may the Lord make us truly thankful" had, for once, been accompanied by suitable expressions of gratitude around the table.

"I had two suitcases," Daisy said. "It was quite a decision what to put in with the sausages and bacon. I've a couple of old skirts that have a distinct suggestion of the smokehouse."

"Nowadays that might be more seductive than Chanel No. 5," her grandmother said; the laughter—and the food—breaking, for a moment, the always tense atmosphere of meals in the Creed household.

Watching the pleasure on her father's face—a little of the slab of butter she'd brought had gone into the mashed potatoes—Daisy felt a moment's regret that she hadn't brought more. But she hadn't dared dip any further into her small reserve of money; the amount she had left until the end of the quarter would allow her to do little more than live, as a dependent, in her parents' house.

"Where is Joan?" she asked. Too long a silence could result in an airing of the real or imaginary grievances usually manifested during mealtimes. Such eruptions in Ireland, Daisy disloyally thought, unpredictable, uncensored, and uncontrolled, were a good deal more interesting than the almost ritual sniping between her mother and grandmother.

"Joan's still at Portsmouth," her father said. "She came home for a weekend's leave in the middle of last month."

"She's become fat," her grandmother said, "and she has a lot of grand new friends."

"One of the Wrens on Joan's shift is Lady Brenda Chadwick," Daisy's mother said. Daisy was unable to tell whether her mother was pleased by the possibility of Joan, if not actively social climbing, at least not quite so dramatically throwing in her lot with the coarser society of the able-bodied seamen she worked with. "The Chadwicks invited Joan to stay with them the last time she and Brenda were given leave."

Daisy watched her grandmother choose not to speculate on the probability of Joan having disgraced herself during the visit; then she watched her mother's equally silent reaction to her grandmother's unspoken thought. She longed to know how Joan had got on, staying with the aristocracy, but it seemed wiser to ask her mother at a time when her grandmother was not present.

"How long are you planning to stay?" her mother asked, her tone the usual one of mild anxiety, little curiosity. It was a question that Daisy had, since she arrived, been expecting but for which she still had no answer. She hesitated, and her mother continued, "It's just—I'm not sure what we're supposed to do about your ration book. I know you've brought more meat and butter than your rations would get you in a year, I was just wondering about procedure."

For the rest of lunch Daisy's mother argued with her own mother about Daisy's ration book, how long it would take to reactivate, and the physical location of the book itself. Daisy's father, after an affectionate but already vague smile at his daughter, allowed his thoughts to drift away. Daisy tried to follow the argument about the ration book; she had no idea where she would be living in three weeks, or what she would be doing, but if it were in England she would need a ration book. She was grateful to have the first practical step on the unknown road she was to take indicated.

She became aware that the other three were looking at her slightly reproachfully; after all, it was her ration book they were agonizing over. There was the pause that preceded a change in subject.

"She's put on a little weight," her mother said defensively—of Joan, Daisy hoped. "They feed them pure starch."

———

"I'D LIKE A DAY return to Farnham, please."

It was the second time that week Daisy had bought a railway ticket; she paid for this one with the exact money, using up the loose change in her handbag rather than breaking a ten-shilling note. There were two people behind her at the ticket office, a middle-aged woman in a dark blue uniform and a slightly younger man in a tweed suit whose drawn face and slight frame declared him unsuitable for military service. Both, without speaking, managed to convey impatience and the suggestion that important official business was being delayed by Daisy's selfishness. There was no train waiting at the platform but, nevertheless, Daisy came away from the ticket-office window flustered and flushed. The day was warm and she could feel sweat dampening her dress. She found a seat in the shade and sat down to wait for the train.

Her family had shown, about her excursions, the kind of curiosity that conveyed mild criticism rather than interest in her actions. Her mother seemed hurt that Daisy had apparently no sooner arrived home than she had set out for London. Her grandmother had sniffed a little, and several times wondered at the frivolous way Daisy appeared to be spending money, gadding about. Her father's "Where are you going today?" required no answer since, without pausing, he followed the question, with "I had been hoping we might take a walk together."

To her mother and grandmother Daisy had lied, leading them to believe she was going to visit a Nugent cousin with whom, despite never having mentioned her in letters home, Daisy had become friendly. She had also allowed them to believe she didn't have to worry about the cost of traveling. Of the two lies, the second came hardest; she was well aware that she could soon be dependent on her father. Unless—unless the action on which she was now embarked, this irresponsible long shot, paid off in some way she was unable to imagine.

The train—smoke, iron, and steam—came slowly out of a short tunnel in a low hillside and more slowly stopped in the station. Although Daisy had traveled many miles by train since she had stayed in Westmoreland, she now thought of the platform where Patrick and James had vied for her attention, and the train she had taken in triumph after a weekend of uncertainty, humiliation, and snubs. She thought, although it was not much more than a year ago, how young they had all been and, although both the men had been in uniform, as though it had happened before the war.

At Farnham, Daisy had to wait for a bus. She brushed her hair and removed a smut, courtesy of British Railways, from her forehead. She was bareheaded; two days before she had tidied herself in front of another waiting-room mirror, adjusting her hat and striving, not quite to her satisfaction, for the image of a young married woman of respectable family, possibly clergy. Today she was trying to look no less respectable, but young, attractive, and not too married. She glanced at her wedding ring; Patrick had put it on her finger and she had never taken it off. She wished, for a moment, she had brought gloves.

The bus stopped at every village and, often, several times in between. Daisy was in no hurry; she knew, although not precisely, where she was going but still did not know what she would do or say when she arrived. Without ever making a real plan, she had gradually been drawn toward a course of action, the result of which she could not, even in fantasy, imagine. For a long time Daisy had missed her husband; now she felt the need for a best friend.

Hayfields and hop pickers. Old-fashioned public houses with self-conscious traditional names. England. It was getting close to lunchtime and Daisy felt the first pangs of hunger. She thought how pleasant it would be, were circumstances different, to sit in a cool, dark pub and sip half a pint of beer and eat a cheese-and-chutney sandwich. But she was unable to imagine who her companion might be and, returning to the present, she remembered that with shortages and her nonexistent ration card she was lucky to have two apples in her bag.

Getting off the bus, she walked up a road, its hedges overgrown, with fields on each side. The first house was a working farm and, after looking carefully at it for a moment, Daisy continued. After the farm, the road became narrower and the surface rougher. Daisy looked at her watch; half past one, not a good time to arrive for an unannounced visit. She should probably wait an hour. She soon came to the gate of a field where the hay had been cut and was stacked into haycocks. She pushed the heavy gate open a little, squeezed past it into the field, and walked along the edge until she found a shady patch under the hedge. She sat down and slowly ate her apples, leaning against the grassy bank under the hawthorn hedge. The ground was dry. Despite the wind and rain over the Irish Sea, it had not rained for some time in southeast England. Daisy's frock was cotton and she was barelegged—she had laddered her last pair of nylon stockings getting onto the train on the way back from London two days before—so she didn't worry about sitting on the ground. The print on her dress had faded and her sandals were worn. For her expedition to London she had worn her Sunday clothes, but after much thought she had decided it would be better to make this journey informally clad than to arrive having hobbled through the countryside in high-heeled shoes and creased linen.

Daisy was tired and the sun was warm. She was excited, but not in a hurry. Sitting, taking pleasure from the sun on her face, she thought about her lack of urgency. She wanted to sit quietly, as Russians do—or, at least, as the fictional Russians that Daisy had read about did—before embarking on a journey. A moment of calm, of drawing together all the strands of herself that had become unraveled and extended by logistics, arrangements, nerves. Very soon her life would change forever; she should not allow this moment to be lost in a cloud of anxious activity. It was as it might feel, she thought, if she were playing roulette, in a foreign country, where she didn't speak the language and had no friends or acquaintances, and had just placed every penny she owned on a number. It might well be, in such a case, that one would be glad to have the wheel spin for a very long time to postpone the consequences of the result. She didn't know whether the thirty-five to one odds the roulette table offered was a level of probability for which she would be grateful.

"I'M DAISY NUGENT. I would like to speak to Andrew Heskith."

The woman who opened the door looked at Daisy for a long moment, but her blank expression did not suggest any curiosity about her unexpected visitor. It was more as though the woman, who seemed to be a little older than Daisy's mother—in her early-to mid-fifties—was intensely preoccupied. The events of the next few moments took place so slowly that Daisy was able to notice, and later remember, every detail of the woman's appearance: her dark blue cotton dress, a prewar design, had a pattern of small sparse flowers. Her gray hair, a perm growing out, and a little yellow, was held back by the kind of hairnet that purports to be invisible. There were nicotine stains on the first two fingers of her right hand; and her hands were rough, swollen, and discolored in a way that suggested both outdoor work and the scrubbing of pots and pans.

"He's—in the conservatory—do you know your way? It's along the corridor, and turn right at the end."

The house was larger than it had seemed from the front, extending back to a depth greater than its width. The corridor was unlit, but two doors opening from it spilled a little light, allowing Daisy to see a dark wooden chest, some sporting prints, a group of small brass objects—their function unclear and perhaps they were purely ornamental—that might have come from India. Had Heskith's father been in the Indian Army? And his mother? Even apart from an almost visible class difference, it did not seem possible the woman she had just met could be Heskith's mother, could have produced a son with such hard reserve, such depths of control and strength. Maybe a widowed aunt—she had worn a wedding ring.

Daisy walked slowly along the corridor, aware that the woman behind her had not moved from where she stood in the hall. But she did not feel as though she were being watched. The feeling of heightened awareness continued; she could feel the wooden floor beneath the thin rug—Indian?—and the increasing distance from the silent, but not seeing, woman behind her. And the decreasing distance between her and the man she had come to see. The man who would be astonished to see her and who would shortly react in a way she could not imagine, even in fantasy, to her arrival.

What was he doing in this house? Could he still be on sick leave? It had been much easier than she had imagined to obtain his address; Daisy had found herself with her carefully rehearsed story unfinished. The hall porter at the Royal Overseas Club, apparently relieved that he did not have to make arrangements to forward the package had, Daisy thought, rather irresponsibly given her Andrew Heskith's address. She remembered now the look on Heskith's face, how his expression had become primitive, even to the extent of his jaw projecting a little, as desire removed the veneer of civilization from his face. Suppose he didn't remember her at first, suppose she had to remind him who she was?

The door to the conservatory was ajar, and Daisy, forgetting to breathe, pushed it open. She paused in the doorway, surprised. Daisy, with distracted parents and little in common with her sister, had read her way through the novels in the bookshelves that lined the walls of the upstairs corridor. Seeking a view of the world other than that presented by her mother's favorite authors—whose eighteenth-century sensibility Daisy, as an early adolescent, found inadequate for her emotional needs—she had dipped into the romance and melodrama that had sustained her grandmother when she had been Daisy's age. She had read Ouida and Marie Corelli, secretly, aware that her mother and grandmother, for quite different reasons, would disapprove. She had, she supposed, been searching for information about life, by which she probably meant love, and these novels, now too dated even to entertain, had failed her. But they had left romantic associations with conservatories. Conservatories were where the heroine was kissed by a guardsman, where she was proposed to by a hero with an impressive title. A conservatory suggested palm trees, a discreet fountain, flimsy evening dresses, champagne, men with moustaches (that association not so attractive to Daisy, who found facial hair on men repulsive), eluded chaperones, small secret bowers, rendezvous.

If the woman in the hall had directed her to the lumber room, Daisy would have been more prepared for the furnishing of the room she was entering. That the room was not intended to serve purely for storage was evident only in two screens, to either side of the door, neither quite concealing furniture, trunks, packing cases, some large old-fashioned china jugs and basins, a cracked mirror, and a lamp with a torn shade. Daisy absorbed every detail of the room of piled junk. The atmosphere was depressing; the room suggested that when the family had moved into the house they had pushed their furnishings through it, using what they needed as they went, and that the residue had arrived, unsorted, in this room; there was an overall feeling this was caused more by despair than laziness or untidiness.

Daisy glanced behind her. The woman still stood in the hall. Daisy had to assume that if she had failed to follow the simple directions she had been given, the woman would have reacted in some way.

Ahead of her, between the temporary walls of the screens and discarded furnishings, there was light, and she moved toward it. As she rounded the corner she began to see plants. Nothing exotic: some geraniums whose dead leaves and flowers needed picking off; a malnourished vine; a straggling bougainvillea whose blossoms and light green leaves rose from the dead growth of the previous year. Not a palm tree in sight, although outside a monkey puzzle tree again suggested an Indian connection—but surely, since it was quite large, a connection from earlier than Heskith's father's generation. Maybe Heskith had come from a long line of Indian Army soldiers, and had, perhaps, spent his childhood in India. It didn't seem likely to Daisy; she had been at school with girls who had been sent home to English boarding schools when they became too old to be educated in India; the girls, who won every prize for swimming or diving each sports day, had been in some way visibly different, although not in a way Daisy could have found words to describe. A texture of skin? A certain stoicism? A sense of their own separateness?

Daisy moved quietly and slowly toward the light and plants; she could sense the presence of another person in the room.

"Hello," she called out, not loudly. Her voice was tight and nervous and, to her, sounded false. She tried again. "Hello."

No one replied, but there was a quiet creaking sound; it came from the other side of the tattered screen. Now, she thought, now. In a moment it will all be over and I'll know. But during the

seconds it took her to reach the end of the room, she knew that
what was about to happen would only set her onto one of two
equally unimaginable paths. Heskith would either accept her or he
would not. In the first scenario, she would find herself under the
protection—to use an old-fashioned term, but she couldn't think
of a more accurate contemporary one—of a man she scarcely
knew; in the second, she was without any plan for her future.
There might be, probably was, a third possibility, but she hadn't
imagined it.

One deep breath and she turned the corner. The creak she had
heard a moment earlier was repeated. A man she had never seen
before sat on a time-darkened wicker chair, his feet on a foot-
stool, and his knees covered by a plaid rug. He was no older than
her father but, in the same way as had been the woman who
opened the door to Daisy—and to a far greater extent—lacking in
life.

Shock, Daisy thought, and remembered she had had the same
thought about Heskith on the evening of the night he had come
to her room. The man who was looking at her, his expression
devoid of curiosity, was, or had been, shocked; so had the woman
who probably still waited, lacking volition, in the hall.

"I'm Daisy Nugent," Daisy said, after a moment. "I wanted to
speak to Andrew Heskith."

The man nodded, but did not speak. He lifted one thin mottled veined hand as though he were about to make a gesture, then,
helplessly, hopelessly, let it fall again.

Daisy had the sense that she must choose her questions carefully, that she could only expect a limited amount of this man's
attention before he wandered back into the apathetic daze from
which she seemed to have woken him. There was no book or
newspaper on the wicker table beside him; only a glass of water,
two bottles of pills, a framed photograph, and a small brass bell.

He must, she thought, spend his days dozing or gazing out at the overgrown garden outside, its lawn unmown, its herbaceous border bedraggled, and its unstaked plants beaten down by the wind.

"You are Andrew—Mr. Andrew Heskith?" she asked, aware there was probably a military rank by which she should have addressed him.

The man nodded in the same manner he had a moment before, and she understood he had already answered her question.

"Do you have a son?" she asked.

Although he did not immediately answer, the expression in the man's eyes changed. He glanced at the photograph on the table, an officer in uniform, dark, handsome, and unknown to Daisy.

"Crete," he said. The first word he had spoken. Then his attention wandered away from Daisy to the garden behind the cobwebby window.

CHAPTER 20

A FAMOUS SCANDAL," Edmund was saying, "long before my time. In fact, I was young enough for my parents to try to conceal the entire story from me. It took me weeks to piece the bare outlines together. Of course, the aftermath and some of the ramifications went on for the better part of a year."

Daisy glanced around the table; having missed the beginning of the story through her own inattention it seemed likely she would, like Edmund, have to piece together the missing parts.

It was Daisy's first evening back at Shannig. She was pale, tired, and inattentive, to an extent that she assumed was visible to the others. She had, the previous night, for the third time, crossed the Irish Sea. A journey she had made accompanied by the painful and humiliating knowledge that she had been in love—had believed herself to be in love—with a man whose name she didn't know. And that it wasn't only his name that was unknown to her, since he had been playing a part during the few days they had spent under the same roof. She knew what he looked like; she knew what he felt like; she knew the intensity and urgency of his sexual nature. And that he suffered. Nothing more. Pride made her think in terms of having believed herself to be in love, but it was as painful as though she had lost the love of her life.

There had been a gale that had allowed her to realize that the first two times she had crossed, the sea had merely been rough. Lying awake, not only sick but frightened, thinking of the eighteenth-century Nugent family drowned making the same crossing, Daisy had tried to reassure herself that the boat would not have embarked had there been any danger. That in 1941, despite the possibility of submarines lurking beneath the dark water, the crossing from Wales to Ireland was not a hazardous one. But she knew that her life, one of the most comfortable and secure in Europe, no longer held the expectations of safety to which she had been brought up. The boat had suddenly lurched in an unexpected direction and Daisy, trying to ignore a background of moans and prayer—the two other women in the cabin had had their rosaries in their hands for the past hour—was slammed against the metal wall on the inside of her bunk. She felt herself a small cork on a cold dark sea. An infinitely reduced, pale metaphor for the hundreds of thousands—the millions—of human beings thrown randomly from one side of their lives to the other then back, often to death. Refugees crossing and recrossing borders. The turmoil in her own life was caused by the farthest ripple at the edge of the pond of world events. And it wasn't going to get better until the war was over. How long could it continue? Everyone seemed to think it would be years; long enough to change everything. Long enough not to wait passively for it to end and to see then where she stood once the smoke cleared.

She had continued to be afraid until the boat reached the shelter of the Wexford coast, afraid but not in a way that prevented her thinking clearly. She was not by nature a complainer, and she understood that her life would seem—was—enviable by the standards of the great majority of the rest of the world; nevertheless, she was sad and deeply unhappy, and there was no one who felt it his business or responsibility to see to her happiness. Happy endings, she reflected, as the boat maneuvered to tie up at the dock at Rosslare, were a novelistic convention; in life, what was needed was a happy beginning or middle.

"Where did they go?" Corisande asked, more as though she were providing a cue than seeking information. Daisy made an effort to focus her attention; there was nothing in her thoughts she had not been over a hundred times.

"That was the depressing part. I thought they should have gone to Biarritz or Le Touquet—places I had never seen a photograph of, let alone been to, but the right kind of address if one were going to engage in wife swapping. But Scotland? St. Andrews? A hearty breakfast, eighteen holes of golf in the rain, drinks at the clubhouse, and then Sodom—well, not Sodom, I suppose, but Gomorrah. It sounded so middle-aged."

Corisande laughed, and Daisy longed to ask who they were talking about, but it was Mickey who spoke.

"They were middle-aged," he said, not raising his eyes from the excellent steak-and-kidney pie Edmund's cook had sent up. Daisy thought that he disapproved of the subject and, even more, of the lighthearted manner in which it was being discussed.

"Of course they were, although one of the women proved she was young enough to conceive a child," Edmund said.

Daisy refused the second helping of the pie that a moment before she had been planning to take. It now occurred to her that this story was being told for her benefit. She wondered how the subject had been introduced while her thoughts were elsewhere. And if she had been imagining a little more weight put on Edmund's last words; she had not imagined Corisande's glance in her direction. At the same moment and for the first time she tried to imagine what would have happened if she had found herself pregnant after her night with the man she still thought of as Heskith.

"They weren't all as attractive as I first imagined. Two of the women were beautiful—I spent hours poring over the family album and the illustrated papers, hoping for a photograph—but the men were ordinary. Hunting types. I'd been imagining thin moustaches and sleeked-back hair."

"I remember being frightfully cross when I was eighteen and asked to stay by Peg Daley for a hunt ball," Corisande said. "Grandmother wouldn't let me go. And she wouldn't say why."

"Wasn't she was the one that caused all the trouble?" Edmund asked. "Was she was the one that got pregnant?"

"No, it was her husband—her original husband, Willie Power, who was supposed to have got Jimmy Musgrave's wife pregnant. Whether he did or not, we'll never know. Their son—if he is—has red hair and doesn't look like either of them."

"So there were three messy English divorces and two low-key English remarriages and a permanent place for all six of them in Anglo-Irish folklore."

"One of the couples survived the scandal?" Daisy asked, unable to imagine how, after this holiday during which wife swapping—premeditated? unpremeditated?—had occurred, the couple who had stayed married had managed to go on together.

"Not at all," Edmund said. "When the reshuffle was over, Jimmy Musgrave and the original Mrs. Daley got the short end of the stick. Skimper Daley married Peg, Willie Power married Nan Musgrave, and—It sounds like one of those conundrums people try to confuse you with after a heavy lunch on Christmas Day."

"Where are they all now?" Daisy asked, mainly because she didn't want her silence to suggest any association with the characters described.

"The Powers—he's some kind of a relation of Hugh Power—an uncle or cousin—"

"First cousin, once removed," Mickey said, his disapproval not preventing him from providing accuracy where it was lacking.

"So, Hugh Power's first cousin, once removed," Edmund continued, "his new wife, and the red-haired child all went to Kenya. They live in Happy Valley and I'm sure they fit in there very well."

"Peg Daley hunts a pack of hounds over the most barbed wire in Ireland and curses at her husband in front of the entire field if he gets in her way," Corisande added. "Jimmy Musgrave gets up late, has lunch six days a week at the Cork Club, and stays in the bar until they throw him out when they close. Ann Daley is still as cross as she was at the time, but she has rather a lovely garden. She lives in Westmeath. Ambrose is good to her; he sometimes takes her racing at the Curragh."

Daisy understood she had been told that a scandal involving sexual misconduct remained alive even in the memories of those too young to have heard it as news; that if you were quick enough and tough enough to weather the storm and brazen it out, some kind of future, possibly in another country, was possible; and that if you ended up with what Edmund called "the short end of the stick," you might as well be dead.

It was Daisy who broke the short silence that followed Edmund's story; a silence, she thought, allowed to linger while she was supposed fully to grasp its message.

"I wonder if it might be possible for me to take the pony and trap over to Dysart Hall tomorrow afternoon?" And added, as Corisande opened her mouth and drew breath, "I need to discuss some business with Ambrose."

CHAPTER 21

DAISY GAVE THE tired pony a flick of the reins to encourage her to trot smartly up the avenue. Yellowing sunlight warmed Dysart Hall and the approach of autumn was in the air. The house, with its closed, shuttered wing. Armistice Day. The day they had learned of James's death.

Daisy had rehearsed what she planned to say to Ambrose. He was not a man often held accountable for his actions. A quick wit, social skills, and his air of authority seemed to allow him to skim above not only awkward social situations, unreliability with women—Daisy still wondered what had taken place between him and Corisande—but also, it now seemed, complicity in a murder. She noticed that it was Ambrose whom she held responsible for both his and Edmund's actions. She knew it was Ambrose's gun—where else would Edmund have got the gun left for Heskith at Dunmaine? She knew instinctively that Edmund answered to Ambrose not only because Ambrose had greater presence and personal authority, but because she believed, without any evidence—since she was hardly going to invoke Maud as a witness—that Ambrose was his superior in some hierarchy, in some secret, probably unacknowledged, possibly informal, part of wartime English intelligence. She tried not to consider the possibility that the assassination was something they had dreamed up themselves and carried out on their own initiative.

Ambrose was in the stable yard, talking to the vet, when Daisy drove in. He watched approvingly as she brought the pony to a halt outside the stable doors and handed the reins to a groom who stood waiting for instructions from Ambrose or the vet. The two old Labradors loitered at Ambrose's side. Although she had no wish for even a minimal additional responsibility, it occurred to her it was unusual there was no gun dog or cat living, indoors or out, at Dunmaine.

Daisy had not anticipated a witness to her meeting with Ambrose and she found herself returning his greeting just as warmly and, soon afterward, laughing at an entertaining account of some domestic disaster entirely of his own making. She told herself she was waiting for the moment they were alone to call him to account for embroiling her in his machinations and—although she would not use these words—ruining her life.

In Ambrose's study, sitting by the fire, as Daisy literally and metaphorically drew in breath to begin, he interrupted to offer her tea. She said she didn't want any, but he rang the bell. Now she had to wait until his elderly parlormaid arrived. But while the kettle boiled on the old range, while the potato cakes were browning in the cast iron skillet, while Ambrose continued to be as witty and amusing as though he had a large and appreciative audience, while Kitty carried the heavy tray along the flagged corridor and across the hall, Daisy had time to think.

Kitty set down the tea tray on a low table in front of the fire. Daisy waited until Ambrose leaned down to put the silver hot water jug on the hearthstone before she spoke.

"Guess who I ran into in London? A friend of yours."

———

AFTER DAISY'S FAILURE to find Heskith at the defeated and dying house near Farnham, she had gone home. Afterward she had no memory of the journey back to her parents' house.

"Are you all right, dear? You look very pale," her mother asked, her usually preoccupied expression now one of concern.

"I'm fine; I have a bit of a headache."

"Too much sun. Why don't you go upstairs and I'll bring you an aspirin."

Ever since Daisy could remember, her mother, seemingly oblivious to the dangers of tuberculosis, infantile paralysis, or diphtheria—the not common but always possible and often fatal illnesses of childhood—had protected her and Joan against sunstroke and from indigestion caused by eating cucumber and freshly baked bread.

Now, for the first time, Daisy agreed that she might have overdone the sun, and allowed herself to be sent upstairs to bed. The next morning she claimed a residual headache and, by the evening, was composed enough to rejoin the subdued tempo of rectory life.

Dinner was silent until Daisy's father asked her about her plans. To cut off a renewed discussion of her ration book, Daisy, speaking without thought, said that she was looking forward to spending a week with her family and that then she must return to Ireland. It was only as she spoke that she realized that this was what she was going to do, should do, had no choice but to do. She felt guilty and deceitful returning to the house she had left— fortunately not announcing her departure as permanent—as though returning to a betrayed husband after she had been rejected by a lover. Being rejected by a lover, she thought, would be a couple of steps up from finding out that the identity of that lover was not substantial enough for her to consider herself rejected.

Daisy allowed herself to be lazy and indulged by her parents for the rest of the week. She lay on a sofa in the study pretending to read as her father wrote letters and dealt with parish business; she sat on a stool in the kitchen, doing small pleasant tasks—podding beans, chopping parsley—while her mother cooked; afternoons were spent in her grandmother's sitting room, listening to the wireless and eating biscuits. She went to bed early and then woke in the night and tried to think of one moment in the future for which she felt any enthusiasm.

She left the rectory in the late morning of the following Tuesday to take a train to London in order to take the boat train from Paddington. On Monday morning she had gone to the post office and withdrawn the remains of her pre-war savings account—thirty-five shillings—just enough to make up the difference between what she had in her purse and the fare back to Ireland. Having so little money made her feel young, vulnerable, and frightened.

Paddington Station was crowded and noisy. Daisy bought her ticket and then, not quite sure which platform she should go to, stood still as the crowd surged around her. The faces of the passers-by were set and preoccupied. She wished there were someone she could ask for directions but the only person she could see wearing a Great Western uniform was behind a grilled counter with a long queue waiting for her attention.

Then she saw him. Quite close to where she was standing, he was looking up at the board that announced departure times of trains and the platform from which they were to leave. She watched him, not moving, as the rush of adrenaline coursed through her body, until he turned in a direction that would take him away from her, into the crowd of monotone uniforms. Without a thought for her suitcases, she pushed her way through the ungiving crowd until she could stretch out a hand to touch him

on the arm. At her first touch he didn't react, unable to differen-
tiate her attempt to grab hold of him from the jostling of other
passengers struggling through the station. Daisy reached out
again, this time even less effectually. She felt as though she were
in a particularly painful recurrent dream, one about loss, aban-
donment, and powerlessness. Then, for a moment, the crowd in
front of her opened a little and she pushed her way forward,
earning an elbow in her ribs from a red-faced middle-aged
woman with two heavy shopping bags. She was at his side, then
a little ahead of him when he saw her. He stopped, so did she;
around them the crowd subtly adapted its course, now accom-
modating them in its flow.

His expression was one of mild puzzlement; it continued long
enough for Daisy to consider the possibility that he didn't recognize her. Then for a shorter moment his look was one of shock and
fear before he smiled and expressed surprise and pleasure. Daisy
found herself tongue-tied as she realized that if this was his reaction to an accidental meeting, how much greater would have been
those emotions if she had succeeding in arriving on his actual
doorstep rather than following a wild-goose chase to Farnham.

"Mrs. Nugent—Daisy, what are you doing here?"

Daisy, seeing how impossible the truth was, that she had
crossed the Irish Sea to find him, said that she was taking the boat
train on her way back to Ireland.

"Where is your luggage?" he asked, his question, though
pedestrian, not unreasonable.

Daisy gestured vaguely behind her.

"Let me help you with it," he said. His face was still pale but
his voice was steady.

Daisy followed him back through the now slightly abated
crowd to where she had abandoned her suitcases. She felt numb
and shocked and very stupid, ashamed that she might have

imagined he would have welcomed her arrival, planless, to cast herself on his mercies. She now knew three things with absolute certainty: that he was complicit in the murder of Sir Guy Wilcox; that whatever his name was, it wasn't Andrew Heskith; and that she wasn't going to confront him with either of these facts. Even less likely was she to tell him that she loved him to an extent that made the rest of her life essentially meaningless. He had called her Mrs. Nugent before he realized that after their night together it would have been kinder to seem to think of her by her Christian name. She followed him as he picked up both her suitcases and made off in the direction of the platform. He bought a platform ticket and they went onto the comparatively uncrowded area beside which the train waited.

"Thank you so much," she said, giving him leave to go although she was silently crying out for him to stay, to make a sign, to say something, to touch her.

"Let me see you onto the train," he said, and carried her suitcases up the steps and into the carriage. He lifted them onto the overhead rack and turned toward her. She stood between him and the door to the compartment. She knew it was the last possible moment to say anything but, although she drew in breath to speak, there was nothing to say. He looked at her inquiringly and, losing her last chance, she lowered her eyes.

"Good-bye," he said, shaking her hand. Daisy looked at him imploringly and after a moment he took her head in both his hands, kissed her briefly on the forehead, and left the carriage.

"YOU'LL NEVER GUESS. Andrew Heskith."

Having set the silver jug by the fire to keep warm, Ambrose slowly rose to an upright position. His face was a little darker than his usual high blood pressure, too much whiskey, weather-beaten ruddiness. Kitty stood patiently by his side; Ambrose started to pour the tea.

"Really?—Milk? Sugar?—In London?"

"Milk, no sugar, please. Yes, I ran into him at Paddington Station."

"By accident then?" Ambrose asked, his tone and expression carefully casual.

"These potato cakes are wonderful. I wonder if your cook would give me the recipe? I really have to do something about the food at Dunmaine—when I get back. I wanted to talk to you about that."

"Thank you, Kitty, that will be all," Ambrose said.

"May I have a little more milk?" Daisy said, delaying Kitty as she turned to go.

There was a pause while Ambrose waited to hear more. Daisy said nothing, waiting until she could be sure there was enough tension for Kitty to register it. As the maid reached the door, Daisy spoke again.

"I need to ask your advice," she said at last.

"Anything," Ambrose said. Daisy thought his casual tone concealed a measure of relief.

"And help," she added firmly. "It's about Dunmaine."

Daisy noticed with amusement Ambrose's almost concealed relief changing to almost concealed irritation.

"Yes," he said, "I'll be happy, of course, to do anything within my power to help you."

"I'm sure that will be more than enough," Daisy said, her tone a little firmer than that she usually employed when speaking with Ambrose. "It's important that we start the repairs and rebuilding as soon as possible. Before the weather gets bad and Edmund gets stuck with us—Mickey and Maud and me—for the winter—"

"These things take time—" Ambrose said cautiously. It was

clear to Daisy that he had not even thought of work starting on Dunmaine until spring. She realized that if she weren't determined it was more than possible that Dunmaine would never be repaired and would, in a year or two, become just another ruin. It was possible, this also a new consideration, that this was what Ambrose, as executor of the estate, with equal parts idleness and pragmatism, was planning. The insurance collected, the house knocked down—or more likely left to crumble on its own—and the land sold. The estate wound up, Ambrose relieved of his responsibilities, and the Nugents forced to make an evolutionary leap into the postwar realities of the twentieth century. It wasn't necessarily a bad idea; but it was not what Daisy wanted.

"I know they do," she said sweetly. "That's why I need your help. Since you are the executor. I need to hurry along the insurance, pin down a builder, arrange for the bank to let us have enough of the insurance money in advance to pay him. Then I want to move back and start taking in PGs seriously."

"Look here, Daisy, it mayn't be quite as easy as that."

"I think it is, once we put our minds to it."

"But—"

"I wonder—could I have another cup of tea?"

And as Ambrose reached for the teapot, Daisy pushed her advantage.

"So if you get started on that, I'll tell the maids they'll be back at work before Christmas. I've taken the opportunity to dismiss Mrs. Mulcahy."

"You've sacked Mrs. Mulcahy?" Ambrose's eyes widened with admiration.

"Yes, it was obvious she wasn't interested in learning how to cook well and, as you said, there's no use in having PGs unless you're prepared to feed them properly."

"But where're you going to get all these PGs?"

"I thought I'd ask you to help with that, too." Daisy paused, and smiled as she said with no particular emphasis, "You were so good at it last time."

THREE DAYS AFTER Daisy's visit to Dysart Hall, Ambrose arrived at Shannig with a Labrador puppy and the news that the bank had agreed to a loan against the insurance payment so that repairs could be started right away on Dunmaine. He had already spoken to a builder who would come, the following day, to see Daisy and make arrangements to begin work. It wouldn't, of course, be quite as easy as that, but Daisy was ready to meet each problem and battle of wills as it came up.

"He's almost house-trained," he said, handing her the puppy. "I brought him just in case the builders aren't inconvenience enough. Last time I had them in, I had no staff and couldn't be doing with making them pots of tea so I gave them gin. They stayed for three months."

Ambrose stayed for tea and then a little gin. Corisande sat beside him, talking of people and places that Daisy didn't know and, it seemed, pointedly excluding her from the conversation. She sounded overbright and amusing in a high-strung way; it seemed to Daisy that an unhappy anger lay just below the surface of her charm. When Edmund came in a little late for tea, two pink patches began to appear on Corisande's cheekbones, and she snapped irritably at him when he made a fuss of the puppy at Daisy's feet. He smiled at her without quite paying attention, poured himself a cup of tea, and sat heavily on a chair at Ambrose's end of the sofa. They started to talk about the price of bullocks and whether Edmund should introduce sheep into the higher fields bordering the moorland. Corisande remained silent, her knuckles white where she held her cup. After a little while Edmund stood up.

"Time to introduce this little fellow to my dogs and find him somewhere to sleep."

Ambrose stood up also and followed him out toward the stables. Daisy rose when they did and went upstairs; she had no wish to be left alone with her jealous sister-in-law.

Daisy sat beside the window writing to Patrick and her grandmother. The window was open to the summer evening and she listened for the crunch of gravel that would announce the return of the two men. But Edmund came back to the house alone through the side door and went straight upstairs to change for dinner.

The evenings were becoming shorter and the light was pale and faded when they sat down to dinner. Corisande was cold-faced and silent; a sulk was in progress.

"Your puppy is a nice little lad, comes from a good line," Edmund said cheerfully, seemingly oblivious to the tension in the room. "What are you going to call him?"

"I hadn't even thought of that yet; I've been describing him for Patrick."

It seemed possible that Edmund and Daisy might be condemned to spending the rest of the meal thinking of possible names for the dog and occasionally, and rhetorically, tossing a "What do you think?" at the silent Corisande.

"I've been writing to Patrick, too," Corisande said, the breaking of her silence ensuring the complete attention of the other two. "I wasn't quite sure whether I should mention your trip to England, Daisy. I didn't know what you'd told him."

Daisy looked at Corisande, startled. She wasn't sure how to reply. It would be easy to tell the truth, that she had spent the ten days at her parents' house, but she was less concerned about her ability to answer Corisande's implied question than the accusation that lay behind it. She was afraid that a disingenuous reply would enrage Corisande's jealousy to further and possibly more accurate accusations. And she was well aware that any words spoken, even in anger, could never be unsaid and would make her position in the Nugent family uncomfortable and her continuing stay at Shannig impossible. Nevertheless, it was the first time Corisande had made her the specific target of her spite and Daisy thought it might be as well to make sure it was the last.

"Whyever not?" she asked pleasantly and not at all as though she were calling a bluff.

"Shut up, Corisande," Edmund said before Corisande managed to say a word. His tone was firm, reasonable, and seemed totally lacking in anger. "Shut up and, for a change, think before you speak."

"I only—" Although the malice in Corisande's voice was still there, it had become defensive.

"Don't be vulgar. How would you like it if Daisy started asking you impertinent questions? You and I, or even Mickey here"—for a moment they all looked at the startled Mickey—"have things we don't necessarily want dragged out and discussed in public."

Corisande flushed. Daisy braced herself for a show of temper before she realized that her sister-in-law was instead holding back tears. Daisy thought of the unpaid dressmaker's bills, the bits and pieces sold off from around the house, and was reasonably sure that these were not the secrets that Corisande was thinking about. It seemed more likely that she and Edmund were thinking of a secret of his that Corisande would prefer not to know, a secret that might have grave consequences for him and would ruin her dreams of prosperity and security. Edmund certainly knew that Daisy had seen the gun that he—or had it been Corisande?—had concealed in the dressing case and had chosen not to speak of it. Ambrose must have told him about Daisy's visit to Dysart Hall and her certainty that he would comply with her wishes. Edmund had plenty of nerve, although perhaps not as much as Ambrose.

Daisy was reasonably sure that all three of them—and perhaps even Mickey (who knew how much he knew?)—were, in quite different ways, thinking of Ambrose.

CHAPTER 22

THE SHORTEST DAY of the year. Daisy looked down at the frozen field that sloped away from the end of the lawn. The ground was hard, frozen solid. In the morning there had been a crisp white frost that made the remaining blades of grass appear to retain some promise of life; now they lay, yellow and brown, lower to the ground and offering no possibility of sustenance to cattle or horses. The day had been cold, bright, and sunny, but now, well before the end of the afternoon, the shrubbery Daisy was leaving was already dark.

Daisy's arms were full of holly, the branches hard and cold, the leaves green, dark, and alive, and with fewer berries than Daisy had hoped for. Tomorrow, perhaps, she could add some mistletoe to the Christmas decorations she was arranging at Dunmaine. But since the mistletoe grew on the high inaccessible branches of an ash, she would need help with it. A ladder or, more likely, a well-thrown rope. Patrick had written about mistletoe in his first letter to her at Dunmaine, a letter written not a week after their marriage.

Daisy sighed. There were often now days that seemed over-loaded with symbols of the past, or a little too heavy with irony to be quite fair. Then, a moment later, she smiled as Conrad, the black Labrador—no longer quite a puppy—came out of the bushes to meet her.

Feet crunching on cold gravel, Daisy approached the glassed-in porch that provided an inefficient buffer between the windswept east side of the house and the chilly boot room; a pale light from within shone yellow through the icy and not quite clean glass of the porch. A light had gone on in the drawing room and in one of the upstairs rooms, the guest room now refurbished for paying visitors. The first of whom, a Miss Sealy-Hewitt, had arrived late that morning; Daisy had left her resting to recover from a rough crossing.

Dunmaine, still was not completely repaired, but was lived in once again. And more hers than it had ever been. Ambrose had set in motion the process that made the repairs possible, and Daisy, present each day, had orchestrated them in such a manner that she and Mickey had been able to return to the house. Now they were entertaining their first paying guest; one of several recruited by Ambrose. Daisy was not quite sure how he had done it; by writing to his friends, calling in favors, or, for all she knew, the expense of an advertisement in the *Times*. Maud remained, for the time being, at Shannig with Edmund and Corisande. For once, the words "for the time being" did not mean "indefinitely," the definition even more firmly established by Daisy than by Corisande.

Daisy set the holly down on the floor of the porch and, using the bootjack, she stepped out of one boot, the sock half off, and onto the doormat, preferring its dried muddy surface to the frigid tiles that covered the floor. The shoes that she now put on were as cold as the tiles, and, closing the doors that were supposed to keep out the cold behind her, she quickly went along the corridor and into the far from warm but noticeably less chilly hall.

A dying fire glowed in the grate of the large fireplace that could never really warm the area since the stairs led up to a large window and a landing. Any heat that rose to that level was immediately dissipated by the drafts emerging from the corridor on either side.

It was teatime, and Daisy opened the door to the drawing room, both to make sure that tea had been served and, if the scene that met her eye didn't deter her, to have a cup herself.

Daisy's grandmother sat in a low armchair behind the tea tray. Mickey and Miss Seally-Hewitt had cups of tea and plates with bread and butter, and Mrs. Cooper, immediate duties fulfilled, had taken up her knitting. A cheerful fire both warmed and lit up the area in which they sat. Mickey was explaining some aspect of climate and soil to Miss Seally-Hewitt who, Daisy realized with relief, was a fellow gardener. Her grandmother was silent, counting stitches under her breath as, on four thin steel knitting needles, she turned the heel of a tightly knit, small stitched sock. Without involving herself more than greeting her guest and inquiring about her recovery from the journey, Daisy was able to drink her tea and leave.

THE EVENING BEFORE she returned to Ireland, Daisy had tapped at the door of her grandmother's room and inclined her ear to hear an invitation to come in. Instead, she heard the sound of the wireless.

Sad, lonely, and feeling, despite the remains of a hot summer's day, the chill of misery and exhaustion, Daisy had gone to visit her grandmother. She knew that she was going to have to start putting a good face on the following days and was almost looking forward to a quiet hour in her grandmother's room. It was her intention to encourage reminiscences of the past and, even if she could not quite pay attention, at least she would allow her grandmother some moments of mild indulgence and herself a restful undemanding time.

About to knock a little louder, she realized she was hearing the familiar voice of Lord Haw-Haw. Daisy hesitated, amused and a little shocked. It was considered unpatriotic to listen to the propaganda of the English-speaking programs broadcast from Germany—although some of them, further to undermine morale, purported to originate in England—but many people, for a variety of reasons, did so.

William Joyce, the most famous and, in a sense, popular of these broadcasters, was known and hated all over England. Because of his voice, rich, confident, and convincing, he had been nicknamed Lord Haw-Haw. Each day he told his English audience of ships sunk, soldiers dead, civilians bombed, that Germany would starve them into submission; and he did so with apparent pleasure. That the population of the battered and hungry country he addressed should have, with a humor suggesting something almost akin to affection, have so nicknamed him, was a sign that that resilient country, starving or otherwise, would never admit defeat.

Nevertheless, listening to Lord Haw-Haw was an unwise and frightening activity usually indulged in guiltily and in secret. Daisy's disapproval of her grandmother's listening habits was not unconnected with her own embarrassment that William Joyce was generally believed, in addition to having been a Mosley Fascist, to be at least in part Irish.

She knocked again, this time a little louder. The voice on the wireless ceased and her grandmother bid her enter.

Her grandmother sat, her hands uncharacteristically idle, in the armchair beside the now silent wireless. Daisy thought for a moment that the woman in front of her had aged since she had last given her her full attention. Then she saw that her grandmother's eyes were pink and that she held a small handkerchief, instead of her usual knitting or needlework, in her hand.

Daisy wondered for a moment if everyone in the whole world was unhappy. Her grandmother was not heartbroken in the way that she, Daisy, was, but she was lonely and frightened. Daisy knew there was little she could do to make herself feel better, but to comfort her grandmother would seem like a small blow against the forces of misery. She sat down beside her and, for the first time since she was a child, took her grandmother's hand.

"Granny," she said, "I am going back to Ireland tomorrow. Until Dunmaine is repaired I don't have a home of my own. When I do, I hope you will come and stay with me for a long time. For as long as you like."

"ONE OF THE Coopers from Sligo?" Ambrose had asked, when Daisy's grandmother had first arrived, and on being told neither she nor Daisy's dead grandfather had any Irish connections, he had treated the old lady with his unfailing courtesy but no further curiosity.

The Nugents, without welcoming Mrs. Cooper, seemed to accept her presence without question. Daisy realized that the eccentricities of one's own blood relations could, if one developed the ability, be judged by the same standards as those of one's in-laws; even so, she still found herself closing her eyes during some of her grandmother's more opinionated conversational pronouncements.

Her grandmother had accepted her invitation on a temporary basis while she ostensibly looked for a suitable—by which she meant inexpensive and genteel—residential hotel, but Daisy

knew that her grandmother had taken up residence for the rest
of the war. At the very least. Her bossy supervision, a small
weekly contribution to the household economy, and assistance in
its reorganization apparently had become part of the arrangement. Mrs. Cooper imagined that on Patrick's return there would
be a reassessment of the arrangement; Daisy knew that such a
reassessment would have to be made by herself—by the new
tougher version of herself—and that she would probably have to
weigh up the financial and organizational advantages of her
grandmother's presence against the frequent embarrassments of
her unsubtle English way of dealing with family, friends, and
staff. Unsubtle and English had, of course, been exactly what
was needed to reorganize the household now without Mrs. Mulcahy. Mrs. Cooper, inspired by the comparative plenty of unra-
tioned food, was training Kathleen to cook and Kathleen's
younger sister, Dolores, to take over the duties formerly performed by Kathleen. On Kathleen's day off, Mrs. Cooper cooked
dinner; the ease with which she did so—an apron over her very
English afternoon dress the only concession—and her expertise
in other areas of housekeeping preventing the belief (the undoing
of Mrs. Mulcahy) that anyone employed at Dunmaine was indis-
pensable.

The fires that burned most of the day in the grates of every
room at Dunmaine that was in use were a recent innovation. The
wood burned came from dead trees that had grown at Dunmaine
and was extravagant only in terms of labor; the occasional sod of
turf was added with an economical hesitation.

Mickey now took responsibility for all outdoor work—apart
from the hens—at Dunmaine. With the help of Philomena's
grandson, he would, in the coming year, make sure the garden
continued to provide vegetables and fruit for the house, and that
the avenue and lawns were maintained. For now, he saw that the

cows were milked, and the horses cared for; and that firewood was sawed, split, and carried into the house.

Daisy took care of the hens. They lived in a long fenced run with a sturdy wooden henhouse in the garden; even in winter they required little more than a bucket of hot mash each day. She collected the eggs—at this time of the year they were sparse—and occasionally chose an old hen for the pot.

Up the stairs, the carpet and the stair rods still bearing traces of the fire or, rather, the extinguishing of the fire. In time, the carpet should be replaced and, rather sooner, the stair rods would need to be polished. Both tasks were on lists Daisy kept on her desk. One for future expenditure; although the list was long, it was her plan and expectation that in time it would become shorter. The other was of larger tasks that would be fitted into the household when there was time; not immediately, since when Miss Sealy-Hewitt left another middle-aged spinster was expected. Then, in the new year, for the first time, Dunmaine would entertain two paying guests simultaneously. By Daisy's calculations, now that her grandmother was a minor financial contributor to the household, a second paying guest represented clear profit.

Daisy put another log onto the small fire smoldering in the grate and sat down at her desk, as she did at the end of each day when she wrote to Patrick. First she reviewed her accounts, not because she sought information, but because they reassured and satisfied her in the absence of someone else with whom to discuss her aspirations and small triumphs. Once a week she allowed herself, in a letter to Patrick, to mention the progress of her plan that should gradually make Dunmaine solvent, that should allow Patrick to come home to a house that was no longer just marking time before it need be sold.

Closing her account book and drawing some writing paper toward her, Daisy dipped her pen in the inkwell and wrote,

Dearest Patrick,

Four days to Christmas. Today I cut the holly for the hall
and dining room. Please God, next year you will be here to
enjoy them with us.

She paused. Surely it would not be long now. Not now that
America had come into the war. The word "us" was one that
would require some definition and decisions when the war was
over and Patrick returned. After the immediate question of
whether "us" should continue to include Daisy's grandmother,
the whole question of the paying guests would have to be
addressed. Would Patrick expect Dunmaine to be as it was when
he left it, or would he—if not welcome—admire, applaud, be
grateful for, the manner in which Daisy now ran the household?
The former way, she thought, Irish; the latter, English. "English"
in the slightly pejorative sense she occasionally heard used by the
Anglo-Irish, its meaning usually, although not always, synony-
mous with "middle class." Or would he see the change as one of
the unavoidable evils of postwar life; a view that would allow
him, all of them, to sigh nostalgically over the Good Old Days
when they had all lived on the edge of a financial precipice, the
bank manager and butcher impatient but not importunate, held
at bay by nothing more concrete than the arrogant self-confi-
dence of the Anglo-Irish and their own habit.

She thought it likely that the Good Old Days would, by and
large, be the reaction the Nugents would settle on. Although it
irked Daisy to think that her work and improvements would be
classified as symptoms of the end of those happier times, it was not
an unreasonable reaction. Although she should not have been old
enough to understand the principle, she knew that the Good Old
Days meant—more than pleasanter, easier, more civilized times—
"when we were young." The Good Old Days being defined, by the

one who remembered, not so much by the circumstances as by the golden haze of hope, energy, sexual possibility, and novelty of experience that surrounded them.

And Daisy, ten days before the beginning of the New Year—1942, with its continuing fears of war and tired hopes of peace—was not yet twenty-three years old. But she no longer felt herself young. During the long, late summer days at Aberneth Farm, pleasantly physically tired, aware of her own strength and the new muscles in her upper arms and in her calves, full of confident and excited hope and expectations of a new, surely better and more exciting future after the war, her spirits high with health and a new sense of freedom, Daisy had consciously felt her own youth.

And yet, surely she was not so physically changed. She got up and crossed the room to her dressing table, where there was a large looking glass with two smaller hinged sides. Daisy was in the habit of sitting in front of it and brushing her hair; her images reflected sometimes made her wonder about Patrick's mother who, she thought, had sat in that seat and looked into the same glass. Apart from Corisande's one reference to her on the way to Sir Guy Wilcox's funeral, Daisy's dead mother-in-law had never been mentioned. She knew only that after Patrick's father had been killed in the Great War, she had lived here with her children and Maud and had survived her husband for long enough to teach Corisande how to make a funeral wreath.

Daisy looked at her reflection with more care and interest than she had done in some time. Her face had changed. It was still young, pretty, unlined; her hair was still dark brown and curly. She weighed perhaps three or four pounds more than she had when she had spent most days in hard physical labor. But that weight did not show in her face; it had served only to slightly round her body, to make her less of a girl.

Her own was not the only image in front of Daisy. There was a framed photograph of Patrick; it had been taken a year or so before she met him. When she was not looking at this portrait, she always imagined him in uniform rather than the tweed jacket, lightly striped shirt, and countrified tie that he had put on to have his picture taken. There were also some smaller photographs and snapshots of her family; one, framed, of her parents, the others stuck into the side of the looking glass. And a chalk drawing of Patrick. It was newly framed and stood a little apart from the others.

When Patrick's letters had stared to come again, four months after the delivery of fourteen letters at once—all but one that he had written home since he and Daisy had married—they came one by one. The second long silence had been broken with a letter from a new prisoner-of-war camp. The wound that he had written of so casually had become infected and he had been transferred to a camp with better medical facilities. Although Daisy was well aware that his letters were censored, she believed his assurances that he had received good, if fairly primitive, care. He walked, he had written reassuringly, with a slight limp but was otherwise completely healthy again.

His portrait suggested otherwise. From the beginning of December, post had come more frequently; frequently enough for those writing not to feel that every question answered, every event commented on, every wish for a birthday or festival was hopelessly out of date and largely meaningless. In the most recent letter, Patrick had enclosed the drawing that a fellow prisoner had made of him—the portrait that now stood on Daisy's dressing table. The paper had been smoothed out as carefully as possible, but the lines from where it had been folded into four were still visible.

The style, as well as the medium, were similar to the drawings

Daisy had spent long afternoons looking at in the *Illustrated London News,* the publication now subscribed to, ostensibly for the paying guests, at Dunmaine.

Daisy was often surprised by the level of talent of the amateur artists who depicted the prison camps. A line or two would sometimes show a detail that would tell her more about the men and their limited, makeshift surroundings than any of the breezy, rather banal, captions beneath could hope to. It was such an amateur artist who had drawn Patrick. The differences between the portrait and the photograph on the other side of the looking glass were considerable, but they were the result of the artist's expertise rather than his lack of it. It was clearly the same person; the bone structure was unchanged, as were the eyes and the shape and expression of the mouth, but the portrait was of an utterly changed man. The physical differences were startling, although only part of the overall effect. Patrick had lost weight and his face was gaunt. His hair had started to recede on both sides of his head and there were new lines on his forehead. His nose, from loss of weight, had become more prominent, and his eyes seemed to have sunk deeper into their sockets. Since the drawing had arrived, Daisy had tried to find in it the Patrick she had, not so long ago, watched shaving; suffused with desire, she had watched him draw his mouth in, his lips over his teeth, and scrape the shaving soap off with a cutthroat razor. Instead, she could see what he would look like when he became old. And he was already shockingly older.

She looked back at her own reflection. She had not aged in the dramatic way that Patrick had, but she was not unchanged. Looking with a new awareness, she could see that the harder line of her mouth had changed her face more than she had imagined. She glanced at the drawing and then back to her reflection, trying to see what Patrick would see when he came home. If he were to come home now, if the war were to end that day. But it wouldn't, and when he came home he would not be as he appeared in the drawing. The changes she could see would still be there, but in a more extreme version. And she, how would she be? Not physically as changed as her husband, and probably not psychologically as changed, but not the girl he had said good-bye to on the second day of their honeymoon at Aberneth Farm. While one could argue that the firmer line of her mouth might denote strength, there was something lacking of the old Daisy. In the eyes, perhaps, there was no longer a readiness for fun, the awareness of infinite possibilities, an openness, a welcome that would spread to a smile. She knew that she still longed for affection but willingness to love no longer showed. *I have learned to compromise,* she thought, *and it shows.*

The thought, the realization, made her sad. Sad, but she accepted the truth without self-reproach. The changes to her life, a life that was not turning out the way she had expected, were similar to those she saw around her. She knew that people lived with secrets, with small guilts, with shame. She hadn't thought she would be one of them. When Patrick came home it would be as difficult for him to recognize in her the girl he had married as it would be for her to accept the stranger in the drawing as her husband. And they had promised to spend the rest of their lives together.

She had no doubt that they would. They were both decent people, of goodwill, and they had loved each other once. The war, far from over, was drawing a thick black line through their lives, through the century, through history. After it, nothing would ever be the same.

ACKNOWLEDGMENTS

I am grateful to Max Nichols, Frances Kiernan, Hope Dellon, Mike Nichols, Susanna Moore, Anne Grubb, and Jenny Nichols for their help and advice. I am also indebted to Desmond Fitzgerald, the Knight of Glin, for his assistance with geographical details of the South of Ireland. And to my mother, the late Cynthia O'Connor, who was a Land Girl in Wales at the beginning of World War II.

The title of this novel is taken from *The Family Reunion* by T. S. Eliot.

READING GROUP GUIDE

1. The characters in *This Cold Country* are kept apart by differences in class, nationality, religion, and political belief, but not by money. Why do you think this was the case? To what extent do we now believe ourselves to belong to a classless society? Or has our society replaced class with money as a measure by which people are judged?

2. The year is 1940; we know who won the war, but it is easy to forget that the characters in this, and other novels with similar settings, do not have the advantage of foresight. Their lives are a delicate balance of the immediate and personal existence of the individual and their responsibilities as citizens of a nation at war. How do the feelings of the characters in this book compare to the sense of national and personal vulnerability felt for the first time by many people in this country?

3. When James comes to Daisy's bedroom do you think of him as a hot-blooded young man who doesn't consider the consequences of his actions toward Daisy? Or is he a cold-blooded seducer, a cad? Or do you think that he is aware of "war and its brutal suggestion that time was, even for the young, a commodity no one

could afford to waste"? How do you think war changes people's view of conventional morality?

4. Do you think Daisy is unwise to marry a man she hardly knows? Or do you think that she is right to have taken marriage and temporary happiness where she could? How limited do you think her chances of either would be if she had waited until after the war?

5. After the war, many people looking back said it was one of the happiest times of their lives. Do you believe this to be true? Does each of us have a place where we belong, a right time and place in history?

6. Daisy recites "Dover Beach" to herself when she is afraid. But the message of Matthew Arnold's poem is not so optimistic. What is he telling us?

7. The Anglo-Irish family that Daisy marries into represents the generations after Irish independence who once were the privileged classes. Now they have neither political power nor money. How do you think they managed to live? And why do you think the shopkeepers and merchants allowed them credit for so long?

8. Mickey and Corisande have, in different ways, flawed characters. Are they a product of their historical environment? Does this background account for certain gaps in Patrick's character?

9. "You may be surprised by how differently they read." Mickey is speaking about two history books, one English the other Irish, that describe the same events. What does Daisy learn by comparing the two?

10. Maud lives in the past. Daisy thinks happy beginnings and middles are worth more than happy endings. How do these attitudes compare with your own?

11. Ireland was a neutral country during the Second World War. How much does this neutrality owe to Ireland's previous relationship with England?

12. The population of the Republic of Ireland is approximately three-and-a-half million; yet the Irish have written a disproportionate amount of the world's great literature. Wilde, Shaw, Sheridan, Joyce, Beckett, O'Casey, Elizabeth Bowen, Maria Edgeworth, William Trevor, Goldsmith, Yeats, Frank O'Connor, Swift, Synge and Seamus Heaney—four of them Nobel Prize winners—are among the most famous. Why has such a small island produced such a wealth of literature? Why has the Anglo-Irish minority produced such a large proportion of Irish literature?